Jeffrey, Elizabeth.

**The thirteenth
child.**

$28.95

DATE			

A Selection of Recent Titles by Elizabeth Jeffrey

THE THIRTEENTH CHILD

Elizabeth Jeffrey

This first world edition published 2009
in Great Britain and in the USA by
SEVERN HOUSE PUBLISHERS LTD of
9–15 High Street, Sutton, Surrey, England, SM1 1DF.
Trade paperback edition published
in Great Britain and the USA 2009 by
SEVERN HOUSE PUBLISHERS LTD

British Library Cataloguing in Publication Data

Jeffrey, Elizabeth
  The thirteenth child
  1. Sisters - Fiction 2. Twins - Fiction 3. East Anglia
  (England) - Social life and customs - 19th century -
  Fiction 4. Domestic fiction
  I. Title
  823.9'14[F]

ISBN-13: 978-0-7278-6759-9   (cased)
ISBN-13: 978-1-84751-136-2   (trade paper)

All Severn House titles are printed on acid-free paper.

Typeset by Palimpsest Book Production Ltd.,
Grangemouth, Stirlingshire, Scotland.
Printed and bound in Great Britain by
MPG Books Ltd., Bodmin, Cornwall.

Acknowledgements

I am indebted to Glen Jackson for the loan of documents regarding primary school education in Victorian times. Also to the staff at Answers Direct, Essex Libraries' central enquiry service, for their prompt and helpful replies to my emails asking for information. *The Victorian and Edwardian School Child* by Pamela Horn was also very useful and informative. Finally, thanks to my agent, Jane Judd, for her careful reading of the manuscript and helpful comments.

One

It was a warm day in May in the year 1880. Eva turned her head and gazed at the two tiny forms lying in the battered wooden cradle.

'Oh, Minnie,' she said to her sister with a sigh. 'My Joe'll kill me when he gets back and sees I've had two this time.'

'Don't be daft. It's not your fault. He put 'em there, didn't he?' Minnie replied sharply. 'He should have been more careful. Seems to me he only has to throw his trousers on the bed and you're up for another one.'

'But, Minnie, don't you see?' Eva's voice was edging towards desperation. 'This makes thirteen. Joe promised he'd leave me alone after this one because it was gonna be the twelfth. He said he wasn't gonna risk having thirteen children because it would be unlucky. You know how superstitious fishermen are.' She rolled her head on the pillow. 'God knows what he'll do when he finds out it was twins this time, especially if he gets a bit of drink inside him.' She shuddered. 'I wouldn't put anything past him.'

'When's he due back?'

'Any day. They've gone to the Terschelling grounds after oysters. Usually takes best part of a fortnight because it's such a long way. I don't know why they have to go all the way to Holland for oysters. There's plenty enough round the coast here, I'd have thought.'

'They'll go wherever there's oysters to be dredged. You ought to know that. My William would have been with them if he hadn't gashed his hand down to the bone on the last trip. He doesn't like his fishing smacks going to sea without him.'

'Is it healing?'

'Yes. He's better in health than temper now. He always gets grouchy if he's away from the sea for too long. You'll see, he'll be off with them on the next trip whether it's properly healed or not.'

Minnie got up from her perch on the edge of the sagging bed and peered into the cradle with her head on one side. 'They're not a bit alike, are they, considering they're twins. The bigger one's dark, like Joe, and the little one's fair, like you. At least . . .' She turned and looked at her sister's long braid lying over her shoulder. 'Like you used to be before your hair turned grey.' She turned back to the cradle. 'The dark one looks healthy enough but the little one looks as if a puff of wind'd blow it away. Which one was born first?'

'The dark one.'

'Yes, I can believe that. It looks as if she took all the nourishment she wanted and the little one got what was left.' Minnie gave a shrug. 'Well, I wouldn't worry too much about what Joe'll say when he gets back and finds he's got thirteen children, Evie. I don't reckon that little one'll live long enough for him to see her, if that's any comfort.'

'Oh, don't say that, Minnie. I've already buried five over the years. I don't want to have to bury another one,' Eva said quickly, with a complete change of mind. 'No, I'm sure Joe won't mind, not when he sees them both.' She paused. 'Pity they're not boys, though,' she added miserably with yet another change of mind. 'He always complains when I have another girl.'

Minnie straightened up and looked round the bedroom. It held very little, only the sagging double bed and the cradle, which stood in a corner beside a rickety chest of drawers. There wasn't room for anything else except a chair with a rush seat under the window, where a dark blue curtain hung, mended until it could be mended no longer. The floorboards were bare except for a small shabby rug beside the bed. Hanging on a nail above the chest of drawers, a faded sampler Minnie recognized from her childhood bore the legend 'Home Sweet Home' in laboriously worked cross stitch and its partner, stating 'God is Love', hung slightly askew over the bed. Everywhere was spotlessly clean and neat although the sheets on the bed and the shawl that wrapped the babies were patched and grey with constant washing.

She smoothed a straggling strand of hair away from her sister's face. Of the two of them Eva had been the prettier sister. She had been tall and slim where Minnie was short and inclined to plumpness; her hair had been thick and wavy where Minnie's was straight. People used to compliment Minnie on being 'the sensible one', saying Eva was a bit of a 'fly-by-night', predicting darkly that she would come to a 'bad end', not understanding how much shy, retiring Minnie envied her vivacious younger sister's outgoing personality. But a hurried marriage to Joe Furlong followed by almost constant pregnancies had turned Eva into an old woman before her time. She was not yet forty but she looked sixty.

Minnie didn't envy her now. Married to Joe's elder brother, William, a prudent man who, unlike his young brother, neither smoked nor drank but looked after his money and now owned his own fishing smack and another besides, she knew herself to be secure in the love of a good man, with a comfortable home in the better part of the town's working-class district. Her one regret was that they had never been blessed with children, something that had always puzzled her in view of her sister's fecundity.

'I'll go and make us a cup of tea, Evie,' she said. 'I brought a few tea leaves with me.'

'Ah, that'd be a real treat,' Eva said gratefully.

But before Minnie could get to the door a girl of not more than eight years old came in, carefully balancing two cups without saucers on a tin tray.

'I used the tea leaves you brought, Aunt Minnie,' she said. 'Was that right?'

'Yes, dearie, I was just on my way to do it,' Minnie said, taking a cup from the tray. 'Ah, you know how to make a lovely cuppa tea, Daisy.'

'Yes, she's a good girl,' Eva said, sipping hers gratefully.

'And what do you think of your new little sisters, Daisy?' Minnie asked.

Daisy put her head to one side. 'I thought they'd be alike, being twins, but they're not. Not a bit. They're tiny, too, especially Jemima.' She looked towards her mother. 'That's what I call the little fair one till she gets her proper name,' she explained.

'Oh, I think it's a nice name,' Minnie said, smiling at her. 'And what do you call the other one?'

'I call her Sophie, because she's dark. We had a story at school about two little girls called Jemima and Sophie and I thought they were nice names. I'd never heard anybody called that before,' she added thoughtfully.

'That's what we'll call them then, if your dad doesn't want something different,' Eva said. 'Like you say, they're nice names. Unusual.' She smiled at her daughter, revealing several gaps where teeth had once been. It was no more than Daisy's due, since she would bear the brunt of their upbringing. It was Daisy who would often have to lose precious schooling in order to look after them and her small brothers so that Eva could earn money, either from scrubbing oysters or gutting herring or salting sprats, according to the season, to make up for what their father poured down his throat. The older children were out at work, Betty was in service and Archie had followed his father into fishing. They all contributed what they could, except for

Frank, the eldest, because he was already married with a wife and child of his own to support.

There was the sound of heavy boots downstairs and a deep voice called, 'Minnie, are you up there, my girl?'

Minnie looked at Eva, a puzzled frown on her face. 'That sounds like my William,' she said. 'I wonder what he wants. He doesn't usually come visiting. I'd better go and see.' She drained her tea hurriedly and got up to kiss Eva. 'I'll come again tomorrow,' she promised.

Downstairs there was the rumble of William's voice interspersed with Minnie's higher tones. Finally Minnie was heard to say, 'No, you'll have to come up and tell her yourself.'

A minute later she appeared again, this time with William, looking reluctant and uncomfortable, behind her. He was a small, wiry man, with a weather-beaten face, thinning brown hair and a thick moustache that covered the whole of his top lip. He was wearing a thick reefer jacket and moleskin trousers and he was twisting his cheese-cutter cap in his hands, one of which was still heavily bandaged.

Minnie went over and sat down on the bed and covered Eva's hand with her own. 'William's brought bad news, I'm afraid, Evie,' she said quietly. 'I thought he'd best come up and tell you himself.'

Eva looked from Minnie to William, who was chewing at his moustache like a dog with a bone.

'My boy, Archie?' she whispered.

He shook his head. 'No, Archie's all right. He'll be back on the next tide.' He cleared his throat. 'It's *Flora May*. They reckon she's gone down with all hands. There was a bad storm out on the Terschelling grounds. The boats got scattered when they went out into deep water to ride it out and when it was over and they all met up again, *Flora May* was missing. All they found was her dinghy and a couple of spars.' He sniffed, chewed at his moustache and gazed unseeingly out of the window until he had his feelings under control. He had suffered a double loss because *Flora May* was one of his two fishing smacks and Joe, his irresponsible, drunken, yet hard-working and lovable younger brother, had been one of the crew.

'All hands drowned?' Eva said disbelievingly. Yet she knew as she spoke that it was true. Fishermen rarely learned to swim, and the heavy leather sea boots and thick woollen sweaters – often knitted to a pattern that would identify where they had come from – meant they would be quickly dragged down in the icy seas. An ability to swim would only prolong the agony. Most wore one gold earring, which would pay for a decent funeral if they were later washed up on shore. Not many were.

William nodded, risking a brief glance at his sister-in-law. 'I'm sorry, Evie, girl. This has come at a bad time for you – well, any time's a bad time for news like this, but you know what I mean. Twins, and that . . .' His voice trailed off and his eyes slid away.

Eva closed her eyes for a moment, then gave a weary sigh and opened them. 'It's no more than I expected,' she said without emotion. 'I knew something like this would happen.' She nodded towards the cradle holding the twins. 'Joe always said thirteen was his unlucky number. That's why he promised there wouldn't be any more after this one. Only this "one" was really two, so he's got his unlucky thirteen, anyway. Not that there's ever been that much luck in this house.' She gave a deep sigh followed by a ghost of a smile. 'Joe wasn't afraid of much, but anything with thirteen in it scared the wits out of him. You know how superstitious fishermen are.' She nodded towards the cradle again. 'They were born on the thirteenth, too, so maybe he was right to be scared.'

'The storm was on the thirteenth, as far as I can make out,' William said gruffly, 'so that must have been when the smack went down.'

'There you are, then.' Eva laid her head back on the pillow. She didn't cry. What was there to cry about? She had lost a husband whom she had married because he had made her pregnant and he had done little for her over the years except keep her that way. Well, he'd been right in one thing: there wouldn't be any more children. That was something to be thankful for.

She turned her head towards William. 'You said my Archie was safe?'

'Oh, aye, he's safe. He's on the *Alice May*. He should be home before nightfall. You know I never let father and son sail on the same boat, Evie,' he added gently.

Minnie and William left then. As they walked home William said, 'We'll do what we can for your sister, Minnie. Help her as much as she'll allow. But five children under ten . . .'

'Under ten! Young Daisy's not nine yet!'

'Ah. That's far too young to be expected to look after the little ones while Evie's at work. It'll make the little mite old before her time. She should be at school.'

'She's no different from a lot of other children, Billy. A good many girls have to stay off school to help out at home, and boys have to stay off school and work if there's a copper to be earned. It's a wonder some of 'em learn anything at all.'

'Reckon you're right, matie,' William said, using his term of affection for his wife.

They walked on in silence for a while, then Minnie said thoughtfully, 'There's one thing we might be able to do, William. If Evie would let us, that is. We could take one of the new twins and bring her up.'

'What? You mean adopt one of them?'

'Oh, no. That wouldn't be right. She would still belong to Evie and I'd never dream of trying to take her place in the child's affection. We'd just give her a home, feed her, clothe her and look after her for a few years. Just to take a bit of the burden off Evie.'

William tramped along beside her in his heavy boots without speaking for several minutes. Then he said, 'If that's what you'd like to do, matie, and if Evie is happy for you to take one of the babbies, then I won't stand in your way. I know you've always wanted your own, but that was not to be.' He took his wife's hand in a rare public gesture of affection. 'I've always reckoned you'd make a good mother, Minnie.'

Two

Jemima had always known that she and Sophie were twins. But they were not twins like Bobby and Bertie Miller up the road, who were as like as two peas in a pod and were hardly ever apart. Those two boys even seemed to know what the other was thinking. She and Sophie weren't like that. They didn't even look alike. Sophie was pretty, with dark curly hair and blue eyes, while Jemima's fair hair was as straight as a pound of candles and her eyes were a greenish brown that somebody once told her was called hazel. And when Jemima looked in the cracked mirror over the mantelpiece she could see that she wasn't pretty like Sophie; she was pale and skinny and her features were pinched. She looked undernourished. Which she was, most of the time.

And, far from knowing what Sophie was thinking, Jemima couldn't begin to imagine what went on in her twin's mind.

Another odd thing was that they didn't even live in the same house. Sophie lived with Aunt Minnie and Uncle William in a nice house at the other end of the town while Jemima lived with her mum and Daisy and the boys in one of the pokey little cottages by the river that got flooded at least twice every year. And it wasn't any good trying to keep the water out when the tide came up high, because as fast as you barricaded the front door with bags of sand and dirt the water crept up the passage and in at the back. Not that it mattered; there wasn't anything in the house of any value and it was interesting to see from the water mark on the wall whether it had come up as high this time as last.

Every week Aunt Minnie brought Sophie to the little cottage in Brown's Yard to see them. Jemima knew Sophie didn't like this. She always clung to Aunt Minnie, sitting on her lap and complaining that the house had a funny smell. Yet she wouldn't come out to play on the quay with Jemima and the others, saying she didn't like mudlarking because she didn't want to make her pinafore dirty, which Jemima thought very odd. She had never before met a child who didn't like playing in the mud. From the way her mum looked down her nose at Sophie she seemed to think it was odd, too. Or perhaps she just wanted to be rid of her so she could talk about grown-up things to Aunt Minnie.

Sometimes after Aunt Minnie's visit there would be a bundle of Sophie's outgrown clothes left behind for Jemima. Mum usually sold most of these before Jemima had a chance even to try them on, saying they were miles too small, which wasn't true because Sophie was taller and fatter than Jemima. But Mum always let her keep one or two bits, because otherwise Aunt Minnie would start asking questions, and they fitted perfectly.

There was one thing that Jemima knew without knowing how she knew it – perhaps that was the twin thing – and that was that Sophie didn't like her. She found this very odd, because she knew you were supposed to love your brothers and sisters, especially if you were twins. So Jemima tried to like Sophie, even though it wasn't always easy. She would offer to let her play with her most precious thing, Raggie Annie, the peg doll Daisy had made for her and which never left her side. But Sophie turned her nose up in disgust at Raggie Annie because she was a bit grubby and when Jemima went to play with Sophie at her house, Aunt Minnie had to remind Sophie to let Jemima hold *her* doll, which was a large china doll called Angela that had corners and couldn't be cuddled properly in case you rumpled its smart clothes.

Jemima loved Aunt Minnie's house because it didn't smell of fish and it didn't have shrimp heads littering the floor in the summer like their house did when Mum picked shrimps for potting at the fish factory. Aunt Minnie's house had a lovely smell, of floor polish and cakes baking and freshly ironed clothes. It seemed a very big house to Jemima, with stained-glass panels in the front door that made pretty patterns on the black and white tiled floor of the hall when the sun came through. The staircase at one side of the hall had a red patterned carpet instead of the bare boards Jemima was used to and there were doors to two rooms on the other, with the kitchen and scullery at the far end.

Jemima always went to tea with Sophie on their birthday. Jemima loved this; all the year she looked forward to May 13th, counting off the days until it was time to dress up in her best clothes – she didn't care that they were Sophie's cast-offs – and hold Daisy's hand as they walked up to Aunt Minnie's house.

They had tea in the dining room, which Aunt Minnie said wasn't often used, because their birthday was a Special Occasion. The dining room had a carpet on the floor and four chairs covered in green plush round the big, bulbous-legged table, which had a snowy white cloth that crackled with starch and was set with sandwiches and jelly and a birthday cake that always said HAPPY BIRTHDAY SOPHIE AND JEMIMA. Only this year it said HAPPY 5th BIRTHDAY SOPHIE AND JEMIMA because they were both five and five was an important age. Jemima thought it was all wonderful and she ate and ate until she thought she would burst, while Sophie complained that she didn't like potted-meat sandwiches and she had wanted red jelly and not green.

After tea Sophie proudly showed Jemima her new doll's pram although she wouldn't let her wheel it. But Jemima didn't care; she found Sophie's old hoop and was happy to bowl it round the garden and to swing on her swing, which Sophie didn't seem to mind. They didn't have a garden at home, only a poky back yard paved with uneven bricks, so it was a real treat to run on the grass and smell the flowers. When Daisy came to collect her, Jemima had no trouble in remembering to say, 'Thank you, Aunt Minnie, I've had a lovely time,' because it was true, even though Sophie had sulked most of the afternoon.

Aunt Minnie smiled and gave her a warm, lavender-scented hug and a kiss and said she was glad she had enjoyed herself. 'Now you're five you'll soon be able to come and see us all by yourself,' she said encouragingly, giving her another hug. 'We'll like that, won't we, Sophie?'

Sophie squirmed her way under Aunt Minnie's arm, pushing Jemima out of the way. 'I'm not letting her play with my dollies,' was her answer.

'Why does Sophie live with Aunt Minnie and not with us, Daisy?' Jemima asked on the way home, when she had finished telling her sister all about the birthday tea they had just celebrated and how she had swung so high on Sophie's swing that she could see right into the next back garden.

Daisy looked down at her little sister happily trotting along beside her. 'I reckon it's because Mum couldn't afford to keep both of you,' she said carefully. 'You know Dad was drowned the day you were both born. Well, with two new babies to look after it would have been a bit . . . well, she wouldn't have been able to work at the fish factory, would she?'

'Well, why didn't Aunt Minnie take both of us, then?'

'Oh, she couldn't have managed two babies. Anyway, you were too tiny for Mum to let you go.' Daisy smiled down at her little sister. 'You were just like a little doll. You needed a lot of looking after.'

'You've always looked after me, haven't you, Daisy,' Jemima said innocently.

'Not all the time, dear. Only when Mum had to go to work.'

'I always remember it being you,' Jemima insisted.

Daisy didn't argue. 'Well, I couldn't have managed two little rascals at once, could I? I was only just over eight when you were born, remember.'

Jemima thought that over for a few minutes, then she said, 'When Mum has one of her funny turns she says it was my fault Dad drowned because I was the thirteenth child.' She looked up at Daisy, frowning. 'But I've counted and counted and I can't make it come right.' She counted off on her fingers. 'There's Frank, then Betty, then Archie, then there's you, then Johnnie and Freddie, then Sophie and me. That's only eight. How can I be the thirteenth child if there's only eight of us? Where are the other five?'

Daisy stopped in the middle of the dusty road and stared in admiration at her little sister. 'How did you work that out, Jemma? How did you do a sum like that and you only just five years old?'

Jemima looked at her in surprise and shrugged. 'I counted it all up on my fingers. I can count to twenty as easy as pie if I use my toes as well. And then if you fold some fingers down, when you count up the rest that tells you how many you've got left.'

'Who taught you to do that?'

'Nobody. I just worked it out for myself.'

Daisy shook her head in amazement. She had missed so much schooling over the years through looking after her young brothers and sister that she had difficulty in counting to ten. 'Come on, I'll show you where the other five are.'

They turned back the way they had come, through the little kissing gate and into the churchyard. It was a dim, gloomy place, overhung with yew trees, and some of the tombstones were very old and covered with moss or ivy. Jemima shivered and clung closely to Daisy as they made their way between graves decorated with rather grubby-looking winged angels with clasped hands, or large ornate crosses entwined with anchors or cherubs.

'There,' Daisy said at last, as they came to a simple stone over-shadowed by huge stone memorials on every side. She pointed to the names, which she knew off by heart although she couldn't actu-ally read them. 'Tommy and Jane, Sidney, Alfred and Ivy. They're the other five in the family.' She ticked off on her fingers. 'Tommy and Jane both died of measles, Sidney had scarlet fever, Alfred fell into the water off the quay and drowned and Ivy died when she was three months old. I can remember Ivy but the others were all older than me and I don't remember them at all.'

'Oh, I see.' Jemima counted on her fingers and then looked up at Daisy. 'So that's how it makes me number thirteen, because Sophie was born before me so she was number twelve.' She shrugged her thin shoulders. 'I 'spect that's why Mum doesn't like me much. She keeps saying number thirteen's unlucky.'

Daisy bent down and gathered her into her arms. 'Well, I don't agree with her. *I* think thirteen's my lucky number. I wouldn't be without you, Jemma, not for all the world. And when I go into service next year you'll be the one I shall miss, more than all the others put together.' She gave her a kiss to prove it.

'I shall miss you, too, Daisy,' Jemima said, her eyes filling with tears.

'Now, now.' Daisy picked up the corner of her pinafore and dried her sister's eyes with it. 'Don't start to cry, sweetheart, I'm not going for a long time yet.' She gave her a little shake. 'Come on, you're a big girl now and you'll be starting school tomorrow. You'll like that, won't you?'

Jemima sniffed and smiled through her tears. 'Yes, I'll like that.' She reached into her pocket. 'Auntie Minnie gave me a piece of birthday cake to take to school for my lunch tomorrow but you can eat it if you like.' She pulled out a rather squashed piece of cake wrapped in a paper serviette.

'Are you sure you don't want it, Jemma?' Daisy asked, her eyes lighting up at the sight of it.

Jemima rubbed her tummy and grinned. 'I already had three pieces at Aunt Minnie's.' She pointed to it. 'Hurry up and eat it or you'll have to share it with the boys when we get home.'

Daisy took a bite. 'Mmm. Happy birthday, Jemma.'

Later that night, after Sophie was tucked up in bed, Minnie looked across at her husband, dozing on the other side of the hearth, his newspaper on the floor beside him where it had fallen. They were sitting in the warm, comfortable kitchen where they mostly lived, she in her high-backed padded wooden Windsor elbow chair, he in his scroll-armed, button-backed armchair. A child's basket chair with a tapestry cushion stood nearby. The only sounds in the room were the ticking of the grandfather clock in the corner by the door and the clicking of Minnie's knitting needles. Sooty the cat was curled up on the hearthrug between them, oblivious to everything.

'I don't know what to make of young Sophie, Will,' she said thoughtfully, dragging another length of wool from the ball. 'You'd think she'd enjoy having her sister to tea on their birthday, wouldn't you? I made them a nice little tea, with jelly and that, and set it all out nice in the dining room. I thought that'd be a real treat for Sophie because we don't use that room much but she was a sulky little madam today.'

William opened one eye. 'Jealous, I reckon,' he said. 'You've always made a lot of the child, matie, and I reckon she didn't like the idea of having to share you with her sister.'

'Oh, do you really think so, Will? That would be a pity, them being twins, and Jemima such a little scrap of a thing. And after all, it's only once a year.' She put down her knitting. 'Come to think of it, Sophie wouldn't let Jemima play with her bricks, either. And wouldn't let her touch her new doll's pram. And when I told her she must share her toys with Jemima she flew into one of her tempers, naughty little puss.'

'I reckon you've made too much of her, matie. Spoiled her.' He picked his pipe out of the rack and began to fill it from his tobacco pouch.

'Oh, I haven't, Will,' she protested. 'All I've done is give her plenty of love.' She was quiet for a minute, then she added, 'I'm afraid Jemima don't get a lot of that from Evie, poor little mite. My sister's got a real down on that child, more's the pity.'

William looked at her through a haze of tobacco smoke. 'I don't know about that, but from what I can make out your sister's getting a sight too fond of drink. There's always one or other of her young-sters at the jug and bottle counter of the Rose and Crown after her jug of porter. And it ain't a small jug, neither.'

Minnie sat up straight in her chair. 'William Furlong, what are you saying about my sister? Are you saying she's taken to the bottle?'

'I ain't saying nothing,' he said mildly. 'Only what I've seen with me own eyes and heard with me own ears.'

'Oh, dear,' Minnie said, deflated. 'What shall I do?'

'You'll mind your own business, matie. That's what you'll do,' her husband said firmly. 'You do quite enough for that family as it is.'

Three

The next day Jemima was so excited at the thought of starting school that she couldn't keep still.

'Oh, do stop hopping about, Jemma,' Daisy said as she tried to fasten the blue serge dress and white pinafore that Aunt Minnie had given her. She stood back. 'There, I think you'll do. Now, I'll just give your boots a rub over. They're a bit scuffed but we can't help that. Are they big enough?'

'Yes, they're a bit too big, really. Sophie's feet are bigger than mine,' Jemima said, looking down at them.

'Better that than too small,' Daisy said cheerfully. 'You'll grow into them.' She picked up the hairbrush and brushed her little sister's hair and fastened a ribbon in it. 'That's nice. You've still got a bit of curl left from where I put the curl papers in ready for your birthday party yesterday so your hair's not quite straight today.'

'I dunno why you're making such a fuss.' Eva was sitting at the kitchen table, her head in her hands, the empty porter jug at her elbow. 'And don't make so much noise. My head's thumping like a hammer. You'll have to call at the factory and tell them I'll be late in. The thought of the stink of fish makes my stomach churn.'

'You'll feel better if you go and lie down for an hour, Mum,' Daisy said over her shoulder. 'Go on, back to bed. I'll make sure the boys are tidy for school.'

'You're a good girl, Daisy.' Eva staggered to her feet and made for the front parlour where she slept. She glanced at Jemima as she passed her. 'Mind and keep that pinnie clean,' she snapped. 'You needn't think you'll get a clean one every day just because you're at school.'

'She looks a treat, doesn't she, Mum?' Daisy said proudly, smiling at her little sister, rosy-cheeked from having her face scrubbed under the tap in the yard. 'Aunt Minnie gave her the clothes for school as a birthday present.'

'What, new ones?' Eva stopped in her tracks and gaped. 'Well, she needn't think she's wearing new clothes for school . . .' She made a lunge for Jemima but Daisy was quicker and stepped between them. 'Run outside, Jemma. Wait for me on the quay. I won't be a minute.'

'Only the dress and pinafore. The boots were Sophie's, Mum,' Jemima heard Daisy explaining. 'And Aunt Minnie is paying the penny a week for school so Jemma won't have to stay away if you can't afford it.' She didn't hear any more as she ran out of the yard on to the quay to wait for her sister. She loved Daisy more than anyone else in the whole world. Daisy looked after things. She could make the boys wash their faces and scrub the yard. She knew how to deal with Mum when she had one of her turns; she didn't get frightened like Jemima did and she was the one who could stop Mum hitting the boys when they aggravated her. She dreaded the day when Daisy would leave home to go into service and sometimes she had a little cry at the mere thought of it. She sat down on a bollard, carefully wiping it to make sure there was no mud on it to spoil her new dress, and a few minutes later her brothers Johnnie and Freddie joined her, their faces shining and their hair still damp under their caps from Daisy's efforts with them under the yard tap.

Daisy hurried out, rolling down the sleeves of her dress. 'Now, you two boys run along to the fish factory and tell them Mum's had one of her turns so she'll be in later. Then come straight to school. If you run you won't be late. Got your pennies for school? Good. Go on, now. And don't lark about on the way,' she called after them. 'You don't want to get a black mark on your first day back.'

She took Jemima's hand as a bell began to ring in the distance.

'That's the school bell,' Jemima said, looking up, her brown eyes wide with apprehension.

'Yes. But don't worry. It means we've still got five minutes. We'll be there in plenty of time if we take a short cut through the churchyard.' She took Jemima's hand and hurried her up Rose Lane, through the churchyard and into the High Street, past Cate's the Butcher, where despite the fly papers the meat was already covered in flies, past the greengrocer's and Baxter's, where Mr Baxter was just opening up his ladies' and gentlemen's outfitters, and over the railway bridge. There they joined the stream of children hurrying down School Lane to the sprawling red-bricked building next to the railway line, all anxious not to be late.

Still holding her hand, Daisy rushed Jemima round to the infants' playground.

'Please, Miss Peel, this is my little sister, Jemima,' she said breathlessly. 'It's her first day.' She gave Jemima a swift peck on the cheek.

'You'll be all right now, dear. Wait for me at the gate after school. Don't dare go home without me.' And she was gone.

Miss Peel was quite young, tall and thin, with curly black hair piled on top of her head in a thick bun from which curly wisps escaped. She was wearing a loose smock over a long purple pleated skirt.

'Ah, yes. You're the other twin, aren't you? I must say, you don't look in the least like your sister, though.' Her rather sharp features softened as she smiled at the anxious little girl in front of her and Jemima thought she was the most beautiful lady she had ever seen, with smooth, creamy skin and large grey eyes. And she had the kindest face. Miss Peel pointed. 'Look, Sophie's over there. She doesn't look very happy so I'm sure she'll be pleased to see you and you can tell her that you'll be sitting together in class. You'll like that, won't you?' She smiled encouragingly again.

Jemima's heart sank because she knew Sophie would hate having to sit next to her. But she couldn't tell Miss Peel that so she summoned up a weak smile. 'Yes, Miss. Thank you, Miss.'

Miss Peel watched her run over to Sophie's side. She knew the history of the twins and it saddened her that they lived such different and separate lives. She was determined to keep them together at school as much as possible.

To Jemima's surprise, Sophie was dressed exactly the same as she was, in a dark blue serge dress and stiff white pinafore. The only difference was that Sophie's shoes were new. More surprising still was that Sophie was even more nervous than she was. She snivelled and clung to Jemima's hand as the whole class walked two-by-two into the classroom. This was a large high-ceilinged hall, with tall windows that were much too high to look out of and brick walls that were dark brown at the bottom and a dirty greenish-blue at the top. A black line, just above Jemima's head, marked where the two colours joined.

The room was divided into two classes, with 'top infants' at one end and 'bottom infants' at the other. Jemima and Sophie were put in 'bottom infants' and sat together on the tip-up bench attached to a desk for two. Sophie had to sit down first to keep the seat from tipping up again because she was bigger and taller than Jemima, whose feet barely touched the floor. At the end of the classroom there was a raised dais with a large blackboard on a three-legged easel next to Miss Peel's desk. Jemima looked round at the rest of the class. Several of them were 'new' like her and Sophie and a few of the others were still snivelling. Jemima was determined not to snivel, although she felt a bit like it. Instead she felt in the pocket of her pinafore where she had hidden Raggie Annie. Her hand closed round her peg doll. It was comforting to know that she was there. It was also comforting to know that Daisy and the boys were somewhere in the building although she had no idea where to find them.

Miss Peel called the register and they each had to call 'Present' when their name was called. After that they had to chant the two times table several times as Miss Peel pointed to the numbers on the blackboard. After the second time Jemima knew it off by heart but most of the other children found it more difficult.

The morning passed quickly. At break time they were all sent out into the playground. Jemima looked for the boys and Daisy but their playgrounds were on the other side of the school and although she could hear the big children shouting as they played, she didn't know how to reach them.

Sophie still clung to her. She had stopped crying now but her face was all streaked with tears.

'When do we get our presents?' she hiccuped.

'What presents?'

'Well, we all had to call out "present" if we wanted one, didn't we?'

'No, silly. It wasn't to *get* a present; it was to say that we were here, we were present.' Jemima knew this because Daisy had warned her.

'Oh, I thought we were going to be given a present.' Sophie's eyes welled with tears again.

'Now, don't start crying again. Come over to the water fountain and I'll wash your face for you.' Jemima took her hand. 'You'll feel better then.'

'But I haven't got a face flannel or towel,' Sophie complained.

'Oh, come here. I'll dip the corner of my pinnie into the water.' Jemima scrubbed at her sister's face. 'Now dry yourself on your pinnie. There, do you feel better now?'

Sophie nodded and gave her a watery smile. 'Would you like one of my jam sandwiches?' she asked. 'Aunt Minnie gave me enough for you as well.'

'Oh, wouldn't I, just!' Jemima said, her eyes lighting up. Apart from the fact that she was always hungry it was the first time Sophie had willingly shared anything with her.

Going home with Daisy after school, Jemima recounted all the things that had happened, how one little boy had cried so much he had to be taken home, how another boy had been naughty and had to stand in the corner, how a little girl had wet her drawers and how she had looked after Sophie when she cried because she thought she was going to be given a present and Sophie had shared her jam sandwiches.

'And what about you, Jemma? Did you like school?'

'Oh, yes. I learned my two times table as easy as pie. Miss Peel says I'm very bright. What does that mean, Daisy?'

Daisy hesitated. 'I reckon it means you pick things up quick.'

Jemima shook her head vehemently. 'Oh, no, it can't mean that, Daisy. I never pick things up that don't belong to me.'

'Not that sort of picking things up, silly.' Daisy laughed and gave the hand she was holding an affectionate shake. 'I meant you're quick to learn. You must be; look at the way you taught yourself to count. And now you say you've learned your two times table on your very first day.'

'Mm. P'raps I'll be a teacher, like Miss Peel.'

'Would you like that, Jemma?'

'Reckon so. Can I go to school tomorrow?'

'Oh, yes. You'll have to go every day except Saturday and Sunday. If you don't the Attendance Officer will come round to find out why.'

'Is that the man who comes round to see Mum when Johnnie stays off school to go and help with the harvest on the farm?'

'Yes, that's right.'

Jemima was silent. She hoped she wouldn't have to stay off school for anything. She hadn't liked the Attendance Officer; she didn't want him coming round after her.

The weeks and months seemed to fly by. Jemima loved school. She quickly learned her alphabet and how to spell simple words and she amazed Miss Peel with her grasp of addition and subtraction. Sophie learned her alphabet with difficulty; she couldn't spell and even simple sums defeated her without Jemima's help. For her part Jemima couldn't understand why Sophie found sums so difficult, because it seemed like common sense to her.

But she had to be careful not to say this to Sophie because she knew Sophie still didn't really like her and only insisted on sitting next to her so that she could copy her work and stay at the top of the class with her. Jemima didn't mind sitting with Sophie but she didn't like her work being copied so it was all a bit tricky. Sometimes she wondered if she should tell Miss Peel but she didn't like the thought of telling tales, so she kept quiet. One day she deliberately put a wrong answer, which Sophie copied. Miss Peel didn't say anything but she moved Sophie to sit with someone else. Next time there was a test Sophie was nowhere near the top of the class.

But Jemima's honesty came at a high price because once Sophie found she was no longer able to copy her sister's work she stopped sharing her jam sandwiches, and sometimes Jemima went quite hungry.

The day when Daisy would leave home and go into service loomed nearer and nearer. She was to go and work for Mrs Clarke in a big house at the top of the hill as soon as she left school on her fourteenth birthday. Anxious that Jemima should be able to manage without her, Daisy began to teach her to get ready and take herself off to school every morning because she knew that their mother was unpredictable, to say the least, and she couldn't rely on the boys to help her, much though they loved their little sister.

'You will be sure and come back, won't you?' Jemima said, with a sob in her voice, kissing her sister goodbye before she went off to begin work for Mrs Clarke.

'Course I will. I've told you that. Every week, without fail.' Daisy gave her another hug.

'Don't you worry. She'll have to come home to bring me her wages,' their mother said smugly. 'When she brings a bit of money in perhaps I shan't have to work my fingers to the bone at that old fish factory. I shall look forward to that.'

And so shall I because then perhaps the whole house won't stink of fish, Jemima thought to herself, but wisely she didn't say anything.

Four

The years went by and life was hard without Daisy. Daisy had swept the floor; Daisy had carried the hot water into the wash house for a 'good wash' as opposed to the daily rinse under the tap; Daisy had kept the boys in order and Daisy had looked after Mum when she had one of her turns. Jemima was beginning to realize that Mum's turns had quite a lot to do with the jug of porter that had to be fetched from the Rose and Crown when there was enough money to pay for it and she vowed that when she was old enough to be sent for it she would accidentally drop the jug. But she knew she wouldn't do that because there was no telling what Mum might do to her if she did. She was already used to being slapped and pinched and twice she'd been locked in the coal hole. She hadn't liked that, because it was dark and dirty even though there was no coal in it. Daisy had rescued her both times and washed her all over in nice warm water and dried her tears as she asked her what she had done to deserve such treatment. Jemima said she thought it was because she'd torn her frock, but she wasn't really sure and she hadn't known which tear Mum meant because the frock was already a mass of patches and tears.

Jemima cried every night when she went to bed because she missed the comfort of cuddling up to Daisy in the big bed and she didn't know who would rescue her from the coal hole now that her sister wasn't there. She resolved to be especially good and helpful to Mum from now on.

She learned to sweep the floor, although the broom handle was taller than she was and the broom hadn't got many bristles left. She made sure that her bedroom was always neat and tidy, just as it had been when Daisy was there to share it with her. She learned to do the ironing, heating the iron on top of the kitchen range and spitting on it to make sure it was hot enough. She didn't often burn herself and when she did Mum said it served her right for being careless. She washed the dishes, making sure to grate enough soap into the water to dissolve the grease but not too much so that Mum hit her for being wasteful, and drained them on the tin tray before she dried them and put them away on the shelf that she could only reach by standing on a chair.

In her spare time she ran errands for the neighbours, earning herself a farthing here, a ha'penny there. She kept the money in a tin under her mattress and when she had enough she bought herself a bar of Pears soap, the sort she had seen at Aunt Minnie's when she'd been there to tea on her birthday, because it smelled so nice. She wrapped it in a piece of flannel and hid it behind a loose brick in the wash house and every Sunday night she took a pan of hot water out there and washed herself all over with her lovely smelly soap before carefully wrapping it in the piece of flannel again and putting it safely back in its hiding place.

The boys never helped; they weren't expected to. They were getting quite big now, and soon Johnnie would be starting work either on the farm or on the fishing boats. Freddie, although he was two years younger, was nearly as tall as his brother. Jemima knew the Attendance Officer was always calling about one or other of them, but they would rather be out working on the farm picking up stones or scaring the birds than learning their multiplication tables at school and Mum didn't care. In fact, it suited her better because she had to pay for them to go to school whereas they earned money working on the farm, so she always made up some excuse or other.

Then one day, just before Jemima's twelfth birthday, everything changed completely.

It was the day Jemima arrived home from school and found her mother busily scrubbing the kitchen floor. And as if that wasn't enough, the horrible flowered porter jug was lying smashed in the yard, so Jemima knew something dreadful must have happened. She went in very warily, stepping round the parts of the floor that had already been cleaned. It wasn't difficult to see where that was.

She waited apprehensively, saying nothing, expecting a tirade of abuse, but her mother didn't appear to be cross. She looked different, somehow, and it took Jemima several minutes to realize that it was because she had washed her face and combed her hair.

'Is there anything you want me to do, Mum?' she asked at last, in a small voice.

Eva sat back on her heels and brushed back a strand of hair with her forearm. 'There. That's beginning to look better, isn't it? Time it had a bit of a birthday.' She looked up at Jemima and almost smiled at her, which was unusual. 'Yes, you can take that bag of picked shrimps over there down to the factory. And don't come back without the money for them.'

'Do you want me to ask for another lot?' Jemima hated it when her mother picked shrimps on the kitchen table, because the shells spilled on to the floor and didn't get swept up for days unless Jemima did it and the table was never scrubbed so the stink lingered. It was better when she went to the fish factory to work, because at least some of the stink had a chance to melt away in the air on the way home.

Eva took a deep breath and said brightly, 'No, not today. We'll manage. Daisy'll be home tomorrow and she'll bring her wages so we'll be all right for a day or two.'

'What happened to the jug, Mum?' Jemima risked the question. She was desperate to know but almost afraid to ask because something dreadful must have happened for the precious porter jug to be broken.

'Aunt Minnie smashed it when she was here this morning.' Her mother sounded quite matter-of-fact.

'Oh, dear.' She hoped they hadn't had a row. She liked Aunt Minnie, not just because she gave her Sophie's cast-offs and paid for her schooling, but because she was so kind. 'But what about your medicine?' That's what it was always called, although Jemima had grown to learn the hard way that it was nothing of the kind.

'I'm not going to drink any more of that.'

'Not ever?'

'Not ever.' Eva got up off her knees and emptied the bucket of filthy water on to the yard, where most of it ran down into the drain. She wiped her hands on the sacking apron she was wearing and pulled back her shoulders. 'I shan't have time for it. I'm going to see about taking in a lodger.'

Jemima bit her lip. It was not a word she was familiar with. 'What's a lodger?' she asked at last.

'Somebody who'll pay to come and live here. Aunt Minnie says they're looking for lodgings for men who've come from away to work at the shipyard, now that it's reopened.'

Jemima looked round the room, at the grubby wallpaper and dark brown peeling paint. She couldn't imagine that anybody would want to come and live in their house, let alone pay for the privilege. 'Is that why you've scrubbed the floor?'

'Yes. I've cleaned right through the house. I can't offer to take in lodgers unless the place is smartened up a bit.' As she was speaking she was taking the chairs off the table where they had been stacked while she scrubbed the floor and Jemima saw to her surprise that the table had been scrubbed as well. 'Go on,' her mother said, waving her away. 'Don't stand there gawping, run along with those shrimps. And when you get the money for them you can call at Bellman's for two meat pies and get a couple of potatoes from Wick's as well.'

Jemima didn't ask any more questions. Something must have brought about this transformation in her mother – she couldn't imagine what and didn't dare to ask, but whatever it was could only be a good thing.

And Eva would have died rather than admit to her daughter what had transpired between herself and her sister that morning. It still made her blush with shame to recall the scene.

When Minnie arrived Eva had been sitting at the kitchen table picking shrimps, her hands moving automatically as she stared at nothing in particular. She hadn't even realized her sister was standing in the doorway watching her. The pile of shrimp heads and tails was growing, spilling over on to the floor as the heap waiting to be shelled diminished and the basin of shelled shrimps filled. Her hair was wispy and unkempt, because she hadn't bothered to comb it, her face unwashed and lined, her overall torn and dirty. The telltale porter jug stood at her elbow. Empty.

Minnie's gaze had shifted to the room. It was sparsely furnished, just the table with four odd chairs round it and a bench against the wall, the kitchen range that needed blackleading, an armchair piled with laundry waiting to be washed. The clock on the mantelpiece, where it jostled for position in the dust with sundry cheap ornaments, was half an hour slow. On the floor was a dirty piece of cracked linoleum with the pattern worn off and there was a threadbare peg rug in front of the stove. The room had a stale, fishy smell about it. Minnie had thought of her own clean, comfortable home and had shaken her head in despair.

'Oh, Evie, look at you! Look what you've come to!' The words had sounded sad rather than angry.

Eva's head shot up at the sound of her sister's voice and she wiped her nose with the back of her hand. 'How long have you bin standing there?' she'd asked. There was anger in her voice.

'Long enough.' Minnie came into the room and sat down opposite to her, first making sure no shrimp heads had fallen on to the chair.

'What do you mean?' Eva stared at her.

'I mean I've been standing there long enough to realize it's high time you pulled yourself together, my girl, and stopped trying to drown your troubles in porter. Now young Daisy's not here to look after things your house is an absolute disgrace. You worked that poor girl half to death while she was at home and now you're trying to do the same to Jemima, poor little mite. It's not right, Evie, and you know it.'

Eva shrugged. 'Jemima's got to do her share, like everyone else. I can't do everything. I'm not like you. I don't have a husband to keep me; I have to work for a living. It takes me all my time to earn enough to pay the rent and buy a few scraps of food. I'm not very good with money, it just seems to disappear,' she added miserably.

'You'd make it go a good deal further if you didn't keep filling that,' Minnie said sharply, nodding towards the porter jug.

'I need it. It's my tonic.' Eva's eyes filled with tears of self-pity. 'You don't know what a struggle I have, trying to keep my head above water, Minnie,' she whined. 'Everything seems to get on top of me, and I don't get a lot of help from the children. Frank's married and already got one baby and another on the way, so he needs every penny he can earn. Betty's in service in Chelmsford; she sends me a bit now and then but not often. I think it's a case of out of sight, out of mind as far as she's concerned.'

'Well, what about Archie? He's still at home.'

'When he's here. But he's signed up for the Royal Navy so I reckon that's the last we'll see of him. It's probably the best thing for him. You know what he's like, can't bear to be away from the sea. Mind you, he's always been generous when he's got it. He'd always give me a few bob when he got a share-out, but I shan't get that now. And Johnnie's only just started on the fishing boats so he doesn't earn a sight.'

'Your Daisy's a good girl, though,' Minnie said. 'Does she still come home every week?'

'Yes.' Eva's expression softened. 'And she gives me most of her wages. That girl's a real blessing to me. She'll usually give the house a bit of a clean and help with the laundry while she's home.'

Minnie clucked her tongue impatiently. 'You're not fair to that girl, Evie. She has to work hard enough for the Clarkes, without you expecting her to come home and slave for you. And there's poor little Jemima, trying to sweep floors and burning herself with the flat iron when she should be playing with her dollies like Sophie does.' She glared at her sister. 'You should be ashamed of yourself, Evie Furlong. And it's no good sitting there and complaining that it's all too much for you. If you weren't always sozzled with that,' she pointed to the porter jug, 'you'd be quite capable of managing. You've let drink addle your brain.' She leaned over and picked up the porter jug and took it into the yard and smashed it on the stones. The last drops of dark liquid trickled between the cobbles. 'There. Now if you want to drink yourself to death you'll have to lick it up off the cobbles.'

'That's my best jug! What did you do that for?' Eva shrieked.

'To bring you to your senses.' Minnie came back and sat down again. 'Oh, Evie, your house used to be as neat as a new pin when Joe was alive. What's happened to you?' she said sadly.

Eva put her head in her hands. 'It was the twins did it,' she said, her voice muffled. 'Well, Jemima. Joe always said thirteen was unlucky. Thank God he never knew I was carrying twins before he drowned.' She looked up. 'See? Like I said, the thirteenth child, born on the thirteenth, the very day my Joe was drowned.' She gave a little shudder. 'I never took to that child,' she added almost under her breath. 'And I've never had a stroke of luck since the day she was born, so my Joe was right.'

'Oh, for goodness' sake, don't be so ridiculous. You've let that superstition get hold of you and rule your life. It wasn't the child's fault she was number thirteen. And you looked after her well enough when you thought she was too little and weak to survive.'

'Yes, well, you'd taken the other one, hadn't you? I had to have something to look after.' Eva automatically resumed her shrimp picking.

'So why don't you look after her properly now? From what I can make out she's a bright little thing.'

'Is she?' Eva said without much interest.

'Yes, Sophie says she often used to help her with her sums.' Minnie glared at her sister. 'You ought to be ashamed of yourself, Evie, the way you neglect that child. I'd take her to live with me now, bless her heart, if I hadn't just taken in a lodger.'

'A lodger? You've taken a lodger?' Eva's hands stopped working and she stared at her sister.

'Well, they've just reopened the shipyard again and they need lodgings for the tradesmen who've come from away. I've got a spare bedroom so I asked William and he said I could take a lodger if I thought I could manage it, although it's not that we need the money. So I've got Mr Banks, he's foreman shipwright, living with us for the time being. He's a very nice, respectable young man, got a wife and small children living in Kent. I expect they'll move this way before long.'

Eva was hardly listening. Her eyes were shining. 'I could do that. I could take a lodger, couldn't I? Now Daisy's not here I could sleep with Jemima and let the bed in the front room downstairs to a lodger.'

'Not unless you smarten this place up,' Minnie said flatly. 'You'll never get anybody wanting to come and live here, the state the place is in. And look at you! You're no advertisement for a decent home.'

Eva ignored that. 'Do you know anybody else who needs lodgings?'

Minnie looked round. 'Nobody who'd pay to come and live here.'

'Don't worry, I'll clean it up.' Suddenly, Eva was becoming more animated than Minnie had seen her for a long time, sweeping the shrimp heads from the table into a bucket, although she ignored the bits that had fallen on the floor. 'And Daisy'll be home tomorrow. She'll help me. How much would I get a week?'

'I don't know. Depends who you get and how much they're prepared to pay.'

'Oh, if only I could get away from that fish factory,' Eva said. 'I hate the stink of that place.'

'Well, I don't know that a lodger would pay enough for you to give that up,' Minnie said with a frown. 'But if you're prepared to give up the porter . . .'

'Oh, I shall. I shall do that.' Eva came round and kissed her sister, leaving a strong scent of stale fish. 'Thanks, Minnie. I'm glad you smashed that jug. I swear I shan't touch another drop of porter. You'll see. I'm gonna turn over a new leaf. I shall get the place cleaned up and then I shall offer to take a lodger.' She beamed with pleasure and Minnie saw the ghost of her pretty young sister behind the haggard face.

'I just hope you'll stick to your good intentions,' Minnie said without much hope.

'I shall. I'm determined to turn over a new leaf, Minnie. I just needed something . . . something to work for, to look forward to, I suppose. Well, now I've got it. You just wait and see,' Eva said.

Minnie opened her purse and took out sixpence. 'Well, here's a start for you. But you've got to promise me you won't spend it at the jug and bottle.'

For a few seconds Eva looked longingly at the smashed jug on the cobbles. Then she squared her shoulders. 'I promise, Minnie. On the soul of my dead, departed Joe, I promise I'm going to turn over a new leaf and I won't touch another drop of strong liquor.'

By the time Jemima arrived home Eva's transformation had begun.

Five

Jemima took the bag of shrimps and hurried along the quay to the fish factory. She couldn't imagine what had brought about such a change in her mother; she hadn't once shouted at her, or hit her, and Jemima had never before seen her on her knees scrubbing the kitchen floor. She suspected it may have had something to do with the smashed porter jug, but she felt it wouldn't be sensible to enquire too closely about that in case it upset things again. She thought a bit more and decided it was more likely something to do with taking in a lodger. She couldn't think of any other reason why her mother would bother to clean the house. Usually, what cleaning was done was left to Jemima.

She started to run. She ran past fishermen in thick Guernseys working on their smacks, hopped over mooring ropes that stretched from the boats to the iron bollards and skirted coils of rope and a pile of rotten sprats. She didn't care. The porter jug was smashed, the house was clean, Mum was in a good mood and they were to have pie and potatoes for tea, instead of bread and scrape. If this was what having a lodger meant she was all for it.

She stopped when she saw her two brothers. Johnnie was mending fishing nets and Freddie was hanging precariously over the edge of the quay racing driftwood boats on the water.

She watched for a moment, then said, 'We're going to have a lodger. And pie and potatoes for tea.' She turned away, saying over her shoulder, 'And you'd better not go home covered in mud, Freddie, because Mum's scrubbed the kitchen floor.'

They both stopped what they were doing and gaped at her. 'Cor. Pie and potatoes,' Johnnie said, a grin spreading across his pinched face. At the same time Freddie asked with a frown, 'What's a lodger, Jem?'

She went back and stood over them, her hands on her hips, the bag of shrimps over one arm. 'Somebody who'll pay to come and live at our house,' she said importantly.

'Pay? To live at our house? Don't be daft. Who d'you reckon's gonna do that?' Johnnie sneered derisively.

'Ask no questions and you'll get no lies told you.' She spoke sharply because the same thing had occurred to her. She turned away before they could question her further and nearly bumped into two men walking along the quay nearby. They were wearing suits and bowler hats, which was unusual: men who loitered on the quay always wore jerseys and moleskin trousers and cheese-cutter caps. The two men smiled at her but she ignored them and ran off to deliver the shrimps, remembering that her mother had drummed into her that she must never talk to strangers.

After waiting for ages to be paid at the fish factory, she ran to the shops and bought the pies and potatoes and hurried home, fearful that her mother's mood would have changed and she would accuse her of dawdling and take the strap to her.

But to her astonishment the two men she had bumped into on the quay were sitting at the kitchen table, their bowler hats in front of them on the freshly scrubbed table, while Mum fussed with the kettle and teapot.

'Ah, here's the young lady,' the older of the two men said as she walked in. But before she could speak her mother had snatched the shopping out of her hand and pushed her roughly outside the back door.

'What have I told you about talking to strangers?' she demanded in a fierce whisper, gripping Jemima's arm till it hurt.

Jemima looked up at her in terror. She might have known the good mood wouldn't last. Visions of the coal hole rose before her, although she didn't know what she'd done wrong. 'But I haven't been talking to strangers, Mum,' she whimpered. 'Honest I haven't.'

'Then how did those two men know I was thinking of taking in lodgers?' Jemima felt her arm shaken roughly at every word her mother uttered.

'I dunno, Mum.' Jemima began to tremble and her voice rose. 'I only told the boys. They were out playing on the quay. P'raps they told those men. I didn't. I didn't tell another soul . . .' Her voice trailed off and she glanced nervously up at her mother. 'I remember now – they were walking past when I spoke to the boys. P'raps they heard what I was saying.' She shook her head. 'But I didn't tell them, Mum. I never spoke to them. Honest.'

'All right, then.' Eva let go of Jemima's arm and pushed her inside.

The older of the two men looked up as they entered. Jemima noticed that he had thinning black hair and a moustache like Uncle William's. He had quite a kind face and now he smiled at her as he took in the situation. He turned to Eva. 'I hope we're not getting this young lady into trouble for talking to strangers, ma'am. Fact is, we overheard her telling her brothers you were thinking of taking in lodgers, so since we've just come off the train and we're looking for lodgings, we asked the boys where they lived and came right along.'

'You might have told me that before,' Eva said, her voice sharp because she had been put in the wrong.

'Well, ma'am, beggin' your pardon, we've only bin here a few minutes so we ain't had much chance. But to get back to what we was saying before the little maid came back, if you'll be so good as to take us, me an' my boy Sam here'll be glad to pay the goin' rate and be thankful to think we're set up with somewhere to lay our heads so soon after gettin' off the train. Y'see, there's no work where we come from down south and we heard the shipyard here has just opened again and they were looking for tradesmen. Well, I'm a boilermaker and Sam here's an apprentice blacksmith so we came to try our luck and I'm glad to say we've both bin taken on.'

'Well . . .' Eva was hardly listening. Her mind was on the fact that two lodgers would be double the money with not that much more work. They looked respectable enough, clean and properly dressed for men in their walk of life. And there was the double bed upstairs . . . Things really were looking up at last. She permitted herself a small, smug smile of satisfaction as she smoothed her overall, part of her mind registering that she was glad she'd changed into a clean one, and took a deep breath.

'I was really only thinking of taking one lodger, but if you wouldn't mind sharing a bed . . .?' She smiled at them hopefully, at the same time trying to keep her lips together so as not to show the gaps where her teeth had fallen out.

'Not a bit, ma'am,' the older man answered, clearly relieved. 'Sam won't mind sharin' with his old dad, will you, boy?'

'No. As long as I've got somewhere decent to kip, that's all I ask,' Sam replied. He grinned, showing a full complement of large, rather horsy teeth.

'Well, then. I dessay we can manage to 'commodate the both of you,' Eva said, putting on what she hoped was a businesslike voice. 'You can have the front room upstairs. You'd better come and take a look, make sure it'll suit you.'

The three of them clattered up the uncarpeted stairs.

'Where am I gonna sleep, Mum?' Jemima asked anxiously, after the two men had approved the room and the price, and gone to fetch their belongings from the railway station. 'That's where me and Daisy have always slept and that's my room now.' She didn't mind the thought of Mr Starling sleeping in her bed, he seemed quite a nice man, but she was uncomfortable with the thought of his son sleeping there. He was a taller, thinner version of his father with slicked-back hair and a bit of a weaselly look about him that she didn't much like.

'Not any more, it isn't, so you'd better fetch your bits and pieces downstairs. Make sure the chest of drawers is empty; Mr Starling and his son'll need somewhere to put their stuff. I'll make you up a bed in the front parlour next to me,' Eva said carelessly. 'I've got a bit of blanket and we can put coats on the floor. That'll do for you for the time being. I want to keep an eye on you if we're going to have two strange men in the house.'

Jemima knew better than to complain.

But it wasn't for long because Freddie was due to leave school. He was being taken on permanently by the farmer where he had for years scared the birds and picked stones when he should have been at his lessons, and he would be living in. His last task before he left was to fetch his bed down the stairs into the front parlour for Jemima.

'Well, you won't be needing it any more,' Eva said as she supervised. She was not sentimental about her children leaving home.

It was nice to have a proper bed again although Jemima didn't much like sleeping in a room with her mother because she snored. Other than that life was much better with the two lodgers in the house; her mother was more cheerful and there was always a good meal on the table in the evening. Of course, Jemima had to help keep the house clean and the ironing and washing-up were always left to her, but that was nothing new.

The big iron mangle with its fat wooden rollers was kept in the yard just outside the back door, covered up with an old coat most of the time to keep it clean. Eva used it as a wringer on wash days to squeeze the water out of the wet washing, then, when the things had been hung on the washing line to dry, they were carefully folded and the sheets and pillowcases and towels were mangled between the heavy rollers to smooth out the creases. Jemima had been in charge of mangling the dry laundry ever since she was tall and strong enough to turn the handle. It was very hard work so one good thing about having lodgers was that Sam would sometimes offer to turn the handle of the mangle for her on a Saturday afternoon.

But she had to be careful because he was inclined to show off and turn the handle too fast.

'Do you like my new jacket?' he asked as he was helping her one Saturday. 'I got it from Baxter's, opposite the church. Smart, don't you think?' He looked down and brushed a hair off the lapel as he spoke.

'Yes. It's very nice.' She didn't look; she was too busy making sure there were no creases in the sheet before she fed it between the rollers.

'Oh, come on, get a move on. I'm meeting my pals at quarter past two.' He began to turn the handle faster and faster.

Suddenly Jemima screamed.

He stared at her. 'What's the matter?'

'My finger! You're jamming my finger. Roll it back. Roll it back!'

'Oh, Christ!' He reversed the handle to release her hand.

Her mother rushed out, followed by Mr Starling in his braces.

'Now, look what you've done!' she shouted. 'You've put blood all over my clean sheets! Why couldn't you be more careful?' She elbowed Jemima out of the way. 'Now that one'll have to be washed again.' She snatched it out from between the rollers and bundled it through to the wash house.

'Let's have a look at you, dearie,' Mr Starling said to Jemima, as she stood nursing her finger, trying to stem the blood with her pinafore. 'Oh, that looks a bit nasty. You come inside and sit down; you look as white as that sheet you were putting through the mangle.' He helped her in and sat her down by the fire, then fetched water from the tap and bathed her finger and bound it up with a piece of clean rag, talking to her all the time as she tried not to cry with the pain of it. 'There,' he said when he had finished. 'I don't think you'll lose the nail.' He turned to his son, who had followed them in. 'Fine help you are, you great oaf. You need to look what you're doing instead of standing and preening yourself in your new finery.'

Sam's jaw dropped. 'Well, I like that! My fault, was it! I was only trying to give the girl a hand till it was time to go to the football match. I shan't bother in future, I can tell you.' He pulled out his watch from his waistcoat pocket. It was a cheap one that didn't keep very good time but it looked impressive. 'It's time now, so I'll be off. Sorry about your finger, Jemmy,' he threw over his shoulder as he went off.

Jemima glared at his back. She hated him calling her Jemmy. In fact, she didn't like Sam much at all. He wasn't a bit like his father, who was a kind, gentle sort of man who didn't mind helping with the washing-up and took an interest when she practised her writing or did sums at the kitchen table.

'I think a cuppa tea is called for, don't you, dearie?' Mr Starling said, pulling the kettle forward on the hob. He shook his head and said, half under his breath, 'I wonder your mother lets you do heavy work like that and you only a slip of a girl. But there, it's none of my business, I suppose.' He busied himself with the teapot.

'Will I still be able to write, Mr Starling?' she asked anxiously, examining the bulky dressing on her middle finger. 'I've got some marking to do.'

He turned and smiled at her in surprise. 'Marking? You? How do you manage that?'

'We-ell,' she drew the word out, torn between pride at what she could do and fear that it might make trouble for Miss Peel. She decided to trust him. 'Miss Peel's mother is ill and I'm very good at sums so she lets me mark the sums for the little ones. They're only very simple ones, adding and taking away. They don't do things like long division and long multiplication.'

He poured the tea and gave her a cup and sat down opposite with the half pint mug he always had his tea in. 'Well, I never. And can you do long division and long multiplication, dearie?'

'Oh, yes. But I'm in Standard Five. I'm supposed to be able to do that.' She thought for a bit. 'Lots of people can't, though. Some of them don't even know their tables.'

'And do you?'

'Oh, yes. I know them right up to my twelve times table. I can do the thirteen times, a bit. But I have to cheat and count up on my fingers for some of it.'

He shook his head. 'Well, I never,' he said again.

She drank some of her tea. Then she leaned forward. 'Miss Peel says when I'm thirteen I can be a monitor.' She leaned back to see his reaction.

'Well, I never,' he repeated for the third time, looking suitably impressed. 'And what, exactly, is a monitor?'

She frowned. 'Monitors help out when there are too many children for one teacher to manage. I think I shall be working with the infants. Miss Peel will tell me what she wants me to teach them. I like her. She's nice.' She drank some more of her tea. 'I should like to be a teacher, when I grow up. Miss Peel says I would be a good teacher.'

Alf Starling was about to say 'well, I never' for the fourth time but he changed it to, 'Yes, I reckon she's right. I reckon you're a clever little girl. Do you know any geometry?'

'No. What's that?' She was immediately interested, her throbbing finger forgotten, which was exactly what Alf Starling intended.

'Shapes. Angles, triangles, squares. I have to do a lot of that kind of working out in my job.'

'Will you show me?'

'Course I will, dearie.'

Eva came in. 'I've put that sheet on the line to dry. I hope it won't rain. Oh, you are careless, Jemima, messing it up like that.'

'I don't believe Jemima was to blame, Mrs Furlong. It was my Sam,' Mr Starling said quickly. 'He wasn't watching what he was doing. However, I've bound up her finger and with luck she won't lose the nail.'

Eva's jaw dropped. 'Lose the nail? Was it that bad?'

'Her finger was jammed in the rollers. Of course it was bad,' Mr Starling said. Jemima had never heard him speak so sharply before. 'You didn't see it. You were too busy worrying about your sheet.'

'Yes. Well. I didn't want it to stain and get iron mould.' Eva shrugged her shoulders, embarrassed. 'Is there any more tea in the pot?'

Jemima smiled at Mr Starling and he winked at her. She knew she had found a real friend.

Six

What Jemima didn't tell Mr Starling – in fact what she didn't tell anybody – was that Miss Peel always gave her a few pennies when she helped with the marking. She saved these pennies carefully, hiding them behind the brick in the wash house along with her Pears soap, and with them she managed to buy real, proper shampoo for her hair.

She had found it quite difficult marking the children's books this time, hampered by her damaged finger, and when she took them back on Monday she had to apologize that the ticks and crosses weren't quite as neat as usual.

'Oh, dear. Your poor finger. And your right hand, too,' Miss Peel said sympathetically. 'Well, I can see what a problem writing is, so would you like to go and help the little ones chant their tables and then you could perhaps read them a story.'

She had to pass Sophie's desk on the way to the infants' class.

'Teacher's favourite,' Sophie hissed from behind the desk's open lid. 'You'll miss the history test, lucky thing. What date was the Battle of Hastings?'

'1066,' Jemima hissed back.

'I hate history. Don't see why we have to learn it.' She banged the lid down again.

Jemima went on to the infants' class where she spent a happy morning teaching them to chant their two times table, pointing to the figures she had written up on the blackboard. It was much easier writing large figures in chalk with her injured finger than trying to use a pencil and paper. For once she agreed with Sophie, because teaching the little ones was much more enjoyable than a history test, although unlike Sophie she did enjoy their history lessons. Then she read a story, giving all the characters different voices: Father Bear a deep gruff voice, Mother Bear a slightly higher one and a tiny squeaky one for Baby Bear. She loved seeing the children sitting cross-legged in front of her, hanging on to every word, open-mouthed in fear when Goldilocks was nearly caught and clapping their hands when she jumped out of the window and escaped. Jemima knew then for sure that this was what she wanted to do with her life. She wanted to be a school teacher.

A month later it was The Birthday. She always thought of her and Sophie's birthday in capital letters but she no longer looked forward to it as she had in the past. This was partly because she was no longer perpetually hungry. In the year since Mr Starling and Sam had come to live with them her mother had been forced to cook proper meals for the two hungry men, which meant that Jemima ate well, too. But of course she didn't tell Aunt Minnie this because she didn't want to spoil her aunt's pleasure in preparing a special birthday tea for them. She even still made blancmange and jelly because she knew Jemima had liked it as a little girl.

This year Jemima had saved up her pennies from helping Miss Peel and had bought Sophie a length of tartan ribbon for her birthday.

'I bought it with my own money,' she said proudly as she handed it to her.

Sophie received it without enthusiasm and handed her the book Aunt Minnie had bought for her to give, saying, 'I think this was quite expensive so you'd better look after it. It's got maps of everywhere in the world.'

'Oh, an atlas! Thanks, Sophie. Thank you, Aunt Minnie.' Jemima's eyes shone as she hugged her aunt. She knew better than to hug Sophie. 'I always look after my books,' she added for Sophie's benefit. Not that she had many, but Mr Starling had given her a book of Hans Christian Andersen's Fairy Tales for Christmas two years ago and she had read it and read it, over and over.

Aunt Minnie gave her a new blouse and there was also a parcel of Sophie's outgrown clothes. They would need letting down and taking in; Jemima was now taller than her sister but she was still as thin as a lath whereas Sophie had grown quite plump.

Tea was not easy. Sophie made it plain that she resented Jemima's presence even though it was their birthday, and the fact that Aunt Minnie made her so welcome only made things worse. Jemima loved Aunt Minnie and she couldn't understand why Sophie should be so unkind when their aunt had taken so much trouble over their birthday.

'Miss Peel says I'm to be a monitor, now I'm thirteen,' she told Aunt Minnie as she carried the dirty plates through to the kitchen after tea.

'A monitor? What's that?' Uncle William asked from the depths of his armchair as she passed. He wasn't out fishing for once because his sails were being mended.

'It means Miss Peel will teach me and then I'll go and teach what I've learned to groups of the younger children.'

'That sounds very grown-up,' Uncle William said, puffing on his pipe.

'Yes. I already teach the infants if Miss Peel is busy,' she said proudly. 'Miss Peel says I can become a pupil-teacher when I'm fourteen and if I pass the exams every year I'll be a proper teacher after four years. So that's what I hope to do.'

'My word, you seem to have it all worked out.' Uncle William was suitably impressed. He turned to Sophie. 'And what are you going to be, dearie? Have you made up your mind yet?'

'No, of course she hasn't,' Aunt Minnie swiftly answered for her. 'She's still got another year at school. There's plenty of time before she needs to think about that.'

'I only asked,' Uncle William said mildly.

Minnie put her hands possessively on Sophie's shoulders. 'Now, you're going to play one of your pretty pieces on the piano for your sister, aren't you, lovie? I'm sure Jemima would like to hear you play, wouldn't you, Jemima?'

'Yes, please. I would,' Jemima answered dutifully.

'All right, then.' Pleased to be able to show off her superior talents, Sophie went to the piano and spread her new pink taffeta dress out carefully on the piano stool before starting to play.

Jemima listened attentively. She didn't know much about music except when she'd heard Miss Peel playing the piano for the children to sing hymns or to march to at school but she felt that the very pretty pieces that Sophie was playing would have sounded better if they hadn't been thumped out like a hammer knocking nails in. Nevertheless she clapped politely when Sophie finished.

'Have you ever thought you'd like to learn to play the piano, Jemima?' Aunt Minnie asked.

'How can she? She hasn't got a piano,' Sophie pointed out unsympathetically.

'She could come and practise on this one,' Aunt Minnie suggested.

Jemima could see from her sister's frown that she didn't like that idea at all. 'I don't really think I would have time to do that, thank you all the same, Aunt Minnie,' she said. 'You see, I shall have to go to Miss Peel's house three evenings a week for extra lessons so that I don't get behind with my studies.' She didn't add that her mother would regard piano lessons as a complete waste of money.

In spite of Aunt Minnie's kindness Jemima was relieved when it was time for her to walk home. As she walked she reflected what a good person Aunt Minnie was, always ready to do a kindness and to think the best of people. Jemima wondered if Sophie appreciated the love and care her aunt and uncle lavished on her; sometimes it didn't seem like it. But if she'd been the one who'd been shouted at and beaten and shut in the coal hole she'd appreciate what a good home she had. That was the difference between being the twelfth child and the thirteenth.

But Jemima wouldn't have changed places with her. Not for anything. Because Jemima had something Sophie would never have: Jemima was clever. She knew this without any sense of conceit and she knew it was a gift that all the money in the world couldn't buy.

Sophie knew it, too, and she didn't like it.

'Aren't you going to help your aunt with the washing-up, Sophie?' Uncle William asked after Jemima had left.

'In a minute.' Sophie was looking through her birthday presents, sorting out the ones she liked from the ones she didn't.

'It's all right, dearie, I've nearly finished,' Aunt Minnie called from the scullery. 'You don't want to be washing up on your birthday. Play us some more of your pieces on the piano. I'll be able to hear from out here.'

'No, I don't want to. I'm busy reading.'

'Do as your aunt says.' Uncle William wasn't usually sharp with her but she was getting to be a lazy little madam. In his view Minnie wasn't nearly firm enough with her. It was the one thing he and his wife disagreed over.

'No. I'm going upstairs to put my things away.' Sophie flounced off.

Minnie came in, wiping her hands on her apron. 'There. Now you've upset her, Will. And on her birthday, too.'

'She's thirteen. She ought to help you a bit more, especially now you've got Mr Banks to look after.'

'Oh, Mr Banks is no trouble, Will.'

William stretched over and put his arm round his wife's ample waist. 'Nothing is ever any trouble as far as you're concerned, is it, matie? That's why you get put upon by that little minx upstairs.'

'Well, she's all we've got, Will.'

'Aye, she's all we've got, matie.' He leaned back in his chair and stoked up his pipe.

Daisy was at home when Jemima arrived back from the tea party. She was sitting at the kitchen table talking to Sam Starling.

'Oh, I'm glad you're back,' she said, getting up and giving her a hug. 'I managed to get an hour off to come and wish you a happy birthday but I shall have to be getting back soon. I was afraid I'd have to go without seeing you. Did you have a nice time at Aunt Minnie's?'

'Yes. Aunt Minnie is always very kind to me,' Jemima said. 'And look, she gave me a new blouse. And there was an atlas from Sophie, although I reckon Aunt Minnie paid for it. I gave Sophie a tartan hair ribbon. Paid for out of my own money,' she added proudly. It was the first time she had been able to take Sophie a present of any kind, since her mother always said there was no money for fripperies and anyway Sophie got more than she needed from Minnie and Will.

'And where, pray, did you get the money for hair ribbons?' her mother asked sharply.

Jemima shrugged. 'Errands an' that,' she said vaguely. Her mother still didn't know that Miss Peel paid her for marking and Jemima didn't want her to find out.

'Hm.' Eva picked up the teapot. 'More tea, Mr Starling? Sam? Daisy?'

'No thanks. I must be getting back,' Daisy said. 'I brought you this, Jemma.' She handed Jemima a little package. 'I made it myself. It's to keep your hankies in. There's two hankies inside as well.' She beamed at her sister.

Jemima opened it and found a handkerchief sachet made of blue satin with her name embroidered across the corner in darker blue. Tucked inside were two lace-edged handkerchiefs, each with 'J' in a corner.

'Oh, it's lovely, Daisy.' Jemima kissed her. 'I shall keep it with my treasures.'

'No, no, you have to use it,' Daisy said with a laugh. 'Well, I must be off or I shall be in trouble.'

Sam got to his feet. 'I'll walk back with you, Daisy,' he said casually. 'I need to stretch my legs.'

'Oh, that's nice of you, Sam,' Daisy said, blushing.

They went off, but not before Jemima had seen the knowing look that passed between her mother and Mr Starling.

She hoped they were wrong. She hoped Daisy and Sam Starling were not 'walking out'.

She was disappointed, too. She had wanted to walk some of the way with Daisy so that she could tell her that she was going to be a monitor at school and help to teach the little ones. Unlike her mother, Daisy took her seriously when she said she hoped to be a teacher, so she wanted to share the good news with her. But she wasn't going to share it with Sam Starling as well.

Not that she had anything against Sam – at least, nothing you could put your finger on. But he made her feel uncomfortable. It was little things, like the way he 'accidentally' touched her drawers as they were hanging on the line to dry as he came into the yard. True, the washing line was strung back and forth across the yard so everybody had to duck to get past the washing hanging there, but she had never seen Mr Starling touch anything. Not even a sheet.

But when she put on her clean drawers she had the feeling that they were already dirty, knowing Sam's hands had been on them.

And that wasn't the only thing. Twice when she had taken her kettle of water and candle into the wash house to have her weekly wash-down, she had sensed a face at the grimy little window, watching her. She had quickly covered herself with her towel and sneaked a look out of a crack in the door. There was nobody to be seen, but the back door was just closing.

Of course, it might not have been Sam, but Mr Starling would never do a thing like that and her mother wouldn't bother, so it was difficult to think who else it might have been. Unless she had imagined it.

Nevertheless, after it had happened for the second time, she made sure always to pin a piece of cloth over the window before she started her ablutions.

Seven

It became a regular thing for Sam Starling to walk Daisy back to Mrs Clarke's after her afternoon off. Daisy seemed quite happy with this but it didn't please Jemima at all because it meant that she was deprived of the chance of a precious few minutes' private conversation with her older sister. She could no longer relate to her all the nice things that had happened at school and all the not-so-nice things that had gone on at home because there was never a moment's privacy.

Jemima still didn't like Sam Starling much, with his ferrety face and droopy moustache. Although he was always very friendly, he teased her and she didn't like it. Sometimes if she passed him and his friends as they stood laughing and talking outside the Rose and Crown in the evening or on Sunday afternoon he would call out, 'Here comes my favourite girl. Look, lads, I've made her blush. Oh, look at her, she's even prettier when she blushes.' She hated this and in the end she would go the long way round so she didn't have to pass them. Another thing was that his knee sometimes rubbed up against hers when they were sitting at the kitchen table – it could be by accident, after all the table wasn't that big – but she didn't think it was. It gave her an uncomfortable feeling, like the time she saw him touching her drawers as they hung on the line and when he'd spied on her having her weekly wash-down – she knew it could only have been him. She was always careful now to hang her underclothes out to dry in a place where he couldn't touch them, but she was still wary of him and she was jealous because he was taking up more and more of Daisy's free time. Time that Jemima had always considered was hers. And the odd thing was, Daisy seemed quite happy about it. Jemima couldn't imagine what her sister could see in the man. But there was so much going on in her own life that she didn't have time to be too concerned about it.

Now she was thirteen, she and three other girls had officially been made monitors. This was standard practice in Board Schools since monitors were cheaper to employ than extra teachers. They were told that they would each be paid five shillings a month and for this they would be expected to teach their respective classes what they had learned from their own teachers either before or after school. Jemima was to work with the infants to begin with, under the supervision of Miss Peel, who decided that it would be best for Jemima to go to her house three evenings a week to learn how to teach and manage the children. Added to this, Jemima knew that she must keep up with her own education, studying in the evenings to catch up with what she had missed while she was teaching. Since she was always far ahead of the rest of her class this last was never going to be much of a problem.

Eva was ready to object to her daughter being what she called 'put upon and used as a convenience so the teacher could sit around and do nothing all day', but when Jemima added that she was to be paid a shilling a week, Eva thought it a very good idea, 'and better than sitting in the classroom wasting your time with books an' that.' Jemima had wrestled with her conscience before deciding to tell her mother she would be earning a shilling a week instead of five shillings a month, so that she could keep a shilling back for herself, but she reasoned that given the chance Eva would take every penny of her earnings and she needed a little money of her own for new stockings and shoe repairs if she was to look respectable in front of a class.

Miss Peel lived in a pretty little cottage called 'Sparrows' in Park Road. It was set back from the road and had a picket fence and gate. In spring and early summer the borders on either side of the garden path were a riot of colour, filled with clumps of polyanthus, daffodils and tulips growing out of a carpet of violets and grape hyacinths. Jemima had never seen such a pretty garden.

On her first visit Miss Peel opened the door to her knock and led her into a small living room with the evening sun streaming through the window. In the centre of the room was a round polished table with a big blue bowl of yellow primroses on a crocheted table mat in the centre. Four dining chairs stood round the table and there were two comfortable-looking armchairs either side of the fireplace, where a beautifully embroidered fire screen stood in front of the empty grate. Above the mantelpiece, which was draped with a piece of green velvet hung with gold bobbles, was a large mirrored overmantel with little shelves holding small china and brass ornaments. A multicoloured shawl was thrown over the sofa opposite the fireplace and there was a walnut chiffonier on the wall by the door. This held myriad coloured glass ornaments, which were all reflected in its mirrored back, giving the impression of a rainbow in the room. On a shelf at each end of the chiffonier stood matching oil lamps with pink, etched glass globes. Several rather large pictures hung on the walls, one of Queen Victoria, still in deepest mourning, taking pride of place. A red turkey carpet covered the floor. Jemima had never seen so much furniture in one room before, not even at Aunt Minnie's, and she thought it was the most beautiful and welcoming room she had ever seen.

An elderly lady, pink-faced and with white hair piled softly into a loose bun, on top of which sat a white lace cap, was sitting on a low chair by the window, knitting. She was wearing a dark blue dress with a high neck, quite plain except for a row of tiny pearl buttons from neck to waist. She looked up as Miss Peel showed Jemima in.

'Ah, so you're the young lady Kathryn is always telling me about,' she said with a smile. 'Come over here to the light so that I can take a good look at you.'

'Oh, Mama, don't make Jemima nervous,' Miss Peel said with a laugh. Miss Peel herself was wearing a plum-coloured skirt with a plain front and pleated back and a white frilly blouse. Jemima had never seen her without her smock before and she was amazed at her teacher's tiny waist. She longed for the day when she would be old enough to wear a skirt that swept the floor, like Miss Peel.

'I shan't make her nervous. I simply want to get to know her a little,' Mrs Peel answered. She looked up at Jemima and smiled again. 'You're too thin, child. You need a bit more flesh on your bones, especially as you're tall. But you've got a good face.' She nodded. 'I can see you'll be quite a beauty when you're a little older.'

'Oh, no. It's my twin sister, Sophie, who's the pretty one,' Jemima said quickly. Then she put up her hand to cover her mouth. 'Oh, I do beg your pardon, ma'am, I didn't ought to contradict you.'

'I *shouldn't*, not didn't ought to,' Mrs Peel said automatically. 'And I didn't say you would be pretty, child, I said you would be quite a beauty. There's a great deal of difference, as you'll no doubt discover as you get older. Now, come and sit down, I'm getting a crick in my neck looking up at you.'

Obediently, Jemima pulled a chair out and sat down.

'That's it.' Mrs Peel was still smiling. 'So, you're going to be Kathryn's monitor, are you? And what then?'

'I hope to be a teacher, one day, ma'am. Just like Miss Peel. That's what I should like more than anything else in the world,' Jemima said eagerly.

'Well, a little bird told me you've the brains for it, so we shall see if you have the application.' Mrs Peel looked over the top of her spectacles. 'Ah, I see my daughter is ready for you so I mustn't keep you talking any longer.' She gave her another sweet smile and went back to her knitting.

Miss Peel had the books spread on the table and for the next hour Jemima was totally absorbed in learning what and how to teach the infants. She was so absorbed, in fact, that she hadn't noticed Mrs Peel leave the room until she returned with a tea tray with two cups and saucers, a glass of milk and a mug of cocoa. There was also a plate of delicious-looking cherry biscuits.

'I've called Oliver. If he's finished his homework he'll come down-stairs for his cocoa, otherwise I'll take it up to him,' Mrs Peel said. 'The milk is for you, my dear,' she said to Jemima.

'Oliver is my nephew, Jemima. He's lived with us ever since his mother died three years ago. She was my sister,' Miss Peel said by way of explanation. She leaned forward as she heard his feet on the stairs and said quietly, 'His father pays for him to go to the Grammar School in Colchester. He goes in every day on the train. After that he hopes to go to college.' Then in a louder voice, 'Ah, there you are, Oliver. Have you finished for tonight?'

A dark-haired young man came into the room, ducking his head as he came through the door. Jemima thought he was the handsomest man she had ever seen, with deep-set, dark brown eyes that had a warm, friendly look, a straight nose and a mouth that turned up at one corner when he smiled, as he was doing now, showing white, not quite even teeth. All this she noticed in the first few seconds.

'Yes, thanks, Aunt K,' he said, sitting down opposite Jemima at the table. 'I've been struggling with Latin translation. I don't know why I find it so much more difficult to translate from English to Latin than from Latin to English. But I do.'

'Well, as long as you've done your best you can drink your cocoa with a clear conscience,' Mrs Peel remarked, handing it to him.

Miss Peel introduced Jemima. 'This is my nephew, Oliver, Jemima. Oliver, this is Jemima Furlong. She is to be my monitor at school.'

Oliver immediately stood up. 'How do you do, Miss Furlong.' He held out his hand for her to shake.

'Oh, I don't think we need to be too formal, Oliver, I'm sure Jemima will be happy for you to call her by name. After all, you'll probably be seeing quite a lot of her since she'll be coming three times a week. Isn't that so, Jemima?'

Jemima nodded, blushing, too tongue-tied to speak.

'Very well, Jemima,' he said, smiling at her. 'That's what I'll call you. It's a nice name.'

All too soon it was time for her to go home. It had been a lovely evening; she couldn't remember when she had last enjoyed herself so much. Miss Peel and her mother had been so kind to her and the cherry biscuits were so delicious she'd had to be careful not to eat too many of them. She gave a little bob as she thanked Miss Peel and her mother, shyly said goodbye to Oliver and ran home, full of what she had learned.

Her mother looked up with a scowl from the penny novelette she was pretending to read. 'And where have you been, I should like to know? You know I won't have you roaming the streets till all hours,' she said by way of greeting.

Jemima's heart sank. Coming back to this cheerless room, where nothing she ever did was right, was like being plunged into icy water. 'You know where I've been, Mum. I've been to Miss Peel's house.'

'Oh, yes. I forgot.' Her mother shrugged her shoulders and went back to the novelette. She had been struggling to read it so that Mr Starling wouldn't know she was practically illiterate. She could make sense of some of it.

'Well, aren't you going to tell us about what you've been doing, then?' Mr Starling put down his newspaper to listen. He was always interested in Jemima's activities in a nice, fatherly way.

Jemima told him she was to have a dark blue pinafore instead of a white one, to show that she was monitor, and she was to have a short, pointed stick to point to things on the blackboard.

'And who's going to provide you with a dark blue pinafore? I've got no money for fancy pinafores.' Her mother's head shot up. She was obviously listening to the conversation although she was pretending indifference.

'Miss Peel's mother is making it for me.'

'Hmph.' Eva went back to her novelette.

'Go on, dearie,' Mr Starling encouraged. 'What else?'

Jemima told him everything else that had happened except about meeting Miss Peel's nephew, Oliver, because she didn't want him to think she was comparing him unfavourably with his own son, Sam. But she was. She couldn't help it. She knew that Oliver was a gentleman; he didn't sprawl in a chair like Sam did and he sprang up to open the door for his grandmother and aunt, which Sam would never think of doing. Oliver had got to his feet as a gentleman should when she was introduced to him. He had even offered to walk her home, which she had refused, not because she didn't trust him, but because she didn't want him to see where she lived.

She couldn't say the same for Sam Starling. She wouldn't trust that man as far as she could throw him.

Eight

The weeks flew past. Jemima loved working with the little children, helping them to learn their times tables, teaching them to read simple words, telling them stories. She soon discovered which of them wanted to learn and which didn't, those who were bright – she knew exactly what 'bright' meant now – and those who could never grasp what she was trying to teach however hard they tried.

There was one little boy, Sidney, who suffered from rickets. He was desperate to please Jemima and he worked very hard at his sums but always managed to make one and two equal four and always missed the 'n' out of his name. In the end all the children called him 'Siddy' and the name stuck. But there was no malice in it because they all looked after him and included him in their games, even though he couldn't run like the other children. When a new boy, who was a bit of a bully, tried to make fun of Siddy, the other children soon showed what they thought of him. He didn't try it again.

Miss Peel always kept an eye on her from where she herself was teaching but Jemima had very little trouble in controlling her class; they seemed to know instinctively that she was very young to be teaching them – indeed some of them had sisters who were older than 'teacher'. She knew from Miss Peel that some of them wriggled because they were verminous and she should tactfully sit them a little apart; others had difficulty in concentrating because they were hungry – she could recognize that feeling easily enough herself. But if they became a little overexcited and unruly she did as Miss Peel suggested and made them sit quietly with their hands behind their backs for a few minutes until they quietened. It always worked. And she only had to write a sentence on the blackboard in her best handwriting and say, 'Now, children, it's handwriting practice this morning,' and the slates clattered out. From then on fifteen heads were bent, fifteen pink tongues stuck out of the corner of fifteen small mouths in concentration and the only sound to be heard was the squeak of slate pencils. The results varied but Miss Peel had told her she must always find something to encourage in every child, however poor their work. It seemed to pay off.

But it was very hard work. Teaching and helping Miss Peel all day, then studying, either with Miss Peel or at home on her own, plus helping her mother, meant she was permanently tired. But at least, with Mr Starling and Sam living in the house, there was always a good meal on the table so she was well fed. And she was thankful that her mother had never gone back to her old lazy and slatternly habits of relying on the porter jug to dull her senses. No longer did she leave Jemima to look after things, not caring what state the house was in. Now, with Jemima's help, she worked hard to keep the house spotlessly clean, especially when Mr Starling was at home so she could hear him say, 'My word, Mrs Furlong, you *are* a hard-working woman!' And there was even new furniture; more comfortable beds and armchairs and matching chairs round the table. Oh, yes, things were so much better with Mr Starling and Sam in the house. Jemima hoped they would stay for ever, even though she didn't like Sam. It seemed as if they would because Mr Starling's wife was dead and he had given up the house he'd rented in Kent when he moved to his new job at the local shipyard.

Jemima often saw her sister at school. Sophie hadn't told her but Jemima knew that she had been kept back when the rest of the class moved up in September because her work wasn't up to standard. The days when Sophie could copy Jemima's work had long gone and her teachers knew exactly how capable she was. They also knew that she could have done better if she had worked a bit harder. Sophie just tossed her head and claimed that she didn't care and proved it by misbehaving in class.

One day as Jemima was shepherding her infants back into their classroom Sophie was standing outside her classroom door where she had been sent for being inattentive.

'You're to come to tea on Friday,' she hissed from behind her hand. 'Aunt Minnie said to ask you.'

Jemima paused. 'Oh. That's very kind of Aunt Minnie,' she said quietly. 'Tell her I'll come if I possibly can.'

Sophie shrugged. 'Suit yourself. Aunt Min said to tell you it'll be boiled eggs,' she added reluctantly. Aunt Minnie knew Jemima loved boiled eggs but rarely got them at home and she'd told Sophie to be sure and tell this to Jemima.

Jemima smiled. 'Then I'll have to get my work done early so I can make sure to come. Thank Aunt Minnie for asking me.' It wasn't often she was invited to Aunt Minnie's when it wasn't her birthday but it did sometimes happen.

After tea of two boiled eggs apiece – a rare luxury for Jemima – and jam sponge, which Aunt Minnie knew was another of her favourites, Jemima helped her aunt to clear the table and wash up. Sophie dried a few plates and then wandered off.

'I'm glad she's gone,' Aunt Minnie whispered, glancing over her shoulder to make sure Sophie wasn't within hearing distance, 'because I wanted to ask you if you could help her with her lessons a bit. She seems to be getting rather behind. I expect you knew she'd been kept back when her class moved up a standard?'

'Yes, I knew that.' Jemima bit her lip. 'But are you sure she wants me to help her, Aunt Min?' she asked.

'Well, I haven't exactly asked her. I thought perhaps you could say something . . .'

'I'll try.' Aunt Minnie looked so anxious that Jemima hadn't the heart to tell her that laziness was probably at the root of Sophie's problems.

They finished the dishes and went back into the dining room, where Sophie was picking out a tune with one finger on the piano; lessons had been given up long ago because she didn't bother to practise.

'Aunt Minnie thought you might like me to go through some of your school work with you,' Jemima said tentatively.

'Whatever for?' Sophie looked at her with raised eyebrows. 'You can't start bossing me about. I'm not in your infants' class, you know.'

'No, I know that. And I'm not trying to boss you; I'm trying to help. Because you are a bit behind, aren't you? You didn't go up to standard six with the rest of the class.'

'Oh, that.' Sophie tossed her head. 'I did it on purpose because I didn't like sitting next to Mary Downing.'

'I'm sure you needn't have gone to such lengths, Sophie. Mrs Childs would have moved you if she'd known you felt that strongly about it,' Jemima pointed out, trying not to smile at her sister's feeble excuse.

'Oh, yes, Miss Know-All. Pretending to know what all the teachers think just because you're a monitor,' Sophie said with a smirk.

Jemima ignored this. 'I could still help you, if you like. You don't want to get behind again.'

'I'm not worried about that. I don't care about school. Only another six months and I shall be leaving.'

'Not if you haven't got into standard six, you won't,' Jemima said. 'Nobody's allowed to leave till then, it's the law.' A law that was often conveniently ignored, especially in the case of large families, where earning money was deemed to be of much more importance than learning to read and write.

Sophie looked at her suspiciously. 'Is that right?'

Jemima nodded. 'You know it is.'

She shrugged. 'I'd forgotten. I'll have to pull my socks up, then.' She sighed dramatically. 'I can't wait to leave! What about you?'

'I hope to stay on and become a pupil-teacher,' Jemima said. 'I thought you knew that.'

'Oh, yes, I forgot.' Sophie gave her a scathing look. 'You must be daft.' She returned to picking out an unrecognizable tune on the piano.

Jemima left soon after. Aunt Minnie was worried about her walking home alone when it was beginning to get dark but Jemima reassured her, saying that she always walked home from Miss Peel's in the evening and anyway it was never really dark because the lamplighter had been round and lit the street lamps for most of the way. So she set off quite happily, engrossed in her thoughts.

As she walked, thinking over her visit to her aunt's house, she reflected that she had absolutely nothing in common with her twin, except the accident of a shared birth. She had known for years that Sophie didn't really like her and if she was completely honest she didn't have much feeling for Sophie either. The way she treated Aunt Minnie, who clearly idolized her, angered Jemima. She couldn't understand why her sister didn't appreciate all the love and care Aunt Minnie and Uncle William lavished on her instead of behaving like an ungrateful, spoiled brat.

Sophie wouldn't have liked it if Aunt Minnie had got fed up with her and sent her home to live, as Jemima was sometimes tempted to remind her. She'd never liked coming to Brown's Yard with Aunt Minnie to visit the family when she was small; now she was old enough to come by herself she didn't bother to visit at all. And there was always an excuse for not accompanying Aunt Minnie on her visits. Whether Aunt Minnie ever spoke to her about them Jemima had no way of knowing, but she showed no interest when Jemima tried to tell her that her brother Archie was in the navy, Freddie worked on a farm and Johnnie was only on the fishing boats until he was old enough to follow Archie into the navy. Sophie was aware that Daisy worked for Mrs Clarke, but not that she was walking out with Sam Starling. If they had been a bit closer, like most twins, Jemima could have confided in Sophie that she wasn't happy about this and felt that Daisy deserved somebody better. As it was, she had to content herself with the hope that it wouldn't come to anything.

Almost as if the thought had conjured up the person, a voice behind her said, 'Well, well, well, Jemmy. Fancy seein' you.' It was Sam. He grinned at her in the lamplight.

She was tempted to reply, 'Well, I don't fancy seeing you!' but she bit her tongue and replied instead, 'I've been to my Aunt Minnie's. I'm on my way home.'

'And I've just come from seein' Daisy.' He tapped the side of his nose. 'She manages to sneak out and meet me now and again for a bit of a kiss an' a cuddle.' He grinned. 'Keeps us goin' till her half day.'

Jemima didn't answer. She couldn't imagine anybody wanting to kiss or cuddle Sam Starling, particularly Daisy. She quickened her steps.

'Do you walk back through the churchyard?' he asked conversationally when it became apparent she wasn't going to say anything.

'No. Not when it's dark.'

'It's quicker than going round by the road.'

'Yes, but there's no lamp to light the path so it's a bit creepy with all those tombstones,' she admitted.

'Ah, well, you're with me tonight so you'll have company.' They reached the churchyard and he put his arm round her as he pushed open the big wrought-iron gate. 'I'll look after you.'

She wanted to push his arm away but it was comforting to have him beside her as ghostly spectral figures loomed all around the big shadowy bulk of the church. She knew that in daylight they would be the familiar grubby stone angels she had always known but they had taken on an ethereal appearance in the light of the full moon and there was always the suspicion that there might be one that wasn't there in daylight . . . an extra one . . . one that might move at any moment . . . At that thought she found herself moving closer to Sam.

'What's the matter, girl? Scared?' Sam laughed. His arm tightened round her and his hand moved up a few inches from her waist.

'No, course I'm not scared.' She tried to pull away but his arm held her fast and his fingers curled round her budding breast, its shape barely visible under her thin coat.

'Good. 'Cause you know I'll always look out for you, Jemmy.' His face was close to her ear now and she could feel his breathing becoming heavier as he squeezed her breast and tried to nuzzle her neck.

'No! Leave me alone!' Something akin to panic gave her the strength to twist away from him.

'What's the matter? What have I done?' He stood in the middle of the path, hands outspread, a picture of injured innocence.

But Jemima didn't wait. Suddenly her fear of the living was stronger than her fear of the dead and she ran out of the churchyard, through the little kissing gate, and didn't stop running till she got to her own back door. Before she opened it she paused and adjusted her hat, smoothed down her coat and took several deep breaths. Then she went in.

Her mother looked up. 'What's wrong with you? You look as if you've seen a ghost,' she remarked.

'I've been running,' she said briefly and turned to hang her coat and hat on the back of the door.

Mr Starling lowered his newspaper and looked at her over the top of his spectacles. 'This wasn't one of your evenings to go to your teacher's house, was it, Jemma?' Almost without noticing he had adopted Daisy's pet name for her.

'No, I've been to Aunt Minnie's to tea,' she said. 'I . . .' But before she could say more the door opened and Sam walked in.

'Evenin' everybody,' he said, taking off his hat and flinging it on to the table. 'Oh, you're home before me, Jemmy. I wondered where you'd got to.'

Jemima coloured at his words but he spoke totally without embarrassment. 'I met Jemmy and walked her home,' he explained, sitting down near his father.

'Good boy.' Mr Starling nodded in approval. It was obvious that he idolized his son. 'Come and sit down. Here, you can have the newspaper. I've finished with it.'

Jemima lit a candle and went into the room she still shared with her mother and sat down on her bed. She was thankful she had found the strength to break free of Sam Starling. She hadn't liked his hot, heavy breathing in her ear and she had a feeling that he had wanted to do something to her, but she didn't know what it was. She also had an uncomfortable feeling that if she hadn't broken free she might have found out.

But there was nobody she could tell of her fears and suspicions. Not Mr Starling, because he thought the world of his son and would never believe her. Not her mother, because she would accuse her of being fanciful and very likely box her ears. And especially not Daisy, in whom she had always confided everything, because Daisy

Nine

After what had happened in the churchyard Jemima avoided contact with Sam as much as she could, although living in the same house it was impossible to avoid him altogether. The odd thing was, he was always very nice to her, and treated her in such an easy, brotherly manner that she could easily have thought she'd imagined the whole thing. But when she recalled the way he had touched her breast and nuzzled her neck she felt slightly sick and knew it was not something she could ever have imagined. She was determined never to give him the chance to take liberties like that again, so she made sure she was never alone in the house with him and bought a little bolt for the wash-house door so that she could feel safe when she had what she called her 'private wash-down'. She had a little trouble screwing the bolt on the door so that it levelled up with the keep on the door frame but it almost fitted and as long as she lifted the door when she closed it and gave it a good hard shove, it held firm.

Nevertheless, she always dragged the heavy old cobbler's last, which her big brothers had always used when they mended their boots, out of the corner where it lived and jammed it against the door, just to make certain nobody could get in.

Once these precautions were in place she stopped worrying about Sam Starling and as the weeks and months passed the whole affair slipped to the back of her mind. In any case, keeping up with her own school work while preparing lessons for the infants meant she had little or no time to think about anything else. She soon got into the habit of spending her evenings at Miss Peel's house, even if there wasn't work to prepare. There was always a warm welcome there, with comfortable chairs and shelves full of books that she could read to her heart's content. Miss Peel and her mother seemed to enjoy her company – and of course, Oliver was there too.

He would come downstairs when he had finished his homework and join in with whatever they were discussing and he seemed so interested in what she had to say that Jemima soon forgot to be shy in his presence and even began to argue with him if she thought he was in the wrong, which seemed to amuse him.

At Christmas, which wasn't much celebrated in Brown's Yard, Mrs Peel gave Jemima a new blue pinafore wrapped round a pair of gloves she had knitted herself and Miss Peel gave her a book of poetry.

Anticipating that there might be an exchange of presents, Jemima had made Mrs Peel a pin cushion and matching needle case and given Miss Peel a blotter and a pen wiper she had made herself. She agonized over whether or not to buy a present for Oliver; it would be embarrassing if he gave her something and she had nothing to give him in return. On the other hand, she didn't want to appear forward in buying him a present if he hadn't done the same for her. In the end she used the last of her little store of money and bought him a notebook with a stiff, marbled cover that he could keep as a diary or for odd jottings. It was a very nice notebook that she would be happy to use herself if she didn't give it to Oliver. In the event Oliver gave her Robert Louis Stevenson's *Treasure Island* so she was more than a little relieved to have something to give him in return.

'Oh, that's really kind of you, Jemima,' he said when he saw the notebook. She could see that he meant it.

She flushed with pleasure. 'I though you could use it for odd jottings,' she said, to cover her embarrassment.

'No, I shan't use it for that at all. I shall use it for special sayings that I don't want to forget,' he replied firmly. He grinned. 'I hope you'll enjoy *Treasure Island*. I've already read my copy three times and I expect I'll read it again, so when you've had time to read it we'll be able to discuss it over grandmama's cocoa and biscuits. If Aunt K ever finishes grilling you with school work, that is.'

'Oh, Oliver, that's not fair,' Miss Peel protested, but like him, she was smiling. 'I don't grill you, do I, Jemima?'

'Grill me? No, it doesn't feel like it,' Jemima said thoughtfully. 'I enjoy learning from you, Miss Peel, so it never seems like hard work.'

'That's the sign of a good teacher,' Mrs Peel said from her chair by the fire. She looked at the clock. 'Now, I don't want to hurry you away, my dear, but it's beginning to rain. Have you brought an umbrella?'

'No, I'm afraid I haven't.' Jemima was reluctant to admit she didn't possess such a thing.

'Never mind, dear. You can borrow mine,' Miss Peel said.

'Oh, no, I couldn't do that. You might need it when you come to school tomorrow,' Jemima said quickly. 'I can run. It's not too far.' As she spoke there was a heavy spatter of rain on the window.

'Indeed you'll do nothing of the kind,' Miss Peel said firmly. 'Oliver can walk home with you and he can bring it back. You won't mind doing that, will you, Oliver?'

'Of course I won't. Hang on a tick while I fetch my coat, Jemima.' He raced up the stairs, taking them two at a time.

By the time Jemima had put on her coat and hat and the gloves Mrs Peel had given her he was back, wearing a thick overcoat with a velvet collar. She noticed that even though it was raining he waited until he was outside before putting on his cap, another sign of his good manners.

'I'm afraid you'll have to keep close to me or you'll get raindrops down your neck,' he said, putting up the umbrella and glancing at her. 'I hope you won't mind.'

'No. I shan't mind at all,' she said, trying not to sound too eager.

'Won't mind what? Getting raindrops down your neck or keeping close to me?' he said teasingly.

She hesitated, then said carefully, 'I would prefer not to get raindrops down my neck.' And as she said it she moved a little closer to him.

'Hang on to my arm then.'

A little nervously, she slipped her hand into the crook of his arm.

He squeezed it gently against his side. 'This umbrella isn't really designed to keep two people dry but I'm sure we'll manage beautifully,' he said and she could hear a smile in his voice.

Although the rain was coming down steadily now, neither of them attempted to quicken their steps. After a while he put his free hand over hers and said, 'How old are you, Jemima?'

'I shall be fourteen next May,' she said, surprised that he had asked.

'And I shall be eighteen in August,' he said thoughtfully. 'Then I shall be going away to college for two years.'

'Oh dear, I shall miss you, Oliver,' she said and then bit her tongue, relieved that he couldn't see her blushes. This wasn't the sort of thing a girl should say to a young man and she was afraid he would think she was dreadfully forward. 'I mean . . .'

But he didn't seem to mind. In fact, he said, 'I shall miss you, too, Jemima. Very much.'

She felt a strange fluttering inside as he spoke because he really sounded as if he would miss her.

'Will you still be here when I come back?' he asked.

'Of course. Where else would I be?' she replied, trying to keep her voice steady. 'I hope to stay at school and begin as a pupil-teacher under Miss Peel when I reach fourteen.'

'Ah, yes, of course.' He pushed open the creaking churchyard gate and they went through together. 'I hope to teach, too. I intend to make sure I pass all my exams at college so that I can have my own school one day,' he told her proudly.

'I'm sure you will. You're quite clever enough,' she said, feeling oddly flat all of a sudden. 'Where do you think that will be?'

'Who can tell? Not too far away, I hope. I want to be near enough to keep an eye on grandmama and Aunt Kathryn. And you, of course, Jemima,' he added quietly.

'You don't need to worry about me, Oliver. I think I'll always be here,' she replied, her spirits lifting again.

'That's a relief.' He squeezed her hand again.

With Oliver by her side she hardly noticed they had walked through the churchyard with its ghostly memorials but suddenly they had reached the kissing gate and they laughed as they got tangled up with the umbrella and got drips down their necks as they tried to squeeze through the narrow space together.

'You don't have to come any further. I'm almost home now,' she said when they finally got through the gate.

As they stood together under the umbrella they could see by the light of the street lamp that the rain was slanting down more heavily that ever.

'If I leave you here you'll get even wetter,' he said.

'No, I shan't. I can run the rest of the way; it's not far. Only just down Rose Lane.'

'Well, if you're sure.'

'Yes. Thank you. I'm quite sure.'

Neither of them moved. Then, suddenly, he bent forward and kissed her cheek. 'Well, we've just come through a kissing gate so isn't that what we're supposed to do?' he said. He looked at her anxiously. 'You didn't mind?'

She smiled at him. 'No, of course I didn't.' Suddenly, recklessly, she stood on tiptoe and kissed him back. Then, without waiting to see his reaction she turned and ran down Rose Lane.

She wasn't in love. Of course she wasn't. She wasn't old enough. But she thought Oliver was the best, the nicest, the most handsome young man she had ever known and she couldn't stop smiling because he had kissed her. And she was glad she had found the courage to kiss him back.

She ran into the yard and pushed open the back door, her face flushed with happiness, her coat and hat wet, her hair loose and sparkling with raindrops.

Her mother looked up as she entered. 'You can wipe that grin off your face. I don't know what you've got to look so pleased about,' she said cuttingly.

Jemima closed the door and leaned against it. Even without her mother's biting words she could sense an atmosphere thick with acrimony so dense that she almost felt she could put out her hand and touch it. She looked round the room. Mr Starling was there, sitting in the armchair by the fire looking quite unlike his usual cheerful self; Sam and Daisy were sitting side by side at the table and her mother was scowling at them from the opposite side. Jemima looked from one to the other, afraid to speak in case she made things even worse than they apparently already were. She cleared her throat.

Her mother rounded on her. 'And you needn't say anything,' she snapped.

'I wasn't going to.' She took off her coat and hat and hung them up, moving carefully in case even this action provoked more tension. Then she sat down on a chair by the door in an effort to distance herself from whatever was going on, which was not easy in such a small room.

Nobody spoke for several minutes, giving Jemima time to speculate and wonder.

'Is it Archie?' she whispered at last. Nothing less than a death in the family could have caused such a tense atmosphere.

Her mother's head shot round and she snapped, 'Archie? Archie's all right, as far as I know. Why should anything be the matter with Archie?'

Jemima shrugged. 'I dunno. I just thought . . . well, there's something . . . I can tell . . .'

'Oh, yes. There's something, all right,' Eva said, waggling her shoulders in disapproval. She glared at Daisy. 'Well, since it's you that's brought trouble home, you'd better be the one to tell her.'

Daisy gave Jemima an apologetic smile and reached for Sam's hand. 'It's me and Sam. We're gonna be married, Jemma.'

'Oh, that's nice.' Jemima still didn't like Sam much but she couldn't really see anything wrong with Daisy marrying him if that's what she wanted.

'*Got to* be married, you mean,' Eva said harshly. 'She's brought shame on us, the dirty little slut. She's in the family way.' She had conveniently forgotten that she herself had been married under exactly the same circumstances.

'You don't need to fret, Mrs Furlong. I've said I shall stand by her, and so I shall,' Sam said virtuously, as if none of it was his fault.

'Sam and me's always planned to get married, haven't we, Sam?' Daisy moved closer to him.

'Yes, course we have.' Sam gave a rather uncomfortable laugh because in truth he had been quite happy with things the way they were. 'Jest not quite yet,' he added in an effort to be honest.

'How far gone are you?' Eva shot at Daisy, cutting across his words.

She hung her head. 'I'm not sure. About three months, I reckon.'

'Not sure! You must be sure. When did he . . .?' Words failing her, Eva nodded in Sam's direction.

Daisy shrugged. It was difficult to know exactly which occasion had done the damage since she and Sam had made reckless use of every available opportunity for at least the past ten months. She realized now that she had been lucky not to get caught before. She lifted her head. 'It's all right, Mum. I've told you, me an' Sam are gonna get married as soon as we can get the banns put up. That's right, isn't it, Sam?' It was a statement, not a question.

'Well, you'd better go and see about that tomorrow,' Mr Starling said, speaking for the first time and before his son had a chance to reply. 'The sooner it's done the sooner you can get the ring on her finger, boy.'

Eva did a quick calculation. 'Three weeks for the banns to be read – she'll be four months by then so there'll be no hiding the disgrace she's brought on her family.' Her voice was filled with disgust.

'It'll all come to light when the child's born, anyway, so I can't see it makes any odds,' Mr Starling said. 'Either way, it'll be a nine-day wonder and then forgot when something else happens to whet the gossips' appetites.'

'It's all very well for you,' Eva rounded on him. 'It's not your daughter who's played fast and loose.'

'No, but it's my son, who's just as much to blame. She didn't get in the family way on her own,' Mr Starling pointed out. Even he was getting a little heated now.

'She should have kept herself to herself.' Eva was not to be outdone.

'And so should he, if it comes to that.' Mr Starling knocked out his pipe. 'But we don't serve any purpose arguing where the blame lies, Mrs Furlong. What's done is done. The next question is, where are they going to live? Neither of them have got two brass farthings to rub together, I'll be bound.'

'We thought we might come here for the time bein', if Mum'll have us,' Daisy said in a small voice.

'Oh, did you, indeed!' Eva glared at her once more. 'And what makes you think I've got room for you?'

'We could make room, if you were willing, Mrs Furlong,' Mr Starling said mildly. 'Now your two boys have gone I could have their room at the back and Daisy and Sam could have the room at the front that Sam and me share.'

Eva looked uncertain.

'Of course, they'd have to pay you rent,' Mr Starling went on. 'But no doubt you'd be glad of a bit of Daisy's help around the house so it could all work out quite well. But only if you was willing, of course,' he added diplomatically.

'Hm. I dare say.' Eva wasn't going to give in too quickly. She turned to Daisy. 'Have you given your notice in?'

'No. Not yet. But I will soon.' Daisy didn't add that she'd noticed Mrs Clarke eyeing her waistline recently and she didn't want to add to her shame by being dismissed from her job instead of leaving of her own accord.

Eva sniffed, mollified by the thought of extra rent and more help around the house. 'Well, I suppose that's what you'll have to do, then. You'll have to come and live here with us.' She turned to where Jemima was sitting and taking it all in. 'And you needn't sit there like a stuffed dummy. Get the cups out and make us all a cuppa tea. I think we need it.'

Jemima pulled the kettle forward and reached the cups down from the dresser. She couldn't believe that it was less than an hour since she had parted from Oliver at the kissing gate in such a rosy glow. It already seemed like a distant dream.

Ten

Daisy had enjoyed working for Mrs Clarke, so it was hard to leave the large, sunny house with its high ceilings and elegant rooms and go back to the cramped conditions of the cottage in Brown's Yard. But she was convinced that marriage to Sam would more than compensate and she dreamed that one day they would have their own little home. So, shedding a few tears, she packed her bag and returned home to live. Either out of spite or in a somewhat belated attempt at preserving convention, Eva refused to allow her to share a bedroom with Sam until after they were married, pursing her lips and announcing that 'it wouldn't be right', despite the fact that she was already quite obviously pregnant. A month later, the banns having been called in church for three consecutive Sundays, Daisy and Sam's wedding took place, at eight o'clock on a Saturday morning in the parish church, with a grumpy vicar to minister and only Eva and Mr Starling as witnesses. Jemima was there, too, in her best dress of pale blue organdie, which had been handed down from Sophie, but being under age she didn't count.

Having only a skimpy idea of what procreation was all about, Jemima couldn't really understand what all the fuss was about. She had already seen quite alarming changes in her own body, which her mother had casually dismissed with, 'well, you're growing into a woman now, so you mind and watch your step,' as she gave her the cloths she was to use and told her she would need them each month. She longed to ask somebody to explain why there should be a need to be careful. And of what? At school she had seen girls giggling in corners and she knew from their manner that they were talking about 'naughty' things, but being a monitor she was no longer one of them and so was excluded from their secrets. And her best friend, Florrie, who had lived further down Brown's Yard and to whom she had been able to talk about absolutely *anything*, had gone with her parents to live in Ipswich. Her own mother had obviously said all she was going to say on the subject so there was no help to be found there and she had the feeling that it wouldn't be at all appropriate to speak of such things to Miss Peel and Miss Peel's mother. So Jemima was left in a kind of limbo, neither girl nor woman, aware that there was something she ought to know about but not knowing who to approach to discover what it was. She knew instinctively that it was not a fit subject to be discussed with Mr Starling, or even with Oliver, with whom she could talk about most things.

The only person who might enlighten her was Daisy. But it was very difficult to find a time to talk to Daisy these days because the house was always full of people and Daisy was always busy. She seemed very happy now that she was living at home and Sam was her husband. They shared the front bedroom, which was over the parlour where Jemima and her mother slept and Jemima often heard their bed creaking rhythmically late at night or early in the morning, which puzzled her, especially when her mother grunted, 'Oh, Lord, they're at it again. Why can't he leave her alone?'

This worried her a bit and she hoped Sam wasn't ill-treating her sister. She didn't think this could be the case because Daisy was always singing and they were always kissing and cuddling. And Daisy seemed to be putting on quite a lot of weight.

The opportunity came to talk to Daisy one day, when she was helping to change the sheets on the beds. She ventured to ask, 'Daisy, I thought you were going to have a baby. Where is it?'

Daisy looked at her in surprise. 'Don't you know, Jemma? Oh, lovie, don't you know where babies come from? Hasn't anybody ever told you?'

Jemima shook her head, feeling silly.

'Come and sit here beside me.' Daisy sat down on the bed and Jemima sat down with her. She took Jemima's hand and laid it on her swelling stomach. 'There. That's where it is, growing in there.'

Jemima stared at her in amazement.

Daisy smiled. 'Can't you feel it moving?'

Jemima felt the little fluttering movement. 'Is that it? Is that the baby?' she whispered, her eyes wide.

Daisy nodded.

'But how did it get there? And how will it get out?'

Daisy looked at her young sister thoughtfully. She was nearly fourteen so it was time she knew about these things before she got caught the way Sam had caught her. Not that she had minded, because she loved Sam and had been as keen as he was, although she hadn't anticipated it would result in a baby quite so soon.

'Sam put it there when it was not as big as a pin head and when it's grown enough I shall push it out. There. Does that explain things enough for you?'

'Sam put it there?' Jemima looked at her, frowning. 'How?'

Daisy gave her a hug and then got to her feet looking slightly red in the face. 'I reckon we've said enough for one day, don't you? Come on, let's get these beds finished.'

Jemima knew she hadn't heard the whole story but when she thought about it she could more or less piece the rest of it together for herself from the way she had seen Daisy and Sam behaving when they thought nobody was about. And it went some way to explaining the creaking bed.

She marvelled that she had never wondered about these things before.

Daisy was six months pregnant by the time of Jemima's fourteenth birthday. Of course, there was the usual birthday tea at Aunt Minnie's. It was a special one this year because both Jemima and Sophie would shortly be leaving school and starting work, Sophie having eventually worked hard enough to move up to Standard Six. Aunt Minnie, always kind and thoughtful, had asked Jemima if there was anyone else she would like to invite. Jemima would really have liked to invite Oliver and she almost did but in the end she decided that Aunt Minnie might not have agreed to it and anyway she didn't want to have to share him with Sophie, who would only have shown off and been even more objectionable than usual. So she played safe and asked if she might bring Daisy. Sophie had invited her best friend from school, a girl called Edith.

Since Florrie had moved away and Jemima had become a monitor she no longer had a best friend at school. The other monitors were sort of friends, but that was only because, like her, they were all in a kind of limbo, halfway between teacher and pupil, so didn't really fit in either place. They didn't have much else in common. But this didn't worry her – in fact, most of the time she was too busy to give it more than a passing thought. She supposed, on reflection, that Oliver was her dearest friend, although she flushed to the roots of her hair at the presumption of even thinking of him in such an intimate way. But she treasured the memory of the evening he'd walked her home in the rain and kissed her by the kissing gate, and she couldn't help wondering if it had meant as much to him as it had to her. Then common sense prevailed and she realized their friendship couldn't last. A boy who went to college and became headmaster of his own school would never come back and marry a girl from Brown's Yard, at the slum end of the town.

But common sense couldn't prevent her from dreaming.

On the day of the party Sophie could hardly take her eyes off Daisy's swelling stomach during tea.

'You're preg . . . preg . . . having a baby, aren't you? When's it due?' she asked, staring at it pointedly.

Jemima blushed at Sophie's rudeness but Daisy smiled at her without embarrassment and laid a hand on her stomach. 'In August, I think. It'll be another little niece or nephew for you. Won't that be nice?'

'What do you mean, *another* niece or nephew?' Sophie said, frowning.

'Well, your brother Frank's got children older than you are but they're still your nieces and nephews. And Betty's married now, with children.'

'I don't know them. They're nothing to do with me.'

Aunt Minnie looked stricken. 'You shouldn't say that, lovie; you know I've always tried to . . .'

But Sophie wasn't listening. 'Anyway, I'm not old enough to be an aunt,' she said, putting an end to that conversation. She turned to her friend. 'Come on, Edith, let's go upstairs. I've got some fashion magazines we can look through. There's a lovely pale coffee-coloured lace chemise . . .'

'Aren't you going to stay and help us with the washing-up, dearie?' Aunt Minnie asked as they went out of the door.

'No, Jemima can do that, she's better at it than I am,' Sophie said over her shoulder.

'But perhaps Jemima would like to come and look at your magazines with you,' Aunt Minnie persisted.

'Oh, she wouldn't be interested,' Sophie's voice floated down the stairs.

'She's probably right, Aunt Minnie,' Jemima said with a laugh, to cover her aunt's discomfort. 'Since I don't have the money to buy fancy clothes there's not much point in looking at them.' She began to gather up the plates. 'Come on, let's get this washing-up done, then we can all go and sit in the garden.' She gave her aunt a kiss and managed to bring a smile to her face by saying, 'That was a sumptuous tea, Auntie. You're a wonderful cook.'

'You certainly are,' Daisy agreed, up to her elbows in washing-up suds. 'I don't know when I've tasted such delicious fruit cake.'

Later, when the three of them were sitting in the garden enjoying the last of the day's sunshine, Aunt Minnie rummaged in her capacious knitting bag.

'I've knitted you a few bits for the baby,' she said to Daisy. 'When I can find them . . . Ah, here they are.' She spread them on her lap, little coats, leggings, bootees and woolly hats.

'Oh, Auntie, that's really kind of you,' Daisy said, her eyes lighting up. She got up and kissed her. 'And they're beautifully knitted. I've sewed some long petticoats and dresses myself but I'm not much of a knitter.'

'And I don't suppose Eva's done much for you,' Minnie said dryly.

Daisy shook her head. 'No. She's always telling me I've brought shame on her house and I'm lucky she didn't turn me out,' she said sadly. 'I think she might have done, too, if it hadn't been for Mr Starling. He's a lovely man. He stood up for Sam and me.'

'Hmph. She's got no room to talk about bringing shame to the family,' Minnie said sharply. 'She'd do well to remember that people in glass houses shouldn't throw stones.'

'What do you mean, Aunt Minnie?' Jemima asked, frowning.

Minnie hesitated, realizing her tongue had run away with her. 'Never you mind, child. Just you make sure the same thing doesn't happen to you,' she said quickly. She turned to Daisy and gave her a look that was as stern as her kind features could manage. 'And just because I've knitted you these bits, it doesn't mean I approve of what you've done, my girl. It was wrong and you know it.'

Daisy blushed. 'Yes, I know, Auntie, but me and Sam, well, we love each other and . . .'

Minnie held up her hand. 'I don't want excuses. You should have waited, like any decent couple. I'm a God-fearing woman and I've already told Sophie that I won't have her bringing trouble to my door and she knows I mean it. And your Uncle William said the same.' Her expression softened. 'Not that she ever would, bless her.' She wrapped the baby clothes up in tissue paper and handed them to Daisy. 'There. And I daresay there'll be a few more bits. Not because I approve of what you've done, mind, but it's not the child's fault and I like knitting.'

Daisy got up and put her arms round her aunt. 'You're a dear soul, Aunt Minnie, and I love you,' she said, tears glistening in her eyes.

'Get away with you.' Aunt Minnie gave her a little push, but she was smiling and clearly pleased.

'What did Aunt Minnie mean about Mum?' Jemima asked on the way home, carrying her birthday presents in a bag that held two new dresses as well as a coat that Sophie didn't like.

'I reckon she meant that Mum had to get married. Like me,' Daisy said. She gave Jemima a hug. 'Just you watch out it doesn't happen to you, sweetheart. But it won't happen to you, because you're a clever girl and you're going to be a teacher. I'm real proud of you.'

'I might be clever, but there are still some things I don't properly understand,' Jemima said thoughtfully.

'You will,' Daisy said cheerfully, refusing to be drawn further. 'One day.'

Three months later, Daisy's daughter was born. Mr Starling and Sam, who was looking as white as a sheet, sat at the kitchen table with Jemima while Daisy's moans turned to screams in the bedroom above. When he could bear it no longer Sam went out, muttering that he needed a drink. Mr Starling followed, 'to keep an eye on him', leaving Jemima to sit by herself at the open door in the heat of the August evening, trying to study. At last, unable to bear the sound of Daisy's suffering any longer, she put her books away and went for a walk.

She walked up Rose Lane and into the churchyard where the yew trees threw a cool shade. There was a stone seat in the corner and she went over to it and sat down, a thin, pale, anxiously hunched figure. From where she was sitting she could see among the ornate memorials the small headstone that marked the graves of the five brothers and sisters she had never known and she reflected that at that moment she was poised at a point exactly between life and death, because while she was sitting looking at those graves Daisy was giving birth to the next generation at home in Brown's Yard. It was a profound thought.

She hadn't noticed that someone had sat down at the other end of the seat until a voice said quietly, 'You're looking very pensive, Jemima. A penny for your thoughts?'

She turned in surprise. 'Oh! Oliver! What are you doing here?'

'I've just been to Baxter's to buy some new collars and I saw you sitting here. You were looking rather sad so I thought I'd come and try to cheer you up. So, what's the matter, Jemma?'

'Nothing. At least, not really. Well, my sister . . .' She bit her lip. Then, suddenly overwhelmed, she burst into tears. 'It's my sister,' she sobbed. 'She's . . . Her baby's coming.' Her voice dropped to a whisper. 'It's dreadful . . . I could hear her . . . She was screaming. Oh, Oliver, I'm afraid she'll die.'

Oliver put his arm round her and pulled her head on to his shoulder and let her cry.

'There, there,' he said awkwardly after a while. 'I'm sure she'll be all right. People have babies all the time, don't they?' He wasn't sure whether that was a good thing to say or not because he was quite out of his depth talking about such things.

She lifted her head and gave a sniff. 'Yes, you're right. I expect I'm just being silly.'

Keeping his arm round her he put his other hand in his pocket and took out a large white handkerchief. 'Now, come on, dry your eyes, Jemma,' he said, dabbing her face with it before handing it to her. 'You know I shall be going away to college in a day or two and I want to remember you with your lovely smile, not looking all tear-stained.'

She took the handkerchief and wiped her eyes. Then she sniffed and managed to give him a tremulous smile. 'Oh, Oliver, I shall miss you,' she said, her face crumpling again.

'I'm going to miss you, too, Jemma.' He gave her shoulders a squeeze. 'When I get homesick, and I'm sure I shall at times, I shall think of us sitting round grandmama's table drinking cocoa and eating biscuits.' He made a face. 'Oh, dear, I don't know whether that will make me feel better or worse.' He smiled at her, then took out his pocket watch. 'I really ought to go. Grandmama will be wondering why it has taken me so long to buy a couple of collars.' He got to his feet and pulled her up with him.

'Yes, I suppose I'd better go back, too,' she said with some reluctance.

He took her hands in his and they stood together, each reluctant to be the first to break away.

'Who knows, you may find you're an auntie by the time you get home,' he said at last.

She nodded. 'Yes. Thank you for . . . for everything, Oliver.' Her lip quivered again as she smiled at him.

Suddenly, he leaned forward and kissed her, very briefly, on the lips. 'Goodbye, Jemma. I'll try and write to you sometimes.'

She put her hand up to her mouth where his lips had rested. 'I'd like that. Goodbye, Oliver. And good luck.'

Eleven

When Jemima returned home everything was quiet. She crept upstairs and was amazed to find Daisy lying in bed with her little daughter in the crook of her arm, looking the picture of quiet contentment. Amazingly, the anguish of the past hours seemed to have been completely forgotten. Her face lit up and she held out her free hand to Jemima.

'Where have you been? I've been waiting for you to come and say hello to your new niece, Jemma,' she said.

Jemima tiptoed forward cautiously. 'Are you all right, Daisy?' she whispered, the cries of her sister's suffering still ringing in her ears.

'Me? Of course I am. As right as ninepence,' Daisy said, smiling at her in surprise. 'Just a bit tired, that's all.'

Jemima looked down at the screwed-up little creature that had caused its mother so much agony and marvelled that it could all be forgotten so quickly.

'What are you going to call her?' she whispered.

'Amy. And you needn't whisper, Jemma. You won't disturb her.'

Jemima gave her sister a nervous little smile. 'I'm ever so glad you're all right, Daisy.'

'Course I'm all right.' Daisy lifted her face. 'Come here and give us a kiss. And one for Amy. There, that's better. Now, don't look so worried, Jemma.'

There was a sound of men's voices downstairs and Sam's heavy tread on the stairs. Jemima escaped, leaving the new parents to marvel at their first offspring.

Amy was a good baby. Nevertheless her presence meant that the little house in Brown's Yard was always in a state of turmoil, with wet washing, piles of ironing and heaps of clothes lying around where once everywhere had been tidy and orderly, especially since Daisy came home to live. And of course, there were times when she cried.

This did not bode well for Jemima. Now that she had reached the age of fourteen she had graduated from being a monitor to the chance of beginning a four-year training period as a pupil-teacher at the local school. She would have been excited about this were it not for the fact that her mother didn't regard this as 'real work' and thought she should find herself a 'proper job'.

'I can't have you staying at school when other girls your age are out earning money,' Eva complained when Jemima handed her the form she needed to sign to give her permission.

'But I shall be earning money. I'll be paid five shillings a week,' Jemima explained. 'And if I pass my exams at the end of the year I'll qualify for a ten-pound grant. Just think of that, Mum.'

'Hm. And if you don't pass your exams?'

'But I will, Mum. I'll work hard and make sure I do,' Jemima said earnestly. Eva was still not convinced. She was quite sure that Jemima could earn nearly that much at the fish factory if she worked hard, with the chance of earning extra if she did overtime when there was a glut. Five shillings a week with the promise of ten pounds that might or might not materialize at some distant date in the future might sound good but to her mind it was no more than a sprat to catch a mackerel. She worked on the principle, thoroughly mixing her metaphors, that a bird in the hand was worth two in the bush. The form got pushed to the back of the clock on the mantelpiece to give Eva more time to think up an excuse.

In desperation Jemima told Miss Peel about her mother's antagonism.

'I shall come and see her,' Miss Peel declared.

'Oh, no, Miss . . . I mean, I couldn't expect you to do that,' Jemima said, horrified at the thought of Miss Peel visiting Brown's Yard.

'Teaching is what you want to do, isn't it?' Miss Peel asked briskly.

'Oh, yes, Miss Peel. More than anything.' Jemima was touching in her fervour.

'Then it's worth a fight. I shall come and see your mother tomorrow. You needn't be there if you'd rather not. You can come and take tea with my mother, she'll like that.' Miss Peel smiled at her. 'Don't worry, Jemima. Your mother can't eat me.'

No, thought Jemima gloomily, *but when you see where I live you may change your mind about my suitability as a teacher.*

The following afternoon Jemima fussed around making sure the house was extra neat and tidy before she left for tea with Mrs Peel. Daisy was still upstairs in bed, because her ten days of lying-in were not quite over, and Sam and Mr Starling were both at work, so her mother was left alone downstairs, pretending to read a novel and prepared to be truculent in her objections because she was nervous at the thought of being visited by Jemima's school teacher. At that moment she could have killed Jemima for putting her in such a difficult position and was prepared to dredge up every objection she could think of to this 'teaching lark'.

It didn't take Miss Peel long to realize all that was going through Eva's mind and with a bit of charm and flattery managed to disarm her in a very short time. By the time she left, after a cup of tea and a piece of Daisy's shortbread, she had Eva's somewhat grudging permission for Jemima to 'give teaching a go', at least for a year, and the promise that she would sign the form 'when she could lay her hands on it'. She was not prepared to let Miss Peel witness that she had trouble even writing her own name.

Meanwhile, Jemima obediently visited Mrs Peel, where she managed to swallow a cup of tea and eat a cream cake. But she didn't enjoy her visit like she normally did, her mind too busy imagining what might be happening in Brown's Yard. She wondered how she would ever be able to face Miss Peel again once she knew about her living conditions. On top of all that, she missed Oliver. Now that he was no longer there she realized that the thought of seeing him had been a great part of her enjoyment in visiting Miss Peel and her mother. Even though it was as over-furnished as ever the house seemed somehow empty without his presence. Even Mrs Peel said how much she missed him.

It was over an hour before Miss Peel returned, an hour in which Jemima's stomach churned as she sat and talked to Mrs Peel.

'Well, that's that.' Miss Peel came in, her face wreathed in smiles as she took off her hat. 'You can begin as a pupil-teacher in September, Jemima. For a year, your mother has said. So that's a good start. She says she'll sign the form when she can find it.'

'When she can find it! But it's . . .' Just in time Jemima understood her mother's ruse and bit back her words. 'Only for a year?' she frowned.

Kathryn Peel patted her shoulder. 'If you pass your exam at the end of that year – and I know you will – you will receive the government grant of ten pounds. I'm sure that will encourage your mother to allow you to continue. Particularly as the grant goes up every year. Meantime you will receive five shillings a week.'

'Maybe I'll be able to earn a little extra by doing odd jobs,' Jemima said, thoughtfully.

'I hardly think you'll have time for that,' Miss Peel said with a laugh. 'You're going to be very busy with your school work, Jemima.'

Thanking Miss Peel and with her head full of conflicting thoughts and worries Jemima left and, on impulse, turned her steps to Aunt Minnie's house, to tell her the good news. She felt she owed it to her aunt, who had paid her school pence regularly, ever since she started school. Her schooling would have been very sketchy if it had been left to her mother to find the penny a week.

But Jemima didn't get the chance to speak because she walked in on an argument. Sophie had her bag packed, ready to leave for Mrs Worsnop's house where she was to begin work, while Aunt Minnie stood wringing her hands, begging her to wait till Uncle Will got home so that he could walk with her and carry her bag.

'It's all right, I'll go with her, Auntie,' Jemima offered, since it was obvious that her aunt was too full of misery at Sophie's departure to listen to anyone else. 'We can take it in turns to carry the bag if it's heavy.' She picked it up. 'I'll take first turn.'

Sophie raised her eyes to the ceiling but said nothing and after a tearful goodbye from Aunt Minnie they set off.

'Anyone would think I was going to the end of the earth,' she muttered as the door closed behind them.

'Well, Aunt Minnie's going to miss you; she's looked after you for a long time,' Jemima said. 'Are you going to be a maid at Mrs Worsnop's? I've seen her in church; she looks a bit of a dragon.'

'I'm going as her companion–cum–maid, whatever that is,' Sophie told her. 'And she's not a dragon, she's very nice. It's because she always dresses in black that she looks so fierce. And she's got a lovely house, with thick carpets and curtains and the furniture is all polished.'

Jemima grinned at her. 'I suppose that'll be your job, to polish the furniture.'

'Of course it won't,' Sophie said, her nose in the air. 'Mrs Worsnop says I'll only have light housework.'

'Well, you're not there yet, so you can do some heavy work and carry your bag. Lord knows what you've got in it.' Jemima handed it to her, then brushed her hands together in an effort to get the circulation going again. 'I'll be starting as a pupil-teacher next term,' she couldn't resist blurting out proudly.

'Are you?' Sophie said without much interest. 'I expect I'll earn more than you. Mrs Worsnop's very generous.'

'Yes, I expect you will,' Jemima replied. 'But I've always wanted to be a school teacher.'

'I know. Well, you're clever, aren't you?' It was the first word of praise Jemima had ever heard from her twin.

They reached 'The Anchorage', the large double-fronted house where Mrs Worsnop, a widow of some thirty years, lived.

'Come in with me, Jemma.' At the sight of the house all Sophie's confidence seemed to have evaporated.

'All right.' After what she had gone through earlier in the afternoon Jemima was not in the least worried about delivering Sophie to her new employment. 'Give me your bag. It'll give me an excuse.'

The bag changed hands again and Sophie rang the door bell.

It was opened by a very smart-looking woman in a black dress and white apron. A white cap with streamers was perched on brown hair that was streaked with grey. She gave Sophie a brief smile, which hardly creased her rather austere features. 'You're expected. Madam is in her little sitting room,' she said briskly. 'But I suggest you take your bag up to your room first. Second on the right at the top of the stairs.'

Jemima had never been in such a grand house. She followed Sophie up the stairs to her room, her feet sinking into the thick carpet.

'Is this the right one?' she whispered in Sophie's ear. 'It's very big.'

'It's the one she said,' Sophie answered as they stood in the doorway, looking round.

It was a large room with an enormous wardrobe and a dressing table to match. The bed was covered with the plumpest eiderdown Jemima had ever seen. It was a beautiful shade of pale pink. Gingerly, she tiptoed over to it and sat down, smoothing it with her hand, and nearly fell backwards because the bed was so soft.

'You'll never want to get up in the morning,' she said, thinking of her own narrow bed.

'Mm. It's nice and comfortable.' Sophie sat down and bounced up and down beside her.

'Careful. You'll break the springs,' Jemima whispered. 'Do you want me to help you unpack?'

'No, I'll do that later. We'd better go down and report to Madam. That's what I've been told to call her,' Sophie said.

'*You* have to report to her. Not me. I'm going home,' Jemima said firmly, following her.

'Oh, you can't leave me,' Sophie waited for her at the foot of the stairs. She looked quite frightened. 'Come in and meet Mrs Worsnop.'

'Don't be silly. She won't eat you. You said she was nice.' Jemima looked down at the skirt she was wearing. It was one of Sophie's cast-offs, with braid stitched two inches up from the hem to hide the line where it had been let down. 'Anyway, I'm not smart enough to come in with you.'

'Nonsense. I think you look very nice.' Neither of the girls had noticed the tall, elderly lady who was standing in the sitting-room doorway watching them. 'I take it you're Sophie's twin sister, Jemima?'

Both girls dropped a brief curtsy. 'That's right, Madam,' Jemima said, remembering that was the title Sophie had been told to use.

'Well, come in here where I can look at you both.' She led the way into a room overpowered by dark, bulbous furniture and with large, heavy-framed pictures, mostly portraits of important-looking men, hung round the walls. She sat down in an armchair and motioned them to stand in front of her.

'You're not in the least alike, are you?' She regarded them both through the gold pince-nez that were fastened with a narrow gold chain to a cameo brooch on the front of her dress.

'No, Sophie's always been the pretty one,' Jemima said, almost out of habit.

'Oh, I wouldn't necessarily say that,' Mrs Worsnop said, half to herself. 'Now, Sophie, if you go down to the kitchen Agatha will show you how I like my afternoon tea.' She made a little shooing motion with her hand. 'Run along now. You know the way to the kitchen, don't you?'

'Yes, Madam. I think so.'

'Off you go, then. Agatha will give you your uniform, too. Make sure you put it on before you come back.'

'Yes, Madam.'

Sophie left and Jemima made to follow her.

'Wait a minute. I haven't finished with you, Jemima.' Mrs Worsnop called.

Jemima went back and stood in front of her. The old lady looked her up and down. 'And when will you be starting work, Jemima?' she asked.

Jemima bobbed another curtsy. 'At the beginning of next term, Madam. I'm to start my training to become a school teacher,' she said proudly. Suddenly, the realization hit her. It was true. She *was* going to become a school teacher. Her mother had agreed to her training, at least for a year. Thanks to Miss Peel her dream was going to come true. She couldn't prevent a delighted smile spreading across her face.

'That's very ambitious. Do you think you're clever enough?' the old lady asked dryly.

Jemima hesitated. Miss Peel said she was clever but it would be presumptuous to claim it herself. So she contented herself with saying, 'I intend to work very hard, Madam, because it's something I really want to do.'

'Then I wish you well, Jemima. You seem to have the right spirit for it.' Mrs Worsnop gave her a smile that deepened the creases in her pale, papery skin. She nodded. 'Very well, my dear, you may go now.'

Sophie was nowhere to be seen as Jemima let herself out. She walked sedately down the drive in case Mrs Worsnop was watching, but when she reached the road she began to run, twirling round and round in her excitement because she was going to do what she had always wanted. Then, as she saw three little urchins playing in the road ahead she slowed to a decorous walk, because if she was going to be a teacher she must begin to act like one. But inside she was bubbling over with excitement, blissfully unaware that those bubbles were about to be burst in a surprising and shocking manner.

Twelve

After Miss Peel left, Eva sat at the kitchen table for some time thinking over the visit and trying to figure out whether she had allowed the young school teacher to 'put one across her' or whether she had come out on top in only agreeing to a year's training for Jemima. She was still trying to make up her mind when there was a tap at the open door. It was Mrs Pittuck from three doors down the yard.

'I saw you'd got the school teacher here so I waited till she'd gone,' she said, with an ingratiating smile that showed broken and discoloured teeth. She was a tall, gaunt woman, whose husband regularly blacked her eye or bruised her ribs on Friday nights. They had no children. 'I've just popped along to see the new baby. Is it all right?' She raised her eyebrows questioningly.

Eva took a deep breath. Mrs Pittuck was about the last person she wanted to see at the moment. She didn't like the woman, who she thought was far too interested in other people's business. But she could hardly turn her away. 'Yes, it's all right, you can come in. There's nobody here,' she said reluctantly.

Mrs Pittuck stepped inside, dragging a ragged cardigan round her as if she needed it to keep herself together. 'No, I meant is the baby all right?' She nodded several times, knowingly. 'You know, comin' a month or two early like it did.'

So that was it. Eva refused to rise to her bait. 'Daisy and the baby are both doing very well, thank you,' she replied icily.

'Can I go up?' Mrs Pittuck jerked her head towards the stairs. 'I've brought a little somethin' for it.'

Eva nodded. 'I s'pose so. But don't stay long.' She knew Daisy didn't like the woman, either.

She was back in less than five minutes. 'A fine baby,' she remarked. 'A good size, too, for a—'

'Yes, Daisy's a good mother,' Eva cut across her words without looking up.

Mrs Pittuck sat down opposite Eva without being invited. 'Your Jemima courtin', is she?' she asked, leaning her elbows on the table.

'No, of course she isn't. She's only just fourteen,' Eva said shortly.

She hoped the woman wasn't expecting a cup of tea because she wasn't going to get one.

'Oh, I thought she might be, seein' as the school teacher was here earlier on.'

'What's that got to do with anything?' At last Eva looked up at her, frowning.

'Well, I jest thought she might have come visitin' since young Jemima was gettin' very cosy with her nephew in the churchyard the other day.'

'I don't know what you're talking about,' Eva said brusquely. 'If you must know, Miss Peel was here on business. Not that it's any of yours,' she couldn't help adding.

But Mrs Pittuck was not to be put off. She leaned forward. 'Well, when I saw 'em kissin' an' cuddlin' in the churchyard I naturally thought they was courtin'.' She looked at Eva with a studied air of innocence.

'I think you must be mistaken,' Eva said, getting to her feet and moving towards the door to show the woman out.

Mrs Pittuck didn't take the hint. 'Oh, I don't think so, Mrs Furlong. I seen it with me own eyes,' she said, warming to her tale. 'He had his arm round her an' she had her head on his shoulder. Then he give her a kiss. I was watchin'. I seen it all.'

'Then it's a pity you hadn't got anything better to do than spy on people,' Eva said, her voice sharp. 'Now, I've got to get a meal ready for Mr Starling and Sam and I'm all behind so I'll have to ask you to go. Thank you for calling, Mrs Pittuck.' She held open the door.

Mrs Pittuck had no choice but to get up and leave. 'Well, don't say I didn't warn you,' she said as she walked past, her nose in the air. 'I wouldn't have thought you'd want *another* one bringin' trouble home to you,' she added nastily.

Eva slammed the door on her back. Then she sat down at the table, shaking with rage. How dared the woman come into her house making such accusations!

Then her shoulders sagged. But what if it was true?

She was still sitting and thinking about it when Jemima ran into the house, beaming, and flung her arms round her mother's neck in a rare gesture of affection.

'Oh, thank you, Mum. Thank you for letting me start my training. If you sign the form I'll take it to Miss Peel right now.'

Roughly, Eva extracted herself from Jemima's clasp, her mind suddenly made up. 'You can take that grin off your face and stop dancing about. I've changed my mind.'

Jemima sat down with a thump. 'What do you mean, changed your mind? But you told Miss Peel . . .'

'I didn't know then what I know now,' Eva said enigmatically. She wagged her finger at Jemima. 'I mean what I say. You're not going training, or whatever it's called, to be a teacher. I'm not having you wasting your time trying to get above your station.'

Jemima frowned uncomprehendingly. 'I'm not trying to get above my station, Mum, and I wouldn't be wasting my time learning to teach children. Anyway, you've already told Miss Peel I could. She said you'd agreed I could do it for a year and I thought . . .'

'Well, you can think again. You're not doing it and that's final.' She leaned back and folded her arms.

Jemima swallowed and licked her lips. She realized that no good would be served by shouting and arguing with her mother. 'At least tell me why you've changed your mind,' she said quietly. 'You owe me that.'

For some reason this seemed to enrage her mother even further. 'I don't owe you nothin' – er – anything,' Eva spat. 'You've brought nothing but trouble to me since the day you were born.' This was a lie and she knew it, which only increased her fury. Her voice rose. 'And now Mrs Pittuck, that nosy old besom down the yard, has been in and told me how you were making an exhibition of your-self with that nephew of the teacher in the churchyard the other day, kissing and cuddling for the whole world to see. And doing worse than that, for all I know. You should be ashamed of yourself, you filthy little slut.'

Jemima stared at her mother, wide-eyed. 'Mum! That's a dreadful thing to call your own daughter! Especially as it's not true. I don't know what you're talking about. You say I was kissing and cuddling with Oliver in the churchyard? I never was! I wouldn't dream of such a thing. Anyway, Oliver would never . . .'

'Oliver, is it?' her mother sneered, beside herself with rage. 'Calling him by his first name and you expect me to believe he wouldn't take advantage? Men are men the world over.' She glared at Jemima. 'Anyway, I expect you led him on.'

Now it was Jemima's turn to lose her temper, despite her former resolve. She banged her hand down on the table. 'I've just told you, I don't know what you're talking about. I've never . . .'

'What's all the shouting about?' Daisy appeared at the foot of the stairs, a pale, ghostly figure, wrapped in a blanket and holding on to the door post. 'What's going on down here?'

They both turned and looked at her. 'You shouldn't be out of bed,' Eva snapped at her. 'And what about the baby?'

'She's asleep. And I'm all right,' Daisy sat down at the table, still looking very pale and weak, giving the lie to her words. 'But I could do with a cuppa tea.'

Nobody spoke a word while Jemima pulled the kettle forward, brewed the tea, fetched cups and saucers from the dresser, poured three cups and put them on the table. Then she sat down again. The air was still thick with acrimony.

Daisy took a grateful sip, then looked from her mother to her sister and back again. 'Well? Isn't somebody going to say something?'

'It's *her*. Been playing fast and loose with that nephew of the school teacher,' Eva said, her lip curling in disgust.

Daisy frowned at Jemima, who shook her head wearily. 'She's got it all wrong, Daisy,' she said. 'But I think I know what she's talking about now. I remembered as soon as I saw you standing there. But it wasn't a bit like Mum's making out.'

'Making out?' Eva exploded. 'Making out?'

Daisy held up her hand. 'Oh, for goodness' sake. Let's at least hear what Jemma's got to say, Mum. Go on, Jemma.'

'It was the day you had the baby,' Jemima said, speaking to Daisy and ignoring her mother. 'I was sitting in the kitchen and you were upstairs. Suddenly, you started screaming . . .' She bit her lip, staring at the oilcloth on the table and registering with part of her mind that the pattern had rubbed off in the middle. 'I couldn't bear to hear it so I went and sat in the churchyard. I was so worried; I was terrified you were going to die, Daisy.' She gave her sister an agonized look. 'Oliver came and sat beside me and asked me what was wrong. He was so kind that I burst into tears when I told him. He put his arm round me to comfort me while I cried.' Her voice dropped. 'That's all it was, Daisy.'

'Not quite *all*, from what Mrs Pittuck said,' Eva said, her voice heavy with accusation. 'She said you were kissing and canoodling.'

'That's not true; we weren't,' Jemima said flatly. 'Oliver is going away to college. Well, he's probably gone by now. He just gave me a goodbye kiss.'

'In broad daylight! You should be ashamed.' Eva was determined not to be proved wrong.

'Maybe she should, but you could hardly call it kissing and

canoodling,' Daisy said, trying to smooth things over. 'You know what a troublemaker Mrs Pittuck is. I'm surprised you're willing to take her word against Jemma's, Mum.'

But Eva was so wound up that this had the reverse effect. 'That's right. You take her side,' she shouted, rounding on Daisy. 'You always were like that with each other.' She held up crossed fingers.

At that moment Sam and Mr Starling walked in from work.

'What's going on here? You shouldn't be downstairs, Daisy,' Sam said, going over and putting his arm round her.

'There's been a bit of a row, Sam,' she said, leaning her head against him. She was suddenly tired. The effort of coming downstairs and then trying to inject a note of calm and reason had taken its toll. Her eyes filled with tears. 'Oh, listen, now the baby's crying. I expect she's hungry.'

'It's all right, love, I'll carry you back up to her,' Gently, Sam picked her up in his arms and edged his way up the narrow stairs with her, telling her all the time that she really shouldn't have ventured out of the bedroom.

'It'll be *your* fault if you've upset her and her milk dries up,' Eva jabbed a finger vindictively at Jemima, who was still sitting at the table, trying not to let her tears overflow at the injustice of it all.

Mr Starling looked from Eva to Jemima, then sat down at the table between them.

'Now, what's this all about? Can I help?' he asked quietly. 'I don't like to see you all upsides with each other and they do say the onlooker sees most of the game.'

'No, you can't help, Mr Starling. This is a family matter and my mind's made up,' Eva said, her voice sharp. It was a measure of her agitation that she excluded him from the family.

'Then I mustn't interfere.' He pushed back his chair and made to get up, clearly offended.

'No, wait, Mr Starling.' Jemima held out her hand to detain him. 'Miss Peel came to see Mum this afternoon and got her to agree to me starting as a pupil-teacher. You know that's what I've always wanted to do, don't you, more than anything else in the world. But now Mum's gone back on her word and changed her mind. She says she won't let me, after all.' Her face crumpled. 'And all because of what Mrs Pittuck said . . .' She began to cry in earnest.

Mr Starling sat down again and handed her a rather grubby handkerchief. 'Now, dry your eyes and tell me all about it,' he said, his back half turned away from Eva. He listened intently, his eyes never leaving Jemima's face as she hiccuped out all that had happened and how Mrs Pittuck had interpreted it while her mother sat wooden-faced, saying nothing.

After she had finished speaking he said nothing for several minutes but sat stroking his moustache and rubbing his hands over his nearly bald head. Then he seemed to make up his mind. 'Well, it looks to me as if Mrs Pittuck got hold of the wrong end of the stick,' he remarked. 'Either that or she enjoys making mischief. It seems to me it was all pretty innocent, I must say.'

Eva rounded on him. 'It's all very well for you, Mr Starling, but Jemima's not your daughter. It's not you she'll come running to if – *when* – she gets herself into trouble.'

'Oh, I'm sure . . .' Mr Starling began.

'You're sure! I suppose you were sure your Sam wouldn't get my Daisy into trouble, but he did.'

'That's different.'

'I can't see it's different at all. Anyway, my mind's made up. Jemima's having nothing more to do with those school teacher people. Apart from anything else I can see her getting above herself and I'm not having that. She'll do what I did and go to work at the fish factory.'

'Mum!' Jemima cried, horrified. 'You can't mean that.'

Eva held up her hand. 'I do mean it. Every word. You can go down there on Monday morning and ask for a job. They're always looking for people and it's respectable work and not badly paid.'

'It's horrible, filthy work,' Jemima said, tears running down her cheeks. 'And you know I hate the stink of fish.'

'You'll get used to it.' Eva was totally without sympathy.

All her hopes and dreams shattered, Jemima put her head down on her hands and cried as if her heart would break.

Thirteen

'Oh, for goodness' sake, stop that blethering and help me peel these potatoes,' Eva said, banging the saucepan and a bag of potatoes down on the table. 'Going to work at the fish factory's not the end of the world.'

Jemima lifted her head, wiped her eyes with the heel of her hand and sniffed, her tears spent. 'It would be for me,' she said quietly. 'I'd rather die than go there.' She pushed back her chair and went to sit on the back step, the warm summer evening a sharp contrast to the black mood inside the house.

'Ah, hang on a minute, dearie,' Mr Starling called. 'I've just thought of something.' This wasn't strictly true; it was not an idea that had just occurred to him but rather something he had been uncertain about mentioning, largely because he had very comfortable lodgings with Mrs Furlong and didn't want to antagonize her. But he was so angry at the way she was treating Jemima that he had to speak.

'Well, if it's anything to do with this teaching lark you can forget it,' Eva said rudely. 'She's not doing it and that's flat. Anyway, what's it to do—?'

'Yes, what have you thought, Mr Starling?' Jemima called before her mother could be even ruder to him. She got up from the step and went back to sit at the table again, chewing her lip. If this lovely man had thought of something – anything – that would save her from the fish factory she wasn't going to leave the room until she had heard what it was.

'Well, it's like this,' he said, darting a glance at Eva, who was attacking the potatoes as if they were to blame. 'I saw an advertisement for a young lady shop assistant as I came past Baxter's on my way home from work. I know it's not what you want to do, Jemma, dear, but it would be better than the fish factory . . .' He raised his eyebrows hopefully.

'Oh, thank you, Mr Starling. *Anything* would be better than the fish factory,' she said, darting a venomous look in her mother's direction.

'I can't see anything wrong with the fish factory. I did it for long enough,' Eva said, throwing a potato into the saucepan and sending a shower of water over the oilcloth on the table. 'Well, come on, girl, get yourself a knife and give me a hand.'

Jemima got to her feet. 'No, I'm going to apply for the job at Baxter's, since you won't let me do what I want to. They don't close till eight so I've got plenty of time.'

Her mother looked her up and down. 'Fat chance you'll have of them taking you on,' she sneered. 'Look at you! You look like something the cat's dragged in.'

'Thank you, Mother.' Jemima's voice dripped icicles. She went out, banging the door behind her.

'That was a very nasty thing to say, Mrs Furlong,' Mr Starling snapped. He was astonished that the girl's mother could be so jealous and vindictive instead of being proud to have such a clever and talented daughter.

Eva rounded on him. 'You mind our own . . .' She stopped short, suddenly realizing that to alienate Mr Starling would be to lose her main source of income. She sat down heavily. 'I'm a bit tired,' she muttered by way of apology to him.

Jemima had only gone out to the wash house and she came back a few minutes later for her hat. She had washed her tear-stained face and combed her hair, twisting it up into a bun at the nape of her neck instead of letting it fall loose round her shoulders as it usually did. Fortunately, she was still wearing her best dress, which she had put on when she went for tea with Mrs Peel – could that have been only a few hours ago? She stood in front of the mirrored overmantel and tilted her hat slightly over one eye. Then she turned and stood in front of Mr Starling, pointedly ignoring her mother.

'Do I look respectable enough to apply for the job, Mr Starling?' she asked anxiously.

He looked her up and down, then nodded approvingly. 'You look very smart and very pretty, if I may say so, my dear. And my word, very grown-up now you've put your hair up.' He smiled at her. 'I wish you luck, my child. I hope the Baxters will be sensible enough to employ you.'

'Thank you, Mr Starling.' She bent and gave him a kiss on the cheek and walked out without a glance at her mother.

Francis Baxter – Frank to his family and friends – had inherited the shop from his father. It had originally been just a gents' outfitters, but when Frank had married Elsie Carver, a milliner, some twenty years earlier, she had persuaded him to buy the empty shop next door so that she could display her hats. Over the years the shop had expanded into ladies' clothing and haberdashery as well. Baxter's slogan was, 'If we haven't got it we can get it.' This worked very well, especially as Frank had a sale or return agreement with the largest clothing shop in Colchester and also a promise of next-day delivery from the local carrier, Mr Wyatt.

Frank and Elsie had one son, Richard, who was now eighteen and had always been destined to follow his father's and grandfather's footsteps into the business. He was a pleasant young man, with brown, slightly curly hair, clean, square-cut features and a friendly smile. He was good with figures and polite to customers, but without his father's rather brash, flamboyant, yet at the same time slightly obsequious manner – a manner which irritated Richard beyond measure.

Richard had a very modern, not to say radical, outlook on life. He considered every man to be his equal and treated everyone, from the Squire to the man who emptied the night soil, with the same polite attention.

Jemima had been in the shop a good many times for things like safety pins or elastic, but today, the ladies' and gentlemen's hats, the banks of drawers, the swathes of material artistically draped, the oil lamps hanging from the ceiling, the cards of buttons and hooks and eyes, even the chairs placed at intervals along the counter so that customers shouldn't be in too much hurry to leave, all seemed to crowd in on her and were reflected in the long mirror at the back of the shop, together with a tall, slim girl in a blue striped skirt with braid near the hem and a straw hat tilted cheekily over one eye.

With a start she realized that she was looking at herself. The image gave her the confidence she had lacked and she pulled back her shoulders and lifted her chin as she saw Mr Baxter appear from a door at the back of the shop.

He bustled forward. 'Yes? Can I get you something?'

'I've come in answer to the advertisement in the window, Mr Baxter,' she answered, her mouth dry.

'You mean you want to come here to work?' When she nodded he took a step back and looked her up and down, taking in her neat appearance and rather down-at-heel shoes. 'You're rather young, aren't you? I'm not sure you're *quite* what we're looking for.' He twisted his fingers together in a rather affected manner. 'We were looking for someone . . . what shall I say? A little more *mature,* perhaps?' He put his head to one side and smiled, revealing tobacco-stained teeth under a small, carefully trimmed moustache.

His wife had followed him through more slowly. She was an elegant lady, dressed in the latest fashion, with a long, sweeping, peacock-blue skirt, belted to emphasize her tiny waist, and a pink frilly blouse with leg of mutton sleeves. Her hair, a beautiful golden colour, was twisted into a bun over a frame at the back to make it look thicker and fringed over her forehead. Jemima was almost sure her face was powdered and that there was a trace of colour on her lips, probably to conceal the fact that underneath she was looking pale and tired.

'This young lady's applying for our vacancy, pet,' he said, turning to her. 'But I'm not sure . . . She doesn't really look old enough . . .'

'I'm fourteen,' Jemima said, desperate for the job but determined not to lie to get it.

Mrs Baxter lowered herself on to the chair at the end of the counter and smiled at her so Jemima bobbed a little curtsy.

'What's your name?' She had a nice, musical-sounding voice.

'Jemima Furlong, ma'am.' She bobbed another curtsy.

Elsie Baxter raised her eyebrows. 'Jemima Furlong? But I understood that you were going to train as a school teacher.' She smiled as she saw the perplexed look on Jemima's face. 'Mrs Peel is a very good friend of mine. She's told me about you and how keen her daughter is to help you. So, why the change of mind?'

Jemima bit her lip. 'It's not me that's had a change of mind, it's my mother,' she said, trying desperately not to sound as bitter as she felt. 'She says I must get what she calls a "proper job" and wants me to go and work at the . . .' She bit her lip even harder. Whatever her mother had done to her she couldn't betray her by admitting the awful truth. 'She says I must find myself a job somewhere.'

'So you decided to apply for the job here,' Mr Baxter said and Jemima couldn't make up her mind whether he was being sarcastic, or mocking, or whether that was the way he always spoke. She decided to take his words at face value.

'That's right, sir.'

'What's your arithmetic like? Can you add up a column of figures?'

'If Kathy Peel has been tutoring her I should think that goes without saying, Frank,' Mrs Baxter said.

'Nevertheless . . .' Mr Baxter busied himself with a pencil and paper, which he then handed to Jemima.

She looked at the column of figures and at the answer underneath. 'May I have a pencil, please?'

He gave her the pencil and watched as she ran it up the columns of pence, shillings, then pounds. 'I believe it should be twenty-four pounds, five shillings and fourpence, not twenty-five pounds, four shillings and fivepence,' she said, handing it back to him. She knew he had been trying to trick her and she had checked her findings carefully.

He looked surprised. 'That didn't take you long,' he said. 'And you're quite right.'

'I've always been good at arithmetic,' she said without false modesty.

'Come here, child, I want to look at you,' Mrs Baxter said.

Jemima stood quietly while Mrs Baxter studied her. 'Are your shoes big enough?' she asked at last.

Jemima blushed. 'They're a bit small. I'm trying to save up for some new ones,' she admitted.

The older woman nodded. 'I'm sure we can soon put that right.' She smiled. 'Yes, Jemima, I think you will suit me very well.'

'Oh, thank you, ma'am.' Jemima's face broke into a smile that transformed her from an ordinarily pleasant-looking girl into quite a beauty.

'It's not my business to know why your mother won't allow you to go into teaching. It seems a pity, since my friends have already told me you are a very bright girl. But teaching's loss will be my gain because I think you're exactly the kind of girl I'm looking for.'

A reply didn't seem to be called for so Jemima bobbed another curtsy.

Mrs Baxter nodded in acknowledgement and went on, 'You see, I have been unwell and my doctor says I must rest more and not work so hard, so I need someone who will learn quickly and can take over some of my duties in the shop. Of course, I shall be on hand to help and advise you and my husband and Richard, my son, will be here as well, although of course they have very little to do with the ladies' department – it wouldn't be right. Now, do you think you would like to work here?'

'Yes, please, as long as you're here to help and advise me, ma'am,' Jemima said carefully, adding, 'I'm a quick learner, as a rule.'

'Yes, so I've heard.' Mrs Baxter turned to her husband. 'I believe Jemima will be ideal, Frank. An older women might resent being told what to do.' She had a hurried, whispered consultation with her husband, then turned back to Jemima. 'We should like you to begin on Monday and we shall expect you to live in, of course. Your wages will begin at two and sixpence a week plus your keep, rising half-yearly according to how well you acquit yourself. Does that suit you?'

'Yes, that suits me very well, thank you, ma'am.' It was only half what she would have earned as a pupil-teacher but she would be living in, away from Brown's Yard, and that counted for a lot.

'Good. Bring your belongings on Sunday afternoon in time for tea so you'll be well settled in before you begin work on Monday.' Suddenly, she leaned on the counter and put her hand on Jemima's. 'My smelling bottle . . . in my reticule . . .'

Jemima stepped forward and found the smelling bottle and held it under Mrs Baxter's nose for a few seconds.

'Thank you, my dear.' Mrs Baxter gave her a wan smile. 'I'm sure we shall get on very well together. I shall look forward to seeing you on Sunday, Jemima,' she said as her husband helped her to her feet and escorted her back through the door into their living quarters.

Jemima let herself out of the shop. Of course, working in Baxter's shop was a far cry from being a school teacher but she told herself it was the next best thing. And if she worked hard and saved her money there was always the chance that she could still attain her dream. In the meantime at least she would be free from her mother's carping tongue.

She took off her hat, shook her hair loose and hurried through the churchyard, anxious to tell Mr Starling the good news.

Fourteen

Jemima managed to maintain an air of cheerfulness for the rest of the week, ignoring the fact that her mother was refusing to speak to her. For her part, Eva couldn't understand why, although she had won the battle over the 'teaching lark', she still had the feeling that Jemima had come out on top.

On Sunday afternoon, Jemima picked up the wicker basket containing all her possessions, kissed Daisy and little Amy and gave Mr Starling a grateful hug. Then, without a backward glance, she left Brown's Yard and made her way to the back entrance of Baxter's shop for Sunday tea. Having been to tea with the Peels several times she wasn't particularly nervous at the prospect of tea with Mr and Mrs Baxter, although she was a little apprehensive.

She needn't have been. She quickly discovered that the invitation to 'come to tea on Sunday' was not quite what she had been expecting.

She didn't even see the family. Her tea was served in the kitchen with Dorothy, the cook-cum-housekeeper. She was a gaunt, efficient woman of about forty, whose looks were fierce but whose heart was marshmallow.

'You didn't expect to eat with the family, did you, dear?' Dorothy said, smiling at Jemima's barely concealed surprise.

'Well, they did say . . .'

'Ah, what they say is not always what they mean.' Dorothy tapped the side of her nose mysteriously. 'They're sticklers for keeping up appearances, you know.' She put a plate of warm scones on the table beside a slab of butter and a pot of home-made strawberry jam. 'But you'll be better off down here with me.' She gave a wicked grin that transformed her face and made her look years younger. 'I always make sure the best bits are saved for the kitchen, so you'll be able to share them with me.' She sat down and put her elbows on the table. 'Now, tell me about yourself.'

By the time Jemima had told Dorothy a good part of her life story she had eaten more of the delicious scones than she had intended. 'Oh, I'm sorry.' She looked aghast at the empty plate that had held the scones. 'You must think I'm very greedy.'

'Not a bit,' Dorothy said, her eyes dancing. 'It's nice to see you appreciate my cooking. But tell me, why on earth does your mother think you're bad luck?'

'Because I was the thirteenth child, born on the thirteenth, the same day my father was drowned. I suppose I must have come as a bit of a shock. She didn't realize she was having twins.'

'And what about your twin?'

'Sophie? My aunt took her almost as soon as she was born and brought her up. She's just started work, too. She's to be a companion-cum-maid – whatever that means – to Mrs Worsnop, at the top end of the town. We're not a bit alike. She's the pretty one.'

'Oh, I don't know about that. Nothing wrong with your face.' Dorothy looked at her appraisingly. She got to her feet. 'Now, you probably think I've asked enough questions. Come on, I'll take you upstairs and show you your room. It's next to mine. Up in the attic, of course.'

She led the way up two flights of back stairs. As they climbed the stairs she explained that because the two shops and living accommodation behind had been made into one there were two sets of identical stairs.

'But they didn't bother to knock the attics through so our rooms can only be reached from the kitchen,' she said as they came to a square landing with two doors, one to the right and one to the left. She opened the door on the left into quite a large, whitewashed room with a skylight in the sloping ceiling, which made it quite light. A cheap, battered-looking bedroom suite in light oak was carefully placed so that the wardrobe stood where the ceiling was highest.

'This is your room. You'll have to be careful not to bang your head if you sit up in bed, but you'll soon get used to it,' Dorothy said cheerfully. 'And don't forget to bring up a can of water when you come to bed ready for your morning wash, otherwise you'll have to trek down to the kitchen and back up again with it. Oh, I mustn't forget to tell you there's a dress hanging in the wardrobe for you to wear for work. There's a belt with it in case it's too big round the waist for you.' She put her head on one side. 'Not that it's likely to be. It's one of the missus's cast-offs and the way she pulls herself in to give herself a wasp waist is quite unhealthy, to my way of thinking. It's no wonder she's always ailing. But she might be a bit taller than you so you'd better try it on, in case it's too long, in which case we shall have to spend the evening turning up the hem. Come down when you're ready.'

Dorothy left and Jemima gazed round the room. Her room. It wasn't nearly as expensively furnished and comfortable as the one Sophie had been given at Mrs Worsnop's but it was *hers*. She had never had a room of her own before, with space to put her possessions, few though they were. Gingerly, she sat down on the narrow bed and then stretched out full length on it. Oh, the bed might be a bit hard but this was luxury indeed.

Five minutes later, she realized that Dorothy would be waiting downstairs for her so she hurriedly put on the dress. It was a dark blue silk, with a high neck, a fullness in the sleeves that hinted at leg of mutton, and tiny buttons down the front of the bodice. It was much better quality than anything she had ever worn in her life before. And it rustled as she walked. She'd never had a dress that rustled before. But it was about two inches too long. She held it up carefully as she went down the narrow stairs to show Dorothy.

'Yes, I rather thought so.' Dorothy nodded when she had inspected her. She reached for her sewing basket. 'Go and take it off and we'll set to work. I don't usually reckon to get out my sewing on a Sunday, the Lord's Day, but needs must, I suppose.'

Jemima put her own dress on again and they set to work. It was very pleasant sitting in the kitchen with Dorothy. The door was open on to a warm summer evening and there was no sound to disturb them except the flies buzzing round the fly paper that was hanging from the ceiling. Outside in the yard tubs of geraniums made a splash of bright colour and beyond them a flight of stone steps led up to the garden, where there was a strip of lawn with a flower border and a path with a washing line.

As they talked it was obvious that Dorothy was very fond of Mrs Baxter, although, as she put it, 'she has her little ways.' It was also plain that she regarded Richard almost as a surrogate son, but had little time for the man of the house.

'He's all show and no do, that man,' she said tersely. 'Likes everybody to think he works his fingers to the bone, but I know different.' She didn't elaborate further.

The next day Jemima started work. Unfortunately, it was one of Mrs Baxter's bad days so after a quick tour of the shop to show Jemima where everything was, the way sales and orders were recorded and how to operate the mechanism on the drawer where the cash was kept, she spent the rest of the day lying on the chaise longue in the living room behind the shop. This meant that Jemima was left in charge. It wasn't difficult to see how things were run, and everything was priced. Being Monday there weren't many customers so she had plenty of time to explore all the drawers and cupboards and Mrs Baxter was nearby to advise.

'I'm truly sorry about this,' she said, and Jemima could see that she really was in some pain and her face had a yellowish tinge. 'The doctor says one of my problems is that my internal organs are displaced. He says it's due to tight corseting, but I really can't believe that's true. All women with any sense of fashion lace themselves in, because everyone aspires to an eighteen-inch waist.' She looked down at her own figure, today draped in a loose negligee. 'Although I must admit I don't feel nearly so sick without my stays on.' She gave a rueful smile. 'Oh, dear, what we women suffer in the name of fashion.'

'Is there anything I can get you?' Jemima asked anxiously.

'No, thank you, dear. I have my tonic water and sal volatile on the little table here in case I need them. And my smelling salts are in my reticule. But if you can manage the shop on your own I shall be most grateful. Of course, I'm here if you need me.' She gave another smile, this time a slightly conspiratorial one. 'But for good-ness' sake don't leave the door open. It wouldn't at all do for my customers to see me *en déshabille* like this.' She put out her hand. 'I can't tell you how grateful I am to have found you, my dear. I'm sure you'll do very well and we shall get on like a house on fire.'

She couldn't have known how prophetic her words were.

Richard came through early on. He was quite formally dressed today in a black morning coat and striped trousers, with a discreetly patterned blue waistcoat, a white shirt and high collar. Unlike his father, he was clean shaven. He was not exactly handsome but he had a pleasant smile and nice brown eyes. Oliver wasn't as tall as Richard but he was broader and more athletic-looking, largely due to the rugby he played at school. Jemima knew it was silly to compare Richard with Oliver but she couldn't help it. Neither could she help it if Richard was found wanting in the comparison. But of course she didn't yet know him very well.

'I'm not supposed to stray into this part of the shop,' he confided, 'but since Mama is indisposed I've come to see if there's anything you need to know.'

'No, your mother is very organized; she's shown me where things are,' she said, 'and she's just there in the living room if I have a problem. Is she often ill like this?'

He nodded. 'Yes. Unfortunately. And now she needs to rest even more because of her heart.'

'And who looks after the shop when she's ill? You?'

'Good heavens, no.' He laughed, showing white, even teeth. 'It wouldn't do for me to sell women's unmentionables! Either we have to close this part of the shop or Dorothy steps in for a few hours. But it'll be much better now you're here.'

'Oh, dear. I hope I'll suit.' Suddenly, Jemima felt the weight of responsibility.

'Of course you will. You'll suit me, anyway.' Suddenly realizing what he had said he blushed to the roots of his hair. 'I must go in case you get a customer.' He hurried off to the other part of the shop.

The shop was not busy so Jemima had plenty of time to explore. She was amazed at the things for sale in the ladies' department, things she had never seen – indeed, never even heard of. She herself still wore a simple cambric chemise and drawers under her petticoat but here there were shelves holding new things called combinations, which turned out to be frilly undergarments made either of cotton, wool or silk, combining bodice, petticoat and drawers. She'd never seen anything like that in her whole life before. Then there were vests in various colours, chemises and drawers in different materials, bust bodices, bust improvers and in a cupboard under the millinery shelf were a number of corsets in pretty colours, liberally decorated with lace frills and rosettes to conceal the uncomfortable, stiff boning. Hidden away in a drawer under the counter were packets of 'towelettes' at a shilling a dozen which Jemima puzzled over and had to ask Mrs Baxter, who lowered her voice to confide that they were used by high-class ladies 'at a certain time of the month'. Jemima wasn't impressed; she thought they were a waste of money when most people used rags that could be washed and reused. It was like a different world to her.

'But you see, we serve the Quality, the ladies from the Hall and the Park and all the important families around here, so we have to keep up with fashions and trends,' Mrs Baxter explained. She pointed to the catalogues lying beside her. 'These are what I study to make sure I keep my stock up to date.'

'I see.' Jemima went back to her explorations of the less interesting items – swatches of dress material, from which lengths could be ordered and sent down from Colchester, spools of thread, and reels of ribbon and elastic. There were also sheets of pink paper on which were neat rows of dress pins.

'We give a paper of pins instead of money if the change due is a ha'penny or less,' Mrs Baxter had explained.

Jemima soon learned and the days and weeks flew past. On her half day she often went to visit Aunt Minnie and sometimes Sophie was there, too, so they could compare notes. Sophie was friendlier and more disposed towards her sister now that she felt she was in a superior position to Jemima and she could boast about the various friends' houses she accompanied Mrs Worsnop to and the things they had to eat on their visits, carefully not mentioning that she usually ate in the kitchen with the maids.

Jemima, not to be outdone, told Sophie about things that were sold in her part of the shop and was gratified to see Sophie's eyes widen as she described some of the more outlandish underwear.

'I'll show you when you come into the shop,' she promised.

On Sundays, they all went to church. Aunt Minnie had always attended church with Sophie and sometimes Jemima had accompanied them. Aunt Minnie took her religion seriously and always tried to behave in what she called a Christian manner, being kind and generous to those less fortunate than herself and never speaking ill of anyone.

Therefore, it came as quite a shock to Jemima to discover that the only reason the Baxters went to church was to be seen. They walked up the aisle, nodding to acquaintances as they went, Mrs Baxter wearing her latest hat and leaning heavily on her husband's arm and they sat in a pew with their name on it, for which they paid an annual fee. This was not quite halfway up the centre aisle because there was a definite hierarchy in church seating and they were, after all, only shopkeepers, even if their shop was double-fronted and even if they did supply the Quality. However, Mrs Baxter always put on her best clothes – sometimes borrowed from the shop on Sunday and replaced on Monday – and her latest hat creation, because it was all good advertisement. Mr Baxter was very fond of checks, the louder the better, which he regarded as the height of fashion and Mrs Baxter thought rather vulgar. Over this they agreed to disagree, since if she made an issue of it he would refuse to accompany her at all. Richard never came; his parents' ostentatious behaviour embarrassed him. He spent Sunday morning doing the accounts for the week. Jemima sat with Dorothy at the back.

In contrast to Aunt Minnie's creed of never speaking ill of anyone, Mr and Mrs Baxter usually spent the rest of Sunday taking their ease and discussing who had been at church and what they were likely to be worth financially. Jemima found this quite shocking.

Dorothy always went to see her sister on Sunday afternoon, leaving tea for the family under a cloth in the larder ready for Jemima to serve. Jemima didn't go home; she felt she never wanted to see or speak to her mother again although she knew she would eventually have to face her. But she often met Daisy and they would go for a walk by the river, Jemima pushing little Amy in her pram and telling Daisy about her work in the shop and Daisy telling her of little Amy's latest doings. On the days Daisy couldn't meet her Jemima usually sat in the garden reading the books Miss Peel smuggled in for her under the pretence of buying ribbon. Miss Peel, who must have bought enough ribbon to deck out a maypole, had been almost as devastated as Jemima at her dreams being shattered. The trouble was, it was difficult to explain the real reason for her mother's change of mind. Jemima suspected that the accusations of misbehaviour with Oliver – which, of course, she could never, ever, speak about with Miss Peel – were in reality only a mask for the real reason, which was that Eva was afraid. Afraid of her daughter becoming educated; afraid of her moving out of the social class in which she had been born; afraid not of her 'getting above herself', as Eva put it, but of her getting above Eva. Added to that, she was vindictively jealous. All this Jemima realized without actually putting it into words.

'But promise me you won't give up hope, my dear,' Miss Peel had said, looking stricken as she came into the shop and found Jemima behind the counter.

Jemima had shaken her head, trying not to cry. 'No. I won't give up hope,' she said.

'Good girl. I shall bring you books and you must be sure to read them. Keep up with your studies. You never know what's round the corner. Your mother may have a change of heart.'

'I don't think that's very likely,' Jemima said bleakly.

Fifteen

Jemima had not been working at Baxter's many weeks when her mother came into the shop. She wore a determined, truculent look and Jemima could see that she had come to make trouble, not a purchase. Nevertheless, she went forward to greet her with a smile, as she did with all potential customers.

'You can take that grin off your face,' Eva said curtly. 'I haven't come to buy anything. I've come for your wages. They pay you two bob a week, don't they? Well, where is it?'

Jemima's smile froze. 'But I don't have to give you my wages. I don't live with you any more,' she said, her voice bordering on alarm. If her mother took her wages she would never be able to save up enough for her training.

'Don't make any odds. You're still my daughter and I'm entitled to what you earn. So where is it?' She banged her fist down on the counter.

'No, I don't have to give you my earnings, Mum. I don't live with you any more. I may give you a shilling or two when I've got some to spare, but you don't have to feed or clothe me, so you can't make me give you my money.'

'Oh, can't I, my girl? We'll soon see about that,' Eva said, her voice rising with every word.

'Please, Mum, keep your voice down,' Jemima said, looking round to see if there were any other customers in the shop who might have heard. 'Look, I'll come round tonight. We'll talk about it then.'

'We'll talk about it now!' Eva shouted. 'I'm not leaving this shop till I get what's due to me.'

Suddenly, Mr Baxter appeared from the gents' department. He raised his eyebrows. 'Is there some problem, Jemima? Is this person making herself a nuisance?' He turned to Eva. 'Are you wishing to make a purchase, madam? If not, I suggest you leave the shop. We're not in the habit of allowing our staff to be bullied by customers.'

'I'm not a customer.' Eva shouted. 'I'm . . .'

'Then you've no reason to be in the shop.' Mr Baxter was already propelling her towards the door.

She shook his arm free. 'Take your hands off me. I'm going.'

With a venomous backward glance at Jemima she stalked out of the shop.

He closed the door behind her and came back to where Jemima was standing, looking rather pale.

'Are you all right, Jemima? That was a bit unpleasant for you, I'm afraid. But I don't think we shall see that woman in here again.'

'No, I don't think we shall,' Jemima said. She didn't tell him the woman was her mother; she was too ashamed.

As the weather got colder, Jemima began spending her Sunday afternoons in the kitchen, by the fire. It was a cosy room in winter, with peg rugs on the floor, comfortable armchairs and a chenille tablecloth covering the table when it was not being used for cooking. Dorothy, who usually visited her sister on Sunday afternoons, always kept the brass and copperware on the dresser polished and the stove blackleaded, so the whole room exuded warmth and comfort.

The office-cum-stockroom was in a room next door to the kitchen and here Richard spent most Sunday mornings making up the books and writing the orders. Usually he had finished by lunchtime but occasionally it took longer. One Sunday, when it had taken him longer than usual to balance the figures, he saw Jemima sitting by the fire as he came through.

'Oh, hello, Jemima. You look very peaceful,' he said. 'May I join you for a few minutes?'

She looked up from the book she was reading and smiled at him. 'Of course you can,' she said. 'I'll be making myself a cup of tea soon. Would you like one?'

'I would, indeed. But there's no hurry.' He sat down and stretched his legs out and folded his arms behind his head. 'Ah, this is nice.'

He didn't say any more so she resumed her reading although she could feel his eyes on her.

'You always seem to have your head in a book when you're not working,' he said after a few minutes. 'What are you reading? A penny dreadful?'

She held up a book full of geometric shapes and theorems. 'Not exactly,' she said with a smile.

He gasped. 'Why on earth are you bothering your head with that sort of thing?'

'Because I don't intend to spend the rest of my life standing behind the counter in your mother's shop selling unmentionables;

one day I'm going to be a school teacher,' she said and waited for him to laugh.

But he didn't, he looked interested, so she found herself telling him about her ambition, about Miss Peel and about how her mother had agreed to it and then gone back on her word.

'But I'm still determined to do it,' she finished. 'I shall save my money and when I've saved enough I shall become a pupil-teacher and pass my exams to become a proper teacher. I might even go to college, and one day, you'll see, I shall have my own school.' She stopped, embarrassed. 'I'm sorry. I'm afraid I got a bit carried away.'

He waved his hand. 'No, no, don't apologize, Jemima. Indeed, I have every sympathy. I know exactly how you feel.' He leaned forward with his elbows on his knees. 'I never wanted to come and work in the shop with my father, but from as far back as I can remember I knew I would have to. Being the only son it was impressed on me that it was my duty to carry on the family business.' He looked down at his hands. 'But, like you, my ambition was for something very different.'

'What did you want to do?'

'I wanted to make my living with my music. I've always loved it and my music teacher, Mr Lax, tried to encourage me to make a career of it.' He shook his head. 'Oh, not as a concert pianist; I knew I would never be good enough for that. But I could have made quite a good living teaching and as an accompanist. But my father nearly had a fit when I suggested it. He said I was to join the family business and make a decent living, not mess about trying to earn a few coppers "tinkling on the Joanna", as he called it.' He shrugged his shoulders. 'My father is practically tone deaf. Music means nothing to him.' He looked across at her and smiled. 'So in a sense I suppose you could say we're both trapped, Jemima. Neither of us doing what we really want to do and both of us trying to make the best of it.' He fell silent. He had loosened his collar and his hair was ruffled where he had repeatedly run his hands through it; he didn't look at all like the suave gentlemen's outfitter that he presented to the world when he was in the shop and she liked him the better for it.

'So you don't play any more?' she asked. 'At least, I've never heard you – although, come to think of it, I've seen a music case in your mother's sitting room. Is that yours?'

'That's right.' He shook his head. 'But you won't have heard me play because I don't have a piano at home any more. I go to my old music teacher's house and practise on his Steinway.' He grinned. 'That's a real privilege, I can tell you.'

'Ah, so that's where you go every evening when you've finished here,' she said with a smile. 'I've often wondered where you were hurrying off to.'

'Yes, unless I go and earn a few coppers playing at the pub. I do that sometimes.' His grin widened. 'I must say, though, the pub piano isn't a patch on Mr Lax's Steinway.'

'I can imagine. One day maybe you'll let me hear you play,' she said.

'Yes, one day maybe I will.' He leaned back in his chair and they sat in companionable silence, each with their own thoughts.

But though she had warmed to Richard, it was still Oliver who filled Jemima's dreams every night, and she kept the occasional, rather sketchy letters he sent via Miss Peel under her pillow at night after reading and re-reading them until she knew every word off by heart.

In spite of what she had expected, Jemima found she didn't dislike working at Baxter's and she was a willing and able worker. Mrs Baxter was so pleased with her that after six months she put her wages up and she put them up again at the end of a year. By the end of two years Jemima was earning four shillings a week, most of which she saved in a box under her bed.

She became very fond of Mrs Baxter, who spent as much time in the shop as she could, even though she was often quite poorly, although she never made a fuss. But she learned more about the family during mealtimes and evenings spent in the kitchen with Dorothy, who also held 'the missus' in high esteem.

'Richard told me he plays the piano,' she remarked one evening as they sat finishing their supper of Welsh rarebit. 'But why does he go round to his old music teacher's to practise? Why doesn't he have a piano here? I don't know anything about music but I'd love to hear him.'

'He can't practise at home because his father sold his piano,' Dorothy said, pursing her lips. 'He said it made the missus's head ache. But it wasn't that at all. The missus used to like to hear Richard play. No, he knew how good Richard was and he wanted to put a stop to it.'

'Oh, but that's dreadful,' Jemima said.

'Yes, that's what I thought. Mind you, the old man was probably drunk at the time.'

'Drunk!'

Dorothy nodded. 'Oh, yes. Our Frank likes his tipple, although most of the time he manages to hide it. But you must have noticed his nose.'

'Well, yes, it's a bit red, but I thought it was just his natural colour.'

'It is now! Coloured by drinking too much whisky over the years.' Dorothy gathered the plates and took them over to the sink. 'But he's not too bad except when he goes on what we call a bender. Then he'll hole up somewhere and drink himself stupid for a couple of days.' She shook her head. 'I sometimes wonder how the missus puts up with it, but I suppose she doesn't have much choice, does she, poor thing? She's got nowhere else to go. I think she was quite upset when the piano went, though. I know she used to like hearing Richard play, whatever the old man said.'

Jemima wished she could have heard him, too.

After that she kept her distance from Mr Baxter. She'd never liked the man, since the day she applied for the job and he'd tried to catch her out with adding up a bill, and now she liked him even less. Fortunately, working in the ladies' department, she had very little need to speak to him.

She came into contact with all kinds of people working in the department with Mrs Baxter, whom she did like, very much. She served women from all walks of life, from fish factory girls wanting a penny ribbon to decorate an ageing hat to the ladies' maids of the gentry buying silk underwear. And one unforgettable day Lady Cornwall herself, from the Hall, came in to be discreetly measured for a new corset. This had to be done by Mrs Baxter herself, of course, and in the privacy of her private sitting room. While she was in the shop Lady Cornwall also chose some expensive duchesse satin for an evening dress, ordering it to be sent straight to her dressmaker.

'I usually go up to town for these things but I've sprained my ankle so it was more convenient to come here,' Jemima heard her telling Mrs Baxter in what sounded like a very artificial and patronizing voice as she limped back into the shop. Mrs Baxter, who had forced herself into her best taffeta to show off her nineteen-inch waist for the occasion, followed at a respectful distance. Lady Cornwall held up her lorgnette and looked patronizingly down her nose round the shop.

'I'm really quite agreeably surprised by this little place. Your stock is amazingly up-to-date for a small haberdasher's, and you have some exceedingly nice dress material.'

'Thank you, milady. I always try to order from the best catalogues,' Mrs Baxter told her.

'So I see.' She glanced around and could see that everything was set out to the best advantage, a skill Mrs Baxter was in process of teaching Jemima. 'You have some quite striking hats, too.'

'They are my own creations, milady. Ladies come from as far away as the other side of Ipswich for my hats. You see, I was trained as a milliner.'

'Hm. All very nice. I may return when I need some small thing.'

'We're always happy to oblige, milady.' Mrs Baxter managed a stiff little curtsy as she showed her out of the shop.

As soon as the carriage had rolled away Mrs Baxter collapsed, leaning on the counter. 'Quick, get me my smelling bottle, Jemima,' she gasped. 'Thank you.' She took a long sniff. 'Now, help me loosen my corset. Ah, that's better.' She subsided on to her couch and Jemima dabbed her forehead with eau de Cologne, which she knew she liked.

'Oh, thank you, dear.' She closed her eyes. 'Oh, Lord, that was quite an ordeal. Lady Cornwall has never been in the shop before. Do you think she was impressed, Jemima?'

'She seemed to be. She said she might come back,' Jemima said, frowning. 'What did she mean when she said she usually goes up to town for her things?'

'London, dear,' Mrs Baxter said without opening her eyes. 'The Gentry always call London "town". It makes it sound as if they're always popping up there, which most of them aren't, of course.' She opened her eyes. 'I think we could both do with a nice cup of tea after all that, don't you? I must say I feel quite exhausted. Ring the bell and ask Dorothy to bring it, will you, dear?'

Later, as they sat drinking tea in the little sitting room that doubled as a stockroom for the ladies' department, but had been tidied up and cleared for the occasion, Mrs Baxter said thoughtfully, 'I hope she'll pay her bill. Those sort of people often don't bother, you know, Jemima,' she added, seeing Jemima's astonishment. 'I sometimes think they regard their patronage as sufficient payment. But you can't pay wholesalers with genteel patronage; it's hard cash they want.' She frowned. 'That duchesse satin, it's the most expensive material in the shop, isn't it? And she ordered twelve yards to be sent to her dressmaker. How much will that be?'

'It's five shillings a yard, so that will be three pounds,' Jemima said quickly. 'And then there'll be the corset.'

'That's another five shillings.' Mrs Baxter fanned herself with the latest fashion catalogue. 'Oh, heavens, I hope she'll pay the bill.' She made a face at Jemima's puzzled expression. 'When you've been in this business as long as I have you get to know these things, Jemima. Some people can always be relied on to pay their bills promptly – other shopkeepers, for instance, who know what it's like to be owed money; or the Peels, who would never run up a bill they wouldn't be able to meet; or your aunt – what's her name?'

'Aunt Minnie.'

'Yes, your Aunt Minnie, those sort of people can always be relied upon. Then there are the poor people, who come in for a penny-worth of elastic or a yard of ribbon. If they haven't got the penny they don't come.' She sighed. 'No, it's the rich people, who think they're favouring us with their custom, who pay late, or quite often don't pay at all.'

'Maybe some of them aren't quite as rich as they like people to think,' Jemima mused.

Mrs Baxter gave a knowing smile. 'That's very perceptive of you, Jemima. And you could be right, at that.' She sighed. 'But I suppose the mere fact that they are seen coming into our shop *is* good for business. Not that they're likely to grace us with their presence very often. I don't know whether to be glad or sorry about that.'

Mrs Baxter was right about one thing. For the next few weeks trade in the shop was indeed brisker than usual but after that it settled down and things returned to normal.

Jemima never did hear whether or not Lady Cornwall settled her bill.

Sixteen

Sophie often popped into the shop on her way to the penny library to change Mrs Worsnop's library books or to buy a few yards of ribbon. She still liked to boast about her position, which amused Jemima, who felt that working in a respectable draper's shop was preferable to being at the beck and call of a rich and querulous old lady, although she tactfully didn't say so.

One day Sophie came into the shop with an order from Mrs Worsnop for winter petticoats and flannel drawers.

'Poor old thing, she's not been very well and she feels the cold,' Sophie explained. 'And now winter's coming the house is like a morgue, except the room that she sits in.'

'Do you think she might like to try combinations?' Jemima asked, getting out a sample in warm wool.

'Lord, no. She'd never wear anything like that. They're far too modern,' Sophie said, making a face when she saw them.

'Yes, I suppose they are. They're quite the thing, you know,' Jemima said, showing off her newly acquired knowledge. She dropped her voice. 'We've got some lovely silk ones, all ruched and trimmed with lace.'

Sophie's eyes lit up and she leaned over the counter. 'Let's have a look.'

Jemima took them from the drawer and laid them out on the counter. Sophie fingered the soft, pink silk. 'My, they're gorgeous. And look at that lovely lace. Are they very expensive?'

Jemima whisked them away before Sophie could snag them on a fingernail and folded them expertly as she had been shown. 'Too expensive for the likes of you and me,' she said briskly.

'Ah, but just you wait,' Sophie said mysteriously. 'One day I might be able to afford cupboards full of lovely things like that.'

'Oh, yes? And how do you think you'll manage that? Not on what Mrs Worsnop pays, that's for sure.'

Sophie leaned her elbows on the counter. 'No, but Mrs Worsnop's got this gorgeous godson. He's been to visit her several times this past year and he's so handsome you wouldn't believe. Makes my heart flutter to even think about him.' She laid her hand where she thought her heart was.

'I think I may have seen him. A young man I'd never seen before came into the shop the other day.'

'That would probably have been Toby. He said he'd been to buy gloves in the town. Didn't you think he was gorgeous?'

'I didn't really see enough of him to judge.' Jemima refused to be drawn further.

'Well.' Sophie looked down at her hands and Jemima noticed that her nails were still quite badly bitten, a childhood habit she had obviously not yet conquered. 'I'll tell you a secret. He likes me. He told me so.' She looked up to see what impression this statement had made on her twin.

'How old is he?'

'Twenty-four. Mrs Worsnop got Cook to make a special cake for his birthday.'

'A bit old for you, don't you think?'

'I'm . . . we'll be seventeen next birthday.'

'Where does he come from?'

'Ipswich. He works in a bank.' She gave a self-satisfied little shrug. 'I quite fancy myself as a bank manager's wife.'

'Oh, Sophie! For goodness' sake! Do you really think Mrs Worsnop's godson is likely to marry her maid? Especially if he's a bank manager,' Jemima said, exasperated.

'I'm not her maid; I'm her companion,' Sophie said huffily. 'And he may not exactly be a bank manager yet, but I'm sure he will be soon. Anyway, I shall be married before you, you see if I'm not.'

'I haven't even thought about getting married,' Jemima said, although this was not strictly true because she fell asleep every night dreaming of what it would be like to be married to Oliver.

'Oh, you're not still thinking of being a dried-up old school teacher, are you?' Sophie said, her tone scathing.

'Yes, I'm saving up so that I can begin my training,' Jemima said, refusing to rise to her sister's bait.

'And what does your mother say about that?'

'She's your mother, too, don't forget. But in answer to your question I don't know. I haven't told her.' She didn't add that she hadn't even seen her since she'd paid that disastrous visit to the shop.

'I haven't told Aunt Minnie about Toby, either. Not that there's much to tell. Yet. But there will be. You'll see.' She pointed to her ring finger. 'I'll have his ring on that finger before another year's out, you see if I don't.' She picked up her purchases and swept out of the shop, the train on her rust-coloured grosgrain skirt swishing as she went.

She had certainly looked very attractive with a rust-coloured hat perched on her dark curls and a tightly fitting black jacket with lapels that revealed a froth of lace at the neck of her blouse, Jemima mused as she cleared the counter and put things away. It occurred to her that perhaps she was not being wise in trying to save nearly all the money she was earning for her training. Perhaps she ought to spend some of it on nice clothes and having a good time. The trouble was, there was nobody she wanted to have a 'good time' with except Oliver and he was away at college. The Peels had invited her to spend Christmas with them two years running and she had hoped Oliver would be there too. But on both occasions he had spent the time with his father – once they had gone abroad to Venice and the other time to the Italian Lakes. It was no wonder he was too busy to write to her and she didn't like to ask Miss Peel about him when she came into the shop in case she thought she was being forward. So she nursed her dreams and continued to read the books Miss Peel supplied her with and looked forward to the day when she would start her training and Oliver would notice that she had grown up and become a woman. A woman he would be glad to have by his side to help him further his own career.

One of Jemima's tasks after the shop had closed was to help Richard unpack and check the things that had been ordered from the Colchester shops and delivered by the carrier's cart. Although anything that was needed quickly could be ordered one day and delivered the next, most things came with the twice-weekly delivery. There was usually a large box from Oswald Went, the gentlemen's outfitters, and another from Annabel's, an exclusive ladies' lingerie shop. The more mundane, everyday items came from the Co-op. Apart from the box from Annabel's, which Jemima dealt with, usually watched over by Mrs Baxter, Richard and Jemima worked together, Jemima ticking the lists as Richard unpacked and put things away on the men's side and the reverse on the ladies' side. It all worked very well and after they had finished – and if there wasn't a big order it often didn't take very long – they would go down to the kitchen and drink cocoa while Dorothy nodded over her knitting in her armchair.

'I won't have any cocoa tonight, Jemma,' Richard said one night as she went over to the stove to begin making it. 'I've promised to go and play at the pub tonight. They've got a bit of a party on. Somebody's birthday, I think.'

She sat down opposite him at the table and cupped her hands around her own mug. 'Not really your kind of music, is it, Richard?' she asked.

He shrugged. 'No, not really. But it earns me a bit of extra pocket money, so I can't complain.'

She smiled. 'A case of "he who pays the piper calls the tune"?'

He smiled back. 'Except when they want to pay me in beer. Customers ask for the latest tunes so they can sing along and then they line pints up along the piano for me. I hate it when they do that because I know that most of them can't afford it. I tell them not to but . . .' He spread his hands. Then he gave a quirky little smile. 'I must say my father has no such qualms. When he's there he drinks my share and everybody else's too, if he gets the chance. Then I have to bring him home and put him to bed because he's incapable of doing it himself.'

'And the next morning, when he's got a head the size of a pumpkin, he swears at you for letting him drink so much,' Dorothy put in from her armchair, where she had obviously been listening to every word.

'That's right, Dolly. You've heard it all before, haven't you?' He yawned and got to his feet. 'I've got a bit more paperwork to do before I go down to the pub so I'd better go and get on with it. Thanks for helping, Jemima. I don't know what I'd do without you.' He gave her shoulder a friendly squeeze as he went through to the office and closed the door.

'He's a good lad,' Dorothy said. 'Shame his father insisted on him coming into the shop and carrying on the family tradition.' She shook her head. 'He never wanted to be a shopkeeper, you know.'

'Yes, he told me that. I never wanted to work in a shop, either,' Jemima said, taking the two mugs over to the sink in the corner. 'I wanted to be a school teacher.'

She stood for a minute with them in her hand, then banged them down on the slop stone so hard that one of them broke. 'And one day, I will,' she said through gritted teeth. 'You'll see.'

Dorothy peered at her over the steel rims of her spectacles. 'I don't know about that, but I can see you've broken a mug,' she said mildly. 'You'll have to replace it, you know.'

★   ★   ★

The following week Sophie was back in the shop again, a parcel of library books under her arm.

'My word, Mrs Worsnop must spend a lot of time reading,' Jemima said admiringly.

'No, it's not that. The old trout says I don't get the sort she likes,' Sophie said airily. She grinned. 'I do it on purpose. I get a couple that I know she'll enjoy and the rest that she won't like so I know she'll send me back to change them. I'd rather do that than sit in a stuffy room learning to play bridge with her and her old cronies.'

'You'll lose your job,' Jemima warned.

'No, I won't. She says I make her laugh,' Sophie said confidently. She leaned over the counter. 'You know those lovely pink combinations you showed me last week? Can I have another look at them?'

'Oh, Sophie. They're not the kind of thing Mrs Worsnop would wear and I'm sure you can't possibly afford them,' Jemima said as she opened the drawer that held them. 'In any case, what would you be wanting with silk combinations?'

Nevertheless, she spread them expertly on the counter in the way Mrs Baxter had taught her.

'How much did you say they were?' Sophie asked, fingering the smooth silk.

'Two shillings and sixpence.'

'Half a crown.' Sophie made a face. 'Haven't you got any cheaper?'

'Yes, we've got cotton ones at two shillings,' Jemima said briskly.

Sophie shook her head. 'No, I don't want cotton.' She looked in her purse, the tip of her tongue poking out in concentration. Then she looked up. 'I can just do it if I borrow sixpence of the old trout's money.' She counted it out. 'There.'

Jemima frowned. 'I don't think you should do that, Sophie. Mrs Worsnop might find out before you can pay it back.'

'Oh, I shan't pay it back. She won't miss it. She doesn't count up what I've spent.' She fingered the pink silk again. 'Oh, yes, they're lovely. I can't wait to put them on.' She nodded impatiently at her sister. 'Well, go on, wrap them up.'

'Sophie you shouldn't do this. It's not right,' Jemima said firmly, making no attempt to wrap the combinations. 'In any case, what do you want pink silk combinations for?'

Sophie scowled. 'It's none of your business. You may be my twin, Jemima, but you're not my conscience,' she snapped. Then she relented and smiled. 'Look, if it'll make you feel better I promise I'll pay her back out of my next week's wages. All right? Now, wrap them up for me. And be quick, there's a dear. I'll get it in the neck if I'm out for much longer.'

Reluctantly, Jemima wrapped them up and Sophie left the shop happily clutching her precious parcel.

Jemima went through to the little sitting room behind the shop, where Mrs Baxter was sitting in her usual place on her sofa, making notes in the latest fashion catalogue.

'What's wrong, dear? You don't look very happy,' she asked, looking up anxiously. Mrs Baxter was glad to leave the running of the shop to Jemima because being on her feet too long exhausted her. But she liked to remain handy in case Jemima needed to ask her advice or if important customers particularly wanted to see her.

'I came through to see if there was anything you needed,' Jemima said, not answering her question.

'Oh, I'd be glad if you'd fill my water jug,' she said. 'And when you've done it you can tell me what it is that's troubling you.'

Jemima went down to the kitchen and refilled the jug. As she got back the shop bell was jangling so she put it down and went through, leaving Mrs Baxter none the wiser as to her problems. It was Miss Peel and her mother who had come in.

'I haven't come to buy anything, I've come to see Elsie,' Mrs Peel said. 'Is she in her sitting room?'

'Yes. I don't think she's feeling very well today,' Jemima said. 'But I'm sure it will make her feel better when she sees you, Mrs Peel. Please go through.'

Miss Peel stayed behind. She hitched herself on to the chair by the counter. 'And how are things with you, Jemima?' she asked, regarding her closely. 'Are you keeping up with your reading?'

'Oh, yes, I read whenever I have the time, Miss Peel,' she replied. 'And when I'm not too tired to take in what I'm reading. It's quite tiring, being on my feet all day. I never seem to get used to it.'

Miss Peel smiled. 'Never mind, it's good practice for you. A school teacher spends a good deal of time on her feet, you know.' Her smile widened. 'I take it you're still keen to teach?'

'Need you ask!' Jemima said fervently. 'I'm saving as hard as I can towards my expenses when I'm training. I don't spend much on myself and I get all my meals free so I'm able to save most of my wages,' she added by way of explanation.

'It's not my business, I know, but do you have to pay your mother anything?' Miss Peel asked tentatively.

Jemima's expression hardened. 'I don't have to pay my mother because I don't live with her. In fact, I don't have anything to do with her.' She paused, then added, 'You may have heard from Mrs Baxter that she came in here and made a scene, asking for my wages, soon after I came here to work. Mr Baxter had to come through and ask her to leave the shop. She hasn't been back since and I haven't been to visit her.'

'Oh, you poor girl.'

Jemima shrugged. 'It doesn't worry me. I often see my sister Daisy. We go for a walk by the river most weeks on my half day. She's got two children now and another on the way. She moved into the cottage next door to my mother when the old lady who had lived there died. She seems very happy.'

'That's good.' Miss Peel paused. 'Oliver is coming to see us next week. I wondered – would you like to come and have tea with us while he's there?'

Jemima coloured. 'Oh, I – yes, thank you. That is, if you think he might like to see me?'

'Oh, I'm sure he would. He always asks after you in his letters.' She got up from her chair. 'Would Thursday suit you? Thursday is your half day, isn't it?'

'Yes, Thursday would be lovely. I'll let Daisy know I shan't be seeing her.'

'Good. About four o'clock, then. Now, I must collect my mother. We've still got shopping to do.'

Seventeen

During the following days Jemima agonized over going to the Peels'
house to tea. Not that she was worried about taking tea with Miss
Peel and her mother; what worried her was that she had nothing
suitable to wear and she didn't want to appear shabby and badly
dressed in front of Oliver. The truth was, for the past three years
she had been single-mindedly saving her wages towards paying for
her training and had paid little attention to buying new clothes for
herself. She had bought a pair of boots when the others wore out
and new underclothes and stockings when the others could no
longer be darned. Other than that, she only had the dark blue
dresses that Mrs Baxter provided for her to wear in the shop and
a single skirt in blue serge and a white blouse, both of which had
seen better days.

She considered waiting until Thursday and then sending a message
to Miss Peel to say that she couldn't come because she was ill but
that was a coward's way out and she didn't consider it for long.
She also wondered if she might borrow a skirt or dress from Sophie,
but Sophie was shorter and fatter – not that those were the words
Sophie would have used to describe herself – and her clothes
wouldn't fit.

There was a pretty green gingham dress in the shop, which Jemima
liked very much. It had dark green ribbon at the neck and three
bands of the same ribbon round the hem of the skirt, which was
gored with pleats at the back. Jemima had a tiny waist and she knew
the dress would look well on her. But she was reluctant to dip into
her savings to buy it.

'Why don't you borrow it for the afternoon?' Mrs Baxter asked
when she saw her looking at it for the umpteenth time.

'Oh, no, I couldn't do that!' Jemima said, horrified. 'I might spill
something on it.'

'Very well. What's it marked up at?'

'Fifteen shillings,' Jemima said wistfully.

'Well, you can have it at cost. Can you afford ten shillings?'

Jemima still looked doubtful, thinking of the hole it would make
in her savings.

'It would look very well on you. Especially if I made you a little green hat to go with it for nothing. How about that?'

Jemima couldn't resist such an offer. 'Yes. Oh, thank you, Mrs Baxter. That would be lovely.'

'Good. Now, I'll make a list of the bits I'll need for the hat and you can try on the dress.' Elsie Baxter was more animated than Jemima had seen her for some time and in no time at all she created a perky little hat out of green gingham, dark green ribbon and buckram with a spray of artificial lily of the valley nestled in the crown.

On Thursday afternoon, wearing the dress and with the little hat worn tipped over one eye as Mrs Baxter said it should be, Jemima set off for Miss Peel's house. As she left Richard was just getting on his bicycle to go for a ride.

'My, you do look pr . . . nice,' he said admiringly and the look in his eyes, a look she had never seen there before, made her blush. 'You must be going somewhere special.'

'I'm going to tea with the Peels,' she said.

'Ah, your school teacher friends.'

'That's right.' She didn't add that it was only special because Oliver would be there.

It was three years since Jemima had seen him and Oliver had changed quite a lot. He was a man now, his dark hair was cut quite short and he had a substantial moustache. To Jemima he seemed somehow bigger – he had clearly put on a little weight – and even his voice was deeper; his presence seemed to fill the little room. But his deep-set brown eyes still held the same twinkle and when he smiled his teeth were still a little crooked, just as she remembered. He was just as handsome, too.

He was wearing a smart brown tweed suit and before they sat down to tea he asked his grandmother's permission to take off his jacket, revealing a fawn waistcoat with a gold chain through a button-hole attached to a watch in the left-hand pocket. To Jemima's admiring eye he looked every inch the prosperous schoolmaster and she had to make a conscious effort not to keep looking at him.

But as tea progressed, with cucumber sandwiches, followed by crumpets and Jemima's favourite biscuits, she forgot to be shy and the conversation flowed just as it used to in the old days. Most of the talk was of schools and teaching, which made Jemima even more impatient to save enough money to begin her own training.

Oliver made them laugh with stories about his days at college and his first days as a 'proper' teacher, as he called it.

'Oh, I was very green,' he said with a laugh. 'But I've learned. I keep a cane on my desk and the children know I won't hesitate to use it.' He leaned back expansively in his chair and stuck his thumbs in the armholes of his waistcoat.

'Not too often, I hope, Oliver,' Miss Peel said, keeping her voice light although there was a hint of warning in her tone.

'Oh, no. Not too often,' he replied, smiling at her.

Jemima had prepared her answer for when Oliver asked her how her training was progressing, as she was sure he would. Obviously, she couldn't tell him the truth, that their last meeting in the church-yard had been totally misconstrued so her mother had refused to allow her to begin teaching, because she wouldn't want Oliver to feel in any way to blame. Neither would she want him to think she regarded their friendship as being anything more than just that, friendship. So she had intended to brush the question off with an airy, 'Oh, I thought it best to wait until I was a bit older and had a bit more experience of the world before I began teaching.'

But to her surprise he didn't mention it.

He did, however, apologize for writing to her so seldom.

'I'm sorry, Jemma, I'm always meaning to write, but there's so much else to do, so much studying, that there's never time. And I'm a very bad correspondent, you know.'

'You don't need to apologize, Oliver. I didn't expect you to have time to write to me,' she lied. 'I know what it's like because I'm busy, too.'

'Yes, I daresay your studies keep you occupied. And no doubt Aunt K keeps you up to date with my exploits. I write to her every week. Well . . . er, most weeks,' he modified his words.

All too soon it was time for her to leave. Fortunately, Oliver didn't offer to accompany her home so she didn't have to go into long explanations as to why she was living at Baxter's. As she walked home she couldn't help thinking that Oliver had changed. He was so full of his new life, so anxious to tell them all that he'd been doing that he hadn't actually asked her anything at all. Perhaps Miss Peel had already told him her circumstances, or perhaps he simply assumed she had begun her training.

If only it were true, she thought with a sigh.

She went down the passage beside the shop and let herself in at the garden gate. Richard was there, in his shirt sleeves and looking slightly grubby, with his bicycle upside down on the grass.

'I got a puncture and had to walk home,' he said ruefully. 'And then I had to find out where the hole was and mend it. It's taken me hours.' He pushed his hair back, leaving a greasy streak, and smiled at her. 'You still look very smart and pretty so I guess you've had a pleasant afternoon. I like your dress, Jemima, it brings out the green flecks in your eyes.' As he said the last words he turned away and bent over his bicycle again, embarrassed.

She went indoors. Richard was a nice man, she reflected, taller and slimmer than Oliver and of course not so handsome although he had good teeth and a nice smile. She crossed the kitchen deep in thought. Oliver had seemed very worldly wise and confident; he appeared to know exactly what he wanted and how to get it. She recalled the way he had pressed her hand when she left. Was it a message? She rather thought it might be.

'My word, you're looking very pretty today, Jemima. Is that one of our dresses? I seem to recall seeing it in the shop window. I hope you haven't spoilt it, dear. Do make sure and press it before you put it back.'

She turned. Frank Baxter was standing in the doorway to the office, leaning against the door post. She had never liked the man since he tried to catch her out on the day she applied for the job, although she had to admit she had been glad of his presence when her mother had made a scene in the shop. Nevertheless, she still avoided him when she could. This was not usually very difficult since he rarely came into her department.

'It's my dress. I didn't borrow it, I paid for it, Mr Baxter,' she said coolly as she reached the door to the stairs. 'You can ask Mrs Baxter. It was she who suggested I might like to buy it.'

'Ah, that's all right, then.' He sat down at the kitchen table. 'Sit down, Jemima. You're not in a hurry, are you?'

She turned back. Was he going to tell her that her work wasn't satisfactory? As she passed him she caught a whiff of spirits on his breath. Six o'clock on a Thursday afternoon and he had already been drinking.

Gingerly, she sat down opposite to him, glad the table was between them.

'Dorothy's gone to see her sister,' he said, his words very slightly slurred. Remembering her mother's drinking days she realized that either he was only slightly drunk or he was very practised at concealing it. 'An' Elsie's resting. Elsie's always bloody resting these days; I dunno what's the matter with the woman.'

'She's not very well,' Jemima said. 'You know the doctor says she's got a bad heart. But she's got other problems, as well, poor lady. I thought you knew about that.'

'How would I know?' he said with a shrug. 'She doesn't tell me anything, these days.' He leaned his elbows on the table and wagged his head at her and she realized that he was indeed quite drunk. 'Doesn't let me into her bed, you know. Not any more.' He lifted his hands. 'Wassa man to do? A man's entitled to his con . . . conju . . . con-ju-gal rights.'

She got to her feet. 'You shouldn't be talking to me like this, Mr Baxter,' she said firmly. 'What goes on between you and your wife is really no concern of mine.'

She made for the door to the stairs but to her consternation he lumbered to his feet and made to follow her. 'You're looking so pretty today I thought you might be nice to me, Jem . . . Jemima,' he said, his voice perilously close to a whine.

'Then you're quite mistaken, Mr Baxter,' she said, keeping the door closed and her back to it. 'And if you come a step closer I shall call Richard.'

He gave a lascivious grin. 'You'll have to shout very loud, then. Richard's out on his bike.' He took a step towards her as he spoke.

'That's where you're wrong, you drunken old sot. Richard was in the back garden and heard every word you've been saying.' Richard stalked in and went straight over to his father and with surprising strength got hold of him by the collar and hauled him through to the office.

'Stay there, I'll be back in a minute,' he called over his shoulder to Jemima, then just before he slammed the door, she heard him say furiously to his father, 'Where did you get it from this time, you disgusting old bugger?'

Jemima sat looking out at the tubs of geraniums, trying to keep her mind off what had just happened. Dorothy had made the area quite pretty, with geraniums all the way up the steps to the garden, and she noticed absently that one of them had been knocked over. She realized that Richard had probably taken those steps two at a time when he heard his father's words. She didn't want to imagine what might have happened if his bicycle hadn't had a puncture. She twisted her hands together; they were still shaking.

She got to her feet and lit the gas under the kettle. Perhaps a cup of tea would make her feel calmer. She was just pouring it when Richard came back, looking more dishevelled than ever, his face still thunderous.

'Oh, yes, please. Pour me one, too. I feel in need of it.' He slumped down in the chair his father had vacated ten minutes earlier. 'I'm really sorry about that, Jemima,' he said.

'Does he often get drunk?' she asked, trying not to let the cup rattle on its saucer as she gave it to him.

'Too often,' he replied tersely. 'I've stopped going to the pub to play the piano because he used to drink the beer they insisted on giving me. But he's always really preferred spirits.' He gave a sigh. 'It's a real problem.'

'Does your mother know?' She held her cup to her lips and hoped he wouldn't hear it rattle against her teeth.

He shook his head. 'I think it would kill her if she found out. She knows he has "headaches". She thinks it's migraine.' He put his elbows on the table and ran his hands through his hair, which was already standing on end. 'I often think I'd like to escape; I never wanted to go into the business in the first place, as you know, but he said it was my duty and Mum backed him up. Now it's me that runs the bloody thing because he's precious little help.' He put his hand out and took Jemima's. 'I really don't know how I'd manage without you, Jemima,' he said. 'Especially now Mum's ill, too.'

She let her hand lie in his for a few seconds and then drew it away under the pretext of picking up her cup. This was not what she wanted. Working at Baxter's was a means to an end, not an end in itself. And she certainly didn't want Richard to fall in love with her.

'You know I'm only working here to save up money for my teacher training, don't you, Richard?' she asked gently, anxious that he shouldn't harbour false hopes.

He gave her a quirky smile. 'I thought you might grow to love . . .' He hesitated. '. . . Like working here so much you'd change your mind about that,' he finished.

'No, it's always been my ambition to become a school teacher,' she said firmly.

'It was always my ambition to get a living with my music,' he told her, 'but things don't always work out the way you expect.' He paused. 'Or hope.' He paused again. 'Or want them to,' he added, his voice bleak.

She got to her feet. 'Dorothy will be back soon. I'd better go and change my dress so that I can help her cook dinner,' she said, putting an end to the conversation.

He nodded and did the same. 'I'd better make sure there are no more bottles hidden in the office and then get on with the interminable paperwork.'

'I believe it's liver and onions tonight. Your favourite.'

'That's something to look forward to, anyway,' he said without enthusiasm.

Jemima went upstairs and took off the green dress and hung it carefully in her wardrobe. It had been quite an eventful afternoon, she thought as she put on her old dress to go and help Dorothy. After such a pleasant and stimulating couple of hours with Oliver at the Peels' house the encounter with Mr Baxter had been an unpleasant shock. What might have happened if Richard hadn't been there didn't bear thinking about. Poor Richard, she felt so sorry for him; he was making the best of being trapped in a life he hadn't chosen. But pity was not enough. She wasn't in love with him, although she had the feeling that he was in love with her and she was quite sure that if she had shown him even the slightest encouragement this afternoon he would have proposed to her. But then she would be just as trapped as he was.

Eighteen

Before she went downstairs again Jemima pulled the tin box from under her bed and counted her savings. The money for the green gingham dress was the most she had taken from it in the three years she had worked at Baxter's. Of course, there had been money for shoe repairs and darning wool and she'd had to buy new stockings when her old ones couldn't be darned any more. In the end she'd had to buy new knickers too, although not until she was ashamed of the old ones, and not until there was a cheap offer in the shop. Even then she had begrudged one and sixpence a pair for them. But she couldn't find it in her heart to regret spending ten shillings on the lovely green dress even though it had made a hole in her savings.

She found a pad and pencil. She wouldn't be able to rent a room in Colchester under at least three shillings a week, more if she didn't want to live in a slum, then she would have to buy food, candles for lighting, probably her own crockery and perhaps furniture . . . And she would have to buy more clothes; she couldn't stand in front of a class of children looking poverty-stricken and down-at-heel and the green dress wasn't at all suitable for the classroom. Her earnings as a pupil-teacher would be five shillings a week to begin with, plus what she had saved. She divided the money in the box into three because it would take three years as a pupil-teacher before she became a fully fledged school teacher with a proper wage. It was a pathetically small amount for all the expenses it would have to cover.

With a dejected sigh she replaced the money and put the tin back under the bed. Maybe another year? She would give herself until she was eighteen. Surely by that time she would be able to manage if she didn't spend any of her earnings. Maybe if she did extra work Mrs Baxter would give her another rise. But what extra work could she do? She was running the ladies' department practically single-handed as it was. What Mrs Baxter would do when she left to begin her teaching Jemima couldn't begin to imagine. She knew she would have to give her plenty of warning so another girl could be trained to take her place but it would be a long time before she could rely on anyone else the way she relied on Jemima.

Another year. A year to try to keep well out of Frank Baxter's way; to make sure she was never anywhere alone with him. She shuddered. She couldn't bear the thought of risking another fiasco like that afternoon's. What she would have done if Richard hadn't come to her rescue didn't bear thinking about. Richard. There was another problem. She must gently try to discourage him from falling in love with her. She would hate to disappoint him if he was harbouring hopes that she might marry him.

She was sure she could cope with all that. After all, forewarned was forearmed and it was only for another year. She could almost begin to count the days. And she had almost forgotten! At the end of her first year's training she would receive a ten-pound grant if she passed all her exams! And another, bigger one each subsequent year of training. How could she have forgotten something so important!

Feeling much more optimistic, she looked in the mirror to tidy her hair. It was thick and blonde and she had taken to wearing it waving back and then twisted into a loose bun on the top of her head. A few wisps had escaped and as she pushed them back into place she examined her features. Her eyebrows arched smoothly over her unusual hazel-and-green eyes. She put her head on one side. She would never be beautiful, not even pretty like Sophie – her mouth was too wide – but her nose was well-shaped, she had good teeth and her skin was smooth.

She stood back in contemplation. 'In a year's time you'll make a very good school teacher, Jemima,' she said to her reflection. Then she hurried downstairs to the kitchen.

The summer wore on into autumn. Frank Baxter seemed as anxious to avoid Jemima as she was to avoid him and she guessed he was ashamed of his behaviour, which suited her very well. As Christmas approached the shop was busy with people coming in for gifts, both small and large, for their loved ones. Jemima had decorated the shop with bunches of holly that Richard had gathered from the woods and he had also managed to find a small Christmas tree to put in the window. She had discovered some tiny red candles in a drawer and she had clipped these to the branches and hung little imitation parcels wrapped in brightly coloured paper. She also scattered a few of the little parcels among the other items displayed, giving the whole window a festive look. As she worked she recalled the Christmas she had spent with the Peels when Oliver was there, the ambitions she had cherished and the presents they had exchanged.

She still had the book Oliver had bought her, *Treasure Island*. She kept it with her few treasures, including his letters. He hadn't written to her for quite a long time now. Probably, he still thought of her as a schoolgirl. He would get quite a surprise the next time he saw her, of that she was sure.

She wouldn't be buying many presents this year. Just a small toy for each of Daisy's children – she would gladly spare the money for them from her savings. She had promised to go to Daisy's for Christmas Day because it would avoid the embarrassment of spending the day with the Baxters, who had also invited her, though it was plain from the way Elsie Baxter had worded her invitation that she would prefer it if Jemima went elsewhere. The possibility of having to kiss Sam Starling under the mistletoe was a risk she had to take.

In the event she had a pleasant day. Amy loved the picture book and Charlie was delighted with the tiny toy engine she had brought them and there was a new dress for the baby. She was relieved to see that Daisy and Sam were still very happy together and even more relieved that Sam made no attempt to lure her to the sprig of mistletoe hanging in the doorway.

'I think I'd better warn you I've invited Mum and Mr Starling for the day, as well,' Daisy said a trifle anxiously. Then she smiled. 'Sam won a bottle of sherry at the works' sweepstake, so a glass or two of that should help things along.'

'Don't worry. I shan't make trouble if she doesn't,' Jemima assured her breezily, suppressing the feeling of apprehension that was making her stomach churn uncomfortably at the thought of confronting her mother again after all this time.

At first, Eva ignored Jemima completely but Mr Starling was very chatty, asking her how things were going at Baxter's and whether she was happy there and telling her how he had re-decorated the front room for her mother. At that Eva thawed a little towards Jemima, mainly because she was anxious to let her know she had also got a new suite of furniture – 'settee and armchairs, none of your old second-hand rubbish' – and after that the day went well, largely due to an unspoken agreement between them to bury the hatchet on this one day of the year so as not to spoil Daisy's enjoyment.

But they both knew it wasn't buried very deep and it wouldn't have taken much to dig it up again.

On Boxing Day Jemima had been invited to Aunt Minnie's. Of course, Uncle William was there and so was Sophie. Aunt Minnie, red-faced from working in the kitchen, had cooked a turkey with all the trimmings, which Jemima tried not to contrast with the rather scrawny chicken she had tried not to eat too much of the day before, knowing that Daisy would hope to make it last at least a week.

'Oh, it's just like old times, having the two of you at the table,' Aunt Minnie said, beaming at her two nieces as she handed round dishes of vegetables.

'They're both working girls now, matie, they can't come and go as they please,' Uncle William said. He looked at the twins, so totally unlike each other, sitting one at each side of the table, and he smiled happily. 'But it's right what your aunt says; it's nice to see the pair of you sitting at the table.' He held out his plate. 'I'll have a bit more of that bread sauce, matie, if you'll pass it down. That's one thing I'll say for you, you know how to make good bread sauce.'

'And batter pudding. And roast potatoes,' Jemima said, helping herself to a few more.

'That's right, dearie, you tuck in. You're still as thin as a rake,' Aunt Minnie said with a broad smile. She liked nothing better than having her cooking praised. 'Don't they feed you at Baxter's?'

'Oh, yes. I eat very well,' Jemima assured her with a laugh. 'But I'm on my feet all day so I don't have time to get fat.'

'Not like this one here.' Aunt Minnie looked fondly at Sophie. 'She's getting as fat as butter. Look at her.'

'Yes, I shall have to stop helping myself to the old trout's chocolates,' Sophie said ruefully.

'Oh, Sophie, dear, you shouldn't call Mrs Worsnop the old trout, it's not respectful,' Aunt Minnie admonished her.

'Oh, I don't say it to her face,' Sophie said with a laugh. 'She's not a bad old stick, really. And Toby, her godson, is *very* nice.'

'You watch your step, my girl. The likes of him won't look twice at a girl in your position,' Aunt Minnie warned. 'He's almost Gentry.'

'Well, he doesn't act like it,' Sophie said.

After the meal was finished and the two girls had helped Aunt Minnie with the washing-up they played silly parlour games for an hour before it was time to leave.

'Would you like to walk back a little way with me, Jemima?' Sophie asked as the door closed behind them. 'I've got something to tell you.'

'Yes, of course I will.' Jemima linked arms with her sister. 'Well, what have you got to tell me?'

Sophie hugged Jemima's arm to her. 'Did you notice the locket and chain I was wearing tonight, Jemma?'

'I could hardly miss it, the way you kept fiddling with it,' Jemima said with a laugh. 'I thought it was pretty.'

'The chain is real gold, you know. It's hallmarked. And the locket is gold, too.'

'Oh, yes. You'll be telling me it's set with rubies next.' Jemima obviously didn't believe her.

'It's true. It is.' Sophie paused. 'And Aunt Minnie was wrong when she said Toby wouldn't look twice at me because he gave it to me as a Christmas present.' She stopped and turned to Jemima. 'There, now. If that isn't a declaration on his part I don't know what is,' she said triumphantly.

Jemima looked doubtful. 'Has he asked you to marry him, then?'

'No, not in as many words, but you don't give presents like my locket to just anybody, do you?'

'No. Not unless . . . Sophie, you don't . . . You haven't . . .?' Jemima tried to search her sister's face in the darkness.

'Don't be silly. I don't know what you're talking about,' Sophie said quickly, proving she knew very well what Jemima was trying to say. 'Look, I'm nearly home now. I can see a light in the window. You needn't come any further.'

Jemima stopped. 'All right, then.' She wanted to say more, to warn her, to ask her more about Mrs Worsnop's godson, but she didn't want Sophie to think she was prying. Or preaching. So all she said was, 'Goodnight, Sophie.'

'Goodnight, Jemma,' Sophie said cheerfully. 'And don't worry about me. I know what I'm doing. Next time you see me I'll be wearing a ring, you see if I'm not.'

It was probably true, Jemima thought as she turned and made her way back the way she had come. Sophie always managed to fall on her feet.

The gas lamps cast yellow pools on the pavements, plunging the spaces between the pools into even blacker darkness. As she passed the Greyhound pub the door opened, letting out a shaft of light, a roar of tuneless singing and a young man fumbling with his clothing before relieving himself against the wall. He didn't even notice Jemima. But she wasn't nervous at being out on her own in the dark; she was too busy with her thoughts.

She wasn't jealous of Sophie's good fortune – it wasn't in Jemima's nature to be jealous of her twin – but sometimes she couldn't help feeling that life was a little unfair. Everything that had happened to Sophie, from being taken to live with Aunt Minnie almost the minute she was born, to her job at The Anchorage – although working for Mrs Worsnop could hardly be called a job because she never had any actual work to do – had happened without any particular effort on her part. And now it looked as if she could be in line to marry a prosperous man, a man who would no doubt be even more prosperous when his godmother died.

By contrast, Jemima had never been loved and cherished like Sophie, and it seemed that however hard she worked to achieve her aims, there was always something standing in her way. But she was the thirteenth child, as her mother had never tired of reminding her, so what more could she expect?

Nineteen

Nevertheless, Jemima started the New Year on an optimistic note even though the weather was miserable, damp and rainy. She was humming happily to herself as she put things away in drawers and tidied shelves in the shop one rather bleak Monday morning in early February.

'You're sounding very cheerful, despite the weather, Jemima,' Mrs Baxter said, smiling at her. 'But there, your smile always manages to brighten up dull days. I really don't know what we'd do without you.'

This was one of Elsie Baxter's better days. She didn't lace herself in quite so tightly these days and consequently her health had improved somewhat although she had to rest quite a lot as her heart still gave cause for concern.

Jemima came down the ladder she had climbed to put back a drawer holding silk camisoles. 'That was something I wanted to discuss with you, Mrs Baxter,' she said, smoothing down her dress in a gesture she hoped didn't look like nervousness.

Mrs Baxter raised her eyebrows. 'You're going to ask for a rise in wages?' she asked with a touch of humour. 'Well, I'm sure we could come to some arrangement . . .'

'No, it's not that, Mrs Baxter,' Jemima said quickly, although afterwards she felt she might have been a bit hasty, since extra money, even for a short time, would have been useful. 'It's . . . well, it's that . . .' She took a deep breath and began again. 'When I came here to work three years ago you may remember that I told you I had wanted to train as a school teacher but my mother refused to allow me to do that.'

'Mm. I've always wondered why,' Mrs Baxter mused. 'I think you would have done very well.' She gave Jemima an affectionate smile. 'But teaching's loss was our gain so I've no cause for complaint.'

'I've never given up that dream, Mrs Baxter,' Jemima went on. 'And I've been saving most of the money I've earned so that I shall be able to support myself, along with the money I'll be earning as a pupil-teacher, while I am training to become a proper teacher with a proper wage. By the time I reach my eighteenth birthday I believe I shall be able to manage to do just that.'

'And how much would you be earning as a pupil-teacher?'

'Five shillings a week and the training is for three years.'

'Hm. And when is your birthday? I've forgotten.'

'The thirteenth of May.' Jemima leaned towards her. 'If you advertised for someone to take my place now I would have nearly three months to train her and show her how you like things done. You trained me, Mrs Baxter, but your health now is not as good as it was then and you might not . . .' Her voice trailed off as Mrs Baxter leaned her head in her hand and reached for her smelling bottle.

'Oh, I could never cope with teaching another girl,' she said faintly. She looked up and said with a trace of petulance, 'Oh, Jemima, why do you want to leave us? I thought you were happy here. I was even beginning to hope that you and Richard . . .'

'I have been . . . I *am* very happy here,' Jemima said firmly. 'But my ambition has always been to become a teacher and if I leave it much longer it will be too late. Girls often begin training at fourteen, you know.'

'Yes, I know, I know.' Mrs Baxter waved her hand impatiently. 'I'll have to think about it, Jemima, before I decide what's to be done. It's been rather a shock, you springing it on me like this.' She struggled to her feet. 'Help me back to my room, please. I think I must lie down for a while.'

Jemima helped her back and settled her on her sofa with her smelling bottle and sal volatile before going back into the shop. She had known Mrs Baxter would react like that, which was why she had put off telling her as late as she could. Life was very pleasant for Elsie Baxter now that Jemima had taken all the responsibility of the shop from her. She could lie on her sofa for most of the day if she felt like it, making no attempt to do anything to help. Her health was not good, Jemima was quite ready to concede that, but she sometimes felt that a little more interest and assistance in the ladies' department would help rather than hinder her employer's perceived problems.

Jemima had also known for some time that Mrs Baxter cherished fond hopes that she would marry Richard, thus anchoring them both to the shop. She realized, too, that it would take very little to encourage the same hope in Richard. So she was very careful to keep their relationship from developing into anything beyond being friendly but businesslike.

Life would be so much less complicated when she could leave and begin her new life. She began to count the days.

A week later Sophie came into the shop with the usual bundle of library books under her arm. She bought three yards of knicker elastic, then said, 'It's your afternoon off today, isn't it?'

'That's right. Mrs Baxter has to manage on her own on Thursday afternoons. She doesn't like it much, I can tell you.' Jemima handed her tuppence change. 'Why?'

'Can you come up to The Anchorage? Askew's gone off to see her sister so I can make you tea in the kitchen.'

'Thanks, I'd like that.' This was a rare but not unheard-of occurrence; Jemima had been three or four times since Sophie had lived there and only when the housekeeper was away so they could have the kitchen, which was warm and comfortable, to themselves.

After Jemima had eaten a quick lunch, she put on her dark blue serge skirt, the only one she had, and a white blouse with a high collar and frill down the front. She had bought it at half price in the shop because it had been returned as unsuitable with a dirty mark and two buttons missing, but after washing it and replacing the buttons it was as good as new. She wanted to look her best in case this was to be the day she was to meet Toby, Sophie's potential fiancé. She wondered how long it would be before the engagement was made official.

She put on her woollen cloak, which Mrs Baxter had given her because she was tired of it, and a small hat with a feather and hurried up the road smiling to herself. Sophie wasn't the only one with good news; now that she had made up her mind to leave Baxter's and start her training she looked forward to sharing her plans for the future with her sister. It was strange that momentous changes should be in the offing for both of them at the same time, she mused, but after all, they were twins, so perhaps it was not so surprising.

She went round to the back of the house and Sophie opened the door and led her through to the kitchen. It didn't look nearly as comfortable and inviting as the kitchen at home, as she now thought of the Baxters' house. In fact, it looked quite bare, with a high ceiling holding a laundry rack on a pulley, and a stone floor. A long scrubbed table stood in the middle of the room. But shining copper jelly moulds and saucepans on the dresser and warmth from the large kitchen range at one end made the room seem slightly less austere.

'This is nice,' Jemima said as Sophie took her cape and hat and told her to sit in the large Windsor chair beside the stove.

'Yes.' Sophie glanced at the big round clock on the wall, its brass weights and pendulum gleaming from years of polishing. 'I'll make a cup of tea. The old trout won't want hers yet so we'll have time to drink ours before I have to take hers up.' As she busied herself with the kettle and teapot and getting down cups and saucers Jemima noticed that her movements were jerky and nervous and her nails were bitten down to the quick.

'Are you all right, Sophie?' she asked with a frown.

Sophie smiled, a little too brightly. 'Yes, of course I'm all right. Why shouldn't I be?'

'I don't know.' Jemima gave a shrug. 'You seem a bit nervy, that's all.' She watched as Sophie poured the tea, spilling some of it into the saucer and on the table.

'Oh, damn.' She fetched a cloth and wiped it up. Then she put a plate of cakes on the table and sat down opposite Jemima.

They sipped their tea and ate a cake each in silence, then Jemima said, keeping her voice light, 'I was convinced you'd asked me up here today to tell me you were engaged, Sophie.'

Sophie made a face. 'No, I'm afraid that's not likely to happen,' she replied, her voice brittle. 'I've discovered he's just got engaged to someone else.'

'Oh, Sophie!' Jemima stared at her twin. 'But I thought you said . . . Oh, how dreadful for you. Were you very much in love with him?'

Sophie stared out of the window, biting her lip to keep from bursting into tears. 'Yes, I am . . . I was. He was in love with me, too. At least, I thought he was. I was quite sure he intended to marry me.'

'Did he say so?'

She shook her head. 'Well, no, not in as many words,' she admitted, speaking slowly. Her words speeded up. 'But he came here as often as he could so that we could be together. Even the old trout said he was visiting a lot more than he used to. She thought it was because she's not been very well and he wanted to make sure she left him plenty of money in her will. But I thought he came because he wanted to see me. But I guess she was right; he was after her money.'

'How did you find out he was engaged?'

'The old trout . . .'

'I wish you wouldn't call her that; it's disrespectful. And one of these days you'll say it to her face,' Jemima interrupted with a touch of irritation.

'No, I won't. I always call her madam. Anyway, she had a letter from him today to say he'd got engaged and would be bringing his future wife to see her next week. Silly old fool is already making plans for a party to celebrate.'

'So you'll be meeting his fiancée. How do you feel about that?'

Sophie shrugged; she couldn't trust herself to speak.

A sudden thought struck Jemima. 'Sophie, you didn't . . . I mean he didn't . . . You didn't let him . . .' She couldn't bring herself to voice her fears.

Sophie nodded, not looking at her sister. 'I didn't intend to, Jemma,' she said wretchedly. 'But . . . well, it just happened.' She sniffed. 'He apologized afterwards, can you believe it?' She turned her head away. 'And I was fool enough to tell him it didn't matter, that I was glad. That was when I thought we were going to be married, of course.'

'How many times did you . . .?' Jemima hesitated, embarrassed. 'Just once?'

'Twice.' Sophie's voice was barely above a whisper. She looked up. 'Only twice, Jemma.'

Jemima heaved a great sigh. 'That's twice too many times. You just want to thank your lucky stars he hasn't made you pregnant, that's all I can say.'

Sophie got up from her chair and went and stood looking out of the window. 'That's just it. He has,' she said quietly.

Jemima closed her eyes briefly. 'Oh, my dear Lord. Now what? How far gone are you?'

'About three months, I think.' She turned back and looked at Jemima. 'I thought it didn't matter because we were going to be married anyway and I kept waiting for him to name the day. But he didn't.' Her voice dropped. 'Then this letter came today saying he was engaged to be married.'

Jemima nodded towards her sister's stomach, which she could now see had a very slight bulge. She sighed. 'So, what are you going to do?'

Sophie spun round. 'I don't know, Jemma. I thought you might be able to think of something,' she said, desperation in her voice.

'Well, I suppose you'll have to go to Aunt Minnie. I'll come with you, if you like.'

'Oh, no, I couldn't do that,' Sophie said, horrified. 'She always said she'd turn me out if I brought trouble home, so it's no good going to her.'

'It's worth a try.'

'No, it wouldn't be right. She's been so good to me all my life; I couldn't do that to her, I just couldn't.' She began to cry.

Jemima watched her. She was glad to see that Sophie had appreciated Aunt Minnie's love and care even if she had never before shown it. 'Well, you could try Mum,' she suggested without much hope.

'What, your mum?'

'She's yours as well.'

'It's never seemed like it. I've never lived with her, how could I expect her to take me in?'

'Well, what about Daisy? She's already got three so one more wouldn't make much difference.' Even as she spoke Jemima realized this was unfair to Daisy.

Sophie obviously thought so, too. She shook her head without speaking.

'Well, I don't know who else might take you in,' Jemima said with a sigh.

'Could I come and live with you?' Sophie asked in a small voice.

Jemima looked at her with a mixture of surprise and alarm. 'Oh, Sophie, no, of course you couldn't. I live over the shop. My room is a little attic bedroom. There wouldn't be room for the two of us, let alone a baby. Not that the Baxters would allow it. They'd probably turn me out for even daring to ask.'

'I thought you'd say that,' Sophie said, as if it was all Jemima's fault. 'Well, then I shall just have to go away where nobody knows me.'

Jemima digested that for several minutes. She couldn't think of a better plan so she said, 'Have you got any money?'

'A bit.'

'How much?'

'Two pounds.'

'That's not going to get you very far, is it?'

Sophie shrugged. 'Can you lend me some?'

Jemima hesitated. She had saved nearly enough to begin her training but could she use it for that when Sophie was in such dire need? How would she feel, spending money to achieve her own selfish ambition when her sister might be starving or roaming the streets with nowhere to live? Even worse, suppose she had to resort to selling her body . . . She realized with a sinking heart that she had no choice.

'Are you good with money?' she asked, her voice short.

Sophie shrugged. 'Not very.'

'Well, if I give you some money you've got to promise me you'll open a Post Office account and only use enough for your needs every week. Because what I give you is going to have to last you for more than just a few months, you realize that, don't you? You'll need money for lodging as well as food and things for the baby.'

Sophie frowned. 'How much have you got, then?'

'Ten pounds.'

'Ten pounds!' Sophie's jaw dropped.

'Yes. I've been saving hard so that I could start my training as a teacher. I reckoned I'd got enough so that I could begin after my birthday this year.' She gave a weary sigh. 'But you're my twin, and you're in trouble. I couldn't live with myself if I thought I hadn't helped you out, so you'd better have it.'

'Do you really mean that, Jemma?' Sophie said eagerly. There was no hint of regret for the sacrifice Jemima was making on her behalf.

Jemima nodded. 'When you've made your plans you'd better come to the shop and ask me for it.' She gave a wry, mirthless smile. 'You'd better not leave it too long or I might change my mind.'

Sophie went and put her arms round her. 'Oh, thank you, Jemma. I always knew I could count on you.'

Jemima extricated herself from Sophie's hug and fetched her cloak. She didn't want to stay in her sister's company any longer. She was furious with her for being such a stupid little fool and she felt sick with disappointment because, through Sophie, all her own hopes and dreams had been dashed. For the second time.

Twenty

Jemima wept as she counted out her precious savings for Sophie. Then she went to meet her at the railway station as they had arranged.

'Now, you promise you'll write and tell me your address as soon as you find somewhere decent to live,' she said as she handed the money over.

'Oh, I will, Jemma. I promise,' Sophie said fervently as she kissed her and got on the train to Colchester. But something in her attitude, in the way she had clung to her until the train was on the point of leaving, gave Jemima an awful feeling that she might never see her sister again.

She watched the train steam out with a heavy heart, then went to break the news to Aunt Minnie. She had tried and tried to persuade Sophie to go herself, had even offered to go with her, but Sophie had refused, insisting that it would be no use.

Jemima suspected Sophie was too ashamed to face the woman who had lavished so much love and care on her over the years.

As usual, Aunt Minnie was pleased to see her and busied herself brewing tea and buttering scones, chattering inconsequentially so she didn't notice that Jemima hardly spoke. Jemima drank her tea gratefully and managed to eat a scone to please Aunt Minnie although she had no appetite for it. It was not until after a second cup of tea that she found the courage to impart the news that she knew would shatter their lives.

Fortunately, Uncle William was at home. There had been gales raging in the North Sea and he was sufficiently comfortably off now to no longer be forced to go and fish in all weathers. He sat in his chair, puffing on his pipe and listening intently to what Jemima was saying.

Aunt Minnie began to cry. 'Oh, my poor lamb, she should have come home,' she sobbed when Jemima had finished speaking.

'What? And bring shame on this house after all we've done for her?' Uncle William said furiously, gripping the arms of his chair till his knuckles showed white. 'Not if I know it! We gave that girl a good home and brought her up to know right from wrong and this is how she's repaid us. You warned her. You always told her you wouldn't stand for loose living and I agreed with you. I'm not having you change your mind now she's got herself into trouble, Minnie Furlong. She should have paid heed to what we said.' He knocked his pipe out on the hearth and put it back in the rack. He had never been as blind to Sophie's faults as his wife, although he had never expected anything like this. 'Oh, no, Minnie, she's not coming back here. She's done wrong and she'll have to abide by the consequences. That's all I have to say on the matter.' He leaned back in his chair and closed his eyes.

'But how will she live, Jemma? I don't suppose she's got any money,' Aunt Minnie said anxiously.

'She's got enough to tide her over,' Jemima said enigmatically.

'I expect he – whoever "he" is – has given her money to salve his conscience,' Uncle William said, his voice full of disgust.

Jemima said nothing.

Aunt Minnie leaned towards her. 'She did promise she'd send you her address, didn't she?' she whispered, with one eye on her husband.

Jemima nodded.

'That's all right, then.' Aunt Minnie folded her arms across her ample bosom, nodding smugly. 'As soon as I know where she is I'll fetch her home.'

Uncle William's eyes shot open. 'That you will *not*, Minnie Furlong,' he said in a voice Jemima had never before heard him use to his wife. He banged his hand on the arm of the chair. 'You heard what I said, I'm not having trouble brought home to this house and that's my final word. You've been too soft with that girl all along.'

Aunt Minnie gathered up the cups and took the tray out to the scullery. Jemima followed with the remains of the scones.

'There's ways and means,' Aunt Minnie whispered, tapping the side of her nose. 'Just you let me know when you get her address. At least I can go and see her and see she's got everything she needs.' Her eyes filled with tears. 'Whatever your Uncle William says I shan't sleep easy in my bed till I know she's not in need.'

'I'll tell you as soon as I hear,' Jemima said. But, just as she had feared, Sophie never wrote.

Back in her little attic room Jemima stared into the empty tin where she had stored her money and her dreams. She had been so very near to achieving her goal; she had even begun composing a letter in her mind to the local school to ask if there would be a position for her next term so that she could begin her training. It was the second time now that her hopes had been dashed and her ambitions thwarted. She threw the tin on to the floor and flung herself on the bed and stared up at the ceiling, too miserable even to cry. Maybe she should give up trying; maybe it was never her destiny to become a school teacher, in spite of all her efforts. Maybe she should just resign herself to a life spent measuring out knicker elastic and selling vests and combinations, avoiding Frank Baxter and pandering to his wife. It was a bleak prospect compared with the hopes she had cherished for so long.

Of course, she could have refused to help Sophie. She could have told her she had made her bed so she would have to lie on it. But Sophie was her twin. Even though they had not really been close over the years the bond was there and it was not in Jemima's nature to turn her back on her sister's need. Whether Sophie would have acted in the same way was a question Jemima didn't consider.

When Jemima told Mrs Baxter she wouldn't be leaving after all she was so delighted that she immediately put up her wages, which Jemima found slightly ironic. She didn't tell her employer the real reason she was staying, she simply said that she had changed her mind because she enjoyed working in the shop. It said a lot about Elsie Baxter that she was so pleased to think her life wasn't going to be disrupted now that she had got so used to having Jemima at her beck and call that she didn't even notice how quiet and withdrawn the girl was becoming as she went about her work.

But Richard noticed.

'You're very quiet these days, Jemima, and you look rather pale. Is there anything wrong?' he asked one evening after the shop had closed. He was checking the order that had come by carrier that day as she ticked off the items on the delivery sheet.

'No,' she replied brightly. 'Everything's fine. Was it a dozen stiff collars size fifteen?'

'No, half a dozen. And half a dozen size fourteen.' He straightened up and looked at her, frowning anxiously. 'Are you quite sure you're all right?'

'Yes. Really. Now, what were you saying? Half a dozen . . .' She bit her lip as tears blinded her and she couldn't see what she was writing. She shook her head. 'No, I'm not all right, Richard. Nothing's fine. Everything's just awful.' Tears began to roll down her cheeks and on to the invoice.

'Hey, hey, this is not like you, Jemima.' He took her hands and pulled her to her feet. 'Now, are you going to tell me what's wrong?'

he asked anxiously. 'Is it something here, in the shop? Is it my pa? Surely, he hasn't been trying . . .'

'No, no, it's nothing to do with your father,' she said quickly, shaking her head. 'It's my sister . . .' It all came tumbling out as she told him exactly what had happened and how she had given all the money she had been saving for her training so that Sophie would have enough money to live on. 'The trouble is, although I feel sorry for Sophie I'm angry with her because I've had to give her my money. All ten pounds of it. It had taken me years to save that much,' she added woefully. She glanced up at him. 'I shouldn't feel angry with Sophie, should I? Not when she's in so much trouble.'

'You wouldn't be human if you didn't,' he said wryly. He shook his head. 'Oh, Jemma. I'm so sorry. I know just how much you wanted to teach. I wish I could help. I haven't got much money, but if there's anything else . . .'

'No, there's nothing,' she said quickly, trying to pull herself together. 'It's my own fault. I shouldn't have been so ambitious, I can see that now. A girl from Brown's Yard thinking she could become a teacher . . .' She sniffed. 'It was a stupid idea.' She looked up at him and managed a watery smile.

'It wasn't a stupid idea at all. You'd be quite capable of doing it.' He wiped a tear from her cheek with his thumb, smiling down at her, his brown eyes full of compassion. Then, very gently, he put his arms round her and pulled her to him. When she didn't resist he bent his head and very gently kissed her on the lips. To his surprise she didn't immediately pull away, her mouth moved under his and her arms tightened round him.

'I really didn't intend to do that,' he said shakily when at last he lifted his head.

'It was probably my fault for weeping all over you,' she said with an apologetic little smile. 'I'm sorry.'

'Oh, don't be sorry, Jemima, it gave me an excuse to do what I've been wanting to do for a very long time,' he said. He put up his hand and gently smoothed a strand of hair from her forehead, then bent his head and kissed her again, very long and hard. 'I love you, Jemma,' he said when he eventually released her, resting his cheek on her hair. 'I think I've loved you ever since the day you came here to work, a determined little fourteen-year-old. But I knew what your ambitions were so I didn't think there was any chance that you could ever think of me as anything . . . well, as anything at all, really.'

She didn't say anything for a long time but stood within the circle of his arms, resting her head on his shoulder. It was a comfortable place to be, a place where she felt she would always be safe and cared for. She sighed. It would be so easy to stop fighting, to bow to what Fate clearly had in store for her, to forget teaching, and to forget Oliver, who anyway seemed to have forgotten her.

She lifted her head. 'Richard, I . . .'

He put a finger on her lips. 'Don't say anything.' He turned a little away from her. 'I'm sorry, Jemima, I shouldn't have told you how I feel when things are at such a low ebb for you. It was stupid and selfish of me to let my feelings run away with me like that. You've got quite enough on your mind at the moment without me unburdening myself to you.' He was clearly embarrassed.

She caught his hand again. 'No, it's all right, Richard, really it is. I didn't mind. What I mean is . . .' She put her fingers to her temples. 'Oh, dear. I don't know what I'm saying. I'm sorry, I can't think straight at the moment.'

'I understand, Jemma. Please, just forget what I said.'

She shook her head. 'No, no, I don't want to forget, Richard. It was the nicest thing anyone has ever said to me.' She shook her head again. 'But you must give me time . . . I need to think.'

A smile spread across his face. 'Oh, Jemma, you can have all the time in the world, if you think I might have a chance . . . That you might consider becoming my wife . . .'

She was quiet for a minute, thinking. Then she said, 'Ask me again on my birthday, Richard.'

'When's that?'

'May. May the thirteenth. That's three months away.' She looked at him and nodded. 'I promise I'll give you an answer then, Richard.'

'In the meantime, will you walk out with me sometimes?'

She smiled. 'Yes, of course I will. Whenever you like.' She put up her hand and touched his face. 'And thank you, Richard. Whatever my answer is, thank you for asking me.'

Twenty-One

Jemima hardly slept that night; her thoughts were in too much of a turmoil. She couldn't imagine thinking of Richard as anything other than a good friend. He was kind and thoughtful, a gentleman in every sense of the word; he was hard-working, too, and he took his not inconsiderable responsibilities very seriously. Jemima knew how he covered up for his father when he was too drunk to be seen in the shop – she knew, too, that this was happening more and more often. And he was endlessly patient with his mother, who, as Jemima had grown to realize, was a consummate actress, playing on her illnesses to gain sympathy; sitting on her chair in the shop looking pale and wan one minute and then bustling about looking busy when anyone she wanted to impress came into the shop.

It was all very difficult for Richard. But he was never going to set the world alight; he was not forceful, dynamic, the way she remembered Oliver. Richard was not given to complicated philosophical discussions; rather he was a practical, down-to-earth man.

Yet it had felt so comforting, so safe, standing in the circle of his arms with her head on his shoulder. It was almost as if she had come home. And she had liked his kisses. She had never been kissed like that before and it had awakened sensations in her she had never before experienced. Even the memory of them sent a tingle through her.

But could she face a future tied, as Richard was, to his dysfunctional parents? And was she prepared to spend the rest of her life measuring out elastic and ribbons and selling women's lingerie and hats? Did she want to become trapped, as Richard was, in Baxter's Ladies' and Gentlemen's Outfitters?

On the other hand, what else could her future hold? By the time she had managed once again to save up enough money to break free, would she then be too old to be considered for a three-year training period? Was she prepared to take the risk of having her hopes dashed for a third time?

Then again, if she didn't marry Richard – and if she turned him down she could hardly remain working at Baxter's – and if she had given up all hope of becoming a teacher, what then?

With these thoughts going round and round in her mind she fell at last into a troubled sleep, only to dream of Sophie, dirty and dishevelled, crouched in a shop doorway. She put out a hand to her but Sophie ignored it and stood up, heavily pregnant, and walked away without a word. Jemima watched her disappearing into the distance and woke calling her sister's name, her face wet with tears.

As Jemima had feared, it wasn't many days before Daisy came into the shop trailing her brood of children with her. She leaned over the counter.

'Why didn't you come and tell Mum that Sophie's run off?' she whispered accusingly. 'You went and told Aunt Minnie.'

Jemima frowned. 'Well, Mum doesn't exactly welcome me with open arms, does she? And anyway, Sophie'd lived with Aunt Minnie for nearly eighteen years, so she was more of a mother to her than our mum ever was.'

'You should still have come and told us.' Daisy was obviously aligning herself with her mother. 'You'd better come round tonight.' She hesitated. 'Is it true she took all Mrs Worsnop's jewellery when she left?'

'No, it isn't,' Jemima said furiously. 'Where did you get that tale from?'

Daisy shrugged. 'It's what people are saying. She must have got money from somewhere, to go off like that.'

'You shouldn't listen to gossip.'

'You'd better come and tell us the truth, then.' Daisy turned away. 'Charlie, leave that! You'll have all them hats on the floor.' She turned back to Jemima. 'Will you come tonight?'

Jemima nodded. 'Yes, I'll be round when I've finished here. About seven o'clock.'

Eva and Mr Starling, as well as Daisy and Sam, were all sitting round the kitchen table like members of the Inquisition when Jemima arrived.

'Where are the children?' Jemima asked, surprised to see both Daisy and her husband.

'They're in bed and asleep. They're only next door so we shall be sure to hear them if they cry,' Daisy said complacently.

'Come and sit here beside me, Jemima,' Mr Starling said, fetching her a chair, since nobody else had bothered. 'Would you like a cup of tea?'

'She hasn't come here to drink tea, she's come to tell us what's happened to Sophie,' Eva snapped, glaring at her.

'I would like a cup of tea, please, Mr Starling, since you ask,' Jemima said, looking at him gratefully. 'I've come here straight after finishing a long day's work; I'm tired and I'm hungry because I didn't wait to have my supper before I came. I knew I wouldn't be here long,' she added for her mother's benefit.

Eva didn't move so Daisy got up and made the tea and put some biscuits on a plate.

'They've got to last all the week,' Eva said.

'It's all right, I'll only have one,' Jemima answered, knowing the remark was aimed at her.

'You have as many as you want, dearie. I can always get some more from the shop,' Mr Starling said, pulling the plate towards her.

Eva glared at him.

'Well?' she said, as she watched Jemima bite into a custard cream. 'What's this about Sophie running off with all Mrs Worsnop's jewellery?'

'I'm sure that's not what Aunt Minnie told you,' Jemima said, finishing her biscuit and discovering that Mr Starling had surreptitiously put another one in her saucer.

'No, all Minnie could do was weep all over me and tell me her little girl had run away,' Eva said in a tone of disgust. '*Her* little girl, indeed. Anybody'd have thought she was the one that gave birth to her.'

'Well, it's about the only thing she didn't do for her,' Jemima wanted to reply, then bit her tongue. She hadn't come here to antagonize her mother. 'But it's true, Sophie has gone away. I saw her off on the train to Colchester. Where she was going after that I don't know and neither did she.' She bit her lip against threatening tears.

'Why did she do that?'

'Where did she get the money?'

'Why did she leave a good job with that old lady?'

'Why didn't she say where she was going?'

'When's she coming back?'

The questions were fired at her across the table so fast that Jemima didn't know which of them had asked what. She held up her hand.

'I'll tell you what I know. Sophie came to me because she was in trouble . . .'

'You mean in the family way?' Eva said, aghast.

Jemima nodded and held up her hand as the questions began again. 'It seems she thought the man intended to marry her but apparently he's recently become engaged to someone else. That's all

I know about him. She insisted on going away where nobody would know her. What her plans are, if she has any, I don't know.'

'If she didn't pinch the old girl's jewellery, what's she going to do for money?' Sam asked. 'She can't live on air. Unless . . .'

'I gave her money,' Jemima said quickly, seeing the direction Sam's thoughts were leading. 'I'd been saving up to start my training and I'd just about got enough, I thought. But I reckoned she needed it more, so I gave it to her.'

'How much did you give her, if I might ask?' Mr Starling said.

'All I had. Ten pounds.'

'Whew, thass a lotta gold,' Sam said admiringly.

'I know it is. It took me three years to save it,' Jemima said.

'So what will you do now, dearie?' Mr Starling asked, more concerned for Jemima than her sister.

Jemima shrugged. 'I haven't decided yet.'

'Well, I should think you'll give up any idea of this teaching lark,' her mother said, waggling her shoulders. 'I never did hold with it. Getting ideas above your station.'

'I haven't come here to discuss what I'm going to do. I came to tell you what I know about Sophie.' Jemima got to her feet. 'Well, now you know pretty well as much as I do, so I'll go.'

'Thanks for coming, Jemma.' Daisy accompanied her to the door. 'You'll let us know if you hear any more, won't you?'

'Yes, I'll let you know.'

Jemima went home more depressed than ever.

The following Sunday afternoon she went to see Miss Peel and take back the books she had lent her.

In stark contrast to the welcome, or rather the lack of it, she had received at her mother's house Miss Peel greeted her warmly and invited her into the cosy cluttered living room Jemima remembered with such affection.

'Thank you for bringing them back, my dear. But you should have kept them a while longer. They could be useful to you when you begin your training. Have you decided when you are going to start?'

Her expression changed from eager optimism through concern to disappointment as she listened to Jemima's story, a carefully edited version of the truth, which left out the vital fact that Sophie was pregnant.

'I'm surprised your sister was willing to take all your money,' Mrs Peel remarked from her usual seat by the window.

Jemima shrugged. 'She needed it more than I did. I was just glad that I could help her.' She smiled bravely at them both. 'I was obviously never destined to be a school teacher.' She shrugged again. 'Silly, really, a girl from Brown's Yard, the poverty-stricken end of the town, imagining she could ever become a school teacher.'

'Don't be silly.' Mrs Peel put her knitting needles down. 'It's not where you come from that's important, Jemima, it's what use you make of your God-given talents. Kathryn's father was a shoemaker and I was a cook but we still encouraged her to go to college and achieve her ambition because we knew she was clever enough to do it.'

'Ah, but you see, that's the difference, Mama. Jemima's got no father and her mother gives her no encouragement at all. I was lucky to have you and Papa behind me and I appreciate it.' Miss Peel smiled affectionately at her mother.

Mrs Peel nodded, acknowledging her daughter's words, then she looked at Jemima over the top of her spectacles. 'I still think it's a pity you're giving up so easily, Jemima. You're a clever girl.'

'I'm not giving up easily, believe me, Mrs Peel,' Jemima said with a break in her voice. 'I'm giving up because I can't see any alternative.'

For once she was glad to leave the Peels' house.

As the weeks went by it became a habit for Jemima and Richard to spend Sunday afternoons together. Sometimes they went for a walk by the river, sometimes they went the other way and walked into Colchester to look round the shops. Occasionally, he would take her to the Theatre Royal to see a play or a variety show, which she really enjoyed.

She liked going into Colchester because there was always the chance of seeing Sophie and it became second nature to her to keep her eyes peeled for her sister. Of course, she had no way of knowing whether or not Sophie had stayed in the town but she couldn't help glancing down every side street and alley that she passed in the hope she might catch a glimpse of the familiar dark, curly hair.

'Why do you keep torturing yourself, looking out for your sister, Jemima?' Richard said one day when he caught her craning her neck to see down a narrow alleyway. 'And don't deny it. I know that's what you're doing.'

'I just want to find her. To know if she's all right,' Jemima said with a sigh.

'If she wanted you to know, she'd write to you,' Richard said gently. He took her hand and gave it a little shake before releasing it. 'Don't you think you've done enough for Sophie, Jemima? More than enough, I'd say.'

She bit her lip. 'She's my twin. I can't give up on her.'

'I know, dear.' It wasn't often Richard allowed himself an endearment. He put a guiding hand under her elbow and said briskly, 'Come on, we'll take a walk in the Castle Park. It's a lovely day and you never know, there might be a band playing. We can sit on the grass and listen while we watch the people go by.'

She looked up at him. 'You're very kind to me, Richard,' she said gratefully.

'I'd like to be a great deal more than kind to you,' he said quietly, without looking at her. 'Just don't keep me waiting beyond your birthday, Jemima.'

'No, I won't.' She didn't tell him she still hadn't made up her mind what to say to him. The worrying thing was, her birthday was less than two weeks away.

Twenty-Two

A few days later Aunt Minnie came into the shop.

She sat down on the chair provided for customers and absent-mindedly ordered two yards of Petersham ribbon, twisting her bag in her hands all the time.

'What's the matter, Auntie? Is something wrong?' Jemima asked, measuring the ribbon and cutting it to length, then expertly winding it round her hand and putting it in a paper bag.

'No, no, dear. Nothing's wrong,' Aunt Minnie said, fumbling for her purse. 'Have you heard from Sophie?' she asked without looking up, her voice muffled beneath the hat laden with flowers, fruit and feathers that she had obviously trimmed herself.

'No, Auntie, I haven't,' Jemima said.

'Neither have I. I thought by this time she might have written . . . might have let us know . . .' Her voice trailed off. She looked up. 'I go into Colchester on the train at least once a week, looking for her, you know. But I never see her,' she added bleakly.

Jemima nodded. 'I look for her as well, every time I go. But she might not be there any more, Auntie. She could be anywhere.'

'I know. That's what your Uncle William says. But I can't help it, I have to keep looking.' She dabbed her eyes with a spotless lace handkerchief. 'I do so worry about her, Jemma.'

'I know, Auntie. So do I. I'll let you know the minute I hear anything.'

She watched her aunt leave the shop. She looked just a little more stooped, a little less ample and her hair under the hideous hat had a few more grey streaks in it. She looked the picture of dejection, even from the back.

'Oh, Sophie,' Jemima breathed a silent message to her wayward twin. 'Have you any idea what you're doing to this dear old lady?'

Jemima's birthday dawned on a sky of cloudless blue. She got up and dressed with mixed feelings, remembering the birthdays she had spent with Sophie at the parties Aunt Minnie had tried so hard to make into really special occasions, particularly for Jemima, because she knew that jelly and thin bread and butter were never served in Brown's Yard, let alone cake. But Sophie had never appreciated Aunt Minnie's efforts; she had always found something to complain or be grumpy about. The truth was Aunt Minnie had spoiled Sophie from birth, indulging in her every whim. But Jemima knew that it was only because she loved her so much and wanted the best for her. And now she was suffering for it. Sometimes Jemima almost hated her twin for what she was doing to Aunt Minnie.

Nevertheless, Sophie was still her twin sister and she couldn't help wondering how she was spending today, their shared eighteenth birthday, alone and six months pregnant. But there was no way of finding out.

Resolutely putting thoughts of Sophie to the back of her mind she went downstairs to begin her day's work. Richard was just unbolting the front door to the shop.

'Many happy returns of the day, Jemima,' he said, straightening up and smiling at her.

'Thank you, Richard.'

'Today you'll give me your answer?' he asked hopefully.

She nodded. 'But not right here and now,' she said with a smile.

'No, of course not. After work we'll take a walk by the river where it's cool and we can talk.'

'That'll be nice.' She turned away. She already knew what her answer would be, but only because she could see no alternative. She would marry Richard and spend the rest of her life selling ladies' underwear. The prospect didn't excite her, even though she was quite fond of Richard. Not that he was a man to sweep a girl off her feet and carry her off to his palatial country house in rolling parkland, but then what man was? Heroes like that only happened in books by Jane Austen and Charlotte Bronte, never in real life. She gritted her teeth. There were a few more hours of freedom to be savoured before she committed herself irrevocably to a life chained to Baxter's Bloody Outfitters.

'There were a couple of cards and an interesting-looking package pushed through the letterbox for you, Jemma.'

She turned back. 'I beg your pardon, Richard? What did you say?'

'I said there are a couple of birthday cards for you. I've put them on the side there.'

'Oh, thanks.' She picked up the cards. There was one with a picture of Miss Peel's garden, which she had clearly painted herself. On the back, in neat copperplate writing, it said, 'Many happy returns and good wishes for the future, whatever it may hold. From Kathryn and Gertrude Peel.'

'Oh, wasn't it nice of them?' She handed Richard the card.

'Yes, indeed. They obviously think very highly of you, Jemma.' He grinned. 'Not that I blame them for that.'

She flushed a little and picked up the other card. It looked expensive; the front was embossed with a spray of yellow pansies and blue forget-me-nots tied with a pink ribbon. Inside it said, in Richard's distinctive hand, 'To Jemma, All my love, always, Richard.'

Her eyes filled with tears. 'Oh, Richard, that's lovely,' she said. 'You're so kind.'

'Oh, I want to be more than that,' he said, with an attempt at lightness, which failed miserably. 'Well, what about the package? I expect it's a birthday present. Come on, open it. It looks intriguing.'

She frowned. 'I can't imagine who'd be sending me a birthday present,' she said, puzzled. Then she caught her breath. Could it be that Oliver had remembered her birthday? She wasn't sure he even knew when it was. And it wasn't very likely, since he didn't even bother to write to her now. With hands that were not quite steady she undid the string. It had been wrapped around a large brown envelope that was folded over and over again. 'Whoever wrapped this up didn't intend the contents to fall out,' she said with a little nervous laugh. She put her hand into the envelope and pulled out a small tobacco tin. 'What a funny thing . . .' She gave it a little shake. 'It's quite heavy and it rattles. Whatever can it be?'

'Well, go on, open it and you'll find out,' he said eagerly, nearly as excited as she was.

She opened the lid and her jaw dropped in amazement. 'Look, Richard. Look, it's money. Sovereigns!' She sat down on a nearby chair. 'Someone's given me a tin of sovereigns. I can't believe this.' She shook her head from side to side. 'Who on earth would give me all this money?'

Richard came over. 'There must be a note somewhere to say who they're from.' He picked up the envelope and looked inside. 'No, there's nothing in here.' He smoothed it out on the counter. 'Ah, look, something's written on the envelope. It says, TO JEMIMA FROM A WELL-WISHER.' He turned it over. 'That's all. Nothing else. Strange, isn't it? Do you recognize the writing?'

Frowning, she studied the envelope, then shook her head, still bemused. 'No, I don't. I don't understand it at all. There must be some mistake . . .'

'It can't be a mistake. It's got your name on it.'

'But I can't imagine who would give me all this money . . .'

'How much is it?'

'I don't know.' She stared down at the tin in her hand.

He gave her shoulder a little shake. 'Well, come on, aren't you going to count it?'

'Oh, yes, I suppose so.' She tipped the golden coins into her lap and counted them back into the tin one by one. Then she looked up. 'There are ten,' she said incredulously. 'Ten pounds. That's exactly the amount I gave Sophie. Exactly the amount I'd saved for my training.'

'That narrows it down, because it must have come from somebody who knew that,' he said.

She thought for a minute, then shook her head. 'But I don't know anybody who's *got* that much money, let alone could afford to give it away,' she said, staring down at it. She looked up at Richard, her eyes wide with anxiety. 'And how can I thank them if I don't know who they are? But they'll think me ungrateful if I don't say anything. And another thing, Richard, should I accept it?'

Richard smiled at her. 'I reckon if whoever it is wanted thanks they would have signed their name.'

She nodded uncertainly. 'Yes, I suppose you're right.'

'By the same token, if you don't know where it's come from how can you return it?'

She smiled at him. 'Oh, Richard, you're so wise.'

'Just common sense.' He pointed. 'So what are you going to do with it?'

'I think I'd better take it up to my room and put it safely away until I decide.'

But of course, she already knew.

It was a little difficult telling Richard that evening as they were walking by the river, but she realized that it was no more than he had expected.

'You don't have to explain, Jemma,' he said, laying a finger on her lips. 'You've been given the chance to follow your dream. It's what you've always wanted. Take it.' He took his finger away and kissed her lightly on the lips. 'With my blessing.'

'Oh, Richard.' Her eyes filled with tears, because she knew what the words had cost him. 'I'm so sorry to disappoint you.'

'Let's not talk about it any more.' He took her arm. 'I think there are still some primroses in the wood. Come on, let's go and find them so I can pick you a birthday bunch.'

Lying in bed that night, with a huge posy of primroses standing on her chest of drawers, reminding her by their scent of cool damp woods, she was torn by conflicting emotions. At one moment she was so excited that she thought she would never sleep because she could, after all, achieve her dream; at the next she felt a sense of sadness and even guilt because she had been unable to give Richard the answer he had hoped for. She knew how much she had disappointed him, although he had valiantly tried to hide it under cheerful and bantering conversation.

Her thoughts turned to the tobacco tin, hidden safely in her underwear drawer. Who could have given her so much money? It was the exact amount she had saved and then given to Sophie. She ran through all the people she knew, both likely and unlikely. Most of them, like her mother and Daisy, had probably never even possessed one sovereign, let alone twenty. And given the choice, her mother wouldn't even bother to give her the time of day. Aunt Minnie and Uncle William? She could believe Aunt Minnie would like to repay her generosity towards Sophie, if she had the money. But although they were quite comfortably off now, she and Uncle William were not rich. Miss Peel? Miss Peel wasn't rich, either. In any case, had she told her exactly how much her savings had amounted to? She couldn't remember. She tried to recall the conversation with Miss Peel and her mother, but all she could remember was Mrs Peel's insistence that she should not give up hope. Mrs Peel. But why should Mrs Peel give her money?

Yet the more she thought about it the more likely it seemed that Mrs Peel had been the anonymous donor. Her remarks, her insistence that Jemima was giving up too easily, telling her she was a clever girl and that she should make the most of her God-given talents – it all added up. And the Peels appeared quite comfortably off, as far as Jemima could tell.

She resolved to go and see them as soon as she could, to tell them the good news – as if they didn't already know! – and to let them know she would begin her training after all. She was sure she would be able to tell from their reaction whether her guess was correct.

Twenty-Three

The reaction at the Peels' house was not at all what Jemima had expected. She had expected to see knowing nods and winks passing between them, instead of which both Miss Peel and her mother were genuinely surprised and delighted at her news and had no idea who the anonymous benefactor might have been. They even tried to hazard a guess themselves as to who it might be.

'Well, I can't think of anybody else,' Mrs Peel said at last, when they had exhausted all the likely and unlikely people. 'It's all a mystery.' She smiled at Jemima. 'But a wonderful thing for you, my dear, whoever your anonymous benefactor might be.'

'And whoever it is, they obviously wish to remain anonymous, so we shouldn't waste any more time speculating. So, let's get down to practicalities,' Miss Peel said briskly. 'Now, you mustn't waste any time in applying for a position at school. You have to apply to the Chairman of the Governors, that's Mr Felgate. There's no doubt you'll be accepted, of course; Mrs Childs, as head teacher, is always consulted on new appointments and I know she hasn't forgotten what a good monitor you were. And it's more than likely you'll be able to begin straight away because we're short of a teacher since Miss Grant left to get married at Easter and has gone to live in Manchester.' She clapped her hands. 'Oh, it's all very exciting, isn't it?'

Her excitement was infectious. 'I'll write to Mr Felgate tonight, as soon as I've given my notice in to Mrs Baxter,' Jemima said, her eyes sparkling. 'Then the next thing will be to look for somewhere to live. Obviously, I shan't be able to stay at the Baxters' house when I'm not working there, and I wouldn't want to go home to my mother's . . . Not that she'd have me.' She thought for a minute, then said, as if it was the least of her worries, 'Oh, I'm sure I'll be able to rent a room somewhere in the town for not too much money.'

She didn't see the almost imperceptible nod Mrs Peel gave her daughter before Miss Peel said, trying to keep her voice casual and failing in her eagerness, 'You could always come and live here, with us, Jemima. We've got a spare room now that Oliver has gone.'

'You could pay us a small rent to retain your independence,'

Mrs Peel added, equally enthusiastic. 'And it would be so convenient for you, because Kathryn would be on hand to help you with
your studies, should you need her.'

'And you wouldn't have to borrow my books, you could just
help yourself,' Miss Peel said.

They both looked at Jemima expectantly.

Jemima's eyes lit up, yet she hesitated. 'It's really very generous of
you, but I wouldn't want to impose on your kindness . . . You've
already done so much for me,' she said at last.

'Nonsense,' Mrs Peel said. 'What's a few cups of tea and biscuits?
We'd be delighted for you to come here to live, wouldn't we,
Kathryn?'

'Indeed we would,' Miss Peel said warmly. 'We enjoy your
company.'

It was quite obvious they meant what they said.

'Then thank you very much, I'd love to come and live here,'
Jemima said, beaming at them both.

Miss Peel accompanied her to the door when she left. 'If you're
coming here to live I think you'd better start calling me Kathryn
when we're at home,' she said. She put her hand on Jemima's arm.
'I'm so glad you're coming to live with us. Apart from anything else,
it will give Mama a bit of pin money, because she has no money
of her own. Of course, she doesn't need it, living here with me, but
it will be good for her to have a few shillings to call her very own.'

Further proof, if she needed it, that Mrs Peel couldn't possibly
have been responsible for the money in the tobacco tin.

The next few weeks were very busy. Even so, Jemima kept looking
for signs that might give her some idea as to who the anonymous
donor might be and every night she wracked her brains, going over
everybody she knew, even down to Daisy and Sam, who she knew
perfectly well hadn't got two farthings to rub together; but she ended
up none the wiser. She even had the fanciful notion that Sophie
had somehow landed on her feet with a rich man who had insisted
she return the money Jemima had given her. But when she thought
about that idea more carefully she realized it had rather dubious
implications so she quickly rejected it.

But one thing was certain: it wasn't Mrs Baxter. She was tight-
lipped with disapproval when Jemima handed in her notice and she
made herself quite unpleasant to Lillian, the young girl who was to
replace her.

'Don't worry, she'll come round in a day or two,' Jemima assured her when she found Lillian weeping into a drawer of silk stockings. 'I'm afraid she's taking it out on you because she's cross with me for leaving. Once I've gone she'll be all sweetness and light, you'll see. Particularly when she finds out how efficient you are.'

'But I'm not efficient, that's the trouble. I put lisle stockings in with silk ones. That's why she's so cross with me,' Lillian wailed.

'Well, you've got a lot to learn. You won't get everything right straight away,' Jemima said, giving her a quick hug and smiling at her. 'I did stupid things when I first came here but I soon got the hang of it all. There, now, you've sorted the stockings – you won't make that mistake again, will you? And you've put the camisoles in the top right-hand drawer under the counter?'

Lillian nodded. 'And the woollen combinations in the next one down and the silk combinations in the bottom drawer. Oh, aren't those silk ones pretty? I wish I could afford them.'

'Maybe you will, one day. Now, on the left-hand side what have you got?'

'Vests in the top drawer, bust improvers in the second drawer and nightgowns in the bottom. Corsets are in the big drawer behind the counter and drawers and petticoats in the ones next to it. Ooh, I've never seen such frilly drawers before, some of them . . .'

'Yes, well never mind that. And make sure you never, ever speak outside this shop about the kind of underwear ladies buy. Sometimes you will be quite surprised at who buys what but you must never comment on it. Do you understand?'

'Oh, yes, I quite understand, Jemima.' But Lillian's eyes were dancing in anticipation about the secrets she might learn.

'I'm not for one moment suggesting anything scandalous,' Jemima said quickly, at which Lillian's face fell.

Richard was not impressed with Lillian.

'She's not very quick,' he said to Jemima as they took a Sunday afternoon stroll along the sea wall. 'And she keeps forgetting to write up the order book.'

'Well, she's only sixteen, give her time,' Jemima said. 'She's having to learn quite a lot in a very short time, remember.'

'You were only fourteen when you came to us,' Richard reminded her.

'I know. But I was desperate. I didn't want to end up at the fish factory.' She pinched her lip. 'You know, your mother doesn't help. She gives the poor child no encouragement at all, just keeps giving exasperated sighs when she gets things wrong.'

Richard looked at her with a half smile. 'You shouldn't be leaving us, you know, Jemima. You're throwing the whole place into turmoil. I don't know how any of us will manage without you. Especially me,' he added under his breath.

She picked up his hand and squeezed it. 'I'll come and see you sometimes, Richard.'

His face brightened. 'Will you? Promise?'

'Of course I will, silly.' To cover the unexpected lump in her throat she grinned and added, 'My unmentionables won't last for ever and where else would I buy them?'

When the time came to leave Baxter's, Richard carried her few belongings to the cottage in Park Road and left her at the gate with a brief kiss on the cheek and murmured, 'Good luck, Jemma. I hope you'll be happy.'

She flung her arms round his neck. 'Oh, I'm sure I shall, Richard. But I shall miss you, really I shall.'

He extricated himself deftly. 'Well, I'm not far away if you ever need me,' he said, deliberately keeping his voice light. Then he turned and left her and didn't look back.

For a few moments she felt quite bereft as she watched him walk away. It was as if he was abandoning her to her fate. Then she gave herself a mental shake. It was a fate she had chosen for herself, not a fate he would ever have chosen for her.

She picked up her bag and walked up the garden path at 'Sparrows' to begin her new life.

Kathryn and her mother gave her a warm welcome and both came with her to show her to her new room. This was a very feminine room, all yellow and white, with lace mats on the dressing table, flowers on the window sill and a patchwork quilt on the bed. There were woollen rugs on the polished floor and the furniture was all in matching light oak, which gave the room a light and airy look.

'We've put a small table under the window in case you want to work up here, where it's quieter,' Kathryn said.

'But most of the time you'll work downstairs, I daresay,' her mother added quickly. She sniffed the air. 'Can you still detect the smell of Oliver's cigars, Kathryn? I got Mr Simons to come and redecorate the room to get rid of it but I fancy it still lingers. What do you think?'

'I can't smell anything,' Jemima said, although the question hadn't been directed at her. She was quite disappointed. A lingering smell of cigars would have reminded her of Oliver. 'I think this is a beautiful room. Thank you, both.' On impulse she kissed each of them in turn.

'Oh, one thing I forgot to tell you,' Kathryn said. 'I'm afraid there's no gas up here. We make do with candles or oil lamps in the bedrooms. Mama wouldn't have gas upstairs because somebody told her it wasn't safe, although I'm quite sure it is.'

'I was told of a whole family who died in their beds while they were asleep because of escaping gas,' Mrs Peel said with a shudder. 'I didn't want that to happen to us.'

'Of course it wouldn't, Mama,' Kathryn said with a touch of impatience. 'Gas is quite safe.'

'Well, I would never have been able to close my eyes for fear of it,' Mrs Peel said emphatically.

'I'm quite happy with candles,' Jemima said, before the discussion could turn into an argument. 'It's what I've always been used to.'

Two days later, Jemima began her teaching career.

Mrs Childs, the head teacher, remembered her work as a monitor and appointed her to work with standard one children, seven-year-olds who were in their first year in the Junior part of the school.

'You will instruct them in Arithmetic, English, Geography, History and Music,' Mrs Childs told her. 'These are the books you will use to instruct them from.' She handed Jemima a pile of rather dog-eared text books. 'When the children practise their handwriting they can fill up the page one way and then turn it on its side and write over what they've already done. You understand, we have to be mindful of waste but at seven years old they must begin to learn to use pencil and paper.'

Jemima bobbed a tiny curtsy and turned to leave.

'Oh.' Mrs Childs peered at her over small gold-rimmed spectacles. 'I forgot. Of course, you will be expected to teach the girls needlework. Can you sew?'

'Yes, I can sew.' She could darn her stockings and sew a button on and she was sure Mrs Peel would teach her any fancy stitches she might need.

She hurried off to her classroom, offering up a quick prayer to Someone – she wasn't quite sure who – that she would manage to control a class of twenty-five children just out of infants. As she entered the classroom the smells she remembered so well assailed her nose: unwashed bodies and urine, overlaid by the smell of disinfectant and the stifling smell of chalk.

Ah, it was good to be back.

Twenty-Four

The days flew past. Each day, after the register had been called, the children all stood beside their desks to participate in a compulsory exercise commonly known as 'drill'. This was a system of bending and stretching exercises designed to keep them fit and healthy and only lasted for about five minutes. The girls went through the motions with varying degrees of reluctance and apathy despite Jemima's efforts to instil a bit of enthusiasm, but most of the boys enjoyed it.

After this, they filed into the hall for morning prayers with the rest of the school. Here, they sang a hymn, which Miss Peel accompanied on the piano, then knelt on the hard wooden floor while Mrs Childs said a prayer, and they all joined in with the Lord's Prayer. After that they filed back to their respective classrooms to begin the day's work.

It didn't take Jemima long to discover who were the brightest, which ones were downright lazy and which of them struggled with even the simplest concepts. There were also a few who liked nothing better than to disrupt the class. She soon learned how to deal with them.

More difficult to deal with was a girl called Millie Carter, who she discovered was the young sister of Lillian, the girl who had taken Jemima's place at Baxter's. She was a thin, sharp-featured child, much given to whispering behind her hand to her desk partner when she should be getting on with her work.

At last Jemima could stand it no longer. 'Millie Carter,' she said. 'Instead of whispering behind your hand perhaps you'd like to share your words of wisdom with the whole class.'

Millie gave a shrug and bent her head over her writing.

'I'm waiting,' Jemima said sternly. 'Come along. Stand up and tell us all what you were saying that was so much more important than the work I had given you to do. Stand up when I tell you,' she said, a little more loudly.

Millie dragged herself to her feet and looked down at the floor.

'Well?' Jemima said. She knew she couldn't give in now; she had to make Millie speak or she would lose control of the whole class. 'I'm still waiting.'

Mary Anderson, who sat next to Millie, put up her hand. 'Please, Miss, Millie was saying that you used to work at Baxter's. She said her sister had got your job because you'd got the sack. That's what she was saying.'

'Oh, was it, indeed?' Jemima said. She looked across at Millie, who was bright red and squirming in embarrassment. 'Is that right, Millie? Is that what you were telling Mary?'

Millie nodded uncomfortably, her eyes on the floor.

'Then I suggest that you are a little more sure of your facts before you pass them on. Spreading gossip that is quite unfounded is bad enough, but telling lies about people is a serious offence and could land you in real trouble,' Jemima said quietly. 'Now, as you're so anxious for your classmates to hear your voice, perhaps you'd like to take out your reading book and read to us all.'

This, Jemima knew, was a worse punishment to Millie than making her stand in the corner because it would demonstrate to the rest of the class just how bad her reading was.

Each night over their evening meal she discussed her day with Kathryn, telling her what had gone wrong and what she felt she had achieved.

'Maybe it was unkind of me,' Jemima said when she related what had happened with Millie. 'But I was really furious to think she had been spreading lies behind my back and I thought standing her in the corner would only make her feel more important in the eyes of the rest of the class.'

Kathryn was silent for a bit, weighing up her answer. She never criticized, never said, 'Oh, you shouldn't have done that,' but was always ready with praise and encouragement or with helpful sugges-tions as to how things might perhaps have been handled better. At last she said, 'I think you did the right thing, Jemima. Millie was obviously getting above herself because she knew her sister had taken your place at Baxter's. She needed taking down a peg or two.' She nodded. 'Yes, I think it was the right thing to do.' She smiled at Jemima. 'You handled it well.'

After the meal was finished there were the next day's lessons to prepare and time had to be put aside for Jemima's own studies because there was always homework from the weekly Saturday morning classes held for pupil-teachers in Colchester. It was usually nearly midnight before Jemima could put away her books and slide into her comfortable bed.

Each Saturday morning she caught the train into Colchester and walked to the rather draughty hall in the High Street where the pupil-teacher classes were held. As she walked from the station, carrying her heavy bag of books, she always kept an eye open for her twin, hoping against hope that she would one day catch a glimpse of Sophie among the crowds so that she could talk to her and perhaps persuade her to return home. She paused to look down every side street she passed and always returned to the railway station by a different route so that she could explore as big an area as possible. But she was always disappointed; there was never any sign of Sophie and she came to the conclusion that her sister must have moved on to another town. But where that might be she had no idea. It was as if Sophie had vanished into thin air.

The school closed for most of August and called it the summer holiday. The authorities had originally decided against a long holiday and tried to keep it open but they soon realized they were fighting a losing battle. August was harvest time when children could be employed to help in the fields, which meant that most of the parents kept their children at home anyway, official holiday or not. After all, apart from the money earned from working in the fields, there was the added benefit of the penny a week school fees saved, so it was profitable all round.

For her part, Jemima was quite glad of a few weeks' respite from teaching. She hadn't realized quite how tired she had become and Mrs Peel encouraged her to stay in bed quite late for the first week of the holidays.

'Oh, dear, you're really spoiling me. I should get up and help,' Jemima said with a yawn, as Kathryn woke her with a cup of tea yet again.

'Not at all. You lie here and catch up with your reading for an hour,' Kathryn said. 'I know just how tiring it can be, standing all day in front of a class, till you get used to it.'

'You're both so kind to me,' Jemima said gratefully. 'I don't know how I'd manage without you.'

'Rubbish,' Kathryn said, but she was obviously pleased at the words.

A week or so later, Jemima went to see Aunt Minnie, who she knew would be delighted to see her. She apologized for not visiting more often. 'I hadn't realized just how much work I would have to get through every week,' she said.

Aunt Minnie looked her up and down. 'You're getting even thinner, child. And you're very pale. Are you feeling all right?'

Jemima smiled. 'There's no pulling the wool over your eyes, is there, Auntie? No, as a matter of fact I got up this morning feeling a bit under the weather. So I thought I'd pay you a visit. It always does me good to come and see you.'

'Mm. Well, let's take our tea into the garden as it's such a lovely day,' Aunt Minnie said, fussing with scones and fruit cake.

Jemima followed her outside with the tea tray although she didn't feel at all hungry and wondered how she could eat very little without offending her aunt. Aunt Minnie had remarked on the fact that she didn't look well but she was sure Aunt Minnie herself had lost more weight and her face had a greyish tinge.

'What about you, Auntie, are you well?' she asked as she sipped her tea.

Aunt Minnie shrugged. 'Well enough, dearie,' she said with a sad little smile. 'But I do miss my girl. If only I knew where she was . . . If only I knew she was well and happy . . . It's the not knowing, Jemma, that's what gets me.' She looked at Jemima hope-fully. 'You haven't seen her, I suppose?'

'No. I'd have told you if I had.' Jemima sighed. 'I look for her every week when I go to Colchester for my class, but I never see her.' She hesitated. 'Do you still . . .?'

Aunt Minnie shook her head. 'No. I don't go looking for her so often now. Uncle Will got so angry with me for going every week that I had to stop.' She gave a ghost of a smile. 'I still have a little trip there on the train now and again, though, because you never know . . .' She dabbed her eyes with the corner of her apron. 'Oh, dear. I do miss her so.'

Jemima crumbled a piece of fruit cake on her plate. 'I know, Auntie,' she said sadly.

Suddenly, Aunt Minnie frowned. 'What's the matter, Jemma? Isn't my fruit cake to your liking? You always used to say . . . Child, what-ever's the matter?'

As she was speaking, Jemima bent double, clutching her stomach. 'I don't know what's wrong with me, Auntie. I didn't feel very well when I got up this morning but I thought if I walked up to see you I might feel better. But now I've got this awful pain . . .'

Alarmed, Aunt Minnie helped her to her feet. 'I think you'd better come inside and lie down for a little while, child. Come along, I'll help you upstairs and you can get into Sophie's bed till you feel better. You certainly don't look at all well.' She kept her arm round Jemima as she dragged herself up the stairs. There, she helped her

off with her shoes and tucked her into Sophie's bed. Then she went
downstairs to fetch a hot-water bottle and a powder: Aunt Sophie's
remedy for most ills.

When she returned Jemima was curled up on her side, fast asleep.

She felt her forehead, then tucked the hot-water bottle in beside
her and sat down to watch over her, reluctant to leave her, in case
she woke. As she lay sleeping, Minnie studied her niece. She was
eighteen now, a grown woman. Oh, where had all the years gone?
With her features in repose Minnie was sure she could detect a
slight, very slight, resemblance to her twin. Of course Jemima was
as fair as Sophie was dark; Jemima was slim where Sophie was —
had been — inclined to plumpness; the two girls had never been
in the least alike, despite being twins, yet now there was something . . . Was it the shape of her nose? The set of her jaw? The
line of her mouth, relaxed and slightly open as she lay sleeping?
There was something in her features that reminded Minnie of
Sophie. She couldn't tell exactly where the likeness lay, but it was
definitely there. She gave a great sigh. If only Sophie was here
so they could stand side by side.

Suddenly, as if she knew she was being watched, Jemima's eyes
fluttered open and any likeness was gone. She smiled as she saw her
aunt sitting by her side. 'Oh, I've had such a lovely sleep, Auntie,'
she said, sighing with contentment and snuggling further into the
covers.

'That's good, dearie.' Aunt Minnie got to her feet and bent over
her. 'And how's that pain? Is it any better?'

'Pain?' Jemima frowned and rubbed her abdomen. 'Oh, that's gone.
I must have slept it away. I haven't got a pain at all now. Except a
hunger pain. I'm absolutely starving.' She began to sit up in bed.

Aunt Minnie frowned. 'Are you sure it's quite gone?'

'Oh, yes. That sleep's done me the world of good.'

'Well, I never. I wonder what it could have been. Indigestion?'
She lowered her voice although there was nobody else in the house.
'Could it be your time of the month?' she whispered.

Jemima nodded. 'Yes, I reckon that's what it was, although I don't
usually have anything more than a slight headache. I've never been
doubled up with pain like that before.' She smiled. 'But I really do
feel better now, Auntie. Is there any more of that fruit cake?'

'Oh, I think I can do better than that, dearie, if you're starving.'
Aunt Minnie got to her feet. 'Come downstairs when you're ready
and I'll make you scrambled eggs on toast. How would that be?'

'Oh, lovely.' Jemima looked up at her. 'You're spoiling me, Auntie.'

'It's nice to have somebody to spoil again,' she said.

Thoughtfully, she left Jemima and went downstairs. When she reached the kitchen she reached down the calendar and made a mark against the date. It was August the thirteenth.

Jemima never had a recurrence of her 'illness' and, refreshed by her late rising and her sleep at Aunt Minnie's, she got down to her studies with renewed vigour. It had never worried her that most of the other pupil-teachers of her age were in their final year whereas she was only just starting her training. She knew she could never catch up with them and her only concern was that she should get good marks in the yearly examinations, which were held at the end of October each year. In fact, she worked so hard and got such good results that her tutors agreed she should sit the first year's examinations after only six months, although they warned her not to expect very high grades. In the event, her grades were so good that she was awarded a ten-pound grant towards her following year's expenses.

She was well on the way to achieving her heart's desire.

Twenty-Five

At the first opportunity, Jemima went to tell Richard the good news. He had been so supportive, in spite of his disappointment when she had chosen a teaching career rather than marriage to him, that she felt he deserved to know that all her hard work had paid off. She appreciated that few men would have been big-hearted enough to rejoice with her when she received the mysterious gift that had made this possible, as he had done, even though it had sounded the death knell on his own hopes.

And anyway, she liked Richard and she missed their Sunday afternoon walks. He had become like an elder brother, in whom she could confide her dreams and ambitions, however far-fetched and unlikely they might be, and to whom she could tell her troubles and worries. She felt sad and a bit guilty that she had been so busy studying that she had barely seen him since she'd left Baxter's.

'There's no need to apologize, Jemma,' he answered when she said as much as they walked along by the river on a cold, late November Sunday afternoon. They were both huddled into warm winter coats, and were wearing fur hats and long scarves against the sharp wind that was whipping the water into frothy ripples and turning the tips of their noses red. 'I understand, really I do. You started your training later than most so you've got a lot to catch up with.' He put his hand under her arm and squeezed her elbow. 'I really admire you for what you're doing, Jemma. You haven't let anything stand in the way of what you want to do.' He gave an almost imperceptible sigh. 'I only wish I could say the same.'

Impulsively, she turned to him. 'But it's not your fault, Richard. Being the only son you weren't given any choice, were you? Your career was mapped out for you almost before you were born. Nobody asked you what you wanted to do; it was simply assumed you would go into the family business, so deciding for yourself wasn't an option. That's right, isn't it?'

'Yep. Right on the button. It never even occurred to me to question whether I might have preferred to do something else. And now it's too late, because I'm stuck. I couldn't possibly abandon Ma and Pa, the state they're both in. Pa can't even begin the day without a shot of whisky now and by the afternoon I have to keep him out of the shop altogether or he'd lose us all our customers.'

'Oh, Rick . . .'

He turned to her, a broad smile on his face. 'Nobody's ever called me that before, Jemma. I like it.'

She smiled back, a whimsical little smile. 'It doesn't help your situation much though, does it? And when you talk of not being able to abandon your parents, it makes me feel like I've abandoned you.'

'Oh, no, not at all, Jemma,' he said quickly. 'You mustn't feel like that. Things tick along all right. In fact, the business is doing very well at the moment. And Lillian's still with us, although she refuses to live in.'

'Why is that?'

He was quiet for a minute, then he said, 'I believe she had some kind of encounter with my father on the stairs, which he vehemently denies. I don't know the details, but knowing what Lillian is like I would hazard a guess that, whatever the circumstances, he was not entirely to blame. However, it resulted in her refusing to live in any more and a rise in pay that she most certainly didn't deserve. A small price to pay, I suppose. At least she's still working for us, even if she is incompetent and my mother can't stand her.'

'Oh, dear.' That was not what Jemima had heard from Lillian's young sister. According to Millie, Lillian was now the prop and mainstay of the firm and would soon be joining it on a permanent basis when her engagement to Richard was announced. That news had caused a surprising stab of jealousy to shoot through Jemima, although she knew it was quite unwarranted because the best thing in the world for Richard would be to have a wife by his side to share his problems.

Since Jemima had always known that was not where her destiny lay she knew she had no right to feel jealous if he had chosen someone else.

Suddenly, Richard gave her arm a little shake and grinned down at her. 'Hey, it's not all doom and gloom, you know. We're supposed to be celebrating your success. And I've got some good news, too. I nearly forgot to tell you.'

Her heart gave a sudden lurch. Had Millie been right, after all? 'Well, go on, then. Tell me. What is it?' she asked cautiously, smiling up at him as she prepared to offer her congratulations.

'You remember I've told you that I often visit Mr Lax, my old piano teacher? He's got this lovely grand piano that he lets me play.'

'Yes, I remember you telling me about him.' She nodded, relieved. It seemed an engagement wasn't in the offing, after all.

'Over the years he has done a lot of work as an accompanist, to choirs, soloists, instrumentalists taking exams or performing, that kind of thing. Well, he reckons he's getting a bit old in the tooth for it now, especially as concerts are mostly in the evening and he prefers not to go out after dark. Can't really blame him for that, he's over eighty. So . . .' He paused.

'Yes, go on. So . . .' she prompted.

'He's asked me to take it on instead.' He couldn't keep the pride out of his voice. Then he added modestly, 'He must have told the people he plays for that I'm reasonably competent because they all agreed for me to do it, even before they heard what I could do.'

'Oh, Rick. That's wonderful.' She got hold of his hand and squeezed it. 'When's your first concert?'

'Next Saturday. I'm accompanying a male voice choir. They're quite good. I've already accompanied two rehearsals, which went well.'

'Where's the concert?'

'In Colchester. At the Corn Exchange. They've told me I might even get a solo spot,' he added. 'So I'm practising like mad in case I do.'

'Can I come?' Her eyes were shining. 'I'd love to hear you. I've never heard you play.'

He grinned at her. 'I was hoping you'd say that. I've got a couple of complimentary tickets, so, if you've got a friend you'd like to bring . . .?'

'Yes. Yes. I'm sure Kathryn would like to come with me. Oh, I shall look forward to it.'

'That's good. I'll give you the tickets when we get back.' He glanced at her. 'You will come back with me, won't you? I told Dorothy I was seeing you and she's baked some of your favourite cakes. She'll be disappointed if you don't come and have some.' He grinned at her. 'And so shall I.'

'Just try and keep me away! I'm just about ready for tea and cakes in Dorothy's warm kitchen.'

They walked in silence for a little while, then she slowed her step a little and said, 'Rick, I wonder if I ought to make a bit more effort to discover who gave me that ten pounds on my birthday.

Now I've been given the ten-pound grant I feel perhaps I should pay it back.'

'Mm. I can understand how you feel,' he said thoughtfully. 'I think I'd probably feel the same, if it was me. But we went through everybody we could think of when you first got it, didn't we?'

'Yes, but I didn't actually *ask* anybody, did I?'

'No, but it wouldn't have been appropriate. You could hardly go round asking everybody you know if they'd given you ten pounds. That wouldn't do at all.'

She shrugged. 'No, I suppose not. I could put a notice in the local newspaper, I suppose.'

He threw his head back and roared with laughter. 'That's about the daftest thing I've ever heard, Jemma Furlong. You'd need hundreds of pounds to pay out all the people who would claim to have given you the money.'

'Yes, I suppose it would be a bit silly,' she agreed sheepishly.

'In any case, it must have been meant as a present, not a loan, because there was no mention of you ever paying it back. And quite plainly the giver didn't want you to know who they were or there would have been a signature, or you would have recognized the writing. You didn't, did you?'

'No.'

'Well, then. It was a present that set you on your chosen path, so I reckon the best thing is just to be grateful.'

'I am, Rick. Oh, indeed I am. I'd just like to be able to say thank you.'

'Who knows? One day maybe you'll discover who your benefactor is and you'll be able to grovel at his or her feet.'

'Now you're laughing at me.'

'That's right.' He grinned at her. 'Come on now. Dorothy will wonder where we've got to.'

After a delightful hour with Dorothy and rather too many of her cherry cakes, Jemima went home and told Kathryn about the concert.

'Oh, yes please, I'd love to come,' she said enthusiastically. 'Now, what would be appropriate dress, I wonder?'

Jemima's face fell. She had never been able to afford to spend much on clothes so her wardrobe was very limited. Apart from the blue serge skirt and three white blouses she had bought to wear for school and the green summer dress — still her 'best' dress — from Baxter's, her clothes had all seen better days.

'Don't worry, Jemima,' Kathryn said, seeing her worried expression.

'We're about the same size so I'm sure I've got something suitable that will fit you.'

In the event, Kathryn wore her new costume, a brown gored skirt and yellow jacket with wide brown lapels and a white lacy blouse, and Jemima wore Kathryn's second-best one, which had a pink skirt, flat at the front and pleated at the back with a tiny train and a black fitted jacket, with one of her school blouses. Kathryn wore her short fur cape with a matching hat because the weather was very cold, and Jemima borrowed a similar one from Mrs Peel, which smelled strongly of camphor because the old lady didn't often wear it.

When they got off the train at Colchester they found the town was still thronged with people. Just outside the station a man with a coke-filled brazier was selling roasted chestnuts and there was a crowd round him, more for the warmth of the brazier than to buy chestnuts. Another man a little further on was baking potatoes on a similar brazier.

One side of the High Street was still full of market stalls from the Saturday market although the livestock was all gone. But under stalls lit by naphtha lamps the last of the vegetables and fruit, looking slightly wilted now, were being sold off cheaply and there were still a few stalls selling cheap jewellery and sweets stuck together in sticky lumps from the heat of the lamps. Underfoot, there was so much squashed fruit, cabbage stalks and discarded wrapping paper that Kathryn said, holding up her skirt, 'I think we should cross the road. It's less crowded and filthy on the other side and that's where the Corn Exchange is.'

They crossed the road, which was equally filthy, but mostly with horse droppings, and continued on their way.

Jemima was never sure what made her glance back to the line of market stalls, which were thinning out as traders began packing up for the day, but as she looked she saw by the light of a swinging naphtha lamp the figure of a shawl-wrapped woman with a baby, intent on searching for the last of the cheap vegetables.

'Sophie,' she breathed, unable to believe her eyes.

Almost as if she had heard her name spoken, the woman looked up and her eyes seemed to meet Jemima's across the street. Then she turned away and was lost in the crowd that still thronged the pavement.

'Wait a minute, Kathryn,' Jemima said, and darted back across the street, ignoring the filth underfoot. She pushed her way through, in the direction she thought she had seen her sister take, craning her neck to see over the heads of the people, trying to catch a glimpse of Sophie's shawled head, at the same time glancing along the unlit passageways and lanes that led off the main thorough-fare to see if her shadowy figure might have slipped that way. But there was no sign of her. Sophie, if indeed it had been Sophie, had completely disappeared. Dejectedly, Jemima re-crossed the street.

'I thought I saw my sister across the street,' she told Kathryn sadly. 'But she'd gone before I could reach her.'

'Perhaps it wasn't Sophie at all,' Kathryn suggested.

'No, perhaps it wasn't.' But Jemima was quite certain that it was her sister she had seen.

'Well, there's nothing you can do, Jemima, and we need to hurry or we'll be late.'

'Yes, of course.' Jemima quickened her steps to match Kathryn's.

The concert was a great success.

The hall was full but Jemima and Kathryn were shown to seats right at the front and Jemima tried to put all thoughts of Sophie out of her mind as she gave herself up to enjoying the evening. She hardly recognized Richard, in full evening dress, as he took his place at the grand piano to the side of the stage and she found herself more intent on watching his fingers fly over the keys than on listening to the choir, although Kathryn assured her afterwards that they had been very good.

They managed to speak to Richard in the interval.

'Yes, it all seems to be going very well,' he said.

'When will your solo come, Richard?' Kathryn asked. 'I can't see it on the programme.'

'No. Unfortunately, I shan't be having a solo spot tonight because the programme is already too long,' he said. 'But perhaps it's as well. Some of the music I'm playing is quite demanding so I wouldn't have had time to practise my own music.'

'You're very good,' Jemima said admiringly. 'I'd no idea you played so well.'

'I had a good teacher,' he said. He took out his pocket watch. 'I must get back. The conductor will want a few words with us before the second half begins.' He gave them both a broad smile. 'I'm so glad you were both able to come.'

They watched his coat tails disappear through the crowd.

'What a pity,' Kathryn mused.

'A pity? What do you mean?' Jemima looked at her in surprise.

She shook her head. 'It's a pity that young man has to waste his time running a gents' outfitters when he has so much musical talent. I'm sure, if he'd been given the chance, he could have gone far.'

Twenty-Six

It had been an exciting evening. Jemima had never seen so many people in one place before and some of the ladies looked very elegant in brightly coloured evening dresses and sparkling with jewels. But there were also those, like Kathryn and herself, more modestly dressed, mostly sitting towards the back of the hall. She realized that it was Richard's complimentary tickets that had provided them with such prominent seats. She couldn't help a glow of pride to think that Richard was her friend and she had been amazed at his skill as a pianist. It was typical of him that in all the time she had worked at Baxter's he had rarely spoken of his musical ability, let alone of his exceptional talent.

Later, lying in bed and trying to sleep, her thoughts went back to the woman she had seen in the market. She had only seen her for a few seconds, and that by the dim light of a naphtha lamp, so could it have been Sophie? Yet, as soon as she had breathed the name the woman opposite had looked up, startled, as if she had heard her name called. She had glanced round, and as if pulled by an invisible thread, her gaze had rested on Jemima, standing in the lamplight across the road, watching her. Then the woman had turned quickly away and disappeared into the crowd and the thread was broken.

It must have been Sophie, her twin. Jemima was certain that there could be no other explanation for the strong, almost telepathic bond that had passed between her and the woman on the other side of the street. She only wished that same telepathy would guide her to where Sophie was hiding with her child. But at least she knew she was still in Colchester.

Jemima couldn't decide whether or not to tell Aunt Minnie that she had seen Sophie. She didn't want to raise the old lady's hopes and risk her spending days on end walking the streets searching, as she no doubt would if she thought there was the slightest chance of finding her beloved girl. Aunt Minnie was becoming a little frail now and fruitless expeditions in the depth of winter would do her health no good at all. Yet to find Sophie again might be the very thing to encourage her back to health.

Every night, Jemima tossed and turned in bed, trying to decide the right thing to do. In the end she went to see Uncle William.

He was on his favourite bench on the corner of the quay. Now that he no longer went to sea with his fishing smack he liked to be at the quayside when *Alice May* returned and if she was not due back he just liked to be on the quayside. That was where he felt most at home, where he could smell the salt air, listen to the wheeling gulls and watch the boats on the river as he talked to his cronies.

His face lit up when he saw Jemima and he moved up so that she could sit beside him.

'This is a rare treat, Jemma, girl. How are you?' he said.

'I'm well, thank you, Uncle, but I want to ask your advice.'

He glanced at her, frowning. 'Are you in some kind of trouble, girl?' he asked anxiously.

'No. No. Nothing like that, Uncle,' she assured him.

He nodded. 'That's all right, then. Fire away, my girl. I'll help if I can.'

While he filled his pipe and stoked it to his satisfaction she told him of her predicament over Sophie – or the woman she thought had been Sophie. When she had finished, he sat quietly puffing for several minutes. Then he got up and walked about twenty paces along the quay, turned and walked back. He did this about three times, pacing the deck, something all the old sailors did when they were turning something over in their minds. Then he came and sat down again.

'Your Aunt Minnie is pining for Sophie, that's for sure,' he said thoughtfully. 'I reckon that's what's at the root of her trouble because the doctor can't find anything else much wrong with her. I managed to put a stop to her tramping the streets week after week looking for her and I wouldn't want to risk her starting that up again.' He took his pipe out of his mouth, looked at it and put it back in again. After several more puffs he said, 'We always told our girl she'd be shown the door if she brought trouble home and I'd be inclined to stick to that but . . .' He shook his head. 'It's no good; I don't like to see my Minnie wasting away. And she is wasting away, Jemma. She's nothing but skin and grief. I sometimes wonder if she'll last the winter out.' He put his hand over Jemima's. 'If you reckon it was our girl you saw and you can find her and bring her home, well, I shan't turn her out. You can tell her that from me.'

'I don't know if I will be able to find her, Uncle. I only caught a glimpse of a woman I thought was Sophie.' She didn't want to raise his hopes too high.

He thought for a minute. 'Perhaps you could put a notice in the local paper. That's what people do, isn't it? Then if it was Sophie you saw . . . well, she might see it.'

'You'd really like me to do that, Uncle?' Jemima asked anxiously.

'I don't want to lose my Minnie, that's the truth of it,' he said simply, his eyes bleak. 'So if there's a chance of finding Sophie . . .'

'I'll put a notice in, asking her to come home because Aunt Minnie's ill,' Jemima said.

'Good girl. You do that.'

'Of course, there's no guarantee she'll see it, Uncle.'

'No, but it's worth a try.' He patted her knee, then got up and walked off, his face working with emotion.

Jemima put a notice in the local newspaper, although she didn't really hold out much hope that Sophie would see it. After all, if money was tight a newspaper wouldn't be high on her list of things to buy. But the following Saturday, as she made her way through the market stalls in the High Street to her pupil-teacher classes, an idea came to her and during the ten-minute break she took a sheet of paper and wrote in large letters:

SOPHIE FURLONG
AUNT MINNIE IS ILL
SHE NEEDS TO SEE YOU
JEMIMA

As soon as her classes finished she took the notice to the stall where she had seen Sophie and spoke to the stall holder, who, to her amazement, immediately recognized the woman she described. She asked him if he would pin it up prominently so that Sophie would see it.

'Course I will. She comes and gets her fruit and veg here just before we pack up most weeks, so she'll see it if I hang it right here, under the lamp,' he told Jemima. 'Tell you the truth, I usually keep a few choice bits back for her, although I don't tell her that.' He tapped the side of his nose. 'She thinks they're all leftovers.'

Jemima thanked him, bought two oranges and two bananas and caught the train home.

All the following week she waited for news that Sophie had come back. On Friday evening she went to see Aunt Minnie but Sophie wasn't there.

'Didn't work, did it?' Uncle William whispered despondently, when Aunt Minnie had shuffled out to the scullery to make the tea.

'Maybe it wasn't Sophie, after all,' Jemima said. 'Yet I was so sure . . .'

'We shall just have to think of some other way.' He raised his voice. 'Ah, tea. And have you brought some of your nice cheese scones, matie?'

'Yes, you old rogue.' Aunt Minnie managed a smile. 'But don't eat too many, you know they give you indigestion.'

'Ah, but they're worth it.' Uncle William winked at Jemima.

Mr Starling was already on the platform waiting for the train the next day when she arrived at the station with her bag of books to take to her pupil-teacher class, so when he held open the carriage door for her she got in with him instead of using the 'Ladies Only' compartment in which she usually travelled.

'So, you're a real teacher now, then, Jemma,' he said, smiling at her. He was a little balder than she remembered but his moustache was as thick and black as ever.

'Not quite,' she said, smiling back. 'I have to go to classes every Saturday while I'm still a pupil-teacher. But I passed my first year's exam even though I'd only been teaching six months. So only another two years and I shall be a real teacher.'

He nodded. 'My word, you've done well for yourself, Jemma. I'm real glad you've been able to do what you'd set your heart on, after all. The trouble you had with that money was a real setback for you. Did your sister ever pay it back?'

'No. I didn't expect her to. Anyway, I don't know where she is.' Jemima glanced at him. He had pulled his pipe out of his pocket, noticed the NO SMOKING sign and put it back again. For a moment she wondered if she should ask him if he'd seen her, then decided against it. If Mr Starling had seen Sophie he would have told her before now.

'Is my mother well?' she asked, changing the subject.

'Yes. Her tongue is as sharp as it ever was, but we rub along all right. She feeds me well and keeps the place clean; a man in my position can't ask for much more.' He sounded like a contented man.

'And Daisy? Now I don't work at Baxter's I don't often see her.'

'I reckon her little Amy will be starting school before long, so I daresay you'll see something of her. She's a right little charmer, the apple of her dad's eye.'

'And her grandad's too, by the sound of it,' Jemima said, smiling.

'Well, she's the only girl. The other three are boys. Oh, did you know? Daisy's just had another boy. They're calling this one Reggie. She's a good mother, our Daisy, I'll say that for her. And of course, her mum gives her a hand here and there. It's nice they live next door.'

The train pulled into the station. 'You say you don't know where your sister Sophie is. Don't you ever hear anything of her?' he asked, offering her a hand down on to the platform.

'No, not a word,' Jemima said, hitching her bag on to her arm.

'That's a bit ungrateful of her, after you giving her all that money. I wonder where she is,' he said.

She gave a sigh. 'I only wish I knew.' She glanced at the station clock. 'I must hurry. I don't want to be late for my class and it's right up at the far end of the High Street. It was lovely to see you, Mr Starling.'

He tipped his cap. 'And you, dearie. Now you mind and take care of yourself.'

'I will.' She gave him a wave and hurried off through the crowd to a morning of algebra, English and history. She was glad she had done her homework. Being the oldest member of her class she liked to make sure her marks were always near the top. And she knew that once she got into her class she would be too busy concentrating on her work to worry about Sophie.

The class was a little late finishing. She glanced at the clock. She would have to hurry if she was going to catch the one o'clock train. And if she didn't catch it she would have an hour to wait for the next one. She gathered up her belongings and made a dash for the door and down the six steps to the pavement.

She nearly cannoned into a woman standing at the bottom of the steps.

'Oh, I beg your . . .' The words died on her lips. 'Sophie! Oh, Sophie!' She dropped her bag of books and flung her arms round her sister, enveloping both her and the child she was carrying. 'Oh, Sophie, thank God I've found you.'

Twenty-Seven

Jemima stood back, still holding Sophie's arm, afraid she would change her mind and disappear into the crowd again. Her first impression was that although Sophie was shabbily dressed she looked reasonably clean. She was a good deal thinner and her face was positively gaunt.

She looked down at the sleeping baby, then smiled at her sister. 'And this is your baby. A boy or girl?' she asked gently.

'Girl.' It was the first word Sophie had spoken and there was a hint of truculence in her tone.

'And what do you call her?'

'Jenny.' She hesitated, then said, the words little more than a mumble, 'I called her Jenny because it was the nearest I could get to Jemma.'

Jemima shot her a glance and saw that her sister's eyes were brimming with tears.

'We need to talk, Sophie,' she said quietly. 'Come on, I know where there's a little tea room where we can catch up on things.' She was still holding Sophie's arm and she began guiding her along the road so that Sophie had no choice but to go with her.

Five minutes later, with a pot of tea and toasted crumpets between them, Sophie said, 'I knew you'd seen me that night.'

'Then why didn't you wait to speak to me?' Jemima buttered a crumpet and pushed it across to her.

'I couldn't. You looked so smart, such a lady. How could I?' She looked down at herself.

Jemima followed her gaze to the shabby, well-darned dress that had been smart and up-to-the-minute in the days when she had worked for Mrs Worsnop and the faded shawl that wrapped both her and the sleeping baby. 'That's pretty ironic. What you didn't know was that my clothes were all borrowed,' she said, with a twist of her lip. 'Miss Peel lent them to me because we were going to a concert. We had complimentary tickets because Richard — you remember Richard Baxter? — was to be the pianist accompanying a male voice choir and he wanted me to go. I had nothing suitable to wear, so Kathryn lent me a costume.'

'No. Stupid of me. Of course you wouldn't have money for clothes because I took it all, didn't I?' Sophie said bitterly. 'And ruined your chances of becoming a teacher into the bargain.'

'I never minded. I gave you the money of my own free will,' Jemima said quickly. 'And it didn't ruin my chances. Somebody, I've never found out who it was, sent me ten pounds on my – our – birthday. Ten sovereigns. I couldn't believe it. But it enabled me to begin my training. That's where I've been this morning, to my pupil-teacher class.'

'I knew you'd been to some kind of class. I've watched you go there every Saturday. But I didn't know what it was.'

'Oh, Sophie, if you knew where I was, why didn't you come and talk to me?'

'It's a long story.'

'I'm in no hurry. Have another crumpet while you talk.'

Sophie shook her head. 'No, thanks, I don't eat much these days. But I'll have another cup of tea, please.'

Jemima poured her more tea and pushed it over together with another buttered crumpet, which Sophie absent-mindedly began to eat. 'I want to know about Aunt Minnie,' she said. 'Your message said she was ill and needed to see me. I think you must be mistaken. Aunt Minnie wouldn't want to see me. Not now I've got her.' She glanced down at the baby on her lap, who was still asleep. 'I'm a disgrace.' A tear fell on the baby's cheek and she wiped it away with her thumb.

'That's as maybe. But what you don't know is that after you'd gone Aunt Minnie spent at least one day every week walking the streets of Colchester looking for you so that she could take you home with her. No matter what the weather, that's what she did, until Uncle William put a stop to it.'

'Oh, I didn't know.' Once again Sophie's eyes brimmed with tears.

'Of course you didn't.'

'How can I get to see her and tell her I'm sorry?' she whispered. 'I know Uncle William won't have me in the house.'

'Yes, he will. I've talked to him. He's so worried about Aunt Minnie that he'll go to any lengths to have her well again. It was his idea to put a notice in the local paper. Did you see it?'

Sophie shook her head. 'I don't see many newspapers unless they're wrapped round fish and chips for a treat. But I saw the notice you'd put up at the greengrocer's stall.'

'I'm glad I thought of that. Well, as I was saying, Uncle William may not exactly welcome you with open arms but he won't turn you away, of that I'm sure.'

'I can't blame him for that. I know I don't deserve to be treated like the prodigal daughter.' She gathered the baby to her. 'But I'm not parting with Jenny. Not for anybody. She's mine. I'm not having her sent to an orphanage. I couldn't bear that.'

'Nobody's suggesting you should part with her, Sophie,' Jemima said.

'But Uncle William might want me to . . .'

'Let's take one step at a time, shall we?'

The baby stirred and began to whimper.

'She's getting hungry. I must go home and feed her.'

Jemima got to her feet. 'All right. But I'm coming with you.'

'No.' Sophie looked at her in alarm.

'You don't really imagine I'm going to let you disappear again, do you?'

'I won't disappear. You can wait for me somewhere. I'll come back. But you don't want to see where I live.'

'You mean you don't want me to see where you live. Well, you've no choice. I'm coming with you and then I'm going to take you home with me on the train. Do you owe any rent?'

'Only till the end of the week. I'm not in debt, Jemma,' she added with a hint of pride.

'That's good.' Jemima picked up her heavy bag of books. 'Well, come on. We don't want Jenny screaming the place down because she's hungry. Is it far?'

'No. I've got a room in a yard at the top of Scheregate Steps. We can cut through Pelham's Lane and down Trinity Street.'

The baby was screaming by the time they reached the passage into the misnamed Primrose Yard. It was a stinking midden of a yard surrounded by cottages leaning drunkenly together and with an overflowing privy stuck right in the middle. Sophie went to a house at the far end and up a flight of rickety stairs to a room at the top. There was one small window, from which could be seen the spire of St Nicholas Church and not much else. There was very little furniture: a small bed in the corner, a table and chair and a box just big enough to use as a cradle. It was cold because there was no fire lit but there were a few lumps of coal on the hearth and there was a cupboard in the chimney recess, presumably where Sophie kept all her possessions. The floor was bare but Jemima was relieved to see that everywhere was clean and neat and the bed was covered with a faded patchwork quilt.

Sophie sat down on the side of the bed, unbuttoned her dress and began to feed the baby. Then she began to cry quietly.

'I'm sorry, Jemma. You shouldn't see me like this,' she sobbed. 'You shouldn't see what I've been reduced to.'

Jemima had sat down on the only chair. 'What you've forgotten, Sophie, is that this is nothing new to me. I was brought up in surroundings not much different to this,' she told her. 'Until I was nearly twelve and Mr Starling came to live with us our house always smelled of fish and Mum was drunk more often than not, so it was left to me to keep the place clean as far as I could. I wasn't brought up in a nice cosy house like you were. But you never came to see Mum unless you were forced to so you didn't see what it was like.' She looked round. 'As rooms go, this isn't that bad. Where's the tap?'

'At the far end of the yard.'

Jemima got up and went to look and satisfy herself that it was well away from the privy. She sat down again. 'Is the landlady all right?'

Sophie nodded. 'She's very good. Treats me a bit like a daughter.' Her voice dropped. 'But she has men in. I won't have anything to do with that, although she'd like me to.'

'I'm glad to hear it,' Jemima said.

'Once bitten, twice shy,' Sophie said with the ghost of a smile.

'How have you managed?'

'I couldn't have done, not without the money you gave me, Jemma,' Sophie said earnestly. 'But I got this room – it was cheap because it's not in a very nice area – and then I got work sewing buttons on army uniforms. I had to walk to the Garrison, pick up the uniforms and the buttons, and then walk back with them when they were done. It was hard work because the uniforms were rough and I didn't get paid much. But if I worked at it I could do six uniforms in a morning and another six in the afternoon. But that meant two trips to the barracks because I couldn't carry more than six uniforms at a time. They were very heavy and as I got near my time I could only carry three, so I only earned half as much.'

'How did you manage after Jenny was born?' She nodded towards the baby. As Sophie had been talking Jemima had been studying her. She was a pretty little thing, with a fuzz of fair hair and big brown eyes like Sophie's, but she looked slightly undernourished.

Sophie followed her gaze. 'I think she looks like you, Jemma,' she said, smoothing the little head lovingly. 'She's the only good thing that's come out of all this.' She looked up. 'In spite of everything, I wouldn't be without her, Jemma. I've heard it said that children bring their love with them and it's true.' The baby finished feeding and Sophie buttoned her blouse and sat quietly nursing her.

'Oh, yes,' she said after a minute, 'I was telling you how I managed. Well, one of Mrs Kemble's fancy men made me a box on wheels to cart the uniforms in. I wished he'd made it for me sooner. I think he thought I'd pay him for it with my favours, but he soon found out he was wrong. But I'd got the cart by then so he couldn't very well take it back. I gave him sixpence instead, which didn't please him.'

'What happened when the baby was born?'

'That's when your money was such a blessing, Jemma. I used some of it to pay a woman to look after me; she called herself a midwife but she was a bit rough and ready. Fortunately, everything went all right, and it was an easy birth.' Her mouth set in a hard line. 'It's about the only thing that has been easy since that bastard led me astray,' she said bitterly. Then she looked up, with a puzzled frown on her face. 'It was odd, Jemma. All the time I was in labour I felt as if somebody was there with me, but I couldn't see who it was.' She shrugged. 'I expect it was just fancy, but in a funny sort of way it helped.'

Jemima made no comment. Childbirth was an area quite outside her knowledge. 'How long did the money last?' she asked instead.

'I shall still have five shillings left when I've paid this week's rent.' There was an understandable note of pride in Sophie's voice as she said the words. 'I haven't wasted your money, Jemma. And when, if, I get back on my feet I shall pay you back. Every penny.'

'You don't need to, Sophie. I told you, somebody already has.'

'Haven't you any idea who it was?'

'No. None at all. But obviously it was somebody who knew I'd been saving up to start my training. I just wish I knew so that I could say thank you.' She got to her feet and looked round the room for a clock but there wasn't one. 'Are you ready? If so, we'd better pack your things and go and catch the train.'

'Pack my things?' Sophie said, bewildered.

'Well, you won't be coming back here, will you?'

'I don't know what I'll be doing.' Her jaw set. 'But I'd be a fool to give up this room before I find out whether we're both welcome, because I told you, I'm not parting with Jenny. I wouldn't get another room at the price. But as for packing my things, I've only got what I stand up in.'

'Then you're ready to go,' Jemima said cheerfully. 'Come on, let's go and get the train.'

'Aunt Minnie. Is she very ill? Is she going to die?' Sophie asked when they were safely in a Ladies Only carriage and the train had pulled out of the station. She bit her lip. 'Oh, Jemma, I couldn't bear it if she were to die and I hadn't seen her again. She was always so good to me and I was such a little brat.'

'I don't think she's going to die but she's making herself ill worrying about you,' Jemima said slowly. 'That's why Uncle William was so anxious for me to contact you. I daren't tell her I thought I'd seen you because she would have come looking for you. That might have killed her, in this cold weather.'

The train drew into the station. It was a cold, foggy afternoon as they made their way along the road.

'I'm glad it's foggy,' Sophie whispered to Jemima. 'I wouldn't want anybody to recognize me.'

'It's something you'll have to get used to if you stay,' Jemima reminded her.

'*If* I stay,' Sophie said.

Twenty-Eight

Uncle William opened the door to their knock. The look of relief on his face was quickly replaced by a carefully non-committal expression.

'You'd better come in,' he said by way of greeting. 'She's upstairs, having a bit of a lie-down. You can go up. I'll put the kettle on.'

Jemima dropped her bag of books and followed Sophie up the stairs. At the door of Aunt Minnie's bedroom Sophie hesitated, then knocked and walked in.

Aunt Minnie hadn't heard the knock. She was lying listlessly looking out of the window. Lying on the big bed she looked to be a smaller, more shrunken version of the old Aunt Minnie.

Sophie walked over to the bed and said softly, 'I've come home, Aunt Minnie. If you'll have me, I've come home.'

Aunt Minnie turned her head. It took a brief minute for her to realize that it was really Sophie who stood there, and then, with a little cry, she held out her arms. 'My girl. Oh, my little girl!'

Sophie thrust the baby into Jemima's arms and enveloped her aunt in a great hug. They clung together, rocking back and forth, both of them weeping, Aunt Minnie saying over and over, 'My girl. Oh, my girl, thank God you've come back to me.'

Jemima stood waiting, holding Sophie's baby in her arms. She looked down at the tiny form, marvelling at the perfectly formed hands, little fingers ending in tiny nails, one hand curled over into a tiny fist. Then Jenny's eyes opened. They were a deep, violet blue, with curling black lashes. She stared up at Jemima with a serious expression, as if she were weighing up her fitness to be an aunt. Then, presumably satisfied, she closed her eyes and went to sleep.

Extricating herself from Aunt Minnie's embrace, Sophie turned and took the baby from Jemima and placed her in the crook of Aunt Minnie's arm. 'This is my Jenny,' she whispered with pride. 'And Jenny, this is Aunt Minnie. But I hope she'll be your Nan.'

'I'll go and see if the kettle's boiled,' Jemima said to nobody in particular, experiencing a sudden, strange sense of loss now that the baby had been taken from her.

By the time the tea was brewed Sophie had helped Aunt Minnie downstairs to the kitchen, where Uncle William was sitting in his chair hiding behind his newspaper.

'She's back, Will. Our girl's back,' Aunt Minnie said to him, as if he didn't already know. Once more she was nursing the baby.

'Aye. So I see,' was his non-committal answer.

'Oh, I wish I'd made some scones,' she said inconsequentially. 'I've only got a bit of cake in the tin.'

Sophie went over to her uncle and knelt down beside him. 'Aunt Minnie wants me to stay, Uncle,' she said. 'I'd like to do that; I'd like to stay and look after you both and nurse Aunt Minnie back to health. I'm not the girl I was. What I've been through has taught me how selfish and ungrateful I used to be. I don't think I'm like that now. I'm willing to face the shame of what I've done. I know people will talk and point a finger at me. I'm ready for that.' She sat back on her heels. 'But I won't stay if you don't want me, Uncle.' Her voice hardened. 'And I won't give up my baby. Not for anybody. I couldn't bear to have her taken from me and put in an orphanage. It's for you to decide. If you can't accept us, both of us, then we'll go back where we came from.'

'No, no, you can't do that,' Aunt Minnie cried, cuddling the baby closer to her. 'Not now you're back. You can't leave us again.'

Uncle William looked over the top of his newspaper and gave a sniff. 'I reckon you've got your answer. If my Minnie wants you, you'd better stay.' He glared at her. 'But we'll have no more shenanigans.' He hid behind his newspaper again.

'You don't need to worry about *that*,' Sophie said with something of a shudder.

Aunt Minnie smiled down at the baby. 'You're going to live here and I'm going to be your Nan, Jenny,' she cooed happily. She looked up. 'When was she born, Sophie?'

'The thirteenth of August. Three months to the day after my –' She shot a glance at Jemima – 'our eighteenth birthday.'

Aunt Minnie nodded complacently. 'Just as I thought. Take the calendar down, Jemma, and have a look at August.'

Jemima did as she asked. The thirteenth of August had a ring round it.

'But how could you possibly have known, Auntie?' Sophie said, amazed.

'Because that's the day Jemima came here looking all pale and ill.' She turned to Jemima. 'Don't you remember? You had dreadful pains in your insides? I fetched you a hot-water bottle and you fell asleep. When you woke up you were better.'

Jemima nodded. 'Yes, I remember. I'd never had such pains and I've never had anything like it since. But I don't see . . .'

'You're twins. There's a bond between twins, even when they're apart. I wondered if it was because Sophie's time had come so I marked the date in case I could ever prove it. And now I have.' She beamed at them both.

'And I had this strange feeling that somebody was beside me all the time. I've already told you that, haven't I, Jemma?'

Jemima nodded. 'It must have been the twin thing again.' She frowned. 'It's odd. Because we weren't at all close when we were children.'

Sophie put out her hand. 'Maybe things will be different now, Jemma. I've done a lot of growing up in these last months.'

'And now you're home to stay, thank God,' Aunt Minnie said happily. 'Your old room is all ready for you and there'll be plenty of room for the cradle, when Uncle Will's fetched it down.'

The next time Jemima visited there was a subtle change in the household. Aunt Minnie had regained her health and energy, which was not surprising, but Uncle William had not only fetched the cradle down from the sail loft where it had been stored but he had cleaned it and planed out all the scratch marks and then polished it so that it looked almost new. He had also made the baby an intricate little wooden toy dog with legs and head that moved, which Jenny was far too young to appreciate.

'Hark! Is that the little maid I can hear?' He cupped his hand over his ear as he sat contentedly in his chair by the fire.

'No, Uncle. She's fast asleep in her cradle. Look at her,' Sophie said, as she brought in the tea tray, laughing affectionately at him.

'Well, with all the noise of you womenfolk chattering you'd never hear if she did cry,' he said good-naturedly. 'Have you brought some of those nice cake things you made this morning? They'd go well with a cuppa tea.'

'Give the girl a chance, Will,' Aunt Minnie said with a smile as she poured out the tea. 'The girl's only got one pair of hands.'

'Yes, I'm just on my way to fetch them,' Sophie said, winking at Jemima.

The atmosphere in the room was warm, loving and happy and it was obvious that the baby had found her way right into Uncle William's heart. Sophie was right; she had changed, Jemima reflected as she made her way home. Inevitably her months of shame, of fending for herself, of giving birth with nobody to really care whether she lived or died, had altered her completely. She was no longer the selfish, spoiled ungrateful girl of the past. She was now a loving, caring woman, prepared to repay her aunt and uncle for the love they had lavished on her over the years. She had grown up.

Winter was always a difficult time in school. Poorly clad children, some with no coats, many poorly shod, a few without shoes at all, were more prone to illness. Even those whose parents were so over-protective that they sewed their offspring into their clothes for the winter – sometimes with a layer of wadding in between – were not immune from the diseases that ravaged the school.

Jemima and Kathryn stitched sulphur bags to the hems of their long trailing skirts to discourage vermin from crawling up their legs. This was a habitual hazard in a roomful of children who rarely bathed or changed their clothes. Mr Green, the school caretaker, washed all the floors with disinfectant after the children had gone home every night to tackle the uphill job of keeping the school free from the pests and diseases that were a fact of life of a good many of the children from poorer homes.

'And watch out for the children who keep scratching their heads, Jemima,' Miss Peel advised. 'Head lice can't jump upwards so you'll be less likely to become infected if you always stand over them and don't get down to their level.'

Even so, they both formed a ritual of washing their hair every week and then combing it through with a fine-toothed comb to make sure they hadn't become infested.

Jemima burst out laughing one evening as they were both busy combing through their hair. 'Oh, dear, who'd ever believe the hazards of teaching!'

Of course, not all the children came from deprived homes. It was easy to see which children came from 'good' homes; the girls wore spotless white pinafores over warm dresses and were well shod and the boys wore warm trousers and jumpers and sturdy boots. Unfortunately, they were just as liable to catch diseases as those in rags and soon after Christmas the school had to be closed for three weeks when an epidemic of diphtheria swept through all the class-rooms. Four children died in the epidemic, one of them from Jemima's class.

The children took the deaths with a stoicism that amazed her, but as Kathryn pointed out, death was a fact of life for most of them. Babies died young, siblings became consumptive and faded away, measles took its toll. And that didn't take into account the accidents: fire, falling in the river or under horses' hooves . . .

'Oh, don't!' Jemima pleaded, covering her ears. 'To hear you talking it's a wonder any of them survive!'

At last spring came. The atmosphere in the classroom sweetened as the children who had been stitched into their clothes for the winter were unstitched and the lucky ones even given a bath. The School Inspectors made their periodic round of the school, spending a few minutes in each classroom before being closeted in the office with Mrs Childs to look at the reports and cash books.

Jemima was a bit worried, not knowing what to expect, although Kathryn told her it was only a formality since School Inspectors knew little about what really went on in schools. 'They're only interested in making sure not too much of the ratepayers' money is spent on unnecessary education for the children, nor on inflated salaries for the teachers,' she said.

'Oh, that sounds rather cynical,' Jemima admonished her.

'You just wait till you see them,' Kathryn replied with a grim smile.

Jemima was in the middle of a spelling test when the classroom door opened and four men in tweed suits entered with Mrs Childs; one she recognized as the local builder, another owned a hardware shop, a third was a boat builder and the fourth was Dr Steers, the local doctor.

She quickly gestured for the children to stand to attention but they had already scrambled to their feet as soon as they saw Mrs Childs.

When the children were seated again the men gazed round the classroom trying to look as if they knew what they were looking for, then the doctor cleared his throat and asked if the windows were ever opened.

'Oh, yes,' Mrs Childs said brightly. 'We like the children to have plenty of air.'

Jemima knew better than to contradict her, but when the school was built the windows were all placed high up in the walls so the children shouldn't be distracted from learning by the outside world. Since special poles were needed to manipulate the catches and they had been borrowed for other classrooms and never returned, she couldn't remember the last time they had been opened.

'You can carry on with your lesson, Miss Furlong,' Mrs Childs said quietly. 'The Inspectors are interested in seeing how the children are taught.'

Jemima nodded her thanks and looked round at her class, now sitting quietly with their hands in their laps, looking at her expectantly.

'Who can spell APPLE?' she asked.

A sea of hands shot up so she chose a boy she knew would give the right answer.

'Good. Who can spell ELEPHANT?'

Not so many hands shot up but she knew who to ask to make sure the question was answered correctly.

After two more questions the men began to shuffle their feet and mutter among themselves, then one of them took out his pocket watch and looked at it.

Mrs Childs took the hint. 'Shall we move on, gentlemen?' she said, obviously relishing the fact that they were more than a little out of their depth on her territory.

After they had gone Jemima heaved a sigh of relief and continued with her spelling test. Having seen them she couldn't help sharing Kathryn's cynicism and wondering if the Inspectors knew what they were looking for and, if they did, whether they had found it.

Twenty-Nine

During term time Jemima didn't have much spare time to visit Aunt Minnie and Sophie but she was always sure of a warm welcome when she did and she was constantly amazed at the change in Sophie. Gone was the lazy selfish girl of her youth and in her place now was a caring, loving woman, grateful to be back where she belonged.

One afternoon, after a good-natured argument over who should make the tea, which Aunt Minnie won, Sophie turned to Jemima.

'We're having Jenny baptized on Sunday.' Jemima noticed the inclusive 'we'; clearly it was Aunt Minnie's idea. 'And we'd like you to be her godmother, Jemma.' She hesitated and her voice dropped. 'I've left a blank on the baptism form where it asked for the father's name – well, I couldn't name her father, could I? Not with him engaged and about to be married . . .'

'No, of course you couldn't. Do you think Aunt Minnie knows who it is?'

'I think she's probably guessed. Either that or Mrs Worsnop will have told her because I reckon the old girl must have known what her godson was like and with me leaving in such a hurry she'd have put two and two together. But she's never asked. I think she's just glad to have me back.'

'I'm sure of that.' Jemima smiled at her sister.

'Nearly as glad as I am to be back,' Sophie added. 'I've got you to thank for that, Jemma.'

'You have thanked me by asking me to be Jenny's godmother,' Jemima said. 'I'd like that, very much.'

'It'll be in the afternoon and there won't be any other babies christened at the same time. The vicar thought it best, since there's no father.'

'Does it worry you, Sophie?'

'That I'm an unmarried mother?' Sophie thought for a minute. 'It did when I first came back. I knew people were pointing at me and talking about me behind my back although nobody ever said a word to me. In fact, one or two turned their backs on me. But I reckon I've paid for my stupidity, Jemima. It wasn't very nice, living like I did for all those months, and now I've got a good home with Aunt and Uncle and I'm grateful for it. I'll show my gratitude by looking after them both till the day they die, which, please God, won't be for a good many years yet. Knowing that, I feel I can hold my head up and look people in the eye without feeling guilty.'

'Good for you, Sophie.' Jemima gave her a hug.

Aunt Minnie came in with the tea tray. 'Oh, Sophie dear, I forgot the sugar.'

'It's all right, Auntie, I'll fetch it. Where's Uncle?'

'Still outside rocking the pram. He said he'd rock her off to sleep but I'm sure she's been asleep for ages.' Aunt Minnie grinned at Jemima. 'He dotes on that child, you know. He'll hardly let her out of his sight. Just take a look out of the window.'

Jemima got up and went over to stand beside Aunt Minnie. Uncle William was sitting on the garden bench, his pipe clamped between his few remaining teeth, his cap tipped over his eyes, snoring gently. A piece of string was tied round one hand and the other end was tied to the pram handle. Every now and again, even in his sleep, he gave it a little jerk and set the pram rocking again.

'Silly old fool,' Aunt Minnie said affectionately.

After Jemima had finished her second cup of tea and eaten more of Sophie's delicious cherry cakes than she had intended, she got to her feet.

'I must go. I need to call in at Baxter's on my way home.'

Sophie accompanied her to the door.

'Richard Baxter's nice,' she said thoughtfully. 'I don't know why you didn't marry him when you had the chance.'

'I might have done if the money hadn't turned up so that I could begin teaching, although I really didn't relish the thought of being tied to Baxter's Emporium with a hypochondriac and a drunkard for the rest of my life. Anyway, it wouldn't really have been fair to Richard, would it, because I would have been marrying him for all the wrong reasons.'

'But wouldn't you have liked to marry him?' Sophie persisted. 'Without the Emporium, as you call it?'

She shrugged. 'I never even thought about it because it was never an option. The one went with the other. But you know I'd always wanted to teach, and I couldn't have begun training for that if I'd got married.'

'Yes, you were always the clever one.' Sophie regarded her thoughtfully. 'And are you happy?'

Jemima frowned at her. 'What do you mean?'

'Is teaching as good as you thought it would be?'

'It certainly keeps me busy,' Jemima said with a laugh.

'That's not what I meant,' Sophie said.

'It's a very worthwhile thing to do. Is that a better answer?' Jemima gave her sister a peck on the cheek. 'But if you think Richard is so nice, why don't you marry him yourself?'

Sophie shook her head. 'It wouldn't be fair to burden him with another man's child,' she said seriously. 'It wouldn't be fair to any man. I know I shall never marry, Jemima. I know that.'

Sophie was right, Jemima thought as she made her way to Baxter's. Having an illegitimate child had ruined her chances of marriage. But teaching didn't necessarily mean that Jemima had turned her back on marriage in favour of her career. In fact, her dream had always been that she would marry Oliver and work beside him in his school, bearing his children . . . She shook her head at the thought. Somehow she couldn't imagine Oliver being in the least bit interested in fatherhood. She sighed. Well, she was the thirteenth child, what made her think life would be perfect? She pushed open the door and walked into the shop.

Richard came forward to greet her. 'You're looking very pensive, Jemima, and that was a sad little smile you were wearing as you came in,' he said, keeping his voice light although his expression was concerned. 'A penny for your thoughts?'

She shook her head. 'They're not worth even a penny,' she said, making an effort to match his tone.

'Then is there anything I can get you?'

She smiled, a real smile this time ending in a chuckle. 'No, not unless things have changed, Richard, and you're allowed to sell ladies' unmentionables.'

'Ah. No, I'm afraid I must hand you over to Lillian for that,' he said. He made no attempt to move out of the way. 'Are things all right with you, Jemma?' he asked, still looking concerned. 'You're looking tired.'

'Oh, dear. That's not at all the kind of thing you should say to a lady, Richard,' she said with a reproving smile. 'You should brush up on your etiquette.'

'I flatter myself I know you too well to bother with polite etiquette,' he replied a trifle impatiently. 'So I'll repeat, are things all right with you?'

She nodded. 'I am a little tired, I'll admit. All work and no play makes Jill . . .' She spread her hands.

Lillian appeared from behind her counter.

'Can I help you, Miss Furlong?' she asked icily. 'I'm sure I can be of more assistance to you than Mr Richard.' She tapped Richard on the arm with a rather possessive gesture. 'I'll look after Miss Furlong, Richard. I know you're busy. Haven't you still got some orders to make out ready for the carrier to collect?'

'No, they're done.' Richard hesitated, then dropped a kiss on Jemima's cheek. 'I'll leave you to Lillian's tender mercies, Jemima.' He winked at her. 'Just make sure she doesn't overcharge you.'

'I *never* overcharge people, Richard,' Lillian said primly. 'This way, Miss Furlong. Now, what can I show you?' She led the way through to the ladies' department with a possessive air, which made Jemima, who knew every inch of the place, smile to herself.

Mrs Baxter was sitting on a chair at the end of the counter. When she saw Jemima her face lit up in a way it never had when she worked there and she was anxious to know how her teaching career was progressing.

'You seem to be very well thought of by the children you teach, Jemima,' Mrs Baxter told her. 'I hear nothing but good of you from mothers who come into the shop.' She smiled. 'I suppose I should be pleased, but their gain is my loss. I still miss you, my dear.' She raised her eyebrows in the direction of Lillian, who was down on her knees searching in a drawer for the summer vests Jemima had asked for. 'Things aren't quite what they were,' she whispered. 'I have to keep a close eye on things or the place would be in chaos.' Then in a louder voice, 'Haven't you found them, Lillian? I think you're looking in the wrong place. You put them in the drawer above, if I remember rightly. Yes, that's right.' She heaved a sigh. 'See what I mean?'

Instead of folding them neatly, Lillian thrust the vests into a brown paper bag and pushed them across the counter to Jemima, scattering her change carelessly instead of handing it to her. Then she marched down the shop and began tidying some shelves.

'Oh, dear,' Mrs Baxter said with a sigh. 'Will she never learn?'

'She always treats me like that,' Jemima said cheerfully. 'I think she resents the fact that I still come into the shop. She shows her disapproval in the only way she can without being downright rude.'

'Why on earth should she do that?'

'Because I'm encroaching on her territory.'

'Her territory! I don't know where she gets that idea from,' Mrs Baxter said hotly. 'I have to spend far more time in the shop than I used to when you were here, Jemima, because she makes so many mistakes that I can't trust her here on her own.'

Maybe that's not such a bad thing, Jemima thought, although she wisely didn't say so. But Mrs Baxter was certainly looking less pale and puffy and was more animated than Jemima had seen her for a long time.

When she left the shop she looked for Richard but he was nowhere to be seen. However, there was a notice in the shop window advertising a concert in the Balkerne Rooms in Colchester. Mr Kenneth Harman, violin, accompanied by Mr Richard Baxter, piano. Jemima always tried to attend any concert where Richard was playing. She decided to ask Sophie if she would like to come too, this time.

Sophie was reluctant at first, but Aunt Minnie finally managed to persuade her, insisting that she was perfectly capable of being left in charge of Jenny for one evening.

'And if she won't settle Uncle William will sing to her; that always sends her to sleep.' She darted a wickedly mischievous look at her husband.

He took his pipe out of his mouth. 'Yes, the little maid likes me to sing to her,' he said smugly. 'I can always get her off to sleep.'

Sophie laughed. 'Yes, it's a form of self-defence,' she said with an affectionate glance at him. 'She goes to sleep to shut out the noise.'

'Well, it always works,' he said mildly, stoking up his pipe again.

'And I shall pay for you both to go to this concert as a birthday treat,' Aunt Minnie said, beginning to clear the table.

They had just finished the traditional birthday tea, with jelly and a birthday cake, which Sophie had made and iced under Aunt Minnie's direction.

'But Aunt Minnie, we're nineteen,' she had protested with a smile as they worked in the kitchen together. 'Do we really need jelly and birthday cake?'

'No, of course you don't *need* it,' Aunt Minnie had replied happily. 'But I like you to have it. It'll be just like old times.'

'You're a sentimental old besom and I love you,' Sophie had said, planting a floury kiss on the tip of her nose.

So they fed jelly to Jenny, who loved it, and even sang 'Happy Birthday' to each other, subsiding into giggles before the end. That was something that had never happened when they were children,

Jemima reflected as she hurried home afterwards, because in those days Sophie had always flounced off on some pretext or other.

Jemima had left Aunt Minnie's rather later than she had intended because she had stayed to help bath Jenny and put her to bed. It had been a lovely feeling, wrapping the small, sweet-smelling baby in a soft, warm towel and cuddling her dry and then tucking her into her cot and singing her to sleep. She could well understand Sophie's determination never to be parted from her little daughter whatever happened and for a moment she almost envied her twin. She made her way home thoughtfully and with rather less than her usual enthusiasm to write an essay for her Saturday pupil-teacher's class.

Thirty

Aunt Minnie and Uncle William had bought Sophie a new costume for her birthday. When she protested at the extravagance Aunt Minnie pointed out that now Sophie was living with them she did most of the housework and cooking, so it was no more than her due. It was true that Aunt Minnie had become very arthritic of late, so she had been glad to hand over the running of the house to Sophie while she sat in the sun, happily knitting or nursing Jenny.

'I see you're wearing the costume Aunt Minnie bought for your birthday, Sophie,' Jemima said as she sat opposite her sister in the railway carriage on the way to the concert in Colchester. 'It suits you. I love that dark, sea-green colour.'

Sophie smoothed the skirt. 'It came from Baxter's. I chose it from a catalogue and they ordered it for me.'

'That's where mine came from, too.' Jemima plucked an imaginary strand of cotton from the lapel of her own maroon jacket. 'When I worked at Baxter's I was always surprised how many people ordered their clothes that way. It's very useful.'

'Yes. And Mrs Baxter made my hat, as well,' Sophie said. 'It was only finished yesterday.' She leaned forward. 'Do you think Richard Baxter will marry Lillian Carter?' she asked, changing the subject.

Jemima frowned irritably. 'Lillian Carter? Why on earth should he marry Lillian Carter?'

'Why shouldn't he?' Sophie said with a shrug.

'I'll phrase it differently. What makes you think he might?'

'Well, when I was in the shop collecting my hat she was acting quite proprietorially towards him, and being very coy and come-hither. She's obviously set her cap at him.' Sophie pinched her lip. 'I suppose it would be quite convenient if he married her,' she said thoughtfully.

'Convenience isn't the best foundation for marriage,' Jemima snapped, her words coming out more sharply than she intended.

Sophie raised her eyebrows at her sister's tone but said no more.

All the same, Jemima was surprised to see Lillian sitting near the front with Mrs Baxter when they walked into the concert hall. Sophie nudged her. 'There you are. See? I told you,' she whispered.

Jemima didn't reply but concentrated on finding their seats, which were towards the back of the hall.

She didn't enjoy the concert very much because her eyes kept straying to where Lillian was sitting with Mrs Baxter and her thoughts kept straying to Sophie's words in the train. Was Richard really considering marriage to that silly, affected girl? Usually, when she came to a concert she quickly became lost in the music but today there was little to distract her from her thoughts. The violinist, a middle-aged man with a beard that looked in constant danger of being tangled in the violin strings, was flamboyant both in his dress and his manner; his programme had clearly been chosen to demonstrate his prowess rather than for the enjoyment of the audience. In contrast, Richard's two solos, an impromptu by Schubert and a nocturne by Chopin, were much more tuneful and sensitively played and the audience showed their appreciation by their applause.

In the interval Jemima saw Richard go over to speak to his mother and Lillian. She also saw how Lillian put her hand on his arm and smiled up at him. Proprietorially, just as Sophie had remarked. After a few moments he left them and came over to where Jemima and Sophie were standing.

'Why didn't you tell me you were coming, Jemima?' he asked in quite an accusing tone, after he had greeted them. 'You know I would have given you complimentary tickets. I don't like you being seated so near the back.'

'It's very kind of you to say so, Richard, but you nearly always manage to give me complimentary tickets, so it didn't hurt us to pay, for once. In any case Aunt Minnie insisted on treating us,' Jemima told him. She nodded in the direction of Mrs Baxter and Lillian. 'Your mother doesn't often come to your concerts. Is she enjoying it?'

He made a face. 'Not much. She said she'd like to come since I'd been given a solo spot but she's not a great fan of the violin.' He dropped his voice. 'Even when it's played well.' He sighed. 'That man is so difficult to accompany. His timing is all over the place.'

'Never mind; your solos went really well,' Jemima said enthusiastically. 'I really loved those pieces you played. It was worth sitting through the rest of it just to hear them.'

He flushed with pleasure. 'Thank you for that, Jemma.'

'Yes, I had no idea you were so good,' Sophie added. She put her hand up to her mouth. 'Oh, I'm sorry, Richard. That was a terribly patronizing thing to say. Nevertheless it's true, you are good. Extremely good.'

'Thank you, Sophie,' he said, smiling. 'Flattery will get you every-where.'

'And is Lillian enjoying herself tonight?' Jemima forced herself to ask.

He made a face. 'She's pretending she is.'

'What do you mean by that?' Sophie asked.

'Well, she's a bit out of her depth, to tell you the truth. She's only here so my mother didn't have to come alone. Pa was supposed to be coming with her but when we discovered there would be a bar here my mother and I decided it was probably safer not to risk him coming and making fools of us all.'

'He's still drinking, then,' Jemima said sadly.

Richard nodded, tight-lipped. 'Oh, yes, he's still drinking.'

Suddenly, Lillian came up and tapped him on the arm. 'You're neglecting your mama, you naughty boy,' she said in a silly little-girl voice. 'Look, she's all by herself.'

'She shouldn't be. You're supposed to be with her, Lillian. That's why you're here,' he replied shortly. 'In any case, I have to get back. The second part will be starting in a minute.' He turned his back on her to speak to Jemima and Sophie again. 'I hope you'll both enjoy the second half. With any luck Monsieur Bonard will tone down the digital acrobatics a bit so you can hear the tunes he's supposed to be playing instead of trying to mesmerize us with his improvisations.' He grinned. 'And if he does that I might just be able to keep up with him!'

'Good luck, anyway, Richard,' Jemima said, squeezing his arm.

He gave her a swift peck on the cheek. 'Thanks for that, Jemma.'

On the way home in the train Sophie said thoughtfully, 'It's such a pity you didn't marry Richard when you had the chance, Jemma. He's still fond of you, you know.'

'And I'm still fond of him,' Jemima said. 'I think of him as a big brother.'

'I'm sure that's not the way he sees you, though.'

'No, he probably thinks I'm a stupid girl who's willing to sacri-fice the chance of marriage to become a dried-up old stick of a school marm,' she said lightly.

'Well, at least you haven't sacrificed your chances by putting the cart before the horse like I have,' Sophie said, a hint of sadness in her tone. Then she brightened up. 'But I've got my Jenny. She's all I need.'

And that's something I shall never have, Jemima found herself thinking, as she remembered the warm sensation that had so unexpectedly washed over her when she cuddled Sophie's baby.

The following day when Mrs Peel opened her post at breakfast she clapped her hands in delight.

'Oh, listen to this,' she said excitedly. 'Oliver has an interview for a headmaster's post in Colchester next week and he's written to ask if he can come and stay for a couple of nights. Won't that be lovely?'

'Goodness, yes,' Kathryn said, taking a bite of toast. 'It's absolutely ages since we've seen him and he hasn't written much lately.'

'No, well, I daresay he's very busy,' Mrs Peel said. 'Now, let me see . . .'

'I can move out if you want him to have his old room back,' Jemima said quickly.

'No, no, there's no need for that.' Mrs Peel patted her hand. 'He can have Kathryn's room. You won't mind sharing with me for a couple of nights, will you, dear?'

Kathryn grinned. 'No, as long as you don't snore.'

'I never snore,' Mrs Peel said, quite affronted.

Days at school were always busy so Jemima had no time to dwell on Oliver's impending visit until she got to bed at night. It was years since she had seen him, not since the day she had come here to the Peels' to tea when she was still working at Baxter's. He had been full of his teaching ambitions then and hadn't even asked what she was doing, for which she had been profoundly thankful. But now she would have plenty to tell him because she was fulfilling her ambitions, just as he was. They would have quite a lot in common. She looked forward to seeing him.

He arrived on Thursday afternoon for his interview on Friday morning. Jemima had just got in from school as he pushed open the gate and she was in her bedroom changing out of her school clothes as she saw him walk up the path. He appeared taller and thinner than she remembered and he looked very distinguished in a smart, dark grey Harris tweed suit and with a grey felt hat perched squarely on top of his dark curls. His shoes were polished to a high shine and he carried a cane in one hand and a small Gladstone bag in the other. He looked every inch the successful schoolmaster.

Jemima put on the skirt belonging to her new maroon costume. It was known as an umbrella style, with a plain front and a sweeping train and had three bands of braid just above the hem. Worn with a crisp white blouse with lace cascades down the front and a wide belt that emphasized her slim waist, she knew she looked her best. She brushed her hair and coiled it into a neat bun on top of her head, pinched a little colour into her cheeks with her thumb and forefinger and went downstairs to greet Oliver.

Thirty-One

Mrs Peel and Kathryn were already fussing round Oliver, remarking on how smart and well he was looking, when Jemima walked in. She waited until Mrs Peel had left to make the inevitable pot of tea and Kathryn had plumped cushions and made him comfortable in the best armchair before she went to speak to him.

'It's very nice to see you again, Oliver,' she said with a smile, holding out her hand.

He immediately leapt to his feet to greet her and she was quite amused as well as gratified to see the surprised admiration in his eyes. 'Jemima!' he said. 'My word, how you've changed.'

Kathryn laughed and shook a finger at him. 'Whatever do you mean, Oliver?' she said. 'That's hardly the way to greet an old friend.'

'Oh, dear.' He flushed a little. 'I'm terribly sorry. Did that sound rude? Forgive me, Jemima. I've always remembered you as the rather earnest young girl I knew before I went away to college.' He smiled. 'I've often thought of those erudite discussions – well, we thought they were erudite, didn't we – we had round this very table.'

'That was quite a long time ago, Oliver,' Jemima said, smiling with him. 'A great deal has happened in those years. Look at you, already being interviewed for a headmaster's post.'

'And looking every inch the part, if I may say so,' Kathryn said proudly.

He pulled down his waistcoat. 'Do you really think so? I had this suit specially made for the occasion. It cost me quite a lot of money, too.'

'Money well spent, Oliver,' Kathryn assured him. 'Ah, here's Mama with the tea.'

They sat round the table drinking tea and eating Mrs Peel's cherry biscuits and talking over old times. Each time she looked up Jemima found Oliver's eyes resting on her, a thoughtful expression on his face. After about half an hour she got to her feet.

'You must excuse me. I have an essay to finish and work to prepare for tomorrow. I always use this time between tea and supper for working and I'm sure you have lots of family things to talk about.'

She left the three of them talking and went back upstairs to her room.

But she couldn't settle to her work. She cupped her chin in her hand and sat gazing out of the window. Oliver was back, as handsome and as engaging as ever. His brown eyes held the same warmth and when he smiled he revealed that slightly crooked tooth in an otherwise perfect set that she had always found so attractive. She sighed. She had dreamed about Oliver for so long and now he was here, under the same roof, hoping soon to become headmaster of a school in Colchester. Maybe she would be able to teach in his school once she was properly qualified . . . Maybe he would ask her to marry him and teach beside him . . . She looked at the blank sheet of paper on the table in front of her. If she didn't get down to work she would never even qualify as a teacher, let alone work beside Oliver. She picked up her pen.

After supper of steak and kidney pie that Mrs Peel had cooked because she knew it was one of Oliver's favourite dishes, and raspberry jam sponge, Oliver announced his intention of taking a turn round the village.

'It was a really delicious meal, Grandmama, but I hope you'll forgive me if I leave you and go for a walk now. To tell you the truth, I'm a bit keyed up over tomorrow's interview and I think perhaps a bit of fresh air might help me to sleep.'

'Of course we don't mind, Oliver, dear,' Mrs Peel said.

Oliver smiled at Jemima. 'Perhaps you'd like to come with me, Jemima? Help to take my mind off tomorrow's ordeal?' he asked hopefully.

'Yes, I'll come with you if you'd like me to,' Jemima said, trying not to sound too eager.

'They make a handsome pair, don't they?' Mrs Peel said to Kathryn as they stood at the window and watched Oliver and Jemima walk out of the gate together.

'Now, Mother,' Kathryn said, giving her mother's arm a little shake. 'Don't start matchmaking.'

'Where would you like to go, Oliver?' Jemima said as they made their way down the road.

'Oh, down by the river, I think. It's always nice and peaceful there.'

'Are you very worried about tomorrow's interview?'

He grinned at her. 'No, not really. It was just an excuse to get you on your own so that I could talk to you and find out what you've been doing all these years. We seem to have completely lost touch, Jemima. I don't know why.'

'You've been away. New places. New experiences. We've both changed. Moved on . . .'

'You've certainly changed,' he said. 'When I left you were a shy, skinny little thing . . .'

'With aspirations way above her station in life,' she finished for him.

'I didn't say that.'

'You could have done. It was true.'

'And now?'

'I'm getting to where I've always wanted to be. It's taken a long time but in about another eighteen months as a pupil-teacher I should qualify and be a real school teacher.'

'Why on earth has it taken so long, Jemima?'

'It's a long story.'

'I'm in no hurry. It's a beautiful evening, with a spectacular sunset and a lovely view over the river, I have a charming companion by my side, what more could a man ask? Except, perhaps, a seat on which to sit and admire the scenery. And right on cue . . .' As he spoke they reached a rustic seat placed on the sea wall. He smiled at her as they sat down. 'Right. Fire away.'

She gave him an edited version of her life so far.

'Ah, yes, I remember now. Aunt Kathryn wrote and told me your mother had refused permission for you to go into teaching.' He frowned. 'Why wouldn't she sign those papers? It must have nearly broken your heart.'

She shrugged. 'It was partly out of spite, I think. She never really liked me. I was her thirteenth child and she always said I brought bad luck.' She could hardly tell him the real reason was that she had been seen by a nosy neighbour kissing him goodbye in the churchyard.

'How ridiculously superstitious.' He was quiet for a few minutes, then he said, 'I'm surprised you gave your sister all your savings.'

'She's my twin. She needed the money more than I did. I was glad to be able to help her.'

He turned and gave her a smile that made her heart turn over. 'You're such a sweet and generous girl, Jemima,' he said softly. 'I'm glad it all came right in the end. I'm glad there was a mysterious benefactor to replace the money. Have you never found out who it might have been?'

'No. Never.'

'He left no clues?'

'No. I don't even know if it was a man.'

'Oh, I'm sure it was,' he said confidently. He got to his feet and held out his hand to help her up. 'We'd better be getting back. I don't want to ruin your reputation in the eyes of my grandmother and aunt,' he said with a smile.

Later that night, as she lay in bed going over the events of the evening, particularly the walk by the river, Jemima recalled Oliver's words about her mysterious benefactor. Why had he been so convinced that it had been a man? Unless . . . But Oliver wouldn't have had ten pounds to give away. Would he?

By the time Jemima and Kathryn returned from school the next day Oliver was back from his interview. He was relaxing in the armchair in his braces and beaming.

'Here you see the new headmaster of St Martin's Primary School,' he said proudly, getting to his feet and bowing elaborately.

'Oh, Oliver, I'm so proud of you.' Kathryn went over and kissed him.

'Yes, congratulations, Oliver,' Jemima said warmly.

'It's only a small school, less than two hundred children, but it used to belong to the church so a small house goes with it at a nominal rent. The school is rather rundown, the previous headmaster was consumptive and died quite recently – he was not very old, as I understand it, not much over forty – but his wife kept things going as best she could. She's agreed to stay on as my assistant, at least for the time being, which the Board are quite happy with.' He was talking quickly in his excitement and he went on, hardly pausing for breath, 'The house has four rooms, which can be divided quite easily into two separate dwellings. I went to see it. It shouldn't be difficult to do and there will be quite enough space in two rooms for my needs.'

'Are the rooms a good size?' Mrs Peel asked.

He looked round. 'About as big as this room, I should think. It's all on the ground floor, a square divided equally into four, so all they'll have to do is block up a couple of internal doorways and make another entrance. Mrs Grantley is so relieved at not losing both her livelihood and the roof over her head, that I believe she would have agreed to living in the broom cupboard.'

'Oh, poor woman,' Mrs Peel said.

'It sounds ideal for you, Oliver,' Kathryn said enthusiastically.

'Yes, I think so, too. Of course, Mrs Grantley understands that should I wish to marry and have my wife as my assistant at some time in the future, then she will have to make alternative arrangements. But at least the present arrangement gives her plenty of time to think about that. I met her; she seems a pleasant enough lady. Several years younger than her husband, I would have thought, although I'm not an expert in these things.'

'And have you any thoughts in that direction, Oliver? Marriage, I mean?' Mrs Peel asked archly, with a glance in Jemima's direction. Jemima felt her colour rise, so she was glad she was sitting in the shady part of the room.

But Oliver only laughed. 'That would be telling, wouldn't it, Grandmama?' he said easily. He rubbed his hands together. 'But enough of that. I was almost forgetting to tell you that I've booked four tickets for the theatre tonight to celebrate. There's some kind of variety performance at the Theatre Royal which I thought we might all enjoy.'

'Oh, that will be lovely.' Kathryn clapped her hands. 'What time does it begin?'

He felt in his waistcoat pocket and pulled out the tickets. 'Half past seven.'

'Oh, then I must make sure we have an early supper,' Mrs Peel said, her mind, as ever, on the next meal.

Jemima said nothing. Richard was accompanying a ladies' choir tonight at the Balkerne Rooms and he had given her two complimentary tickets. She stifled a sudden pang of guilt. She rarely missed a concert he played for and there had been some that had been less than enjoyable – the violinist with the beard sprang to mind – so she was sure Richard wouldn't mind. He always said when he gave her the tickets, 'If you're not doing anything else you might like to come.' Well, tonight she was doing something else. Her conscience settled, she began to look forward to the evening.

The variety show was mediocre to say the least. There were two acrobats, one of whom inadvertently fell off the other's shoulder and hurt his foot so he limped through the rest of their act. The funniest thing was that, judging by the venomous looks that they shot each other during the rest of their performance, each was blaming the other for the accident. The audience roared with laughter, which didn't help, because it was meant to be a serious performance. There was a soprano who was quite good although Jemima thought Richard would have been a far better accompanist and she had another fleeting stab of guilt at the thought of him seeing two empty seats where she and Kathryn or Sophie would normally have been sitting. There hadn't been time to give him back the tickets. Then the comedian came on and she forgot about Richard as she laughed at his patter. The final act was a fire-eater. Mrs Peel nearly fainted with anxiety when she saw what he was doing.

'How do we get out of the place?' Jemima heard her whisper to Kathryn. 'I fear we shall all be burned in our seats.'

Jemima smiled to herself. She wasn't worried; she'd noticed that there were numerous buckets of sand placed at strategic points because of the gas lighting, which was far more dangerous although everybody was so used to it that they didn't give it a second thought. Neither did it bother her that most of the variety acts were less than perfect because Oliver had engineered the seating so that she was sitting next to him. All through the performance she was conscious of his sleeve brushing hers as they shared an arm rest and several times he turned and whispered something not very complimentary about the performers, which made her giggle. The fact that she could feel his warm breath on her face and his moustache tickle her ear as he whispered gave her an altogether different sensation.

Thirty-Two

The weeks flew past. Oliver was to take up his new position in September so when term ended and he left the school in Cambridge where he had been teaching he came to live with the Peels until his house in Colchester was ready.

For Jemima this was a magic time. To have Oliver living under the same roof and to see him at nearly every mealtime, to hear him singing in his bedroom as he shaved, to join in mealtime discussions and feel she really had something to contribute, were the stuff of dreams as far as she was concerned.

Kathryn and Mrs Peel were in their element as well. They fussed over him, making sure he had the most comfortable chair to sit in and that the spills to light his pipe were always to hand. Mrs Peel cooked his favourite meals and Kathryn ironed his shirts. Sometimes even Jemima felt that the two women were inclined to smother him with their attentions and it became obvious Oliver was beginning to share her feelings one day when Kathryn and her mother were arguing over samples of curtain material for his little house in Colchester.

'Oh, heavens, does it really matter what colour the curtains are in my house?' he burst out. 'I'm sure it won't worry me, as long as I can close them at night. What do you think, Jemima?'

'I rather like that one,' Jemima said, pointing to a swatch of cream brocade. 'It will make the rooms nice and light.'

'Then that's settled. Cream it shall be. Not that it worries me; as long as I've got a desk, a bed and room for my books that's all I need.'

'Oh, no, dear. You'll need an armchair . . .'

'And a dining table . . .'

'And at least two chairs . . .'

'And a chest of drawers . . .'

'And a carpet . . .'

Oliver heaved a sigh and looked at Jemima with raised eyebrows. 'It's a lovely day, Jemma, let's go for a walk and leave Grandmama and Aunt Kathryn to decide what else I'm going to need in this vast mansion they seem to imagine I'll be moving into.' He grinned at them both. 'Just remember, it's only two rooms and I don't have a fortune to spend,' he added more seriously. He picked up his hat, a straw boater. 'Come on, Jemima. Let's go.'

Jemima didn't need asking twice. She put on her hat, a wide-brimmed straw one decorated with forget-me-nots, and followed him.

'I like that hat,' Oliver said as they reached the gate and turned to wave to Kathryn and her mother. 'It suits you.'

'Thank you, kind sir,' she said, flushing with pleasure.

It was one of those days in high summer when the sky was a cloudless blue and the heat shimmered in the dusty road ahead.

'Goodness, I didn't realize quite how hot it was. We'll go down by the river, it may be a bit cooler there,' Oliver said, taking off his jacket and slinging it over his shoulder. 'Or are you finding it too hot for walking?'

'No, I think it will be lovely down by the river, especially if the tide's up.'

They strolled along the narrow streets towards the river. It was even too hot for much conversation and Jemima was just thinking how nice it would be to paddle her feet in the cool river water, as she used to when she was a child, when they rounded a corner and nearly bumped into a woman pushing a pram.

Jemima smiled delightedly. 'Sophie! I didn't expect to see you at this hour of the morning. I don't think you've met Oliver, have you? Oliver, this is my twin sister, Sophie.'

They shook hands politely, obviously not sharing Jemima's enthusiasm at the encounter, then Sophie turned to Jemima. 'Aunt Minnie's arthritis is always worse in the hot weather and Jenny's been a bit grizzly; she seems to find the heat tiresome, too, so I thought I'd take her for a walk to give Aunt Minnie a bit of peace.' She smiled at Oliver to include him in the conversation. 'We've been down by the river. There's a nice little breeze coming off the water.'

'Good. That's where we're making for,' Oliver said briefly.

Jemima looked into the pram. 'It looks as if the walk's done the trick. She's fast asleep.'

'That's good. Well I'd better go. I've got some baking to do. With any luck I'll get it done before she wakes up. I know you're always busy, but come and see us soon, Jemma.'

'I will. Bye, Sophie.'

They walked on in silence for a while, then Oliver said, 'So that's your twin sister. You don't look in the least alike, do you?'

'No. Sophie's always been the pretty one.' This had been Jemima's automatic response ever since she could remember.

'Are you fishing for compliments?' Oliver asked wryly.

Jemima frowned. 'What do you mean?'

'Well, aren't I supposed to say, "No, you're the pretty one"?'

'No, of course not,' Jemima said crossly. 'I was only stating a fact. Sophie has always been the pretty one. She's always had dark curly hair while mine's this mousy colour and straight as a pound of candles.' She shrugged. 'It's never bothered me because I've always known that although she had the looks I was the clever one, which was much more important as far as I was concerned. Anyway, we've never been in each other's company that much. We weren't even brought up together. She was brought up by our Aunt Minnie.'

'Yet you gave her all your savings,' he said thoughtfully.

'Of course.' She looked at him in surprise. 'She's my sister. She needed the money more than I did.'

'I wouldn't say that. You needed it for your career. Presumably the reason she needed it was in that perambulator. I noticed she was not wearing a wedding ring.' He pursed his lips disapprovingly.

'Yes, things were very difficult for her. The least I could do was to help her all I could.' Jemima frowned. 'But are you saying I shouldn't have given her the money, Oliver?' she asked.

'Indeed I am. She got herself into trouble, she should have been left to get on with it, not come running to you for help.'

'You don't understand. It's quite obvious you haven't got any brothers or sisters, Oliver,' she said quietly. Her voice rose. 'And girls don't "get themselves" into trouble, as you very well know. They get led astray by men who ought to be ashamed of themselves and who get off scot-free.'

'Well, you know what I mean.' He sniffed a little uncomfortably, remembering a girl at his Cambridge lodgings. He didn't think she became pregnant but he was never sure because he left before she'd have had time to find out. He reverted to his theme. 'I hazard a guess that your mysterious benefactor wouldn't have been so generous in replacing your money if he'd known what it had been frittered away on in the first place.'

'It wasn't "frittered away", as you call it,' Jemima said through gritted teeth. 'In fact, it could well have saved Sophie's life because it enabled her to keep her head above water and remain respectable.'

'Respectable! Ha! Is that what you call it?'

'Yes, that is what I call it.' She turned her head away. 'Not that it's any of your business, Oliver.'

'No, you're quite right, Jemma, it isn't.' He took her arm and smiled at her disarmingly. 'Now, we're supposed to be out for a pleasant walk by the river to escape my aunt and grandmother arguing over furnishing my house, so don't let us start arguing over your sister.'

She gave him a brief smile in return but his words rankled. She had never thought of Oliver as being quite so judgemental.

'In any case,' he went on, 'I'm far more likely to listen to what you have to say about it.'

'About what?' she asked, frowning.

'About what I shall need to set up home, of course,' he said, squeezing her arm. 'I wouldn't want to choose anything you didn't like.'

She was confused. Oliver seemed to be sending out conflicting signals. One minute he was disapproving of her actions, the next saying that her opinions mattered to him – almost hinting that she might be a part of the home he was setting up. She was disappointed, too, in having discovered an unforgiving, almost puritanical streak in him.

They walked down to the riverside and found the river at half tide. Gulls and wading birds were busily poking about, weaving patterns of three-toed footprints in the mud, anxious to find food before its source was submerged for the next few hours by the rising water.

'Listen, you can hear the mud plopping,' she said, trying to regain something of the companionship they had started out with.

'Filthy, stinking stuff. Did you know you can drown in it?' he replied.

'No. As children we often went mudlarking. I never heard of anyone drowning,' she said, then realized that they were disagreeing again. It was probably the hot weather making them both irritable. She took off her hat and fanned her face. 'I think I'd like to go home now, Oliver,' she said. 'It's very hot, even down here by the river. I think I'll find a shady spot in the garden and catch up on some of my reading.'

He nodded. 'That's a good idea. I've got quite a lot of paperwork to get through, too.'

Luncheon was quite a subdued meal. Jemima hoped Kathryn and her mother would put the desultory conversation down to the heat, since they didn't have much to say, either. Afterwards she excused herself and took her book down to the end of the garden where there was a seat in the shade of the apple trees, right out of the way of everything and everybody.

She hadn't been sitting there long before Oliver arrived, complete with a sheaf of papers and a rug.

'Do you mind if I join you?' he asked, spreading it out almost at her feet without waiting for her answer. 'You see, I want to make amends. I'm afraid I rather offended you this morning, Jemma.' He got down on the rug and sat looking up at her. 'You know you're the last person I would want to offend, don't you? Please say you forgive me.'

She looked down at him. 'What do you want me to forgive you for? Stating your opinion?' she asked quizzically. 'Everyone is entitled to an opinion, Oliver.'

'Mm. Maybe I was a little insensitive in the way I spoke.'

'Yes, maybe you were, a little.' She didn't say she forgave him and in truth she wasn't sure she had, but her words seemed to satisfy him and he got up and came and sat beside her, his charm and good humour melting away her irritation with him. The sheaf of papers he had brought with him remained untouched and her book remained unread while they talked.

'When do you finish your training and become a fully fledged teacher?' he asked, his arm resting carelessly along the back of the seat where they were sitting.

'In about another year,' she told him.

He nodded. 'That'll be about right. By that time I should be well established in my school, Mrs Grantley will have had time to seek employment elsewhere and I shall have a vacancy for an assistant.'

'Are you suggesting I should apply for the post?' she asked a little coquettishly, putting her head on one side.

'Of course.'

'And what if I don't?'

'I shall demand that you do,' he said, trying to look stern and failing.

'Well, we shall see. I might not pass all my exams.' Laughing, she held up her book. 'And I most certainly shan't if you keep me talking like this.'

'Not another word shall pass my lips.' He was silent for a few minutes. Then he said, 'I'm serious, you know, Jemma. I really want you to come and work at my school when you finish your training.'

He leaned towards her. 'I think we would make a very good team.' As he spoke his lips brushed hers, then he gathered her into his arms and she felt herself melting and drowning in his kisses.

That night, lying in bed and reliving those moments, Jemima remembered the words he had spoken. He hadn't made her a formal proposal, yet how else could she construe his words, other than that he intended marriage?

She stretched luxuriously. She had imagined being kissed by Oliver so many times in the past, but the reality had surpassed her wildest imaginings, shaking her to the very depths of her being. She knew that if he had formally asked her to marry him today she would have said 'yes' without any hesitation at all.

He hadn't asked her – at least, not in so many words – but her answer would be ready when he did.

Smiling gently to herself, she fell asleep.

Thirty-Three

All too soon it was time for Oliver to move into his new house ready for the beginning of the new term. Kathryn and Mrs Peel fussed round him and insisted on helping him to move in, which privately Jemima thought he could well have done without, although he didn't complain. Jemima didn't even offer to help, making the excuse that she had promised to go and see Aunt Minnie, who was not very well.

In truth, she wanted to see Sophie and the baby, too, although she didn't say that to Oliver, who wouldn't have approved.

Jenny was over a year old now and giggled as Jemima sat her on her lap and played 'this little piggy' with her toes and 'round and round the garden' on her hands. After tea, which Jenny would only eat if Jemima fed her, Jemima carried her up to bed and sang her to sleep.

'You should be here every night, Jemma,' Sophie said. 'She obviously likes the sound of your voice, the little madam.'

'Either that or she went to sleep to shut out the noise,' Jemima replied, laughing.

'Ah, that child's brought a ray of sunshine into our lives, and that's a fact,' Aunt Minnie said indulgently. She was always ready for Jenny to climb up on to her lap so that she could recite nursery rhymes to her. 'Bless her, she knows she has to sit still when she's on my lap because Auntie Min's got sore bones.' She had to be helped up to bed these days because the arthritis in her joints was so bad. 'And as for our girl,' she said and looked lovingly at Sophie. 'We couldn't manage without her, could we, Will?'

Uncle William nodded. 'Aye, she's a good girl to us,' he agreed.

Jemima got ready to leave, breathing a prayer of thankfulness that things that had started so badly had turned out so well in the end. Sophie and Jenny had a good home and Aunt Minnie and Uncle William would be looked after to the end of their days. More than that, their house seemed to radiate love, which was more than could ever have been said of the house where Jemima had been brought up. When she thought about it, which wasn't often, she felt quite sad that there had always been so much bitterness in her mother's heart.

'I'll walk to the gate with you,' Sophie said.

'Oh, dear, nothing's wrong, I hope,' she said anxiously.

'No, silly.' Sophie took her arm and gave it a little shake. 'It's just something that's occurred to me.'

They reached the gate and stood on either side of it, Sophie leaning on the gatepost with her arms folded. 'I've been thinking about it and I reckon I know who your mysterious benefactor was,' she said, looking very pleased with herself.

'What, the person who gave me the ten pounds on my birthday?' Jemima frowned. 'Go on then, who do you think it could have been?'

'Why, Mrs Worsnop, of course. Couldn't be anybody else, could it?'

Jemima was still frowning. 'What makes you think that?' she asked doubtfully.

'Well, it was her godson who . . .' She hesitated. 'Led me astray.'

'But she didn't know it was him, did she?'

'She must have guessed. She's not daft.'

'But she didn't know I gave you all my money.'

'Aunt Minnie could have told her. They always used to talk together after church on Sundays so I'm sure Aunt Min would have told her what had happened.'

Jemima nodded slowly. 'I suppose it might have been her . . .' She didn't sound convinced.

'Well, if it wasn't her, who do you think it was, then?'

'I really don't know.' She grinned. 'What I do know is that it wouldn't have been our mother. She wouldn't give me the time of day, let alone that amount of money.'

'I don't suppose she's ever seen that amount of money.' Sophie frowned. 'But I suppose it could have been that man who lodges with her. You got on well with him, didn't you?'

'Mr Starling? Yes, he was always very kind and supportive to me, so I suppose it might have been.' Jemima pinched her lip. Her face cleared. 'But whoever it was didn't intend me to know so it wouldn't be right to go round asking questions.'

'And you're happy to leave it at that?'

'Yes, I'm happy to leave it at that.' She started off down the road.

'Perhaps it was your friend, Oliver,' Sophie called after her. 'He seems very taken with you.'

Jemima didn't reply. It was something she had wondered herself.

The church clock struck seven as she made her way home and she paused and then changed direction. She was in no hurry. If Kathryn and her mother were back they would be full of the day's events and Jemima was in no mood to hear about Oliver's new house; it had been the sole topic of conversation between them for several weeks now and she was tired of hearing about it. They seemed to have taken over and he appeared happy to let them, concentrating on preparing himself for his new role as headmaster. Although it was of her own choosing Jemima still felt left out and if she was honest with herself, not a little jealous, which she knew was quite unreasonable.

So, instead of making her way home she decided to go and see Dorothy at Baxter's. Her kitchen was always warm in winter and cool in summer and there was always a warm welcome from Dorothy, whatever the weather.

She was standing at the table ironing and, as ever, her face lit up when she saw Jemima coming down the area steps.

'Oh, I was just thinking about you, Jemima. It seems a long time since we last saw you here.' As she spoke she put the iron down on the hearth and began folding away her ironing cloth. She smiled at her as she pulled the kettle forward. 'It'll be nice to have somebody to talk to.'

Jemima hadn't the heart to tell her she had already drunk several cups of tea with her sister so she sat down and watched as Dorothy busied herself with cups and saucers.

'Doesn't Lillian spend time down here?' she asked, thinking over Dorothy's last words.

'Lillian! Not her, the little madam.' Dorothy poured the tea, her lips pursed disapprovingly. 'Of course, she doesn't live in like you did, so she's not often here in the evenings, but she'd rather spend her spare time in Mrs Baxter's sitting room; she thinks kitchen company's beneath her. And Mrs Baxter might not like it but she won't say anything because Lillian practically runs her part of the shop now, which suits Mrs B very well because it means she can concentrate on making her millinery creations.' Dorothy took several sips of her tea.

'I can't see why that should make a difference. I used to run the ladies' department, but I still spent my spare time down here with you.'

Dorothy leaned her elbows on the table as she sipped her tea. 'The customers don't like her very much,' she confided. 'She's too bossy. You should hear her, always telling them what they ought to buy. "Oh, no, madam, that hat looks dreadful, you should buy this one."' She gave a passable imitation of Lillian's voice.

'You sound as if you don't like her very much, Dorothy,' Jemima said with a smile.

Dorothy gave a little mirthless laugh. 'You could say that. We fell out in a big way the day she came into my kitchen and told me the best way to make fairy cakes. She told me I should rub the fat into the flour, not beat the fat and sugar together first. I soon sent her packing, I can tell you.'

'I can well imagine.' Jemima tried not to laugh. Dorothy's melt-in-the-mouth fairy cakes were legendary.

'The trouble is,' Dorothy said, putting her cup carefully back on its saucer. 'She's got her eye on Richard – well, one eye on Richard and the other on the shop, more like. I can see what she's up to. She's already wormed her way into Mrs B's good books and she's even made herself pleasant to the old man.'

'Mr Baxter, you mean?'

'Yes. She's nice as pie to him, although most of the time he's so sozzled he doesn't know what day of the week it is. Even lets him put his arm round her. And more, I shouldn't wonder,' she added with a knowing nod. She poured more tea for them both. 'And that's after all the fuss she made when she first came here, refusing to live in because she said he tried to interfere with her. Not so fussy now, is she, the brazen little hussy!'

'What does Richard have to say about all this?' Jemima asked frowning.

'Oh, you know Richard, he doesn't say a lot. And of course, he's always busy, what with running things here and practising for his piano engagements.' Her voice softened. 'That's where his heart is, Jemima, in his music. He spends all his spare time round at his teacher's house.' She sighed. 'But I reckon Lillian'll get her way in the end. I reckon he'll marry her, more's the pity.' She shrugged. 'Well, after all, he's a young man and a young man needs a wife to warm his bed, when all's said and done.'

Jemima finished her tea and left. For some reason she felt heavy-hearted but she didn't know why. Dorothy had only stated the obvious. Richard needed a wife. But not Lillian. In fact, she couldn't think of anybody who would be good enough to marry Richard and she couldn't bear to think of him being unhappily married.

When she got home Mrs Peel and Kathryn were there, drinking a much needed cup of tea.

'Pour yourself a cup, Jemima,' Kathryn said.

Jemima laughed. 'No thanks. I've drunk enough tea this afternoon to sink a battleship.' She gazed round the room. 'It seems odd without Oliver here.'

'I'm afraid we shan't be seeing much of him now,' Mrs Peel said. 'He's got a very nice little home now we've made it comfortable for him. Oh, and by the way he says would you like to call and see him when you've finished your class on Saturday? Your classes are beginning this week, aren't they?'

'Yes, they are. Oh, I shall look forward to that.'

Oliver had clearly looked forward to it, too.

'Jemima! It's good to see you,' he greeted her. 'But I was quite disappointed when you didn't come with Aunt K and grandmama to help me to move in.'

'I thought you would have quite enough whisking skirts around without me adding to them,' she replied with a smile.

'But yours was the one I wanted to see,' he said quietly. He caught her hand. 'There's lots to see. I'll take you over to the school, then Mrs Grantley has very kindly invited us in for a bowl of soup and a chat.' He scratched his chin. 'You'll have to tell me what you think of her, Jemima. I can't quite make up my mind.'

The school consisted of two large classrooms, each with rows of desks crammed together as closely as possible and tiered so that pupils could see and be seen. On a raised dais at the end of each classroom stood a teacher's desk next to a blackboard and easel. Propped against one wall were screens that could be used to divide the rooms into smaller classrooms if there were enough teachers. Between the classrooms was a small staffroom-cum-headmaster's office and out in the playground there was a drinking fountain with a metal cup chained to it and two privies, one for something approaching a hundred girls and one for a similar number of boys. It all looked very shabby and rundown.

'Mrs Grantley has Standards One to Three in the other room and I shall have Four, Five and Six here, in this slightly larger one,' Oliver said, looking round. 'I realize it will take a certain amount of strong discipline on my part to keep something like a hundred hooligans under control but once they understand who's master I don't think I shall have any trouble.' He picked up a cane lying on the teacher's desk and flexed it. Jemima's eyes widened in horror but before she could open her mouth to speak he went on, 'And, of course, the monitors will help both me and Mrs Grantley with rote learning.' He sighed. 'I expect it will work well enough. Anyway, I don't intend to stay here very long. I hadn't realized it would be quite as rundown and poverty-stricken as this. But it will do for a start.'

'I think you're very lucky to have been given a headmaster's post at all after such a short time teaching,' Jemima reminded him with asperity.

'Yes, I suppose you're right,' he said. 'Although, in truth, I think they were desperate to find somebody.'

Mrs Grantley was a plump, motherly figure in her late thirties, calmly efficient. They sat down at her highly polished dining table and she poured them bowls of thick, nourishing soup.

'Of course, the school isn't looking its best,' she said. 'As you know, my husband was ill for quite some time before he died so things got a bit behind. The Board were going to pay for a lick of paint before you came, Mr Simpson, but they've had to spend the money on dividing the school house into two to accommodate us both so I'm afraid we shall have to wait a little longer.' She shook her head, smiling. 'They don't like parting with ratepayers' money for education, which a good many of them think is wasted on the poor.'

'Education is never wasted,' Oliver said firmly.

'No, of course it isn't,' Mrs Grantley agreed. 'But you can't always get these men to appreciate that. Any more than they will acknowledge that children can't learn if they're hungry so there should be food – porridge or bread and jam – available for them when they first arrive in the morning. That's the first thing I learned when I began teaching. But they say that's the responsibility of the parents.'

'Which, of course, it is,' Oliver said.

'Indeed, but a good many of the parents round these parts either have no work or spend what they earn on drink.'

'So the poor children go hungry,' Jemima said. 'I agree with you, Mrs Grantley, it's hard to concentrate with an empty belly.' She knew this from bitter experience.

Mrs Grantley smiled. 'Every Saturday morning I bake a big batch of biscuits which I keep in a tin under my desk. I give one to any child I find has come to school hungry – you can always tell. Hungry children fidget and squirm and can't concentrate. You'd be surprised the difference a couple of oat biscuits makes.'

'I hope you don't think I intend to spend my time feeding biscuits to the little brats,' Oliver said with a trace of sarcasm. 'My task is to feed their minds.'

'One goes with the other,' Mrs Grantley said mildly.

'Not in my school, Mrs Grantley,' Oliver said, putting down his spoon with a clatter. 'The children will come to my school to be educated, not fussed over. If they know there are biscuits in the offing they'll all claim to be starved. No, if they refuse to learn they will be given a good caning, *not* fed biscuits. We need to be clear about that right from the start.' He was growing quite red in the face as he tried not to lose his temper.

'Oh, I don't hold with caning, Mr Simpson,' Mrs Grantley said calmly. 'My husband never used a cane. He was quite sure you could get more out of a child by treating it with kindness than with cruelty.'

'I'm not talking about cruelty. I'm simply talking about a good caning. You've got to knock sense into some of these thick skulls.'

'Perhaps we should wait until you are acquainted with the children before we continue this discussion, Mr Simpson,' Mrs Grantley said quietly. 'Remember, I know them all. I've worked with them for a number of years so I know their parents and the backgrounds they come from.'

'Then perhaps things have got a bit stale and it's time to inject a few new ideas into the school.' Oliver leaned back in his chair and hooked his thumbs in his braces. 'And that's exactly what I intend to do.'

'Well, we shall never agree if you begin thrashing the children,' Mrs Grantley said. 'I could never stand for that.'

'Stupid woman,' Oliver said as he and Jemima returned to his part of the house. 'I'll soon put her in her place.'

'Do you not think you should tread a little gently to begin with, Oliver?' Jemima said as she prepared to leave.

'No, Jemima. I believe I should start as I mean to go on,' he replied. 'And that is to rule with a firm hand. A very firm hand.' He took a step towards her. 'But that's enough of school for the moment. I want to talk about us.'

In the event, he didn't talk at all. He was too busy kissing her.

Thirty-Four

It didn't take Oliver long to settle into his new school. Mrs Peel fussed in her usual way, worrying that he wasn't feeding himself properly, and insisted that he should make it a habit to come to Sunday lunch every week. This pleased Jemima, and Oliver didn't need asking twice. He even bought himself a bicycle so that he could make the journey more easily.

Of course, most of the conversation centred around his new school.

'I don't think I shall stay there long,' he informed them after a few months. 'I know it's a step up in my career but it's never been the kind of school I really want. The children come from very poor homes so it's a waste of time trying to teach them. They're too stupid to benefit from being educated.'

'Oh, I think that's a most unfair thing to say, Oliver,' Jemima said heatedly. She didn't like arguing with him but she felt she couldn't let such a sweeping statement pass without comment.

'Yes, indeed, Oliver, so do I,' Kathryn said, even more heatedly. 'You're implying that it's only people with money who are likely to have clever children and that's quite ridiculous. I've known some very wealthy people who are extremely stupid and some extremely clever children from the other end of the scale.' She smiled warmly at Jemima as she spoke.

He waved his hand dismissively. 'You may be right,' he said, implying that he didn't think they were. 'All I'm saying is that I don't intend to stay in this miserable little school for long. Most of the children are ill-clothed and dirty, and they're badly behaved. Mind you, a few strokes with the cane will soon sort that out, I'm sure.'

'Mrs Grantley doesn't see it like that. She seems very fond of the children she teaches,' Kathryn said thoughtfully.

'That's just the point! Mrs Grantley has no children of her own so she tries to mother these little brats instead of instilling a bit of discipline into them. In my book teachers are not there to be *fond* of the children; they're there to educate them.'

'Spare the rod and spoil the child,' Mrs Peel said quietly.

'Exactly!' He beamed at the three women sitting round the table. 'You'll see, before long I shall have the best disciplined school in Colchester, in spite of Biddy Grantley and her tin of biscuits, which, incidentally, I have forbidden her to bring into the school. What she does outside school hours is not, of course, in my control.'

Jemima bit her lip against a retort but Kathryn wasn't prepared to be so reticent.

'Children can't absorb knowledge if they're hungry,' she said sharply.

'Then their parents should see that they are adequately fed before sending them to school,' he replied. He held his plate out for another helping of apple pie.

'But, Oliver . . .' Jemima began.

'But what, Jemima?' he asked with a smile, his spoon halfway to his mouth.

She shook her head. 'Nothing.' It was quite obvious that Oliver knew nothing about the problems of the poor.

After he had gone Kathryn remarked, 'Poor Oliver, he's got a lot to learn. I rather think becoming a headmaster has gone to his head.'

'He'll settle down and learn a bit of sense before long, I'm sure,' Mrs Peel said complacently. 'What he needs is a good wife. Don't you agree, Jemima?'

'I'm sure he's not ready for that yet, Mama,' Kathryn said quickly. 'And neither is Jemima.'

Jemima smiled but didn't reply, and lying in bed that night she imagined for the umpteenth time what marriage to Oliver might be like. She had been in love with him for such a long time – indeed, ever since they were children – that it had become almost a part of her. And most of the time she was quite sure he was in love with her, although he had never actually said so. Of course, she understood the reason for this. He wanted to concentrate on making a success of his career before taking on the responsibility of a wife. Not that she intended to be a responsibility; she was going to work by his side and be his helpmate, just as Mrs Grantley had worked beside her husband until his death. Like that she would be able to demonstrate to him that more could be achieved by encouragement than by beating. She was a little disappointed that Oliver set such store by the rod. But if he didn't ask her to marry him she could hardly tell him this. It was really quite frustrating.

But she had walked to the gate with him when he left and he had held her hand as if he was reluctant to let her go, saying he looked forward to seeing her again very soon, so it was only a matter of waiting.

During the following week she noticed that there was a poster in Baxter's shop window advertising another of the concerts where Richard was accompanist. She did not miss many of his concerts, which were always held on a Saturday evening. She went into the shop to buy a ticket but, as usual, he gave her two complimentary ones.

'I wish you'd let me pay for them,' she protested.

'Don't be silly. They're a present. I like you to come, and you deserve a reward because you've sat through some diabolical performers at times, haven't you?'

'Yes, but not any more. You're getting quite a name for yourself as a soloist as well as an accompanist so you can be a bit more choosy these days.'

'That's true.' He sighed and glanced round the shop. 'I can command quite a good fee these days. To tell you the truth my playing earns me almost as much as this place makes and certainly gives me a good deal more pleasure. Sometimes I think I'd go barmy if I didn't have a concert to look forward to.'

'I look forward to them too, Richard. I wish they happened more often,' she said with a smile.

'They could, if I had the time. I have to turn down engagements when I get behind with my work here.' He glanced round to make sure there was nobody within earshot. 'I had a real go at my father the other day. I told him he was more of a liability than an asset to the business, that he did little or nothing to help and that he was drinking all the profits away. I said if I had my way I would sell up and get out because I never wanted to be there in the first place. I really lost my rag and said things that I probably shouldn't have done.' He made a face. 'I felt pretty bad about it afterwards.'

She laid a hand on his arm and smiled sympathetically. 'I wouldn't worry, Richard. If I know your father he was probably too drunk to take in half of what you said.'

He nodded. 'Yes, you're probably right.'

Lillian came bustling up. 'Richard, dear, could you help me with the window display, please, if you've finished serving?'

'I'll be there in a minute,' he replied without looking at her. 'And I'm not serving. As you can see, I'm having a quiet conversation with Jemima.'

'How nice for you,' she said icily. 'Well, some of us don't have time for idle gossip.' She flounced off.

He closed his eyes. '. . . eight . . .nine . . .ten.' He opened them again. 'To be fair, she gets on very well with my mother,' he remarked. 'But she does tend to get above herself.' He accompanied Jemima to the door. 'I look forward to seeing you on Saturday, Jemma. Actually, it's quite an important one for me. I get two quite big solo slots.'

'Oh, what are you playing?'

'Beethoven's "Moonlight Sonata" and a couple of pieces by Grieg.'

'I shall look forward to that.'

'Good. I'll look forward to seeing you there. Ah, I've been so busy talking about me I nearly forgot – how are things going with you, Jemma?'

'At school? Very well. It's still quite hard work because my Saturday morning classes are quite demanding, but in another six months they'll be finished and I'll be a fully fledged teacher.'

'And then the world will be your oyster,' he said with a half smile. 'Lucky girl.'

The following Saturday Jemima called at Oliver's house when she had finished her Saturday class in Colchester. She didn't need much of an excuse to pay him a visit – a book to return or borrow, a mathematical problem she needed his help to solve – but today she had the legitimate excuse of inviting him to attend Richard's concert with her.

He was always pleased to see her and usually insisted that she stay and have lunch with him, saying Biddy was only next door so she was just as good as a chaperone. Sometimes after lunch Jemima would tidy up a little or iron his shirts for him. He always protested that this was not necessary but he obviously liked to watch her doing it and she wondered if the same thoughts were going through his mind as she was thinking. If they were he never said so.

She waited until it was nearly time for her to catch her usual train before she said, 'I've got tickets for a concert tonight, Oliver. Would you like to come with me?' It said much for their relationship that she had been a bit doubtful about asking him and had waited until it was time to leave before plucking up the courage to do so.

'What sort of a concert is it?'

'It's one of Richard's concerts. He's accompanying quite a well-known baritone singer and Richard's got a couple of solos.'

He frowned. 'I really don't have the time for that sort of thing, Jemma. I have such a lot of school work to get through.' He ran his hands through his dark curls. 'I hadn't realized the amount of paperwork there would be in this job. I have to fill in forms for everything. I can't spend fourpence without filling in a form to get the permission of the Board treasurer. I think they regard ratepayers' money spent on education as money wasted and I'm inclined to agree with them as far as this school is concerned.' He looked up at her and smiled. 'Look, why don't you ask Biddy Grantley to go with you? I daresay she'd like a night out.'

'But I don't want Biddy Grantley to come with me, Oliver. I want you,' she said boldly.

He looked at her for a minute, then a slow smile dawned on his face. 'Is that an invitation, Jemma?' he asked.

She frowned. 'Yes, of course it is. Richard has given me the tickets . . .'

'That's not quite what I meant.' He got up and took her in his arms. 'It's not quite what you meant, either, is it, Jemima?' he said softly. His face was very near to hers, making her heart pound so that she couldn't think straight.

'Why, yes, of course it is,' she answered a little breathlessly. 'What else could I mean?'

'You could mean that if I come to the concert with you this evening you would come back and spend the night here with me,' he whispered, close to her ear. 'I should like that, Jemma. I should like that very much.' He moved his head and his mouth found hers. For a moment she didn't move, savouring the warmth of his lips against hers, then, suddenly, the implication of his words hit her and she struggled free.

'No! No! That's not what I meant at all,' she said furiously, dragging the back of her hand across her mouth as if to erase his kiss. 'How dare you suggest such a thing! What kind of a woman do you think I am?'

He made a calming gesture with his hands. 'All right, all right, I'm sorry, Jemma. I made a mistake. I mistook your meaning and I've apologized so there's no harm done. We'll be friends, just like we've always been, and forget I spoke out of turn.' He smiled encouragingly at her.

She didn't smile back. 'You wanted me to come back here and spend the night with you, Oliver,' she said coldly. 'You were quite prepared to let me risk putting myself in the same position as my twin sister. For which, I might remind you, you condemned her out of hand.'

'No, no, of course not,' he protested. 'You know I wouldn't do that, Jemma. There are ways . . .' He stopped, flushing.

'No doubt they are exactly the words my sister's seducer used,' she said icily.

He smiled disarmingly. 'But this is different. We're going to be married.'

'Are we? That's the first I've heard. You've never proposed to me, Oliver.'

He tried to take her in his arms again. 'Well, I'm proposing now. Will you marry me, Jemma?'

'And if I say yes, will you expect me to change my mind and stay with you tonight?'

'Well, it would be nice . . .'

'Yes, it would, wouldn't it? But I would prefer a proposal when the main thought in your head was not how to get me into your bed, to put it bluntly. I daresay my sister's lover made the same promise to her, only it turned out that he was already engaged to be married to someone else and Sophie was too naive to see through him.' She took a deep breath and her voice quivered with fury as she continued, 'Well, I'm not too naïve to see through you, Oliver, but I'm disappointed in you. For years I've been thinking I was in love with you, but you've opened my eyes for me and I can see that I have been wasting my love on someone who never really existed. I thought you were my ideal man, loving and caring, kind and generous, but you're none of those things. You're lecherous and you're cruel, taking out your vengeance by beating defenceless young boys whose only crime is that they are slow to learn. Oh, no, Oliver, if you were the last man on earth I wouldn't marry you.'

She turned her back on him and gathered up her things. 'I think you would do well to listen to Biddy Grantley. She could teach you a lot about the best way to educate children. I could tell you, too, although I'm not yet a fully fledged teacher. It's *not* by making them stand to attention and salute you when they see you in the street and it's not by making them quake in their shoes – if they have any – when you walk into the classroom. It's by gaining their respect as a fair and just man. You've got an awful lot to learn, Oliver.'

She left, closing the door very quietly behind her.

Thirty-Five

Jemima was so furious and upset over the scene with Oliver that her first instinct was to go straight home. She strode off towards the railway station but hadn't gone far before her step slowed as her fury began to subside and her thoughts became more rational. For how could she go home and face Mrs Peel, who thought the sun, moon and stars shone out of her grandson's eyes? And how could she face Kathryn, too, who could see no wrong in him? Even more important than that, how could she disappoint Richard, for whom this was a special evening? So she took several deep breaths, pulled back her shoulders and turned back to make her way to the Corn Exchange, where the recital was to take place. When she arrived she went to the ladies' room to powder her nose, tidy her hair and make sure her hat was on straight. Then, satisfied with her appearance, she went to take her seat.

To her surprise she found herself sitting beside Mrs Baxter and Lillian. On her other side was an elderly man that she recognized as Mr Lax, Richard's piano tutor, although she didn't know him well enough to do more than smile and bid him good evening.

'I couldn't miss tonight's concert because Richard's got two big solos as well as accompanying the singer. Did you know that?' Mrs Baxter whispered proudly.

'Yes, he told me,' Jemima answered, smiling.

She greeted Lillian, sitting on the other side of Mrs Baxter, who hardly managed a nod in return. She was clearly annoyed to find Jemima sitting beside them and possessively fussed over Mrs Baxter to assert her superior position. *Oh, what a stupid girl*, Jemima thought wearily.

She settled in her seat and looked at her programme without registering what was on it because her mind was still too full of the scene at Oliver's house – what she had said, what Oliver had said, what she now wished she had said and her fury at Oliver's assumption that she would be prepared to spend the night with him. In her present frame of mind she never wanted to see him again, let alone spend the night with him. Oddly, she found herself impatient to tell Richard all about it because he was the one person she could talk to who always understood. But she knew that tonight was not the night to burden him with her troubles.

The concert began. She watched as he took his bow and went to the piano, amazed, as she always was, at how professional and self-assured.he had become on stage. His evening dress was immaculate, with snowy white shirt-front and starched collar and cuffs, and his hair was carefully groomed. While he was not exactly handsome and had never followed the fashion to sport a curly moustache, he was very personable and he had a very attractive smile, a smile that reached his eyes and made them crinkle at the corners. Unlike Oliver, there was not the slightest hint of arrogance in his demeanour. She pulled her thoughts up sharply. There was no comparison between these two totally different men and it was wrong of her to seek it. She sat back and tried to blank out everything except the music.

During the interval Richard came to speak to them in the little room set aside for important guests. Mrs Baxter was given a seat but Lillian made sure she was standing close to Richard; she liked to be seen with the up-and-coming young pianist and she hung on to his every word and even possessively brushed an imaginary hair from his lapel, which obviously annoyed him, although he was too polite to say so. But he ignored her as far as possible and talked with Jemima and Mr Lax, after formally introducing them, discussing the music, the history of the baritone he was accompanying and the details of his own solos, whether they thought the Beethoven in the first half went well – 'that third movement of the "Moonlight Sonata" is a bit of a swine but I think it came off all right' – and his hope that they would enjoy the Grieg he'd be playing in the second half.

This conversation went right over Lillian's head and she soon got bored with it. 'I see you're wearing the new costume we ordered for you, Jemima,' she interrupted, looking her up and down. 'It looks very well on you but I think you would have done better to take my advice and have the green instead of that muddy brown colour, although I must admit the orange blouse sets it off quite nicely.' Then she turned to Richard and said ungrammatically, 'I think I'd like you to take me and your mother back to our seats now, Richard. My feet hurt in these new shoes.'

'You were silly to wear them here for the first time, then, Lillian. And my mother is perfectly happy talking to the lady sitting beside her. But if you want to go back to your seat I'm sure you can find your own way without any trouble,' Richard said shortly, lifting his eyebrows eloquently to Jemima.

When she had taken herself off and Mr Lax had turned to talk to his mother he said quietly, 'Are you all right, Jemma? I've noticed you're not looking quite yourself tonight. Has something upset you?'

'I'm well, thank you, Richard,' she said, amazed that in the excitement and tension of the concert he had noticed. She smiled at him. 'And, as I told you, I'm enjoying the concert very much.'

'Are you quite sure?' He was frowning, obviously not convinced.

'That I'm enjoying the concert?' She deliberately misconstrued his remark. 'Of course I am. I always do. You know that.'

His eyes searched her face anxiously but she managed to keep smiling. Now was not the time to tell him her troubles although she could tell he was not convinced that all was well with her.

She laid a hand on his arm. 'It's time for you to go backstage again. Good luck with the second half. I'm sure it will go well.' She gave him another encouraging smile.

'He's a very talented young man, Miss Furlong,' Mr Lax said when she resumed her seat. 'If he wasn't tied to his father's business he could go far.' He shook his head. 'Such a pity.' He looked at her and smiled. 'I'm prejudiced, of course. Richard is almost like a son to me. I've taught him all I know.'

'He speaks very highly of you, too, Mr Lax,' she replied.

'He . . .' But there was no time for further conversation as the second half was about to begin and after it ended, to enthusiastic applause, he hurried away to catch his train.

Mrs Baxter had already invited Jemima to wait and travel home with them, which clearly hadn't pleased Lillian, so they waited for Richard, who had things to do and music to collect before he could leave. It suited Jemima very well to catch a later train; she wasn't at all anxious to go home to Kathryn and her mother, whose sole topic of conversation would be their beloved Oliver. Was he well? Was he getting enough to eat? How was he looking? Indeed, her mind was already busy trying to think of somewhere to go the following day so that she didn't have to spend it in Oliver's company while his grandmother and aunt fussed over him like two hens with a single chick. She felt quite sickened at the thought.

'A penny for your thoughts, Jemma?' Richard said as the train rattled on towards home. She was sitting in the corner opposite to him, with Mrs Baxter next to her. Lillian had commandeered the seat beside him and was sitting as close to him as she could without actually sitting on his lap.

She turned from looking out of the window, which only showed a reflection of her own face coming out of the darkness. 'I was just thinking I hadn't seen Dorothy for some time and I wondered if I might come and have Sunday lunch with her tomorrow,' she said thoughtfully.

'You won't be able to do that. Dorothy's gone to her sister's for the weekend,' Lillian said with a note of triumph in her voice. '*I'm* cooking lunch for the family tomorrow.'

'That doesn't matter. You can still come, Jemma. You can have lunch with Mama and me,' Richard said. 'And Father, of course, if he's up to eating anything. Is that all right with you, Ma?'

'Yes, dear, of course it is,' Mrs Baxter said, smiling at Jemima.

'That's all very well, but I'm not sure I can manage . . .' Lillian began, with a face like thunder.

'Oh, surely one extra won't tax your culinary skills, Lillian,' Richard said carelessly. 'You're always telling us what a good cook you are. Tomorrow will be your chance to prove it.' He gave Jemima a wink.

'I could always come early and lend you a hand, Lillian,' Jemima offered, glad of an excuse to leave the house even earlier than she would have done.

'That won't be necessary. I'm perfectly capable of cooking a meal, thank you very much,' Lillian said stiffly.

'That's settled, then.' Richard craned forward in his seat. 'The moonlight seems very bright tonight,' he said. 'I didn't think there was a full moon.'

'No, there was a new moon earlier in the week. I remember because I went outside and turned my money over,' Mrs Baxter said.

'Oh, Mother! How can you be so superstitious!'

She shrugged a little sheepishly. 'I've always done it. It's supposed to bring good luck. Not that it's ever done me much good,' she added.

He frowned. 'Well, that's very odd, then. The sky seems to be quite light over towards the town.'

'I expect it's the reflection of the street lights. The modern gas lamps are much brighter than the old oil lamps used to be,' Jemima said, twisting round to follow his gaze.

'Ah, yes, of course. That's what it is.' He leaned back in his seat with a yawn and closed his eyes, exhausted by the excitement and stress of the evening.

The train pulled into the station and some half a dozen people alighted along with the four of them.

'I should keep away from the bottom end of the town if I was you,' the ticket collector announced as he was taking the tickets. 'According to a bloke who's just got on the train there's a bit of a fire down by the church. Apparently someone's already called the fire brigade but you know how long it takes to round up all the firemen, then they've got to get their boots and helmets on and run down the road with the fire engine. The whole town could be up in smoke before they get the hose unreeled.'

Some of the other passengers laughed at the joke but Richard frowned. 'A fire? Where, exactly?'

'Dunno, mate,' the ticket collector said. 'I only know what the bloke told me. A fire down by the church. One of them old sheds, I reckon.'

'I'd better go and see if I can lend a hand. It sounds a bit too close to the shop for comfort,' Richard said anxiously. 'Will you take my mother and Lillian home, Jemima? I probably won't be long.'

'We can find our way home without your help, Jemima,' Lillian said rudely. She caught Mrs Baxter's arm. 'Come along, dear.'

She hurried Mrs Baxter off with Jemima following. Halfway along the road they met Mr Lax, uncharacteristically hatless and with his coat flapping open, obviously coming to meet them.

'I've just seen Richard,' he said breathlessly. 'Naturally, he's gone to see what he can do to help, but he asked me if I would take you ladies home with me for safety, if you're willing to come, that is.'

'Why? Why can't we go home to the shop?' Lillian demanded, planting her feet apart and her hands on her hips. 'If those old sheds are on fire there's no danger. They're nowhere near the shop.'

'Old sheds? What old sheds? It's not sheds that are alight. It's much more serious than that. Now, if you'll come along with me I'll make you all a nice cup of tea.' He had already taken Mrs Baxter gently by the arm and was hurrying her along the road.

'I'm not coming. I'm going home to my mum,' Lillian said firmly. 'I'll see you tomorrow, Mrs B, when I come to cook the dinner.'

She went off, hobbling in her new shoes.

When they arrived at Mr Lax's house, one of three houses standing alone down a short lane, he ushered them into quite a large room dominated by a grand piano draped with a colourful shawl.

'So this is where Richard comes to practise,' Jemima said, looking round. The rest of the room was quite sparsely furnished but there were two reasonably comfortable armchairs and a matching settee placed round the hearth.

'Yes. Please sit down and I'll make some tea,' he said, refusing Jemima's offer of help.

'I wonder where the fire is,' Mrs Baxter said anxiously. 'They said it was just a bit of a fire so I don't suppose it's anything much. Probably at the pie shop; that's four doors down from us so we should be quite safe. I've always said they're not careful enough with those ovens – the number of times we've had pies from them with burned pastry!'

Jemima couldn't help smiling at Mrs Baxter's peculiar logic but she realized she was letting her tongue run away with her because she was more than a little nervous. Any talk of fire was worrying.

Mr Lax came back with a large tray on which was a bottle of brandy as well as the tea things. He poured a generous helping into each cup after he had poured the tea.

'You may need this, Mrs Baxter,' he said, handing one to her. 'Because I'm afraid I have bad news for you.'

Mrs Baxter put her hand to her breast. 'Oh, no!'

He nodded. 'I'm afraid so. It's your shop that's on fire. And it's a big fire.'

Thirty-Six

Amazingly, Mrs Baxter didn't faint, although she turned very pale. She sipped her brandy-laden tea and her colour gradually returned. 'This'll be the end of Baxter's,' she said, shaking her head. 'I've always been afraid of fire, the kind of stock we carry . . .' Her voice trailed off. 'God knows what Frank will do, seeing his family business go up in flames. Was he there, Mr Lax? Did he see it happen?'

'Doesn't he usually spend his Saturday evenings in the Rose and Crown?' Mr Lax asked.

'Ah, yes, of course. That's where he'll be, drinking himself under the table as our house and home burns down, never mind our livelihood and all we've worked for! Typical of Frank Baxter.' She began to cry, tears running unchecked down her cheeks, at the same time rummaging in her bag for her smelling bottle.

Jemima found it for her. 'Would you like to lie down, Mrs Baxter?' Jemima said gently. 'This is an awful shock for you.'

'Yes, I must say I don't feel very well,' she said weakly.

Jemima led her over to the settee and made her comfortable with the rug Mr Lax gave her.

They left her there and went to the kitchen, which was as neat and clean as Jemima would have expected of the dapper old gentleman. She watched as he filled the kettle and put it to boil ready to wash up the cups. 'Have you any idea just how bad the fire is, Mr Lax?'

He spread his hands. 'It must be pretty bad. It's an old building and as Mrs Baxter said, the sort of things sold there . . .' He didn't need to elaborate further.

'Yes, of course. Oh, dear, I hope Richard is all right.'

'It's his hands I'm worried about,' Mr Lax said, relieved to be able to voice his fears. 'I hope he protects them. He has so much talent . . . If they were to be burned . . .'

She looked at him, her face creased with worry. 'He wouldn't do anything stupid, would he, Mr Lax? He wouldn't try to go in and salvage things . . . After all, it's their home as well as their shop . . . All their personal things . . .'

'That's what worries me, Miss Furlong, but I sincerely hope not.' He smiled at her. 'You're fond of the boy, aren't you?'

She nodded. 'Yes. We've been good friends for a long time.' She looked out of the window. 'I can't see anything from here. I think I'll go and see what's happening. I can't just stay here wondering what's going on.'

'I've already told you, Miss Furlong. It's a big fire. Added to that, the tide is low so they can't use water from the river to help put it out. It could easily burn till morning. Look out of the back door. You'll be able to see the flames from here.'

She opened the door. 'Oh, my God! There'll be nothing left of the place.' She closed the door and leaned against it. 'I do wish Richard would come back. I wish I knew what he was doing.'

'I expect he's looking after his father, if I know Richard.' He poured water into the washing-up bowl and swished suds into it and began washing the cups.

She picked up the tea towel and a cup. 'Tell me about Richard. You were his piano teacher. What was he like to teach? I'm training to be a school teacher, you know.' She spoke jerkily, wiping the cup and putting it down on the table.

He looked at her over his gold-rimmed glasses. 'They're my best cups,' he reminded her with a smile.

'Oh, sorry. I'll be careful,' she said ruefully.

'I've never been a school teacher; I've only ever taught the piano,' he said, seeing her agitation and keeping his voice calm. 'Richard was always a very apt pupil. I knew, right from the start, that he was gifted and I tried to encourage him as much as I could. At the time his mother was not well – she suffered a lot with nervous problems – and his father said she couldn't bear to hear the piano played, so he sold it. I rather think the real reason was that he wanted the money for drink, but that may be unfair. At any rate, I suggested Richard should come and practise here, which really suited us both. He loved playing my Steinway, and it was company for me, as I'd been quite lonely since my wife died.' He smiled. 'In a way, Richard became the son I had always wanted but had never been blessed with.'

'I know he thinks a great deal of you, Mr Lax,' Jemima said, slightly calmer now.

He nodded. 'Yes, and I'm very fond of Richard, too.' he replied. 'I know he is a man of utter honesty and integrity.' He dried his hands and said thoughtfully, 'I lent him some money once – oh, it would have been about three years ago, I suppose. I don't know what he wanted it for, I never asked, but I told him to regard it as a gift. He refused to do that and paid me back every last penny although I knew he wasn't a rich man. It was quite a lot of money, too.'

'How much?'

He looked at her oddly. 'It was ten pounds. Not that it's really any of your business, my dear,' he added gently.

'No. I'm sorry. I shouldn't have asked.' She folded the tea towel and hung it over the rail at the end of the draining board, her movements careful and deliberate. 'I think I should be going, now, Mr Lax,' she said, her voice flat.

'Why, my dear? Don't you want to wait until Richard gets back?' he asked in surprise.

'No. He'll be tired. I think I should go now.'

'It's very late. It's well past midnight . . .'

'I still think it's best that I should go.'

She fetched her handbag from the drawing room. 'Goodnight, Mr Lax. Thank you for your hospitality.'

He followed her to the door. 'I'd much rather you stayed, Miss Furlong. A young lady, out on her own at this time of night . . .' He was still anxiously urging her to stay as she hurried away. He closed the door behind her, puzzled at her sudden decision to leave.

She hurried back to the Peels' house. There was still a glow in the sky from the fire but she didn't go home that way because she didn't want to risk seeing Richard.

She didn't want to see Richard ever again.

She fumbled with her key, her eyes blinded with angry tears, and let herself into the house. Mrs Peel and Kathryn were in bed and asleep so she was able to creep up to her room without being questioned. There, she flung herself on her bed and cried as if her heart would break.

How could he have done this to her? How could he have pretended to speculate with her about where the mysterious ten pounds had come from when he knew all the time that it had come from him? What sort of a fool had he taken her for? All this time she had felt guilty, had felt she had somehow let him down because she had chosen to start her training rather than marry him, when in reality he must have regretted proposing to her and more or less bought her off. Yes, that's what it amounted to: he had bought her off.

And she had thought they were good friends.

She got up very early the next morning because she didn't want to see Kathryn or Mrs Peel and have to explain why she didn't want to see Oliver after his behaviour towards her last evening – was it only last evening? It seemed like years ago.

Oliver, a man who lived by double standards regarding women and who would end up hated and feared by all his pupils. She had misjudged him, as well as Richard.

She left a note to say she was going to see her sister and left the house.

She had to throw gravel up at the window to wake Sophie, who appeared, bleary-eyed at the disturbance, but hurried down to let her in when she saw Jemima standing there, a carpet bag in her hand.

It took several cups of tea and soaked handkerchiefs before she could gather from her sister what was troubling her.

'A fire? At Baxter's? Was anyone hurt? Richard? Oh, Jemma, love, do stop crying. I can't make sense of what you're saying,' she said at last.

Jemima blew her nose and took a deep breath. 'I don't know whether or not Richard is hurt and I don't care,' she said, her voice still trembling on the edge of tears.

Sophie blew out her cheeks. 'Well, that's a new one. I thought you . . . I thought you were . . . friends,' she said carefully.

'So did I. But not any more. Not now I know what he's done.'

'And what has he done?' Sophie was almost afraid to ask. 'Proposed to Lillian?'

Jemima looked up, frowning. 'Not as far as I know,' she said crossly.

Sophie spread her hands. 'Then what?'

'Remember that ten pounds somebody gave me? I've never known who the mysterious benefactor was. Well, now I've found out. It was Richard.'

'Richard!'

'Yes. He borrowed the money to give me and then pretended to be as mystified as I was as to where it had come from.'

'That was very generous of him. So why are you so cross?'

'Because he made me look such a fool.'

Sophie frowned. 'You're not making any sense, Jemma. How can somebody giving you the money to do what you'd always wanted to do make you look a fool?'

'Oh, don't you see? He'd already asked me to marry him.'

'When?'

'Oh, does it matter?' She waved her hand. 'It was after I'd told him that I'd given you my savings. I expect he felt sorry for me so he proposed. I said I'd give him an answer on my birthday. And on my birthday the ten pounds turned up, "from a well-wisher". So, of course, I turned down his proposal and began my training, just as he knew I would.' Her mouth twisted. 'I suppose you could say he bought me off.'

'You mean he never really wanted to marry you in the first place?'

'No, he just felt sorry for me. I felt sorry for him, too, being saddled with a shop he hated and parents who were a constant worry. Well, at least he won't have the shop to worry about now if it's burned down.'

'That's a callous thing to say.'

Jemima shrugged but said nothing.

Sophie frowned. 'I really can't see why you've got yourself into such a state about all this. What does it matter what Richard's motives were? You've got what you wanted, a teaching career. And no doubt you'll marry Oliver . . .'

'No, I never shall.' Jemima began to cry again. 'Not after he condemned you as a loose woman and then expected me to behave in exactly the same way and spend the night with him. I couldn't believe he could be so blatant about it.' She sniffed. 'I don't like his teaching methods, either. He'll end up hated and feared by all his pupils.'

'So your idol's turned out to have feet of clay,' Sophie said wryly.

'You could say he's toppled right off his pedestal,' Jemima agreed, with the first hint of a smile.

There was a noise from upstairs.

'Ah, that'll be Jenny. I'll fetch her down because I don't want her to wake Aunt and Uncle. They don't get up very early these days.'

Jemima wiped her face with the heel of her hand. 'What is the time?'

'Half past eight.'

She went upstairs and brought the baby down, still rubbing her eyes and rosy with sleep. Jemima held out her arms and took her.

'I'll just fetch her a drink of milk and a rusk,' Sophie said. 'I won't be a minute.'

When she came back she said, 'Well, that's the last of the milk. I'll have to nip down to Payne's for some more. I shan't be long. She'll be all right with you till I get back. You can put her in her playpen when she's finished her breakfast. Oh, if she's still hungry when she's finished that, you'll find a biscuit in a tin in the kitchen.' She dropped a kiss on Jenny's head and hurried out.

Jemima fed Jenny, cuddling her and talking to her all the while. Looking down at her she couldn't help being struck by the irony of the fact that this beautiful child was the result of Sophie 'ruining' her life, because if ever there was a happy and fulfilled woman it was her twin. In the quiet of her aunt's kitchen, with Jenny happily slurping her milk and dribbling it down her bib, Jemima felt a sharp pang of envy – bordering on jealousy – for the life Sophie had that she, Jemima, had turned her back on, thinking that she wanted to spend her life doing nothing more than teaching other people's children. But in her single-minded determination to teach she had forgotten that she was also a woman, with a woman's instincts for a home and children of her own. Oh, she had cherished dreams of life in the classroom married to Oliver – she had got that wrong, too; Oliver was now the last person she would want to spend her life with. Too late, she realized that Richard, whom she had mistakenly regarded as nothing more than a good friend, was the man she loved and needed by her side. But the realization had come too late; he no longer wanted her and had been prepared to borrow ten pounds in order to retract his proposal and buy her off. She blushed with shame and humiliation at the thought.

Jenny finished her milk and began to whimper so Jemima carried her out to the kitchen to find the biscuits. Then she frowned, because standing on the kitchen table was a jug, standing with a beaded muslin cover over it to keep out the flies. She lifted the muslin, and could see that the jug was nearly full. Puzzled, she put the baby in her playpen and opened the back door to let the sunshine in. The church bells were ringing. She frowned again. Of course, it was Sunday.

So where was Sophie going to get milk that wasn't needed when all the shops were closed?

Thirty-Seven

Sophie hurried down the road, intent on her purpose. She had never forgotten how Jemima had come to her rescue when she was in trouble. She had literally given Sophie her life back. Well, now it was her turn to help Jemima. Some might call it interference but she didn't care. Jemima was her twin and she didn't want to see her make a disastrous mistake with her life.

She went straight to Mr Lax's house, guessing that the person she wanted to see would be there.

Richard was just finishing a breakfast of bacon and eggs, which Mr Lax had insisted on cooking him. He was dressed in a rather old-fashioned grey suit that was not quite long enough in the sleeves and legs and a white shirt with an uncomfortable-looking wing collar that reached nearly up to his ears.

'Miss Furlong,' he said, surprised, getting to his feet.

'No, please, sit down and finish your breakfast,' Sophie said. He looked so tired and drawn she almost wished she hadn't come. But then she thought of Jemima and knew she was doing the right thing.

'I heard about the fire at your shop, Richard,' she said. 'Was it very bad?'

He pushed away his half-eaten breakfast. 'About as bad as it could be, I'm afraid. Everything's gone. Shop. House. Everything.' He closed his eyes briefly. 'They also found my father in the wreckage.' He shook his head. 'I don't know what he was doing there. He always spends Saturday evenings in the Rose and Crown.'

'Oh, Richard. I'm so sorry,' she said quietly. 'So what will you do?'

'Richard and his mother will stay here with me for the time being,' Mr Lax said firmly, as if he had already had this out with Richard.

Richard shot him a grateful look. 'Mr Lax is very kind. Of course, my mother will be all right when everything's sorted out, because the shop was well insured.'

'And Richard will be able to do what he's always wanted: make his living with his music,' Mr Lax said, trying – and failing – not to sound too happy.

'Of course, that's all in the future,' Richard said with a sigh. 'But I hope so.'

'I know so,' Mr Lax said. He turned to Sophie. 'Can I offer you a cup of tea, Miss Furlong?'

'No, thank you, Mr Lax. I mustn't stay. I just came to . . .' She broke off. Richard looked so tired and worried that she simply couldn't burden him with further problems, not even for Jemima's sake. She turned away.

'Is it something to do with your sister, Miss Furlong?' Mr Lax asked anxiously. 'She did leave here in rather a hurry last night. I wanted her to stay but she wouldn't. I was a little worried about her, I must admit. I wondered if she might be unwell . . .'

Richard was immediately on his feet. 'Yes, I had expected her to be here when I got back. Do you know where she is, Miss Furlong? Is she ill?'

'No, she's not exactly ill,' Sophie said reluctantly. She wished now she hadn't been quite so impetuous in coming to find Richard. She hadn't stopped to think how tired and shocked he would be after the fire. She turned away. 'It doesn't matter. I'll come back later, when you're . . .'

But Richard caught her arm. 'No. Something's wrong with Jemima, isn't it? That's why you've come. Where is she?'

'She's at my house – I mean, at Aunt Minnie's. Maybe you could call round later . . .'

'No, I'll come now.' He picked up a top hat lying near the door. 'Ah, no, I think I'll dispense with that.' He put it down again. 'Right. Let's go.' He held the door open for her. 'You say she's at your house? Why is she there and not at "Sparrows"?'

'Oh, I don't think she'll want to live with the Peels any more,' Sophie said breathlessly as he hurried her along. 'Oliver, their golden boy, blotted his copybook well and truly last night by suggesting Jemima might like to spend the night with him. Since he had been very critical of my situation she saw that as blatantly two-faced on his part and I think she told him so.'

'The ba— Ah, I rather thought something had upset her when I saw her at the concert,' he said, covering up neatly the word he had almost blurted out.

'Added to that, she doesn't like his teaching methods. So all in all, she's discovered Oliver is not the man she imagined he was.'

'And she's disappointed?' he asked.

'No. Not a bit.' She stole a sideways glance at him. 'I think she's come to her senses and realized that her affections lie in a rather different direction. But there's something else I think you should know . . .'

Richard listened intently until she had finished what she had to say but although his face darkened he made no comment. So she said no more until they arrived at the house, when she showed him into the front room, which was obviously rarely used.

'I'll tell her you're here,' she said briefly and left him pacing up and down while she went down the hall to call Jemima, hoping and praying she had done the right thing.

'You didn't buy milk,' Jemima said when she walked into the kitchen, looking at her sister's empty hands accusingly.

'I forgot.'

'You forgot it was Sunday, too.'

'Ah, so I did. I forgot my purse, too. I don't know where I left it.' Jenny began to cry and held up her arms to her mother. 'It's all right, sweetheart, Mumma's back,' she said, picking her up and smothering her with kisses. 'Will you go and see if I left it in the front room, Jemma?' she asked, over the baby's head. 'I can't think where else it could be.'

Jemima went along the hall to the front room. 'I don't think it'll be here; you hardly ever use this room,' she said half to herself as she opened the door. Then she stopped. 'Richard! Oh, no. So that's where she went!' She put her hand up to her mouth. 'Why did she drag you up here, for goodness' sake? As if you haven't got enough . . .' She looked him up and down. 'Richard, what in heaven's name are you wearing?'

'I'm wearing one of Mr Lax's suits because mine got ruined in the fire. You may remember my shop burned down last night, together with my home? Not that you bothered to wait and find out what the damage was.' His expression was stony and his tone clipped and heavy with sarcasm, which sat oddly with the ridiculous suit of clothes. 'The suit doesn't fit very well because I'm slightly taller than Mr Lax and it isn't exactly the height of sartorial elegance but it's all I have at the moment, since my evening suit got ruined and everything else that I – or rather we – owned went up in flames. Including, incidentally, my father.'

'Your father!' She gasped, her annoyance at once forgotten. 'Oh, Rick, I'm so sorry. But how . . .? I mean, I . . . We all assumed he was at the Rose and Crown, where he always spent Saturday evenings.'

'That's what everybody thought. But he wasn't. He was found on the stairs. The general opinion is that he was drunk, as usual, and that he tripped on the stairs as he went up carrying a lamp.' His tone was still brusque.

'The general opinion. You don't agree?'

He shook his head. 'I know my father. I know he was always very conscious of the risk of fire, even when he'd had too much to drink. Understandable, given the nature of our business. No, if he upset a lamp on the stairs I'm sure he did it deliberately, that he intended to burn the place down. But I wouldn't say that to just anyone and of course I could never prove it. Not that I'd want to.' He spoke in an unemotional, flat voice.

Jemima sat down with a bump on the nearest chair. 'But why? Why on earth would he want to do such a thing?'

'Obviously because of what I said to him the other night.' He gave a weary sigh. 'I told you I'd quarrelled with him and told him a few home truths, including the fact that the shop was a millstone round all our necks and he was no help at all. I think he must have taken it to heart and acted on it.'

'Oh, surely not!'

He shrugged. 'Who can tell, the state he's been in these past weeks. But I'll always have to live with the suspicion that I might be to blame for it all, his suicide and the fire.' He went over and stood looking out of the window.

She got up from her chair and took a step towards him. He heard her and swung round. 'It's all right, you needn't waste your sympathy on me, I shall survive,' he said on a note of bitterness. 'Just as I shall survive the fact that you thought I was "buying you off" and that I didn't really want to marry you when I gave you that ten bloody pounds.'

Her jaw dropped. 'Sophie had no right . . .'

'Sophie had *every* right because at least we know where we stand now, Jemima.' His eyes were flashing with temper. She had never seen him so angry. 'To think you had the audacity to assume that the only reason I borrowed that money from Mr Lax to give you was because I'd changed my mind and regretted having asked you to marry me in the first place. That I saw it as a way out.' He banged his fist into the palm of his other hand. 'My God, what kind of a man do you think I am, Jemima?' he said furiously. 'If that had been the case, couldn't you even give me credit for having the courage to tell you to your face?'

She got to her feet. 'But you only proposed to me in the first place because you felt sorry for me,' she said hotly. 'Because I wept all over you after I'd had to give Sophie my savings. Well, no girl wants to be married out of pity.'

'And no man wants to be accepted as second best,' he retorted. 'I knew when I asked you to marry me that you didn't really want to be my wife. I knew your heart was in teaching, not in Baxter's.'

'Then why didn't you just offer me the money, instead of pretending to speculate with me as to who my "mysterious bene-factor" could have been? That was dishonest.'

'Because you would have been so grateful to me that you would have married me instead of beginning your training and I would always have known it was not what you really wanted. I couldn't have lived with that. Second best is no basis for a good marriage. So I gave you what I knew you wanted without burdening you with gratitude.'

'And got yourself off the hook at the same time,' she said bitterly.

'Oh, no, I'm not having that,' he said, banging his fist on the table. 'Can't you get it into your thick little head that I did it because I loved you? If I could have been sure, on your birthday that year, that you could have truthfully said, "Yes, Richard, I'll marry you because that's what I want more than anything else in the world," I would have been the happiest man alive. But I wasn't sure, so I had to take the risk and give you the money so that you could choose. And you made your choice.'

She hung her head. 'I'm sorry, Richard.'

'Sorry for what?'

'Sorry for misjudging you. It was unforgivable.'

'Not quite,' he replied enigmatically.

'And I'm even more sorry for making the wrong choice,' she said, her voice barely above a whisper.

He studied her for several minutes without speaking. 'Are you sure about that?' he said at last.

She nodded. 'Oh, yes. Quite sure.'

'Well, you could easily make amends, of course,' he remarked. 'I'm told it's a woman's prerogative to change her mind.'

She looked up questioningly.

'Oh, come on, Jemima.' He grinned at her. 'I can't go down on one knee in the time-honoured manner because these trousers are too tight, but could you bear to consider marriage to a poor, wandering minstrel who has so little to offer? No home, precious little money, no clothes except those he stands up in, largely because he can't sit down, and his only means of making a crust the talent in these hands?' He held them out to her.

'A not inconsiderable talent, at that.' She went over and took them and kissed each finger, one by one. Then she looked up at him and smiled, her eyes brimming with happy tears. 'Yes, my poor, wandering minstrel, I can bear to consider marriage to you.' She took a step back and put her head on one side, still holding his hands. 'That is, if you can bear the thought of a young school teacher, not quite out of her training, making you a present of a new suit of clothes.'

'Oh, I think I could bear that without any trouble at all,' he said, easing his uncomfortable collar. 'And the sooner the better, because I can't kiss you with this collar on; it's strangling me.'

'Then take it off,' she commanded.

But he already had it unfastened and as he threw it on the table he pulled her into his arms.

Outside the door, Sophie straightened up and tiptoed back down the hall to her little daughter with a broad, satisfied smile on her face.